UNMOORED

UNMOORED

Jeri Parker

A NOVEL

WINTER BEACH PRESS
Brooklyn, New York • Salt Lake City, Utah

Also by Jeri Parker

Uneasy Survivors: Five Women Writers

A Thousand Voices: a Memoir

This is a Winter Beach Press Book

Published in the United States of America by Winter Beach Press
Brooklyn, New York and Salt Lake City, Utah
winterbeachpress.com

Library of Congress Cataloging-in-Publication Data is available

ISBN 978-0-9836294-3-6

Manufactured in the United States of American

First Edition 2015

Cover and interior design by Duane Stapp
Cover art by Jeri Parker

For my grandmother

It's well known that he who returns
never really left,
so I traced and retraced my life,
changing clothes and planets,
growing used to the company,
to the great whirl of exile
to the great solitude of bells tolling.

Pablo Neruda

ONE

He was fascinated with fire all that week, my mother told me. Why didn't I know? "Mother?" I asked. She didn't look up. My voice sounded hoarse and unfamiliar. I was as terrified of what she was going to say as of what overtook him. And I'm back in it.

What will happen is this. I say it to myself, say it because there is something I don't know about it. My father will ask for a candle. She'll get one for him, although she'd hidden them earlier. He has stayed up for two weeks—all day and all night, sitting at the window. No one even remembered he had a window; his room was always darkened. But the last two weeks of his life, he will open the shutters and lie there looking out at the cattle grazing and the light spring breeze lifting the new grass.

He's my father, and I spent more than half my days wishing he weren't. Almost down to his last night. Everything I had decided—about my life and my father's life, even about the century, was changed by his death. Only my grandmother will stay constant.

My father and my mother had quarrelled earlier that last day. I learned of this after, like I learned everything. Later she came into his room to find fire eating at the pictures he'd tacked up on the walls. She took an old towel and smothered the flames and then hid the candles. I see the towel—threadbare, green and white—and the ivory candles going in the bottom drawer of the bathroom vanity, its wood still not painted.

He'll knock on the wall between their rooms at five o'clock in the morning. It will be dark and cold and windy and March, the edge of morning in a little southeast Idaho town that has seen better days. Much better. The next morning, his picture will be on the front page of the newspapers in that end of the state—*The Rexburg Standard Journal*, *The Idaho Statesman*, names I know by heart. March 31, 1992. When I pick up the first of them, I'll see his young face, better-looking than I expect, the son of the man who established those papers.

My mother will come when he knocks on the wall; he's too weak to pound, but somehow she'll hear. She's too weak by now not to do what he wants, even as far as leaving the means of death in his hands. She opens, she's opening the door he has shut. The smoke billows out and the fire alarm shrieks.

My father is lovely calm. It is a great last gift. You'd better get the bucket in the bathroom and fill it in the bathtub and put out the flames, he says to my mother, the oxygen tank around his neck. She does what he tells her; she always has.

"How big was the fire?" I ask when I get there. I can't think. I barely know what I'm feeling. By then the detective is telling us not to have an open casket. They're taking him out that bedroom window that was always closed and shuttered. His room is a black hole. Police, detectives, firemen, insurance agents move in and out of what's left of the house. They are quiet and helpful, unlike the television crews with their telescopic lenses. This must be only a present moment, I'm trying to say to them. Don't make a record of this.

Scraps of my father's life are being piled in a wet heap outside the window. I stand there seeing all of us flat and black and curled at the edges. Here is a piece of paper lying soaked and blackened on the grass. Suddenly even his handwriting has meaning for me, and I study it. Then I hear him singing the words I'm looking at, and I remember my own childhood.

> The orchard, the meadow, the deep tangled wildwood,
> And every loved spot which my infancy knew.

"The policeman got there first," my mother is telling me, "the one that broke the bedroom window and dived in." And I'm listening to my father singing when she says, "The policeman must have been standing on your father when he called out that he couldn't find him. That's right where he was lying." She says it like that, matter of fact, not much emotion but not blanked out, just in the zone I can't understand. I'll never know what happened in there, I think. I might have said it. And I hear him singing:

> The old oaken bucket, the iron-bound bucket
> The moss-covered bucket that hung in the well.

She doesn't cry until we're huddled in a motel and lie silent and cold to the heart, waiting for daylight. "Oh Rennie," she says, and I wonder what to do. I think of my brother, and that makes me catch my breath. *Kent,* I'm saying within. He doesn't know yet, and I wonder how he will understand.

We had it all wrong. We'd thought we didn't have a father, or we might have said we had a father so dark he wasn't worth having, who made a home so tumultuous it didn't count either. But we did, we had him, and for better or for worse, he was our home.

David, the man I'd loved for fifteen years, was gone too by then, and the boy I thought of as my son. And my grandmother, who'd been the reaching light for me, my fixed point.

I lay in that motel room and realized I'd lost the great figures in my life. I am fifty-nine, more than halfway through; it's time for loss. I lay there and told myself breathe in, breathe out. I did that until first light when I slipped away and walked to the banks of the Snake, the North Fork of the Snake, wide and wintery. I studied the river for news of my father, the waters he and I had fished so many times, all up and down that end of Idaho. The river was silver and the sky a mother-of-pearl that had no translucence. If the dark bank of trees hadn't formed a border, it would have been a solid sheet of gray, as slightly varied as the feathers of a pigeon. When the tears came, they came with a sound that announced the end of me as I'd known myself.

I drove back to Salt Lake City when there was nothing left to do and sat at my desk for the next three days, writing what I remembered of my father. I didn't go into my studio. I was like someone in a trance. If I kept writing, I could keep it from always happening, as though I could beat back the flames that had engulfed him. I took that yellow Ticonderoga pencil in my hand and finally words seemed to flow out of my fingers and onto the paper and I was surprised to see meaning emerge. Then I went back to Idaho and spoke at his funeral.

When I could get away from the friends and family that had gathered to remember Blaine England, I walked down to the river. The old sawmill cabin where I'd been a girl and where I'd taken David was at its headwaters, north a hundred miles. I stood looking out over its surface, and it calmed me. Maraya would say to me when she was my housekeeper—actually more friend than housekeeper—"Be cahm, Miss Rennie," and she'd add, "Take the ginger tea," *the* pronounced with a long e̲. And I know what I'll do when I leave. I'll take Highway 20 and follow the river almost to the door of the cabin.

"Above the dam," I say, wondering if my words drift out over the water, above the earthen dam; fifty or sixty miles above it and to the west is my unchanging love, where the sawmill was and where the cabin still stands with its mountains beyond, its paths strewn with the light of morning, the shadow of dusk, the scent of alpine daisies and Douglas fir, of grass and mint and brook. These things are clear to me, and I will go back to them.

If I start from what is clear, I can account for the basics. And I lay out the constellation of my life as I'd known it—what I'm sure of. I am Rennie who will follow the thread of the half-told tales. I am already beyond choice. I've stopped painting. I don't spend afternoons walking the foothills above Salt Lake City. I don't sleep out in the studio in the cold spring nights. I don't have breakfast in a rush, pacing up and down in the greenhouse as I eat so I can be loosened up when I get to my easel. I have forsaken these ways. I'll miss only one thing—the big paintbrush, two inches, natural bristle, very finely made. It will outlive me. It cost most dearly to acquire it, and it has my history now, the colors in deep layers up and down its handle. Fingerprints from a decade of paintings—alizarin and phthalo blue and earth green and rose madder and ochre and cadmium yellow light. It looks as though I mixed the colors from what I see out along the banks of the river, in all seasons, in reflections.

I don't return calls. Some art gallery is trying to reach me, and I mean to get back to whomever it is, but I don't. I don't go to bed at the first dimming of light. I've left Neruda and Borges and Cather and the Book of John on the bedside table. I haven't talked to Thelma, or any other friend.

I do call my twin brother, Kent. He hasn't regained the ground he lost so many years ago, the intellectual ground, and I still think of him as a young boy reaching and fading. I wonder if he'll be spared the searching. Every time I see him, he asks about Daddy. I don't know yet that he is going to ask: Is he still gone? Does he drive his truck? Can we go and get him back? Questions that will tell me what there is to ponder. Of everyone, I will stay near to Kent.

My father Blaine is keeper of the final key. How could I have known that, but I do know it now, know it by instinct. I have nothing else to go on. I had no interest in him or his reality until the last year of his life and he was in full descent. Something more was missing every time I saw him, and at the last I was in a clamor to understand him, finally acknowledge him. I told many tales about him—the colorful, the unbearable. And I see they were all half-told.

My mother is Deborah, afraid and spared. She was afraid of my father. I never thought that would extend to being afraid to save him. Or was she quite clearly afraid of his living? She didn't have much time—the flames were at her own feet, and I realize with some surprise that she spared herself ending in the fire with my father. For whatever reasons, the choice she made was to drop the bucket of water she'd gone for, to turn and to run.

Her mother is the fable-maker Phaedrus, the name I gave my grandmother when I was a young girl. She was the center that holds. Her tales were richly told. She alone raised me on the steadiness of love, what raising she got to do. And for the first time I wonder if it will be enough.

My grandfather is Royce. He chose Phaedrus and she him, with his scent of lemons and late blossoms. And pine and pitch and hard work, outdoor work, his hands smelling like leather when he came in from the mill and took off his gloves. I see him swinging me up into his arms when I meet him on the trail from the mill to the cabin, and that would be almost sixty years ago.

Among the others that steady me now? Carlos is the son I chose, adopted, to the degree I could adopt him. I gave him language as best I could, and he gave me the understanding of language as he learned to speak, if not to hear, his dark eyes telling me as much as his words, "I care, dead or alive."

My friend Thelma Myzeld understood Montana needs more smokers, and I did smoke with her from time to time when I lived in Bozeman, a little more than an hour's drive north of the cabin. She knew as much about Faulkner as ranching. She'd be the first friend I'd call if I were making calls.

Maraya learned to say *dā-em,* hanging onto that first syllable, before she ever left Nicaragua. "*Dā-em,* Miss Rennie, I got lucky," she said to me when she began helping out with my yard and my house, and then my dog Thalo.

David loved me. He loved me in Philadelphia, where I've always said we met, and we loved each other across the East and West and three continents and one island, and then he was gone and with him something I can't name, something deeper than names. I told no tales there, but I wrote about the palpable joy of arrival and the inextinguishable sorrow of loss.

These considerations are what I do know, moorings, little islands of fact in which to anchor while the storm of my father's death—excoriating and unexpected—washes over me. I trace it all out, looking for the balancing point I've lost.

I leave the river when I get cold and go back up the cement steps of the motel with its used-before smell. My mother seems to be asleep when I enter the room, and I sink into the bed. I don't think I'll drift off again, but I do.

The sun was just coming up the next morning when I loaded my car, left a note, and turned right onto Highway 20, heading north. My brother Kent and I used to chirp out, "Turn right because the wolf turns right," when we got to the fork in the road that led to the cabin. It made me smile.

The countryside hadn't changed much over the years. Farmland spread out below the foothills, waiting to be ploughed and seeded and harvested. The cottonwoods and poplars that lined the edges of fields and roadways were still in their winter elegance, no more than the bones of trees, the branches of one so full, the other so spare.

I didn't drive an hour before I saw the Tetons to the east. I never quite expect them; there is no prelude—it's farmland and suddenly that vertical wall rises 14,000 feet into the clouds. It astonishes the senses. Then I was in quaking aspen as I approached Targhee National Forest. I could see the dark green of the pines through their delicate branches. In a few miles it was nothing but lodge poles defining the slant of the hillside down to the North Fork. I was in the Centennials again.

I knew I'd need at least a few provisions, and I made a stop at Elk Creek, grabbing some milk and potatoes and chocolate and water, which is about all that was available. I'd continued driving in a trance-like state, but when I crossed McCrea's Bridge, I became alert and studied the corridor of lodge poles. They cut the road with their long shadows.

Then I climbed the last hill and the breathless feeling came back. I always expected the whole mill camp to be spread through the pines like the patchwork fantasy I remembered. It was a jolt to see one little cabin, the only thing still standing out there in the meadow not far from the mill pond. I noticed how wonderful its lines were—the gables, the stone chimney, the shed roof over the added bedroom. It was graceful and well-proportioned.

When I got to the old wooden door, I pushed it open, murmured my greeting, smelled the familiar scent that wood burning stoves bequeath. I went through those rooms one by one, sat on the high bed with the gold and blue quilt where I had slept, parted the curtain into the room where my grandparents had slept. I held the thin fabric of that curtain in my hand until I was quiet inside. Then I went back into the kitchen and wiped the dust from the blue and yellow oilcloth that covered the table, and I sat at it and looked out over the meadow. Uncultivated. Let me uncultivate myself and join the random transplants seeking sun. They'll be up soon—the dogtooth violets, the mules ears, the larkspur. I'll be here for it.

I cleaned the cabin all that first day. I worked too industriously to feel the cold. When I settled down in the evening, I built a fire in the fireplace. I didn't think about my father when I first looked into the flames leaping and jumping, then I saw him in a room of fire, and I went outside. I should have checked the chimneys anyway. The one in the kitchen was just stovepipe, and it looked compromised, but the stone fireplace chimney could withstand a lot of winter. I was suddenly exhausted, and I went back inside and into my grandparents' room and got in bed. I was too cold to undress. I took off my jacket and slipped under the covers just as I was and fell asleep. I was in a still, quiet, lone place, within and without.

I must have slept for hours; it was dark when I woke. I got up and scrambled into the living room to see if I had a fire left. There were enough red embers in the gray ash to flame up, and I went out to the woodshed and gathered a few more sticks of wood and came in and added them bit by bit. They were sacrament to me. I'd performed these actions a thousand times for my grandmother. "No more nonsense about fires," I said to myself, and I sat in my grandfather's big maroon wingback chair and felt the warmth spread through me.

The last time I'd sat before a fire in this room with its knotty pine walls and its big windows facing the creek, I'd been with David.

And I pick up the conversation I can't seem to stop having with him. "My father is dead, David," I say. "It already seems like a long time ago that you were both alive." I get up and throw another log on the fire.

"Tell me about the best of your days with him," I hear David say. When he said it, we were still lying in the high bed in my room, sun streaming in the window. I'd fixed him a delicious trout and fried potatoes and onions, and then we'd gone back to bed.

"The happy times were here," I'd told him. "Although the coop wasn't bad."

"The coop?" He was laughing and I'm back with him.

"We lived in a chicken coop one winter, honest to God. It would have been about 1938, when we were in Pocatello. On Dirke Street. Infamous Dirke Street. I was just old enough to adore it. Another year and I'd have been in school and probably had the sense to be embarrassed."

"No wonder you're an interesting woman, Rennie," David said, and he had that look of admiration that brought such safety. "Were the chickens embarrassed?" he asked, but I could barely understand him because he was chuckling. He made the most endearing sound when he was amused. I'd have done anything, I must say, to amuse him.

"Yes," I said, "actually the chickens were embarrassed. And of course they were doomed."

He was still laughing—that rich, rolling, easy laughter of his. "There *is* nothing worse than a doomed, embarrassed chicken."

"I have to agree."

"Walk me through it. How did you come to live in a chicken coop? And was it with or without chickens?"

"Without, alas. But the coop remained interesting, very."

It was still cold in the bedroom where we curled—it was early spring at the cabin then too, and I drew the covers up over him. We were propped up on pillows; we loved to lie in bed on a stack of pillows and chatter. "We never knew what my father might come up with," I said when I'd snuggled back down to him. "One time when we were first on Dirke Street, he brought about sixty baby chicks home and put them in the bathtub, and when we returned from school, there they were, cheeping away in their white quarters. We didn't bathe—that is, not in the tub—for weeks." David was saying you're making this up.

"No, too good to be made up," I told him. "My mother was chagrined, but we were enthralled. It was the first time I remember being fascinated by the drama of survival—the joy in it even to ignoring walking over those who drop down."

"This is heavily interesting. You knew chickens by then. I get quite an image of the bathtub," David said. "Not to mention the coop."

"We lived in it. It was still autumn when we took over the coop so we had a chance to get used to its privations before winter." I was laughing one minute and talking in a rush the next.

"When the chickens began to feather and went out to their larger pens, my father said, 'I could really use your help getting this coop ready for us.'"

"'For us!' we squealed. A million-dollar house wouldn't have sounded better to me than living in the chicken coop when I was five."

"I think I could have settled into a coop at that age," David said. "Did the chickens resent you? Give me details. I'm picturing this. This is movie material."

"The chickens didn't live to voice an opinion. That was the bad part. Let's skip that part, because one of them was my pet. Except to say that there was a hen that just wouldn't fall down. Kent and I were sent out with little switches from the willows to try to lead her back in so she could drop over dead in her own yard. But no. She ran up the alley without a head, then she veered off into the cottonwoods. 'How could she see?' we were squealing. 'Switch her back,' my father said, and we chased her, astonished and in that crazy way of kids, enlivened."

David leaned forward and hugged his knees and laughed at this. "Was your hair long?" he said. "I'm getting the full picture."

"It was long and wild and curly. In the photos of that time, Kent and I look like a couple of ragged orphans, and I guess we would be today. The State would sweep you right out of a chicken coop."

David was snickering now, like a boy himself. He sounded a lot like Kent. "Describe it, Bird," he said. He gave it the English pronunciation, barely an *r*. "Kipling called his daughter Behd, did you know that?"

"It's a fine-sounding name," I said. "The chicken coop was decidedly where we had our best times. It was a warren, a true little lair where we curled together against the winter. We didn't have some of civilization's best features, but we didn't seem to suffer for it. My mother had a kitchen and she cooked macaroni, then browned hamburger and put it in, and then threw a whole tomato or two in, and later we'd fish off the skins. And onion. She browned that with the hamburger. The coop would smell so good, and it was warm—we had a butane heater and we'd sit around that heater and eat our goulash and then pop popcorn. We had a table, but we liked to sit by the heater."

"What about the chickens?"

"They were on blocks of ice in my grandparents' shed by the time we moved into the coop. I hate to say. My grandparents lived across the street, lucky for us. Once the chickens were out, we washed the whole coop down with Lysol. This was a decent coop—it was over thirty feet long. First we took those wide knives—putty knives—and scraped for quite a while. Kent and I were semi-devoted to this stage. And then my father was the one who washed it all down with Lysol. He made us stay away when he did that. He'd already taken out the roosting nests. Then we all painted it. Kent was in seventh heaven. His feet hardly touched the ground."

"This is good footage," David said. "Your father had found his Robinson Crusoe, hadn't he?" I turned so I could look at him fully. His enjoyment made me think even more of Kent.

"'Get your brush, Rennie,' my brother would say." I leaned and traced David's hand on the white sheet. "'Come by me, close to the paint,' he'd say every time I drifted a few feet from him. We had four-inch paintbrushes and a bucket of whitewash, and we didn't care where it ended up. We just slopped into it. It could go on the walls; it could go on the floor. The floor was nothing but pieces of plywood put up on blocks because the birds had been right on the ground. And when we had it all white, my father put down some linoleum, a cream-and-green speckled deal. I guess speckled was right for the occasion."

"*Are* you making it up?" he asked. "As you go? I could admire that as much as real."

"It was real," I said to him. "Clear real, although I do make things up. My father was fun through the whole coop era. He had a project and he had everyone involved. Doing something together was our best of times, and in those early years, we had a lot of good times—camping on the North Fork when we fished, hiking in to get a Christmas tree. Christmas was fabulous in there. But first, my father built a set of bunk beds, wide ones, and my mother and father slept on the lower bunk and Kent and I crawled up to the upper. I remember we had blue-and-white spreads, periwinkle blue—what a lovely word periwinkle is."

"Go on and on," David said to me. He looked dreamy now.

"We'd lie in bed and listen to my father sing. It was his favorite time, singing the old songs. 'We are poor little lambs who have lost our way,' and we'd start bleating and then we'd giggle and start clucking. If we were up on our bunk, we'd go into a roosting position. My parents had some friends—Virginia and Val—who came over what seemed like every night, and we'd fall asleep listening to them playing cards, and Kent murmuring, 'I bid, I pass.'

"The one Christmas we were there, we sang for hours. 'Silent Night' was last and we fell asleep to it, and on Christmas morning we woke up to a knock at the door. My dad went over and opened it, and it seemed like all the Christmas cheer in the world spilled in. It was his sister and brother-in-law and they said, 'Get up, get the eggs on, and come on with us to Saint Anthony.' And we had a big breakfast—eggs and bacon and hot chocolate and cinnamon-raisin toast. And then we loaded all of our gifts into the back of their car and drove off, singing all the way."

"Was your mother happy too? It couldn't have been easy for her."

"I just remember us all so snug and content and close, even my mother. Maybe proximity is a factor in animal happiness. There wasn't enough space to turn heavy."

"Let me try that theory out," David said, and he put his arms around me and I was lost in my own happiness with him.

"The dead don't come back, do they, David?" I said to the cooling air. I'd let my fire go out.

I slept late my first morning tucked up in the mountains. It was so cold when I woke, I decided to drive into Pond's Lodge for breakfast. April isn't much better than February that high up. I shivered all the way in, even with the heater at full tilt. The big dining room at Pond's with its pine ceilings and split log trim wasn't much warmer. I sat by the fire—you could get right up to the big stone fireplace—and ordered just what I'd been thinking about, bacon and eggs and raisin-cinnamon toast and hot chocolate. I had time to check out the mounted moose head, the bear, the pheasants, and the elk. They needed dusting. We'd taken better care of them when I worked there as a girl. At least everything was pretty much the same. I was particularly relieved to see the Norman Rockwell prints still hung along that high ledge all around the room, the bark left on the wood frames. I'd had quite a few meals under those prints with David, usually lunch. We were always too late getting away to order breakfast.

By the time my food arrived, I was back to remembering my father and what it was like to leave the cabin with him and my mother when I was a girl. It would be September and they'd come for me and I'd say goodbye to my grandparents and get in the Buick and stare out the window all the way back to Dirke Street.

I literally fell from grace. I fell getting out of the car, I fell going up the steps to the house I'd be in now until summer came again, I fell off the slide at school one year and fractured my skull. I fell off a cliff in a cardboard box and broke my arm just above the wrist and cut my lip. I couldn't stand on my own two feet in the city.

I did learn one very neat trick, and I learned it from my father. I should say my brother and I learned one neat trick because Kent was there when my father taught us to ride the fur of a deer, ride it down to the ground, our faces right in the shimmering red interior. My father would call Kent and me over to him when he came home from hunting and he'd be skinning out his deer and he'd say, "Hey, you two! Come over here and help me," and he'd laugh. He amused himself. I have this trait from him; I can amuse myself with dirt.

Kent and I would venture toward him very carefully by then. We were already afraid of what he might do. We'd forgotten the years of rocking in the old chair, him singing "Tara Talara Tala." It seemed like one morning he'd rocked us in that chair, and the next evening he'd reached out for his fraternity paddle and pounded us. He could slap your bottom with that paddle until you sobbed—the old back draft hnhnhnn that lasted beyond tears. Or he could hit you with the bristles of a hairbrush until you bled. We thought it was ordinary behavior. What did we know.

When my father called us over to help him dress out his deer, we went quaking and clinging to each other. We'd have been as afraid not to go. In this way, my father usually managed to present us with more than one fear at a time. Fear has an offspring or two, you later find, foremost among them resentment, and with it come small fissures in your view of the world, and yourself, the beginning of compromises so infinitesimal you don't see a dam eroding.

My father looked us over when we got to the garage door that first time. He was squinting into the sunlight, bent over a set of drawers he was working on. His hair had dropped down over his eyes, like vines. Hair hanging down like vines. I'd thought Huckleberry Finn and I had the same father.

He stood up and went over to the deer he had hung to age. He limped to it, actually, and I see him drop down a little as he walks. It was October, the moon when the deer paw the earth. My father was always talking about his twins being born in October, the Indians' favorite month, he'd say, and we'd get that line—when the deer paw the earth. He liked all Indians except the ones at hand, the Blackfoot. He wasn't quoting the Blackfoot.

What I see, standing there in the garage, is a deer on a pine-covered hilltop, pawing the earth and then spiralling down from the arrow he's been delivered. While my father reaches up and makes two cuts on the deer hanging from the rafters, I'm hearing hooves pounding and dirt flying—thawp thawp. My father picks me up and lifts me to one of the cuts in the deer hide. My heart is thumping. I never know what he is going to do. I shudder a little when he reaches for me. I smell the wild meat and my dusty father.

"Hang on now," he says, "and take a ride." And he lifts Kent to the other cut. And he brings his knife up to my face, brings it right up to where my hands are holding on to the stiff fur and my head jerks back, as far back as it can go, and he makes quick strokes in front of my face. My eyes can't focus I'm so close, watching the knife in the white that holds the fur to the body of the deer. And then the fur slowly peels away, and I feel myself begin the ride. If I stop, I kick away from the deer's body with my feet, and then the slow, sloopy ride continues.

Then my father turns to Kent and starts his ride. Then he gets it timed so we both ride a strip of hide down at the same time, my father working quickly with his knife, until we have that deer skinned. Our faces are right up in the fresh meat, the coolness in it and the smell of it and the feel of white congealed fat and dark drying blood on our hands.

The deer is like elaborate jewelry inside. Its death or its dead body aren't the kinds of things we fear. A deer always hung in the garage and got dressed out at the end of October or the beginning of November. We think he is beautiful with his red, exotic lining crisscrossed with white ribs. Where the buff color of his fur comes against the edges of red astonishes me, and I will paint those colors together over and over. As I see the deer hanging still and elegant, we are slowly dropping to the ground, and there's something there I'd missed. We'd have done anything for Daddy, and we didn't even know it.

When we went in the house to wash, giggling like bandits, my father coming in behind us, laughing too, my mother looked at our hands, smelled us, and asked, "What in the world..." And she looked at my father, and we wouldn't understand that look for years.

"Riding down the deer," I said. "Riding and riding him down."

I'd gotten so I liked riding the fur, but I felt the strangeness in it, I observed my mother's shock. It added to the heady danger I'd loved. It felt like a forbidden thing to do, and my father had introduced me to it. I knew no kid in that neighborhood—not Carol Ann or even Jim Leish, nobody in that town or probably the state or country—had a father who would hoist his son and daughter up to the first cut on the fur of his deer and let them get their faces in it and skin him out, their weight against his releases.

I see my father laughing. I see what he saw, and the skinny backs of his son and daughter, the dark unruly hair bobbing as they slowly descend to earth, hands and arms covered with blood to the elbow, blood on the tips of their noses—it all comes into view.

I looked out the big window of the Pond's Lodge dining room and tried to bring my attention to breakfast. The river was just beyond and I could see stretches of it through the trees. I'd hardly touched my scrambled eggs. It seemed to distress the waitress. I ordered a second cup of hot chocolate and sat there occupying myself with it and with looking around the room. I catalogued in my mind what had changed—the refinished floor, a counter, no stuffed bear by the fireplace. I wasn't used to having time, and that in itself was unsettling. I felt calm one minute and disoriented the next, and I was back to sorting.

Even when my father was fascinating to us, we were nervous around him. A sense of adventure didn't last a day. We never knew if the next encounter would be an elaborate endeavor or a paddling with the hairbrush. Anything would set him off.

One afternoon not long after riding down the deer, a neighbor, Mr. Leish, told my father how Kent and I had called his boy a Fucker Ducker. It was raining outside, water pouring down the walls of our unfinished cinder block house. Mother said to us after school, "Your father wants me to talk to you." She sat us up on the unfinished kitchen counter and stood between us, terribly uncomfortable, and said, "Did you call Jimmy a bad name?"

"What name?" we said. "Jimmy?"

"Well, two names," she said, moving from foot to foot, shifting her eyes. "They rhyme." Fucker Ducker didn't get uttered for quite a while, and then my father came home. We got paddled with the old fraternity paddle, and then he got out the hairbrush, and we got it with that until our bottoms bled and scabbed.

I did think Fucker Ducker was a good phrase. I also knew I must have said it, must have been lonely wrong, although I couldn't remember making it up or hearing it either, memorable as it was to me. But I had to have been the one. It never occurred to me that Kent might have murmured it somewhere. He didn't have name calling in him, for one thing. He was without malice and without guile. Did I have just enough of each to see that?

Once when my father was rough with us, my grandfather said, "Brother, he'd better not come around me. He'd better never try a deal like that again or I'll mop up the earth with him." I didn't hear him say it or I'd have begged not to be sent back to Dirke Street. I see it lined with hollyhocks and weeds, like our household of narrow ambivalences.

Many years later, my grandmother told me what my grandfather had said. By then I was thirty. "He was all but headin' over there to mop up the earth with him," she said, and as always I laughed at the way she said it, and I paid attention. She expanded your sense of the past, the future, all of it, in that vivid language of hers. I needed another twenty years to begin to know my father, but she made what was anguish somehow interesting.

I never wondered why my grandfather didn't mop up the earth with Blaine England and come to Pocatello and get Kent and me and take us home. We didn't have room for wondering how it might have been. We were working hard managing how it was. A lot had to happen before we saw that excusing my father so much, all of us, played its part in his losing any sense of boundaries and judgment. Down to the last candle. And my mother with him.

As the days put mercy between me and that candle, I begin to think about my mother. I feel myself losing her as well as my father. Is she recoverable? How much judgment can she have suspended and still remain? Or is that my choice? Is she there and I can't find her?

And this unruly saving. Is it begun as much in diversion as in preservation, diversion in the sense of the careful movement around some fragile center? It is not lost on me that these moments of recollection themselves are an act of diversion. So going around one thing leads back to another.

The links I'm looking for are deeper far than beginning middle end. Life seems more like a collection of realities to me than a sequence of them, and, except for the days at the mill, still more like a collection of inventions.

I hadn't locked the cabin door when I'd left, but when I opened it at the end of my slow drive back from Pond's, I remembered someone had mentioned there was a key in the lock to my father's bedroom door that last day. It was an old fashioned lock so it would have been a skeleton key—big and noticeable—a key that could lock someone out. Or in. When I envision it, smoke is coming out of that slim hole, out around the edges of the key, curling out into the hallway, like a call.

I try to get hold of my mind, but I'm asking myself is it this and not the fire itself that has turned me into a backward creature? This last part of our lives reserved for understanding the first? Did my mother and father look at each other across a table at Pond's Lodge and spend an afternoon they will never forget?

I have that wrong. The tense has changed, and I think of my father dead and try to imagine not remembering. I hadn't wondered what his mind went back to until it was almost too late to ask him. I know now that I was trying to ask: Who were you? Of those so close beside me?

It is not a long distance to who am I? Who have I been? And who were David and Rennie? And by how much do the little fictions we had to create alter the large facts? We all ended in the same place. Except for my grandmother and my grandfather. "Stay with them," I say to myself, and I go into the cabin and build a big fire in the wood burning stove. I can't believe how fast it heats up the kitchen. I make a pot of tea and carry it to the table and take my position looking out over the meadow. The sun is already on it, melting the last of the snow.

The only person who saw the cards I was holding was my grandmother. I didn't have to—she'd have known anyway—but one by one I laid them down for her. It began a card at a time, here in Idaho, at her kitchen table, looking out at the meadow that led to the sawmill. "I love someone I shouldn't have loved," I told her.

"I know it," she said. She smelled like cinnamon. The whole kitchen smelled like her—cinnamon and butter and coffee and a fire in the stove. "What's he like?" she asked.

"Everything. Summer. Winter. Everything in between. He takes his grandmother fresh muffins. He bakes for her Saturday night and flies two thousand miles to her Sunday morning with his muffins. And he looks at me. Looks so... And the children. He doesn't..."

"That's too bad," she said. That's how a conversation with her would go. She didn't say I thought you knew better. She listened to what we had—and to what we didn't have.

Little by little, I began to examine how my grandmother handled her life. That was my key, I saw, and no smoke to contend with.

So sitting at the old pine table with its one weak leg and its worn wooden surface, and its blue flowered oilcloth and its history—the pies rolled out, the bread punched down and raised up, the yellow Fiestaware plates set to serve anyone who came to it, high or low, I began my journey, although I hardly recognized it as such. I wanted to do more than keep the glory of those days. I chose, as much as I could choose, to be bequeathed.

That time was like nothing you ever see now. In those days, it wasn't so solitary living out in the murmuring forest in the sawmill camp our grandfather and his brothers had built—those drop-dead handsome five Scottish brothers. There were twenty cabins altogether, snugged in among the trees like small animals, a row along the bottom of the hill for the brothers and a scattering across the top for the hired help. Not one of them had running water or electricity; they didn't seem worth having to us. If the grown-ups felt differently, we never knew it. We were summer's golden children, marching up the hill, buckets in hand, for water. We fought for the chance to be the one to go, and we fought to be the one to light the lantern. We didn't think anything could touch a lantern for eloquence, and we had that right. We lived simply and joyfully. Our main music was the shushushush of the pines rising and falling behind our hollered giggles. We grew up to the murmuration of trees with the smell of wildflowers and the song of birds. We cooked food on a wood burning stove or outside. Dinners and cookouts and camping trips and big Sunday breakfasts and abundant, almost opulent, bouquets of wildflowers and excursions into the Park. We always called it the Park. No one ever said Yellowstone National Park.

Our days were as varied as the colors in the meadow. One morning we hiked, although we didn't call it hiking. We called it going. Let's go. Let's go to Pinecrest Almost. Let's go to Swoon Moon Lagoon. Let's go to Huckleberry Finn. That would be the time we picked berries. The next afternoon we fished. We fished with poles made from willows. It hadn't occurred to us we'd ever pay hundreds of dollars for a fly rod and learn to forget the word pole. We fished the mill pond. We fished Brown Sign and, as our range extended, everything on the North Fork, invariably ending at Coffee Pot Rapids. And we fished the Outlet. Our childhood names, our childhood places. We didn't hike to them. We just set out.

Events came and went—births, weddings, a scattering of deaths, still remote from us. The events we noticed were the circuses we put on, the auctions we went to. The best auction of all time was in the summer of 1943. We wouldn't have known we were in a war if our uncles hadn't been gone and chewing gum wasn't hard to get.

I'd just been taken up to the mill. Kent was there waiting to tell me about the auction when we drove up. I'd come with my grandfather in his lumber truck. Up the line, we called it. Mother, let me go with him, I'd plead. Up the line.

Sure she can come with me, my grandfather would say. Kent is up there and they can both catch a ride down when someone makes the trip.

That was before the unaccountable time that left Kent so dimmed. We were inseparable—he couldn't stand it until I got up there, and I couldn't stand it until I was there with him. I was ten in 1943, a young ten. My grandparents' sons were all overseas, one in the army and two in the navy. We must have been both a distraction and a bother when we came to stay, although nothing seemed to really unsettle them.

We were almost nowhere but the meadow that summer. You could stand in it and smell the alpine daisies and the grasses and the creek beyond and turn and see a wonder every direction—the Tetons rising in the distance to the south, the cabins to the east, the high, astonishing mill facing them across the pond to the west. And north was more forest and the Centennial Mountains and Montana.

Out in the middle of the meadow sat an old pumper truck, and the auction was being held to raise money to pay for it. In the back of the truck was a roll of brilliant oilcloth. It was like a quilt of red and green and blue and yellow with flowers in the squares of color. Some were tiny white flowers and some were funny orange flowers and some were hardly more than a cluster of dots.

When all the tables were up, standing right out in the sun in front of the cabins, Aunt Lucinda sang out, "Roll 'er," and one of the men began at one end of the long tables and rolled the oilcloth until he came to the other end, and there was Lucinda laughing and bringing her teeth down with a snap, punctuating her laugh, her mouth never losing the broad grin, but only still for a minute before she called, "Hold it, got it, move it along," and they were off to the next table. When the shiny bright cloth had been spread over our table, we thought we would die of ecstasy.

"Wow, you've got it figured so *good*!" Kent said to me. "We'll have the *snappiest* booth." We got our lemons out and our sugar and our tub for water and our smaller tub for ice, and then, before the crowds came, we went exploring. The little old commissary and office were straight in front of the cabins, the meadow in between. They were old grayed outbuildings, garages attached to one end of them, and the small granary behind. Items for the auction were piled high, inside and out. There were crates of live chickens, truckloads of firewood split and stacked in cords, a load of two-by-fours, old insulators on weathered posts that had supported the first electric lines in that end of the country. Inside there were worn wooden trunks with brass bands around them and about ten coolers and canteens. In one corner was a brass bed. Lamps of every kind, old and new, were scattered through the room. Lamps were a big part of our lives at the mill where we didn't have electricity. We never used candles. There was a pair I kept coming back to look at. They were kerosene brakeman's lamps, and they said S. P. Co. on them. I asked my grandmother what that stood for.

"Southern Pacific Company," she told me. "The Guggenheims came in here first and railroaded, and they sent for the Harrimans. These are from the Harriman Railroad Ranch. Before that, it was called the Island Park Land and Cattle Company."

I ran a hand along the side of one of the lanterns. It felt slick and cool. "It's one of the most beautiful spots in the whole place," my grandmother was saying. "You can see the Tetons one way and the Snake River the other, the North Forth of the Snake. You know it. You've been out there fishing with your dad eight hundred times."

I'm watching her as I remember, taking what she has to give me, but this time into the meanderings of adulthood, not the directness of childhood. I trace the arc of the lantern's handle and listen. "Oh brother, the strings of fish that used to come out of that place and into my frying pan. The guys could hardly hold them."

"When did the railroads come in here?"

"Let's see, the first line in here was the Bassett Line. Maybe there's a date on these. Look on the bottom."

I turn the lamp as carefully as I can. "Adlake—Kero, 3-45 U.S.A." was written in raised letters. How do I remember? I'm reading them. I'm full of the nights they lit after David hung them in the cabin bedroom.

There was a painting propped up by where my grandfather was unpacking things, and I went over to him. The painting was of an old western saloon that had a sign in the window advertising Beer 5 Cents a Glass. And there was a Charlie Russell there, beat to hell, but a Charlie Russell. Everyone stood around and talked about that painting.

"Beer, 5 cents a glass, maybe we're charging too much for our lemonade," I said to my grandfather.

"That's a long time ago. You can't get a beer for that now, not by quite a few nickels," and he laughed. Laughter as soft as rabbit fur came out of him. He was a glory of a man, glorious to look at and glorious to hear.

Kent found a little wooden jug that had a cork in the top and a wax seal around it. "Look at this," he said to me. "This wax is just *hard*!" I looked at the red wood in Kent's hand. It was beautiful against the brass bands that held it tight, and against his brown fingers. He reached over and gave it to me, and I held it up so I could read the label between the brass bands. The label was brass too, and printed into it was "Packed for" and then in big letters "*VALERIE JEAN DATE SHOP*" in fancy writing, the *h* on *shop* making a big high dip over a tree. There was a scene in a sienna hue of the Valerie Jean Date Shop below the lettering. Green trees and green grass and at the bottom in brass-colored letters against a darker ground was "*California Pitted Dates*" and then in smaller print, "In syrup and Date Brandy Net We. 3 lbs. Alcohol 6 2% by Volume."

David and I were the ones that opened that cask.

"Are they still *in* it?" I remember asking my grandfather. "The dates and brandy?" And for a moment I see clearly the child I was, keen for it, but wary, even here.

"You bet they are," he told me. He'd been over to the shower that was under the boilers at the mill, and he had that smell of limes and lemons and late blossoms. "That's how they used to come, packed up like that, and you'd give it to someone special for Christmas and it was the most outstanding gift you could give."

"How old is it, do you think?"

"Could be thirty years old, could be seventy," he said. "Couldn't be much more than that if I'm remembering when the railroads come in."

I noticed that its auction number was 35A. The lanterns were Number 22. Both of them came up early in the bidding. That was good, I thought. People would still be holding out for the big things.

I dreamed that night of eating dates packed in brandy syrup with a dark-haired man who couldn't take his eyes off me. Yes, I had those girl dreams. We all have them by the bucketful. There was a time when I didn't do anything but invent dark hair, and it turned out to be chestnut going gray.

Everybody put work clothes on the next morning and went out to the fire truck. A funny little man with a cowboy hat that came almost over his eyes veered toward us and handed us pieces of wet or dry sandpaper. Everyone in camp got their piece and went to work sanding the truck slick. Aunt Lucinda was crying out, "Tall people reach high. Middle people do the mid-section. Children do the bottom." It was a very good program, I thought. Did anyone feel lonely? Or harried? Cell phones and day planners and caller ID and automated dialing and Post-Its and call forwarding and call waiting and two dozen pin numbers and passwords—the whole damn world waiting for the number you can't remember and your mother's maiden name—that's more than four decades away. The one phone in camp was a party line—two longs and a short. Our minds were as free as our hearts.

The smell of chicken cooking in the barbeque pits that had been set up drifted out over the day. "It isn't *those* chickens, is it?" I asked my grandmother, who was sanding above me for all she was worth.

"No. Those gray and whites are for the auction. They're in the granary, although why they put them out there I'll never know. I'll be surprised if a weasel didn't get in and have himself a midnight snack."

"Gram!" I cried and spun for the granary. I was panting when I came back. "Okay," I said, out of breath.

"I'd have hated to have you see what a weasel does to a chicken, Rennie," my grandmother said. It was a phrase I repeated a lot of times. There was almost no ground it didn't cover. By the time we were all dirty and sweaty and tired of popping off horseflies, a shiny blue pickup arrived to inspect the fire truck. It had every kind of gear on it, and part of it was closed in.

"She's good! And ready!" The veering man swayed his way along the truck's freshly sanded surface, both hands extended. He ran them over every inch of it. "Men, prepare her!"

His men appeared, dressed in white overalls, and in half an hour, they'd "masked and prepared her adequate to our standards," the dizzy man kept saying. “Everybody stand back now, in fact everybody clear off for about an hour.”

Lucinda was up on a stump, crying, “Children go to the mill pond to clean off, men to the showers, women to their cabins—get your washbasins down, what else can we do?”

And we went out to the pond. We rolled up our pants and pranced and splashed in the water, and we walked logs close to the edge of the pond and glanced furtively back at the camp. We weren’t supposed to be on those logs without some of the pond monkeys around. It was better than the first day of summer.

When we got back, the truck was bright red, the paint still shimmering with wet. It sat smartly in the meadow, and we circled and circled it, seeing our reflections in scarlet. “Split a raindrop,” I said, just like my grandfather. The only thing I would have changed that day was the color red.

That’s when I looked past the fire truck to the bend in the willows. I caught my breath a second time. No one but Kent knew what was out there in the tall grass beside the stream, what we were making.

We got our lemonade stand open and the fiddle band started in. It was “Turkey in the Straw” and “Ma! He’s Makin’ Eyes at Me” and “Waltzing Matilda.”

And suddenly the auction was starting. “Now, ladies and gentlemen, let me teach you how you’re going to bid.” And he held up the first item, a pair of chimes that one of my uncles had made.

"*Who'll* give me ten," he cried. "Ten, ten, ten, *ten* dollars. *There*!" and his hand flashed out in the direction of a bare-headed man in the middle of the crowd. "Now ten, now ten, let's make it *fifteen*, who'll make it fifteen, ten holding, fifteen, fifteen. Now comeagiveme*fifteen*."

I never saw or heard words the same after listening to that nimble-tongued auctioneer singing out his numbers. Mark from Krupp's Ranch got one of the roosters for $10, and he carried the bird around all day, bending over to give it a kiss, his big straw hat dipping down in front of the bird and his mustachios lost under the dip for a moment. Someone bid low on a china cream and sugar set that was hand-painted in gold leaf. The auctioneer swung around, pointed a finger at the bidder, and sang out, "The lord *loves* a cheerful giver!"

The bid jumped. "Sold *out*! Right back there!" rang through the crowd again, the *out* several notes above the rest. It didn't sound like talk at all, and I wandered through the crowd, returning to see my little jug, taking it all in, all the details that I would wear like a shield when I returned to my mother and father and the chaos of Dirke Street.

"Cute little heifer, but she's mean, she's a mean little wife for him," someone was saying. Women stood together and men stood together and young boys and girls stood together. There were men who hugged every woman in the crowd and men who never took their eyes off the item they'd come to bid on.

"Who'll start at ten?" the auctioneer was saying, and I looked up to see my brakeman's lamps.

That's what summer was like. I roamed up and down the auction tables spread through the meadow, the sun warming the forest, my brother, unimpaired, at my side, my grandmother at the center. We could ask any question and have an answer. We could come and go without fear, without reprisal. We could take the biggest bite of the day there was to take.

And in the evening, we came back into this cabin, into the front room, and made a fire in the cook stove and heated milk in the blue enamelled pot for our nightly hot chocolate. Kent and I took our mugs into the living room and sat on the floor between our grandmother and grandfather and chattered about our purchases. Then we ran up and down the path between cabins, calling out our goodnights to cousin Garlene and Aunt Jane and Uncle Tom, all of them. I loved it time out of mind.

Nothing was locked. It never occurred to us that someone could be locked in. No one thought of smoke as anything but what drifted up from a good time.

The time isn't exactly right for the auction. I must have been a little older, but the feeling is just right.

I had a day not unlike it with David. No wonder I'd loved it. It was a mild spring morning in Philadelphia. The arching chestnut trees were still light green and delicate, and I could see the spire of City Hall through the new leaves. Rain had refreshed the streets and rooftops. The city was awakening, and it felt festive and neighborly. It couldn't have been in greater contrast to my little cabin at the end of a trail in the woods.

David took my arm like a kid, not like the diplomat he was. I say diplomat because I can't say more, or say it more precisely. What I say about David could never be verified. "It calls for a particular lunch," he said, and we walked the few blocks to Reading Terminal. When we got to the vast entrance, he stood and breathed it in. You would have thought he was at the crest of a ski run.

There is a language you don't communicate through words, a recognition of nature, of habit, of history—breath and skin and bone are realigning, and they don't go back to what they were before. The words that overlaid that deeper communication were ordinary words. "This way, that way, anything you want,"

David said. "It's all right here." And there it was, spread before us, the terminal's high arched roof covering ten city blocks of fresh fish, flowers, produce, exotic oils, cured meat, raw meat, cookware. Let's say this was in 1967, the year of so much upheaval. We didn't have a sprawling, pulsing indoor market in Idaho even approximating Reading Terminal for another twenty-five years.

As David led me beyond the great doors and down the wide aisle, he ticked off what was displayed. "Mushrooms, sausages, bread baking, goat's milk, cheese—Ami du Chambertin and Pecorino Romano. I think that one was here when I was a boy. Look at that yellow!" A few feet further, he picked up an onion. "*Feel* this," he said, handing it to me. "This—this *wrap!* What a dress it would make." I held that onion and looked at it. Anything closely observed is an astonishment, I thought. God in the details. And I looked back to David. "Did you come here as a boy?" I asked, picturing it as I could, picturing my own childhood.

"I did, I came here with my grandmother." He was using the words that would affect me the most. I was caught up completely in the sights and smells. And David. He leaned down to study a row of asparagus, and I noticed the rich coloring of his skin where it met his lips. I didn't like the word lips in English, and I thought of it in French. *Levrès. Les levrès.* He had a beautiful mouth.

We wandered up and down the aisles until we came to a seafood concession. "Would you like shrimp, crab, lobster?" a man as florid as his seafood asked us.

“I would *love* a crab sandwich,” I said. “Two?” the shopkeeper asked. David nodded. “Add a coffee and a tea,” he said. We stepped up to the red-tiled counter, rested our elbows on its cool surface, and watched our sandwiches whisked together. They were ready instantly, and we took our trays of food to an old table David pulled out from one of the stalls. We sat amid the clatter and commerce and unwrapped our sandwiches, and I mixed a little sugar and a lot of cream into my tea.

“Did you have crab sandwiches here with your grandmother? Was this your favorite?” I asked. And I came to learn about his childhood, that he’d been raised not more than ten blocks from Reading Terminal, that his family was involved with the trains that had come here, that he had had many crab sandwiches with his grandmother. I asked him how it had stayed all open and bustling and gloriously used. And he told me the history of Reading Terminal, exuded it. “Some of these vendors can trace their ancestry back to the first farmers’ markets of the 1600s.”

“The 1600s!” I said. “*Shakespeare* was still a consumer, although he was a ways off.”

“Two months by small ship, smaller than you’d think. London got coffee somewhere in the middle of that century, if I’m not mistaken,” David said, never missing a beat, stirring his own coffee. “And the minute London had coffee, it was loaded into the holds of ships and set sailing for the New World and these farmers’ markets.” His hand, palm down, gestured to the scene before us.

“*Measure for Measure*?” I asked. “And what about tea?”

He liked that, I could tell. His eyebrows went up in approval. And he told me by the time coffee arrived, we were shipping chocolate to Spain and right here was your first chocolate, that stand right over there—Bassett's Ice Cream. And tea. The world had never been without tea. We talked like that all afternoon. I'd never seen him fanciful. I'd known him as the giant in his field, an accomplished man, someone I consulted with, although that's not quite the word—someone of astonishing stature.

He had a wonderfully varied voice, and I listened and ate as he told me there *was* always a market here, more than one, and well before the railroads. And when the Philadelphia and Reading put a terminal in, they kept the two farmers' markets that were already here. "Had to," he said. "The farmers wouldn't leave."

And that was the way he answered my question about its origins—the engrossing lore and then the simple fact: it was started in 1891, seventy-six years ago, about fourteen years before the last of the little Idaho towns up here were being organized—Rexburg and St. Anthony and Ashton. I'd forgotten the question that set it all in motion. In a conversation with David, you just winged along, getting a breathtaking view. I watched his hands, big well-formed hands, hands like my grandfather's. He didn't do a lot with them when he talked, but you were aware of them.

"When do I get to see your paintings?" he said to me as we left Reading Terminal. And that other language was being spoken between us.

"Who gets to see what you do?" I asked. "David?" By then I already loved to say his name.

"What I do," he said. "If it could be enough. But painting—painting calls for your gifts. Calls for grace."

It is David I go to in my sleep. We're still in Philadelphia, telling each other stories over dinner at Kelly's. He turns to me at the doorway and he looks at me, the most searching look. "What do I have to give you?" he says. And he puts his hands over my hands, encircles them, and continues. "'I offer you that kernel of myself that I have saved, somehow—the central heart that deals not in words, traffics not with dreams, and is untouched by time, by joy, by adversities.'"

The remembrance of love comes back unexpectedly—there is no prelude to that either. I sleep for an hour, and when I wake, I lie in the familiar bed and remember walking into that restaurant with David. He was tall and he had a vigorous stride, and it was a pleasure to walk beside him. He had a lot of elegance and a dash of boyishness, a riveting combination.

When we were sitting across from each other, I said "Borges?" I was smiling at a man who knew such lines, remembered such lines and offered them, consorted with poets.

"Yes, Borges."

"I had a bear come to my cabin in Idaho," I told him. "I don't know what brings it to mind."

"Not a grizzly?" he said.

"I wasn't sure at first but we got up close and I determined that he was not a grizzly. He walked in through the double glass doors. I mean *through*. I thought I had a dinner guest."

"He came right into your cabin while you were there—walked through glass?"

"He did. The glass didn't even slow him down. You wonder where you are on the food chain, actually. I've told it so many times in Idaho, there is no one left to tell it to. You don't hesitate to drop to your knees and do a bear scene in Idaho."

"Don't hesitate here." He looked directly at me. I knew I was beyond the reach of anything but his voice.

"If I had gotten to choose between getting younger every year or having a bear in my cabin, I'd have taken the bear."

"Did you decide that after the bear? Does that still count?"

"I did decide that *after* the bear came into my dining room, well, I call it a dining room. Everything counts if the bear is real. I decided it was a twofer—I got the bear and I got much younger. And I got to see his impressive eyelashes."

"I love your youthful mind," he said. "How much younger can it get?"

I could feel myself smiling. I felt joy when I was with David. "I also decided that once in a while you get just what you wanted," I continued. "I've overhauled the idea several times and I now have it down to 'You're more likely to get what you want if you don't know you want it.'" I looked up at him. "I know what I..." I started to say.

He paused. "Tell me more," he said, and I continued.

"He'll appear, but he's got a philosophical context. Think about what-you-wants. They're always paltry. You'll want something reachable, something, when all is said and done, ordinary, like getting younger every year. But if you contemplate it, it's a tedious notion. It was tired several hundred centuries ago. Your imagination hardly has virgin territory to subdue. And then there is the vanity. And the expense."

"The vanity! And the expense!" I was laughing now and so was David. It was the laugh of those who love laughing. I hadn't heard it in myself in years. And I couldn't look away from him. "Tell me stories until dawn," he said. "Go on. On and on."

"My bear cost me nothing," I said softly. And then I resumed with verve. "And I would never have been outrageous enough, outrageous as I know I've been, to ask for a bear to come into my dining room."

"He really *did* come in? Were you in danger?" I could see he felt alarmed for the first time, as though the danger might have stepped up to the little wooden table at Kelly's.

"Yes, he came to the back of the place." We sat there looking at each other as I filled in the details, the bear outside, me stepping onto the back deck to photograph him, his coming to the window, dragging his claws across the screen. "He took that screen with him and left nothing between us but a very thin, old piece of glass. Glass is a liquid, I reminded myself, if just barely. That's when I decided it was too much excitement for him and I slipped into the living room." And I did get down on the floor of the restaurant and show David how the bear climbed the post to the deck, claws coming into view first, and how close I got to that bear, *could see his eyelashes*, and how it reminded me of my cat—the one who likes beer. And I told him, "Kooks came in with her ears in the Number Seven Position. I should have been alert to that."

"Number Seven Position? Is that for terror?" He was stammering with laughter now. "Is there some truth in this story?"

"Oh, plenty of truth. Way too much truth. And plenty of terror for a creature whose history didn't contain a threat bigger than a bear's foot."

"'I offer you my ancestors,'" he said to me.

I looked at him, looked with that directness reserved for one or two people in a lifetime. "I accept your ancestors." The extraneous falls away, and you feel it go. You're where the bear is. You're unfettered, and able. You study him as he studies you. You're strangers, real strangers, suspended indoors together by accident, getting acquainted.

He let my hands go and sat back.

"Where you do take me," I said.

He leaned across the table and spoke so softly I could barely hear him, "You who I want to give—to have everything I have to give." And he returned to Borges. "'Words, any words, your laughter; and you so lazily and incessantly beautiful. We talked and you have forgotten the words.'"

"I don't forget the words, David. I'm afraid I don't forget any of it. At all."

"Did you have to kill your bear?"

"Brian? No, I don't kill bears."

I made a little sound at the thought of bears being killed. "Brian," I said. "His name was Brian." And I was laughing again. "The rangers came directly, trying to get back their reputation." David knew I loved this conjoining of worlds. Wild comes to tame. And that was the afternoon—the laughter and the meaning.

"He was one of those bears with...vision," I said, and I was serious again. "I know how it sounds, but he let me see that about him."

"You know what can't be said. But say it."

"Native Americans believe in vision bears." David had a boyish look as he listened, his face full of animation. I suppose mine was too. But I was watching him. His eyebrows were involved with every word.

"A bear comes to your dining room table. You've built a shelter from the storm and the storm comes right on in. Going where you have to go. The bear can show you what you know but might have missed. You notice his coat. He needs Science Diet."

"Science Diet?" David is on the edge of laughing again. Snickering. "You're making this up?"

I shook my head. "But what you're really noticing is the bear's spirit. You defer to it, actually. You think about him for hours and days and weeks. The fear you feel passes first, and you're awake as you've never been. Then comes the awe, the humility, the gratitude."

"What do I even have to give you?" He spoke carefully, and there was that elegance about him. "'I can give you my loneliness, my darkness, the hunger of my heart; I am trying to bribe you with...'"

He paused. He didn't finish the line. Much later I looked it up, and read, in sorrow this time, "I am trying to bribe you with uncertainty, with danger, with defeat."

"What you have..." he said. "The bear is your totem? He's chosen you, hasn't he? And your longings, the hunger of your heart. If you do know what you want, do you get that too? And the Borges poems? Can I take you beyond them? To the other side?"

He paused for a long time, all the while looking at me, and then he said, "In my heart I will betroth thee unto me in lovingkindness and in justice and in mercies all the days of my life."

"How can I have you?" I heard myself say. "How can I not?"

And we ate together on a marble-topped table in a restaurant that looked a hundred years old. I still see his face, see all of it, down to the painting that hung before us—fishermen pulling in their seines, their boat already fading from view in the gathering dusk. I can remember perfectly the soft colors of the rare oyster plates on the shelves that ran all around the walls of the restaurant, and the line of gold coat hooks that looked like music staffs.

It was the end of day at the cabin as well, still and calm, and cold the minute the sun went down. I got a fire going in the kitchen stove, and then I remembered the stovepipes had looked loose, and I grabbed my grandfather's heavy gloves from the shelf under the washbasin and went outside and secured them. Then I took down the old aluminum washtubs from where they hung on the porch and walked out to a snowbank—I didn't have to go far—and filled them with snow. When I got them back inside and onto the stove, they rocked and stuttered as they heated. "Water," I said, watching it arrive. I'd gotten by until now on the half gallon I'd carried in.

I pulled a kitchen chair near the stove and watched the little water droplets skitter on the hot surface. This kitchen—anything in this cabin—made me remember the last time I was here with David. We always came early in the year when no one was about. Of all the places we'd been together, it was being here with him that was everything to me.

I might have done without David if he hadn't said those words to me. *I will betroth thee unto me in lovingkindness and in jus-*

tice and in mercies all the days of my life. I looked it up. It's slightly different in Hosea.

"And I will betroth thee unto me for ever; yea, I will betroth thee unto me in righteousness, and in judgment, and in loving-kindness, and in mercies.

"I will even betroth thee unto me in faithfulness."

We had those things. I only had them once. I considered myself married to David after I heard those words. The uncertainty, the danger, the defeat would come later.

I knew I'd bring David here to the cabin when I saw his rooms in Philadelphia—a suite of offices, really. He'd taken me to Elfreth's Alley first. "It's the oldest street in the country," he'd told me, and he'd added, "maybe not the oldest *street*, but the oldest *continuously inhabited street* in America." I was completely taken with it. We made our way along its cobblestones through the moonlight. It was no more than a short lane, really. The hitching posts were still in place, and pumps had been left in the front yard, and lanterns along the street. When I got back to the car, I was in ecstasies. "This has the *feel*," I said to David.

And then we drove to his offices on Washington Square. It was a world apart from the push and clatter of Broad and Market or the ruin of the streets that crisscrossed above my apartment house at 2601 Pennsylvania. We stopped under the arching trees at the grave of America's first unknown soldier. "I come here regularly to see if the perpetually burning flame has gone out again," I told him.

"'Freedom is a light for which many men have died in darkness,'" he quoted. And by then we were looking at the inscription.

"This much history—I feel it like the weight of expectation," I said. "It's both a reprimand and a comfort, isn't it? Is it what Will Durant meant—the first lesson of history is modesty?"

He gave me that smile of his, so full of affirmation, earthy and dignified at the same time, and he led me to his offices. An enormous cherrywood desk sat against the far wall, surrounded by bookcases. He told me to wander through his personal room while he sent off a few messages. "It's practically a museum," he said, and opened a door for me.

I was as enlivened by it as I would have been if I'd just dropped into the North Fork of the Snake. Wide windows running floor to ceiling faced the Square. Light streamed in streaks across the Steinway, making its dark wood almost red where the beams lay. I stood entirely still and watched dust particles dance in the shaft of light. When I looked up, I felt myself take some final step.

Along one wall hung innumerable pictures, all in black and white. There were photographs of old sloops beside a lake, of trees, of grayed outbuildings beside a barn, of rutted roads leading through pines and maples to distant hills. Many were of David at the edge of a lake or beside a campfire. In one he was rounding up cattle, but the horse he was on was no workhorse. He was groomed, sleek, both of them ready to step high right out of the captured moment.

When I turned from that wall to another, I found myself looking at a batik framed in walnut. I had only seen batiks stretched and mounted behind glass, and I was glad David had done it differently. In the scene, a milkmaid sat in tranquility, her hands on an equally tranquil cow. The cow's head was turned toward the viewer. I stood looking at the nub of horns on that head and the back of the milkmaid, her braid falling almost to the stool. A gold cat was beside her, no doubt waiting for a squirt of milk from the unusual cow. I could almost feel the colors—a whimsical mix of pinks and light purples and lavenders and ochre daubs and flashes.

Down the wall from the batik were heavy, round, wooden frames—David later told me they were hat forms he'd found in a shop near Kelly's. In them were illustrations from old sheet music. Gloria Swanson was in one, and a woman I didn't recognize, with "Clara Shearer, '37" signed under the picture.

There were more pictures—a young David waving from bridges, trolleys, double-decker buses, and the unforgettable entrance to Reading Terminal. Here was a Philadelphia I'd never know, and it was his history. It overrode what was happening out that window—streets disquieted by age, garbage filling their gutters, the dark and poor huddled by the heat vents of apartments in which white people reclined on cooled balconies.

I went to the piano and put my fingers on the keyboard, thinking what his fingers could make it do. Haltingly, I picked out “The Whiffenpoof Song,” half singing, half saying the words.

> Gentlemen songsters off on a spree
> Doomed from here to eternity
>
> Lord have mercy on such as we—
> Baa Baa Baa

Someone was softly clapping when I finished, and my shoulders jumped as I turned. David stood in the doorway, still clapping. He flushed. I could see the color rise along his neck, and it made everything in me rise.

He joined me at the piano, and this time he played, making the melancholy old tune throb with the brightness and beat of a ragtime melody.

“I didn’t know you played *everything* so well,” I said. “What don’t you do?”

He was riffing and tapping his feet, and we both sang, mountain style.

Rooms—the rooms people occupy. The word means something entirely different to me now—the place where things happen, where people fall in love, where people die.

The room my father was in is always just down the hall at the back of my mind, and I see my mother getting the candle and I'm trying to stop what will happen. Was I too late with not enough? Does that describe us all?

It is entirely improbable to me that my father should die of an accident, apparently an accident, ruled by the police an accident, when he was already struggling to stay alive. And remembering my life with David made me think how thin the tie between my father and me was in those days. In some ways it made me feel less connected to my earlier life as well.

But my deepest thoughts were on gentlemen songsters off on a spree. I wonder if that's how my father saw himself. A gentleman songster. An aristocrat in his own way, a fallen aristocrat. His mother had come from the Midwest, from Missouri, and she'd studied at the Cincinnati Conservatory of Music, which he'd been raised to think was as good as it gets. "Remember you're an England, and never forget the Englands are better than anyone else." That was her idea of upbringing. He knew it was a dreadful thing to have been told, but he told it with a certain arrogance.

He acquired her love of song along with her prejudices. My first memory of him is being tucked beside him in a rocking chair, him singing. If he saw himself as the gentleman songster, I saw myself as a sea urchin. Actually it was two sea urchins I saw snugged in the grotto of my father's chair. Me in one arm, Kent in the other. Kent was crazier about it than I was. And after Kent's accident—or maybe it was more a fading, or an acceptance of a very clear reality—Daddy went back to singing to him like he had when we were children, and he never stopped until Kent was sent to an institution.

Daddy had a rich, full voice. It wasn't high and it wasn't low and it wasn't loud and it wasn't soft. It was like water running over your hand when its temperature is perfectly balanced and you can't say if it feels hot or cold. He always sounded at once soothing and distinctive. There was something sensitive in his singing, and in his speaking voice too, that wasn't in his manner, and the combination was disarming.

He'd sing "Gentlemen songsters off on a spree" like the world had ended and there would never be another gentleman or another songster. Over and over and over, and it couldn't be too many times for me. We had a dog named Mike and he'd sit at my dad's feet, wherever he was. The big old house on Dirke Street—an Idaho house with a fruit cellar and cottonwood trees fifty feet tall and hollyhocks in the alley and a dog named Mike. My father would sometimes come out on the steps in the evening and sing us home. I remember thinking if we ever got lost, we'd follow his voice in, like we followed the whistle at the mill.

Memory. Maybe that's my mother's memory, not mine. When she had us, Mother says my father would tell her goodnight in the hospital and then sing to her all the way down the hall and she'd lose him for a moment and then she'd hear him on the street. Their white house was close by and she could just make out the melody as he walked home. When he came in the morning she'd hear him singing his way back to her. It was "Stardust"on the way home and "Smoke Gets in Your Eyes" on the way back.

Sometimes Daddy would stop being the gentleman songster and he'd kick Mike in the teeth or Kent in the back—anything in his path, down the stairs or up the stairs, whatever direction he was going, his hair hanging down over his face, his fist reaching for stomach or ribs. But it didn't matter. Mike would slink back and sit at his feet. And so would my brother. I don't think I did when I was little, but I don't know. That's what I'm trying to find out.

I didn't when I was older. I defied him. That was in the years when all I could remember was him kicking Mike, and Kent, who began to decline so I could barely stand it. No, I couldn't stand it at all. I can still see my brother's face, more desperate than afraid, pleading for my father to love him again. Kent seemed to require that time in the rocking chair with my father, and he spent hours and hours there for years after I'd abdicated. He'd lie back against my father's arms as a young boy and listen in a kind of ecstasy as my father rocked and sang the old songs. There were small dips worn into the cushioning where Kent and I stood and later sat and a large dip in the middle where my father sat.

I can see the two of them perfectly. I have just combed my brother's hair. He is holding the front of his shirt with his hand in that idiosyncratic way he had once it started—he never let go of it if he could avoid it and he crippled his left hand that way. His right hand was nearly as curled up. He'd carried a package of gum in it from the time he'd lost the thread of things.

My father has dark hair and he wears it slicked back. His face looks considerably like the young Frank Sinatra, and as a child I think there is a real connection because my father sings so well. I say to him, "Why don't you go down to the radio station and sing with Frank Sinatra?"

"The songs are on *these*," my father laughed, holding up a record. "Frank Sinatra's not in town."

That's how I got introduced to records. I learned to pick my favorites out of a stack of a hundred—the red label of *Mexicali Rose*, the tiny nick in the center ring of *Stardust*, the label worn through on *Twilight Time*.

When Daddy's hair dropped down and Kent or Mike got kicked, the good times would fall away, fall into cold, cold Dirke Street. I'd go into the bathroom and run the water and be sick. I'd go outside and kick dirt. But it *wasn't* like father, like daughter, I said to myself. I was not afraid I'd kick a lot of dirt in my lifetime. I wasn't anything *like* my father. I was more like my grandmother. I saw myself being humorous and gentle. I didn't scare anybody. I was nothing like my father, not even in looks. Oh, the dark hair, yes, I said, but I had my grandmother's almond eyes. Didn't I? And her spontaneity.

Lord, you're fervid, I murmured, not believing I was talking to myself. *It's not horse racing*, I said. So was that how I'd worked it out? If he was the loser—and I thought he'd lost most all the time—I was the winner? It was true that the more violent my father was, the calmer I'd become. Not exactly true—true on the exterior. I must have come to depend on the contrast, placed value on the distance between us. That was where safety lay, and the more different we were, the more I knew who I was.

I start to tremble. I remember him singing, singing like one of the Gentlemen Songsters, and I hear him differently. "Too-ra-loo-raloo-ra, Too-ra-loo-ra-li." His mother was Irish, and he'd sung all the old Irish ballads when we were small. "Over in Killarney, many years ago, my Daddy sang this song to me, in tones so sweet and low." I'd forgotten I loved those songs, and I'm astonished how long they've remained in my mind, how much feeling the memories invoke.

The only sound of his voice I have in this world is him singing a song he wrote. He loved Indians, or more specifically, Indian lore, and he'd caught in the melody the stateliness, the metered beat of the Indian chanting he'd heard. It ended in a high, plaintive note. "When Great Father say I go, Spirit stay in Idaho." He sang it into the recorder I brought for him the week before he died. Listening to it stunned me.

I am aware that I am not well. My own life feels jeopardized, and if I'm embarrassed by it, which I am, I'm old enough to know that there are few incentives as compelling as running out of time. I've started something here, and I want to go to the end of it. I've started something that began way before my mother's call, before my father's funeral.

I feel afloat. I feel cast about. I can't bear to think there was safety in dismissal, in remove, and it occurs to me that a child can be negligent as well as a parent. I long to talk to my grandmother.

What is a life? I see the question has implications for me. What is it we do that lasts? How can it be that it simply stops? Can we know the echoes that will remain?

I thought of my grandmother at every turn through those first days at the cabin—beside her stove, on her couch, in her bed. And then I woke the third or fourth morning hearing her. She was telling me about pudding.

Bucket pudding, it was called. My mother made it with suet and eggs and flour, and I think she used a little milk. She used to take a glob of dough about this big—maybe bigger than that—about like this. Then she'd put half a teaspoon of baking soda in warm water—half a teaspoon to a whole one. It was all by guess and by golly. Then she'd put it in a round tin or loaf—anything you wanted. Then you'd bake it until it was done—I didn't tell about the raisins, did I? She put them in. It was like a fruitcake. A dough cake—I don't know the name of it. There was no spices in it.

Then she used to make wonderful soda biscuits, but I don't know how you make them. I still make red mush the way my mother did. Any fruit juices in the house and tapioca. You can throw in jelly too, and it comes out just red. Thick and red and no two batches taste the same. It's better than it sounds—you've had it. Fae calls it Groit Groit or Roit Groit—her family's Danish, and they made it too.

Mother was very very particular with her food. Egg cake—when my father didn't come home, she made egg cake. He wouldn't eat it. He didn't like anything with milk. We called them Ma and Pa when we were little. Then we called her Mother. We never said Mom. We did get so we called my father Dad. My mother wasn't stingy, but she was real nervous to cook for strangers. She done so much sewing it was more her hobby than cooking.

Nobody ever went to your grandfather's home in their life that they weren't fed. Molly used to sit up till midnight ironing all the men's shirts. One of Royce's brothers—I think it was Arch—Arch had a pretty good education—he'd read her novels while she ironed. And Thomas would listen from his big chair by the fire. That would be your great-grandpa, actually. One of those brothers was always living with Molly and Thomas. I never called her Mother. I called her Molly. Everybody did and everybody loved her. They were very hospitable people. She just went ahead and cooked whatever she had.

Pie I could make like nobody's business. Better than my mother or Molly. I'll tell you how I did it. Royce's sister said I couldn't make pie worth a damn, and I was so mad I made pie till I could have told the emperor how to make it, and everybody said it was the best they ever had. In pie you've got the customs of the country, or a region of it. You've got your sugar pies in maple syrup country—Vermont clear right into Canada. You've got your apple pie right across the nation, with local variations according to the crop. You've got your strawberry pie in California where you can get the damn things. Don't ask me what they eat in the East—key lime or something fancy, or is that Florida?

I used to read everything I could lay my hands on, so I should know. I read everything Katherine Anne Porter wrote while my mother was making egg cake or red mush. Maybe I was older then. Maybe it was Sarah Orne Jewett. We called her Sarah Orange Juice so we could remember her name. *The Country of the Pointed Firs*. Of course we'd pick up a title like that. And Eudora Welty came along and that's all we read. When I was twelve, my father subscribed to the *Youth's Companion* for me, and we never had it out of our home when there were children. That and the *Saturday Evening Post*. Your Grandpa was crazy about *Ten Nights in a Bar Room*. We'd all go to Uncle Jim's and he'd read *Ten Nights*. It took him all winter. It was a good book but nothing like *The Golden Apples of*—whatever it was.

> My dad was a reader. If I'd read one book of his choosing, I could read any book of my choosing. He gave me five dollars to read *Huckleberry Finn*. I did have to hide *Les Misérables* to read it. I was enthralled. Dad had us read *David Copperfield*. And we had a fairy book called *The Chatterbox*. And we had.

Then just as clearly as I'd heard her, she was gone. I felt as though I'd been sitting at that kitchen table with her. That's how our talk was. Essentials. I felt steadied, more than steadied. I could see I was beginning to learn how to sustain myself in the face of being my father's daughter, the daughter of a father who might have killed himself, might have had help.

It is my father who is bringing me all the voices of my life, his goodbye in a dark register, his bid for atonement.

TWO

My mother and father started blithely, more blithely than most. *Good looking* comes up a lot in any description of them. I've heard it from friends, family. Your mother was good looking enough to have any guy she wanted. I hear that from everyone, have always heard that. "Nobody could believe it when she chose that tempestuous little Blaine," my cousin Sue told me. I sit at the kitchen table and go over conversations my mother and I have had about my father, conversations when he was still alive in the next room.

I drive back into the lodge and call my mother again. The phone is right out in the open, near the entrance—it's not in a booth. "Tell me about Daddy," I say. "Was he—what kind of guy was he when he was young? Was he flamboyant?" And I think about the word I've used, and I try to think of the totality of my father—a man loved, distrusted, and despised within the circle of his own family.

"Yes, he was what you'd call flamboyant," my mother says. I suddenly have a sense of the history of that word—*flamboyer*, the Old French for to blaze, to flame, and I lose track of my mother's account. Then I'm back with her. "He flew to Detroit in that little sweater-vest he had with the blue and yellow diamonds on it, and he drove a new Dodge back. Nobody else in St. Anthony did that. He was a smart dresser. He dressed like something off the cover of *Collier's*. He was always dressed in a suit and tie and hat, even skiing." I know she is smiling at what comes to mind. "He was real clever. Everybody loved to be around him. He had a beautiful voice, and he made up a song for me." She's smiling that private smile of hers, I'm sure of it. She's gone back and found him. I can hear it in her voice.

"He'd try it, I don't care what it was, he'd try anything. He went up to Bear Gulch one day—he didn't have anything in the way of equipment. We were camping at Ice House Creek, and there was still plenty of snow around and up he went, just walking up the hill in his coat and tie and dress shoes and a pair of skis he'd grabbed from somewhere and some leather straps to tie them to his shoes. Laughing. Our friend Ben was with us, and I said 'No, no, he'll break every bone in his body.'"

It was straight up and down, I remember that. I shift my weight. I wish I had a stool to sit on. I get tired.

"That run at Bear Gulch was just straight up and down. And narrow," she is saying, "that narrow strip between the pine trees, just perpendicular. And Ben said 'No, he won't, not Peaky.' That's what everybody called him. 'He'll come down and he'll get up laughing, and he'll say I'm going to try it again.'"

"Did he?" I lean against the knotty pine wall of the lodge.

“Sure enough, he came down that hill, skis and legs and arms and coat all in a tangle and snow flying up from him, and he came crawling out of that snow laughing his heart out, shaking the snow out of his dark hair, and saying ‘I’m going to try it one more time.’ We had a lot of fun in those days.

“We took a mattress and tied it on top of the car and went over to the Outlet that fall—it was just a little creek late in the year, and we camped beside it after work. You kids went with us a lot, but this time we left you at the mill with your grandparents. We put the mattress down beside the river and made a campfire and had supper. He got up early the next morning, dew still on everything—he was as wet on the bank as he was in the river. He got his waders on and caught the most beautiful rainbow.”

She pauses. “He came yelling up the bank, ‘Deborah, Deborah, come look what I’ve got,’” and there is meaning in her voice beyond waders and fish. I understand she is seeing him before it all unraveled in dark rooms, courtrooms, hospital rooms, and I realize I’ve almost always felt outside their life together.

She continues after those layered pauses. “It started to rain, and we sat there in the rain by our fire and fried that fish and some potatoes and eggs. And then we went back to…” And she doesn’t finish.

“If he was attentive, he was extravagantly attentive, is that how he was?” I ask. And if he was negligent, it was an obliterating negligence.

She always talked about the prominent family he'd come from. He used to go down on the street corner, she'd told me, told me many times, and sell the family newspaper for spending money. They might have been a day old or a week old, but people would buy them from him anyway. His dad would take him to the Horseshoe Bar and stand him up and let him sing, his dark hair flopping in his eyes. When he was at home, his mother had that one message for him: You're an England and you're better than anyone else. "It made him mad, I'll give him credit for that," my mother had said, and I wonder if it confused my father, carried a kind of loneliness.

And my mother's voice comes back into focus. "Your Grandpa England said to me before he died, 'I don't know why we've been so bitter about the Mormons all our lives. Too new an outfit for old Presbyterians. All our friends, the people we did business with, were Mormons, and they were good to us.'" She pauses. "Your grandmother wouldn't speak to me for months after Blaine married me because I was Mormon."

A very dark shadow fell across our household over the word Mormon. I remember being grabbed by one hand, Kent by the other, grabbed by the front of my shirt and raised off the ground, held against the wall by that hand at my collar, my body slumping into my shirt. *"Do you believe some guy went up in the hills—New York!"* My head is being banged against the wall and my body flops around below it. *"Joseph Smith!"* That dismissing derision through every word. *"And dug up gold plates!"* Sneering now, hair hanging down. I glance over at Kent. His body is slumped in his shirt, like mine. He looks straight ahead. "*Book of Mormon! From gold plates dug up by a kid in the hills of New York! Talking to Father, Son, and Holy Ghost! Do you believe that?*" He is screaming. Hair hanging right in his face, in his eyes, long enough to reach his teeth. He's got a toothpick in his mouth. I watch it jump around as he screams. I deplore that toothpick. Kent and I are both silent. Our heads thump against the wall with every word. "*Do you believe that?*" he screams. "*No*," we finally whimper. "*Say it again*," he hisses. "I don't," I say. "*Say it!*" He's out of control, I know that as young as I am, and it makes me quake. I say it. "*I don't believe Joseph Smith dug up the gold plates.*" I slur it. He bangs my head against the wall every time I stop. I'm limp and I hate him. He's made me tell my first lie. Big lie. Lie in fear. I do believe it. I believe anything he doesn't believe. It makes perfect sense to me.

Then he works on Kent.

"Your father would go out to the stray pens with his buddy Blair," my mother is saying. There is something comforting in these memories for my mother, and I stop letting my thoughts wander and pay attention. "They'd get on the horses and ride them out and have a big time. The sheriff told the two of them that day that they were headed right for the reform school, a matter of time, that's all. Question of when. But his father could have gotten him out of anything, just picked up the phone and called Senator Borah."

"Senator Borah was a pretty big name to call," I say.

"That's who they'd call. Blair was your father's main friend all his life. They wrote to each other the whole time Blair was away serving his church in Mexico City. Your father hated the idea of Blair going on a church mission, but he wrote to him, and they fell right back in together when he came home. It wasn't long before military service came up. Blair wouldn't enlist when they wouldn't take your father—he waited to be called up. Your father sobbed in your grandfather's arms when they wouldn't take him." I hear myself make that little sound of sorrow when she says this, and I try to imagine my young father devastated.

"The last time Blair came to the house, your father was literally strapped to an oxygen tank. You were there, weren't you? Do you remember that? I think you arranged it. This is going to cost you a fortune. I'd better hang up," she says.

I shift my weight. I lean against the wall. But I keep her talking. "Finish about Blair," I say. I'm not in a phone booth. I'm just standing beside the counter where you get fishing licenses. Anyone could hear the conversation, but I'm the only one around.

"Blair looked surprised when he saw your dad. He was serious for a moment, then he picked right up where they'd left off. He'd always tried to get your dad to be baptized, and they had this running thing about it. Blair was real cute with your father on the subject. He was the only one who could even mention Mormons. 'We could get the job done down at the river today, Peaky,' he would say. That was his usual line. And your father would say 'It's too damn cold to become a Mormon today.' They hardly varied the script. They'd say the lines they'd said for sixty years, and then they'd laugh."

I smile. Every visit was a new arrangement between them about this baptism if it was the same language. But that last time Blair came to see my father, Blair looked sad, really sad, I remember that, and he varied the script. He looked my father over and said, "How are we going to get this contraption in the water, Peaky?"

I'm focused on my father again, my own memories of him, and I make myself listen more closely.

"And then one day he followed me in his car—him and Whiskey Bill."

"Whiskey Bill," I say, remembering, and I chuckle. They've always sounded like a clever bunch to me.

"My friend Afton had met Squeak Howe at a dance, and he and Peaky and Whiskey Bill all said, 'Come on, come with us.' Listen, this is costing you too much. We better hang up."

"I don't care," I say, although I'm exhausted and a pain runs like a knife up my spine. "Whiskey Bill and Squeak Howe and Peaky." I repeat their names. I've heard them a lot of times. I imagine the end of the '30s. Fred Astaire and Ginger Rogers in *Carefree*, Benny Goodman, Billie Holiday, Ella Fitzgerald. "A-Tisket A-Tasket." Tin lunch pails. *The Birth of a Nation*.

"We said no," my mother is saying. And she tells me how they followed her home, how good looking Daddy was, and funny, and always laughing, always pulling tricks. "He scared me so bad when I was carrying you kids with his getups," she says, "his hair pulled down over his face, the most awful set of fake teeth, and his mother said, 'Don't do that, Blaine, you'll mark those babies.'"

Then she goes through the osteomyelitis—1926, his junior year in high school, the bruised bone playing football, the stay in the hospital in Idaho Falls almost that whole year. "They were still operating on him when we married," she tells me, tells me about the five hours she listened to the doctors chiseling bone, wondering how they'd manage a baby. Two babies didn't cross her mind until she was holding Kent and me.

How young she was, barely out of high school. I'm alarmed at how little I've walked in their moccasins. And what my father went through. "He suffered a lot, didn't he?" I say. The effect of endless pain and no end of worry is not as unfamiliar to me now as it was when I was making up my mind about what kind of man my father was. I'm struck by how little I'd thought of how life *was* for my father, actually was.

"There was just a shell left of your father's leg," she continues. "There wasn't much more than that left of him. The doctors were going to put a steel plate in, and they said 'Let's leave it and see if it grows back.'"

It's hard for me to remember this part of it. "Is that when he started carving himself up?" I ask. I can remember the smell in the room. I shift from foot to foot. I wish I had one of Thelma's cigarettes.

"He used to get abscesses on his legs," my mother is saying. "He had a set of knives, and he'd open himself and drain those abscesses rather than go to the hospital. He'd cry out when he did that. Kent used to just take off, but you'd stay in the corner of the room, watching and trembling from head to foot. I probably shouldn't have let you see that."

"I can't stand to remember it," I say. But I do. I remember his exhausted face, the swelling, that smell, the bucket and the glint of the side of a knife. I shudder, and I think Dear God, this can't have been modern times, and what can I know of what overwhelmed him.

The bartender walks by on his break, and I motion for him to bring me something to drink.

"You come from this," I say to myself. This too. Not just the forest out that window. My mother's voice goes on.

"'How am I going to support a wife and a set of twins?' he'd say to me. He'd had to quit college anyway because his Dad got sick, and he came home to help on the newspaper."

"His jobs?" I ask. I'm always afraid she'll say something I don't want to hear, don't want to know.

"He tried everything there too. He was a surveyor, he was a bookkeeper, he was everything on a newspaper—reporter, typesetter, editor. He could do any of it. He was a gunsmith, he was a machinist, he was a technical writer—that didn't last long. He managed property, he ran a service station—that was even shorter."

As she talks, I run through the list of jobs I've had. Soda jerk, waitress, fishing guide, fly tyer, artist, editor, tour guide, understudy to an anthropologist, teacher of art workshops, researcher. I used to talk about staying in England as a swan upper. Consultant, guest artist, art recorder—or whatever they're called, more or less an informant—assistant professor, art photographer. I should have stayed in England and led the swans up the Thames. A favorite line of mine comes to mind. "It's good to be shifty in new country." Simon Suggs, that old frontier tall talker. I'm like my father, I think.

"He wasn't too steady, that's one thing he wasn't." My mother talks through my list. I was old enough to see that before he packed us off to California. He was getting himself fired fairly regularly by the end of the forties.

"He was a complete gun nut," she says. "He and Valda. Virginia would come home and say I smell vinegar. That crazy Blaine and Val would sit in their living room and shoot out the back door and occasionally they'd hit the kitchen cabinets, and there went the vinegar."

"'Deep Purple' was our favorite," my mother says, and I know she has that dreamy look she had when she was a young woman.

I drift off, imagining a man who could love a phrase like "Deep Purple Dreams," and I hear him singing.

> When the deep purple falls over sleepy garden walls
> And the stars begin to flicker in the sky
> You come back, what is it, haunting my memory

And I lose the lyrics, something, something, "Breathing my name with a sigh."

What is this to me? If I know what happened in that fire, in their history, will it change who I am? But it has already done that, and I think again of having felt distinguished by the difference between my father and me, by my indifference to him. That barrier reef has washed away.

When dreams become nightmares—that's a long slow road, a tortuous road. That's the road that is always different. It takes time. What is Tolstoy's line? Everyone is happy in the same way. Their tragedy is all their own. Maybe I've improved on what I don't remember.

All that my mother talked about on the phone happened early in their lives. The deep purple dreams hadn't faded.

On the drive back to the cabin, I think about the particulars I've avoided. If my father killed himself—just say it, I say to myself, but I avoid the word suicide in my mind. To take one's life—I pose it that way—to choose to stop, and then who knows what. And the edges of choice. Was he getting enough oxygen by then to make a conscious choice? The word conscious…"Look at it," I say to myself. "And how conscious were you of where he was?"

My father was preparing to make a choice, I'm sure of that. What else does a parade review of your life mean—the yearbooks, the scrapbooks. Asking himself what is life? Barely room on the bed for him. And the weapons, the 30-06 under the bed. The pistol. The sawed-off 4-10 he'd fired to get my mother's attention. Because that is the last version—not "called to her," as she first said. Or was that always my version? The knives. I see those weapons charred, lying in groups on the lawn outside his bedroom window. Deborah, there's a fire in here, he would have called out. And then the gunshots that she did hear. And the arsenic. He'd laid out his options, that's what it looks like to me. And there were, no doubt, bottles and bottles of pills in his bedroom.

And matches. But would he have tipped the candle over? It fell somehow—it didn't jump off the bedside stand, and I see it begin to feed, its yellow mouth nibbling the edge of the white sheet, see the scorch, the gray ash spread, the orange tongue of flame leap up, as though out of nowhere.

And I wonder how he got on the floor. Did he fall, or did he get himself down there to swipe at those rising flames? Mother said that's what he was doing when she came to the door, hitting at the flames with his hands. But to *light* the fire, he would have had to lower himself to the floor, and I'm not sure he could have done that, and reach for the candle and hold it to the sheets, hold it almost under the bed—that's where the fire started. Or tip it over, push it over, drop it.

I'm shivering. I pull the car to the side of the road. I wish Kent were well enough to talk to. I sit and watch the light fading in the pines.

Could she have helped? I can't imagine she turned a key in the lock and walked away, listening to his calls. Or held a candle to a bed sheet herself. Would they have looked at each other? Would he have begun to give her last orders and instead glanced up to see the price of tyranny? Or could she have paused at the doorway before coming in? The door was shut, she said. I think she said that. But it was never shut. Or at least, not usually. That fatal few more seconds. She wasn't fast. And she wasn't decisive.

I don't like the word martyr. That's how she saw herself.

The past isn't over, it isn't even past. Faulkner has it right as you can get it. Maybe knowing its hand in our lives comes when everything must count? When the words you use keep back the smoke?

But atonement. Beautiful in its look—its length, its round shapes, its hills and valleys. Slow and lovely to say, as though saying it would grant infinite dispensation. The mystery of an act or series of acts that *make up for*, *make it right*. Almost incomprehensible. Do we grant it in our minds, or is it a reality, a phenomenon that can change the color of things?

I get back onto old Highway 20 thinking of the history of the roadways along here—Highway 191, a spur of 91, that leads into West Yellowstone, and the original, the Yellowstone Park Highway. When I get to Kilgore Road, I turn west and quiet down. I stop at the mill pond and look out over the meadow. It's already the end of April, and I haven't noticed the little yellow dogtooths pushing up through the damp ground. I walk to the edge of those familiar waters. I know enough about optics to know that water reflects the color of the sky, with some local modifications. In this case, gray.

That crazy Thelma Myzeld had a few words to say about gray water. And atonement. And Faulkner. "Faulkner wasn't always Faulkner," she'd said, out of the blue, or so I thought. She was a friend you laughed with. I hadn't expected her to say such a thing. It quieted me to remember it. "Go by accretion," I tell myself, and I hear her saying, "That goddamned Ray is looking for his goddamned jacket. I told him, 'Wear the moment as a garment and forget the goddamned jacket.' Moths and dust. Go read *The Sound and the Fury.*"

I was still thinking about that crazy Thelma Myzeld the next morning. I'd have gone right to the phone and called her if I'd known where she was. Or called my grandmother if she was where you could call. In all the years I had her, she was the first person I tracked down to talk to if something struck me funny, and even the thought of Thelma Myzeld did. My grandmother's commentary on funny things, Thelma Myzeld in particular, took you to another level. I knew a long time ago Phaedrus was a guide to enhancement, if not embellishment.

One of our best conversations was about Thelma Myzeld, and that's what I woke up laughing about. I'll be hearing from Thelma

Myzeld one of these days. That's with a long *i* and the accent up front—*my'*-zeld.

"Wait'll you hear Thelma Myzeld's latest," I had told my grandmother. This would be when I was still in Montana, decades ago.

"Thelma My Foot. It sounds like one of those friggy fedderings of yours." She made me laugh and I was already laughing.

"Thelma's got another one," I said. "Bed raggled."

"Bed raggled," she said, said it slowly. "That's a hard one. Bed raggled." I could hear my grandmother mulling it over, and I was sniggling away at the other end of the line. We'd talk for an hour long distance and think nothing of it.

"Bed raggled," she said again, the accent heavily on bed.

"A sportscaster from Pocatello said it, tried to say it. 'The team came out looking pretty...' That's your last clue."

"Pretty...be*draggled*"

"*Very* good. Nobody is better at this than you," I said to her.

"Remind me how you got started on this mispronouncing stuff with your Myzeld."

"Thelma Myzeld got me started, and that's how she got her name. I never did get *Missled,*" I told my grandmother. "She had to explain it in detail, but I never called her anything else after she came right up to me and said—I'll try to imitate her low smoke of a voice, 'I Myzeld. It should have been *miss* pause *led,* but I *miss* pause *read* it in class. I Myzeld in fifth grade, standing up reading to not one but *tha-ree* groups. It should be Myzled, but it's too hard to say. *The fair damsel was Myzeld.* I was lucky to get damsel right.'"

My grandmother was snickering. She was a good snickerer—we both were. "I remember you telling me about Myzeld now," my grandmother said. "Where did you ever find her? She puts me in mind of our cook, Edith."

I was in Bozeman then. I knew my grandmother had heard the account, but I told her again. "I met her when I was looking for an apartment close to the University, and she turned out to be one of the best friends of my life. She had this crazy ad in the paper and I called. 'I'm inquiring about a good place out of town in the trees, vices required,' I said. It was hard to handle my sense of irony—that's almost the word. But it would have been my response to her irony.

"'That one.' Her voice was so low you could hardly separate the words. Not low so much as smoky. 'Do you smoke?' she said. She made me laugh and it wasn't a very funny time in my life.

"'I do occasionally smoke. Will that count?' I said. 'But I hardly ever drink.' That's what I told her, although it wasn't quite true. And she said, 'That's too bad. I kind of wanted a real smoker.'

"Kind of wanted a real smoker? 'Could I come meet you?' I said.

"'I don't know if you'll be wild enough for me, but come on over,' Thelma Myzeld said, and that's how we met."

My grandmother was laughing just the way I had. "Did she ever go by the name of Edith? I'm scared to ask what you two got up to? Go get yourself some supper, and I'll fix your grandfather an onion sandwich. I've got sweet Vidalias. I wonder how she would have pronounced that." And we said goodbye, but I was still hearing Thelma Myzeld after I hung up.

We drank tea all that first morning after we met and every morning I was in Bozeman. And the last week I was in town, I said to her, "Come shopping with me. I need a special gift."

"Special gift," Thelma said. "It's love, isn't it."

"Yes, it is love." I smiled. She was the closest thing to a confidante I had in all the years I loved David.

When I got to her place, we had our usual tea. "What was your worst mispronunciation?" she asked, picking up the old game. "I should say misreading because you have to misread to mispronounce." Several fields below whiskey baritone. Just veered off like that, always did.

"R-glees," I said.

"R-glees?"

"Argyles." I chuckled, and so did she.

"I should have had that. I can't believe I let that slip by." And she lit a cigarette. "Try this. Unched."

"Unched." I made my deliberations. After a few sips of tea, Thelma Myzeld repeated, "Un*shed*."

"Unshed?"

"*Unshed* tears." Thelma Myzeld was in her glory. Un pause shed was the way she put it. "The fair damsel was myzeld, but her tears were unched."

That's when I gave her bed raggled. That elevated me. And she came back to the shopping. "What size do you need?" she asked.

I put my arms out. "Tall. Good size."

"You've got it bad. This calls for Ray's cashmere." And she left the room and back she came with a gorgeous cashmere jacket. Deep and lush. It looked like it had never been worn.

"It's lovely," I told Thelma Myzeld. "That's exactly what I'm looking for. Where did you get it? Can you find something like this in Bozeman?"

"You're not in Butte, honey," she said, whiskey-rich. "We're not going shopping. We don't need two of these."

"You mean give this to…? But it's Ray's. I couldn't…"

"You can. That's the bliss of it."

She ran an ad—this was years after I kind of wanted a real smoker. "See it to hate it" was all there was to it, and she put that in the paper under Unfurnisheds and I knew she was true stuff. She called that week and said, "Wouldn't you know someone from Utah took it. I'll have to get out the sweet peas."

"Sweet peas?" I said. I was laughing at her as always.

"Old Bozeman custom. I spared you when you arrived. Haven't you run into the Sweet-Pea-Capital-of-the-World talk?"

"I have heard sweet peas come up," I said.

She gave a little snort. "That's how we used to meet visitors—go down to the train station with bouquets of sweet peas. Women, of course." She lit a cigarette. "God, what kind of impression would that *make*?"

"Give me one of those Camels," I said. By now I could light my own properly. I only got about four a year smoking with Thelma Myzeld.

I was on my way to Utah then, and she sat me down and said, "This Utah you're going to. You know it's not part of the West. Here are your western states: Colorado, Montana, Wyoming, Idaho. Not Utah, maybe parts of southern Utah. It has nothing to do with geography. By the way, Ray came home last night and said he had a lead on his jacket." Spluttering laughter. "A *lead!*"

"The Utahn?" I asked when I saw her again.

"Utahns. They never come in singles. Usually not twos. I looked them over and gave them my line."

"The poor Utahns," I say. "Poor maligned Utahns. You never think you're a Utahn if you move there from somewhere else. The carrot snappers."

And I remembered what my grandmother had said. "I'm a Utahn if you count my beginnings, and I don't think I am. I'm all Idaho. But this Thelma Myzeld knew how to live her life. She was *occupied* in living the whole thing."

And I tell her something else Thelma Myzeld said. "Know my mother and father?" she'd repeated once when I asked her about her parents. "You mean, understand them? I know I don't know *them*. I don't even believe I *came* from them."

Thelma Myzeld said she'd save my place indefinitely, and she never rented it again. She always had two or three places to rent, but she kept mine. And then I came back to her place one time and she was gone without a trace. I didn't hear from her for years and years. But once I'd met her, I knew I had a friend for life. She could amuse herself no end with her tiltings with language, but she took you just as you were, made you feel welcome, shed new light on belonging, whether you were from Utah or Idaho or Singapore.

Father wasn't always father, either. It comes as a relief to me to think of him flying off Bear Gulch. I did that. I know what took him down that hill, and back up. What he was before—I have that in me.

And what he was during. I have that in me too. I'm not only my grandmother's child. I notice the acknowledgment doesn't alarm me.

It sweeps over me how generous-spirited my grandmother was toward my father, a man who caused her daughter such relentless pain. And her first grandchildren. She could have maligned my father; my mother did.

But she didn't vary, not even with someone like my father. She was abundant—downright, impartial, loving and fun-loving, a celebrant, an encourager of the heart and the habits of the heart. She said at the last, "I had a wonderful life all the way through." That was the jewel she gave us. We bore no burdens for her. We were free to bask and thrive in her love of life, which included all of us, included me, just as I was, just as I am. I haven't been that generous-spirited with my father.

He brought an Angus calf into the kitchen one night when I was home from college. He brought that calf into the house, fevered and shivering. He made a bed for it in the corner by the stove. I watched. "Bring me blankets," he said.

"From the bed?"

"Sure, yeah, three or four."

"*Blaine*," my mother said. He prepared a bottle of milk and warmed it, shook a few drops against his arm to test the temperature. I stood in the doorway of my bedroom and watched for hours. He was soft with that little calf, lying beside it to keep it warm and then bringing in hot water bottles. Finally the two of them fell asleep and I crept to my bed, astonished.

I lay awake wondering what I felt. I wanted to go in there and lie down beside them. I told my grandmother about it years later. "What did you think?" she asked me.

"I wanted to be that little calf, I guess that's it."

"Your father doesn't know how to do that for you," she said. "The calf can't jump away from him."

And the richness of her spirit helps me to see myself as more than an invention. It brings to mind my being the parent—mother, or surrogate mother—to Carlos, the son I chose, my student in the years I taught the deaf, and then my son.

I'd told Carlos that story about my father and the calf.

"Inside?" he chirped, his face alight with the pleasure of such anarchy. "Calf in the kitchen? By the sink?"

"No," I said, chuckling at his view of it. "In the corner by the stove. My father turned the oven on and left the door open to help warm the calf."

"By the stove," Carlos repeated, his voice full of significance. He made me see it more clearly. It was wonderful, really, to have a calf in the kitchen. And a father so unrestricted by conventional behavior. I didn't see my father lead it in. I wish I had. Maybe he carried it in.

"My father fed the calf from a bottle," I told Carlos. "Practically all night."

"Bottle? For babies?" Carlos was beside himself. His voice was sliding through octaves on single words. He was a crack lip reader by then, or I should say speech reader.

"Yes, a baby's bottle. He made the holes in the nipple larger. And the calf sucked just like he would from his mother."

"Calf sucking bottle?" I could see Carlos study the scene in his mind. "You wonderful Rennie," he said to me, and I felt my heart fill. I was something like Phaedrus to him, and I hadn't realized it.

After I'd met Carlos in a classroom, if I wasn't with David, I was with him. I was learning what language is, and what it was to have a son. You had to remind yourself he wasn't fictional—wasn't Huckleberry Finn. Even when he became sick, very sick, his dark eyes harbored the secrets and exploits of the boys who are born to be hell-raisers, the boys who light out for the territory. His black hair was the last thing to change. It stayed barely curled in front and tucked around his ears and neck in the back in a way that made you want to ruffle it.

He wasn't much past twenty when he lay in his hospital bed or sat up in a big reclining chair and told me about his childhood and how he lost his father. He had on maroon and white regulation pajama bottoms, but the T-shirt was an original, faded and cut down, way down, to spare him suffering in the hot hospital.

The dash and verve that had distinguished him had been stilled. The rebel he'd been in school—those days were over. I know he missed them; I did myself. I watched him create someone else to be in a body he hardly knew. But nothing changed his large heart, his quick intelligence, his forest eyes that came to know everything.

"Tell me about your first friend," I said, wanting to pass the time with him as he struggled against renal failure.

"Well, I don't remember my first friend. I guess Manuel my friend, because he live close my house. Manuel and I was with for twelve years."

"What kinds of things did you do?" I was loving to see him rally for a moment.

"Trouble, trouble, all the time trouble." His voice was still high, birdlike.

"At home? At school?"

"Everywhere," he squeaked.

I gave him a notebook and pencil. "Write these things down for me, will you?"

"What's it for?" he asked, his voice going high on *for*. He was so charming I put my face down by his and nuzzled him the way I had when he was a boy.

The next night he handed me his notebook. I thought he'd written more about his friend, but he'd done something that captured his whole life. I ran my eyes over the list he'd made, stopping at the pivotal moments, at least for me.

7825 I get new kidney
7320 My son charil. Last time I see him 2 ½ months old
7219 should I married Cathy but I drop it
6714 I went to Montreal Ca R
6310 Rennie and I was Friend
552 my father was gone on the earth

When I looked up, I asked him about the numbers. “Year, age,” he said.

“Year? Age?”

“I am 25. I get new kidney.” He had a slightly scoffing manner. But I was glancing over that outline of a life, thinking of what he had done.

“‘My Father was gone on the earth.’” I read his words aloud. “You’re eloquent,” I said, and I let him sense the meaning. Even in the dim light, I could see his eyebrows raised in questioning.

Carlos—who missed the father he hadn’t known. He was two the year of a snowstorm and a train and an old car and his father trying to get home from work. He had the newspaper clipping of that night, and he’d shown it to me as though it established something. Not drunk, not a knife, I thought. An accident and my father was gone on the earth. And he drew and painted his famous red car. That quirky red car looked both alarmed and able, like it could meet a train but make it on to the next life.

Even deaf and disadvantaged, Carlos was in the business of creating a place in the world and a way of communicating all his own.

I'd spent a lot of springs with Carlos, one of them right here in this cabin watching May push the remains of winter aside, and I was seeing the same reclamation. The meadow was fresh with new growth. Every day added another hue. The yellow dogtooths were still up—the crazy little flower. It looks like a fabulous Provençal headdress with its flaring yellow petals under the bell-shaped crown—I guess you'd call it a crown. You can't look at one without wanting to draw it. They last longer than I remembered, coming up through the patches of snow and thriving into the beginning of June.

The mountain hollyhock near the creek was about an hour from blooming. The bottom spikes were almost open; you could see the pinkish white emerging from its green wrapping. My grandfather used to tell me that the deer will be getting ready for their fawns by the time you see the hollyhocks come out. It thrilled me that he knew about flowers, let alone what was happening in the forest as they bloomed.

"I'm staying up here," I told the dogtooths on one of my strolls through the meadow. I went to Pond's and made some calls. I wasn't that far from Ashton, and I got back in the car and drove in that direction, south. My mind was humming. If I could find a way to get water to the cabin, I would be very comfortable. It used to be easy for me to go up the hill to the well with buckets two or three times a day. The thought made me wonder how my grandmother had done it—cooked for a family and multiple guests, washed clothes for everyone, kept the cabin and all of us shining clean.

When I got to Ashton, I went to Don's Plumbing and Heating. It was on Main Street with everything else. It could have been any little Main Street in the West in the last eighty years. I asked a young man if there was someone who knew about siphons. "Go another twenty miles to St. Anthony," he said. He was studying me; I could see that he thought he knew me and I felt how little I wanted to be known. "Go to Housley's and ask for Wes. He'll know what you need."

I knew they would have what I needed the minute I walked in the door; the smell alone confirmed that. Even in that wide place with its high ceilings, you could pick out the distinctive smell of copper and machine oil. I liked seeing the wooden compartments with their various rows of metal fittings—elbows and right angles and couplings—threaded, tapered, graduated in size. And the same thing repeated again in copper, in brass, in black plastic, white plastic. Then there were the coatings—sealants, glues, lacquers, lubricants. The men had an efficiency that was reassuring. This was an ordered universe, and I lingered in its safety and possibility. It wasn't part of the world that was changing so fast you couldn't get a handle on it—it would look just like this if you came back next year. Or next decade.

Wes was out, I was told, and I went back to my mud-splattered Scout and drove around until I found Chiz's. I was hungry just thinking about what Chiz would be cooking. Rumor had it that she'd stayed when she was released from an internment camp after the war and ever since she had been preparing food in a tiny kitchen for the fifteen people who grabbed a seat at the counter, plus take-out. I parked and went in. There was one red leatherette stool left. I glanced up at the bulletin board although I always had the same thing—Chow Mein & Shrimp, $7.65. I ordered it.

Conversation is always good at Chiz's and it wasn't long before the guy next to me said, "Good shrimp." I didn't mind talking to him. He was toothless and cheerful for all the world, and maybe not quite sober. "Shrimp you want to cherish," he said. "I remember when I thought I'd never see another shrimp."

"Further inland than this?" I said to him. He made me smile.

"Oh no, not further, deeper. Deep in a foxhole eating rations."

"The war?"

"That was a very good word for it. I happened to long for shrimp some of those muddy nights."

Just then my steaming plate arrived. "Will you forgive me if I dig in here?" I asked, reaching for one of the crispy shrimp.

"No pun intended, I'm sure," he said, raising his wild eyebrows.

"Oh, I didn't mean..."

"Quite appropriate, really." He had some dash to him.

I was eating with vigor. I was clearly not getting enough food in my little camp.

"You work with pumps and that out in these farm fields?" I asked.

"Oh, that I do, I fully do," he said. "Practically invented irrigation." I could see that the subject was dear to him.

"I'm trying to get water to an old cabin up the road," I told him.

"Took you for a little homesteader. Yi got the look. Not a bad look, either. Don't mean to be familiar. How you goin' about it?"

"There's a creek—Mill Creek—not too far away. I don't know if it's much higher than the cabin. It winds through the willows and grass and goes through a pond. Then it crosses a meadow and I think it climbs slowly from there. If it does, it's barely a climb. I tried to gauge it but you're going up and then down. There's water closer but I know I'd have to go up a ways."

The old fella's face changed—lit up, really. "If it's uphill—it don't have to be much. Gravity for ya." He got out a pencil and began to sketch. He made a quick lick of his tongue along the edge of his lip as he worked. By the time he was finished, I had an elaborate little drawing of what was possible. I thanked him and asked if I could buy his lunch.

"You from around here?" he said in reply. I laughed and headed back to Housley's.

Wes was a no-nonsense guy. He started laying things up the minute I walked him through the sketch, penciling in a few notes and additions as he went. "Let's start with ten rolls of ¾-inch black plastic pipe, flexible enough. You'll want to put it in something to strain it at the intake, keep the sand out. Maybe a brook trout." He didn't crack a smile. "You might try this." He walked over to a bin and came back with a heavy metal fabrication that had a kind of Y in it. "Farmers use this in irrigation. You'll want to cut out some big plastic water jug for a feeder—to feed the water in and put this in the end, and see if that don't put enough pressure behind that water, give it a little head, to make it to your place. Put this right down in the creek and lay rocks around it and under it. Secure it. Here, take this screen and screen off the end of your jug. You'll want to cut it right out so the water can fill it and flow into the pipe." I had a feeling that was one of his longest speeches. He had a fully attentive audience for it.

I was ecstatic. I couldn't stay within the speed limit driving back to the cabin. I hadn't thought what I'd do to get the water from the pipe into the cabin. I'd forgotten to mention a barrel. Just as well—I'd see if I could get water there before I went any further.

As soon as I parked under the pines, I began walking off the route I'd take. It was late—it would be dark in half an hour, and I had a hard time staying clear of broken limbs and stumps and gopher holes. I tried to mark out a level trail until I could find a good climb so the water would have some drop. The bright blue camas were still out, their sepals and petals almost the same color. The Indians in this part of the country roasted them for dinner. My grandfather had told me that too, in his husky voice.

I saw a rose fairy slipper growing up out of a decayed stump and took it for a good omen. I'd never seen one before. It's an orchid. I couldn't believe it could grow at 7,000 feet. "A beautiful little omen for you," I said to myself. Right near there I came to a spot in the creek that was sandy and deep. There were plenty of rocks around—along the creek bed and up the side of one bank. They varied in size from that of a baseball to a small dog. "This is it!" I slapped my leg. "This is the intake!"

I went back to the cabin, already hungry again, but I sorted all my gear on the back porch before I made a cheese sandwich. I was thinking of Chiz's shrimp. I wondered how she got fresh shrimp so far inland. And that made me think of my little friend.

Water tumbled in my dreams that night, from Trevi Fountain to Coffee Pot Rapids. I lay in bed wishing I had had the chance to bring water to my grandmother. And I hear her again, "Water—it divided more people than divorce."

I had one other wish—I wanted my dog with me something awful, and I knew it wouldn't be long before I went for her.

The next morning I walked the route I'd traced out, eating a leftover baked potato on the trail. There was a fallen log at the head of it. I hadn't noticed it last night and I vowed not to walk out here without good light. The log crossed over the creek right at the intake I'd planned, which would be handy. I sat down on it and surveyed the area, looking to see if the columbine had bloomed yet. The distinctive plants were everywhere but no flowering had begun. Another week or two. This would be a prime piece of ground to keep up with the wildflower season. My grandmother had white columbine all around the cabin and in flower boxes under the front windows. "They're buttercups, you know," she said to me and smiling asked, "Don't you love the thought? When they flower, the meadow will take on extravagance," and I anticipated the array of colors they'd add to the pale yellows and pinks and blues already splashed through the new green.

On the walk back, I recited what would follow the columbine. The mule's ears would come up and the meadow would turn yellow overnight. When the sun fell on those yellow petals, they'd radiate light themselves, beaming out of the tall sage green leaves—the leaves that turn and dip. I could remember exactly what the meadow would smell like then—tangy and spicy, and when they dried in August, you'd get the heaviest scent of the summer and the greatest crunch when you walked through them.

I noticed a scattering of sego lilies in the danky spot near the pond. They looked like delicate tulips with their white petals turning almost unnoticeably to shades of purple. The Indians made bread from their bulbs. Mormon pioneers wouldn't have survived their first winter in the West without them.

Birds were dipping and soaring above the meadow. They're out all day long now that it is warmer. The hummingbirds dart about like they are losing their minds—you see them almost every day—and the killdeer call. With their white chests and black collars, they look like little ministers. The robins join in.

I could really hear them when I got up close to the cabin, where they nest in the eaves.

Everything was thriving, I noticed. "Take a lesson," I murmured. Even the grasses were thriving, battling it out with the flowers. I don't know much about grasses except that there are almost as many varieties of them as there are orchids. I'd never taken time to notice the grass underfoot but I still had time. I'd heard they cover more of the earth than anything. Thank God it isn't all asphalt.

I sat on the porch of the cabin and looked out over the meadow when I got back. In its mix of flowers and grasses were huckleberry bushes and Oregon grape and what we used to call bear-berry bushes. I didn't miss the whimsy and abandon and elegance. How had we accustomed ourselves to just grass, and usually only the ubiquitous Kentucky Blue—the mandatory sheet of green in every American city, with its call to trim and edge and clip and fertilize? Who wouldn't love the ten thousand things going on out here? Even so, I knew mankind had played his role in most meadows. Where there was a clearing, fertile ground had been prepared for a seed to drift in.

It's not terribly unlike a family, and I picture the deep violet camas, the spiky, conspicuous flower of middle summer, finding its place. And I'm surprised to realize I wouldn't choose to take my father out of his place in my family. I couldn't do without him any more than I could do without Carlos, or Kent, or David, or my grandmother, and there is comfort in the thought, more than comfort.

I walked along what was left of the path to the commissary the next morning and sat on the old log railing at the edge of the meadow. My grandmother had run the commissary, and I see her in that little store behind its wooden counter, taking orders for groceries and filling those orders. Sometimes I'd stepped behind that counter, polished by all the cans and sacks of beans that had slid across it, and I'd gotten the items off the shelf as she called them out—Dutch Boy cleanser, Arm & Hammer baking soda, sacks of Idaho russets, cans of Green Giant beans. She had a playfulness in everything she did. Nothing was just a task to her. "Spam, Brillo pads, Hershey bars." I was saying these things aloud, but it was her voice I heard as I walked back to the cabin, remembering what a day with her had been like, hearing our morning chatter as clearly as though we were there together again.

"You even laugh in the mornings," she is saying as I come out of my bedroom, rubbing my eyes and sniffing the coffee and the bacon air, and I laugh too. I've got my yellow socks on, and my hands go automatically from my eyes to my hair, making the combing motion through it.

"What have you got me by?" I say, chuckling as my grandmother lifts the back of my shirt.

"Looks to me like size nine. Do you always wear it on the outside?"

"Cripes and Snipes! Have you got me by my label? Am I inside out? I hurried too fast."

I see my grandmother move around to the front of the stove and push the bacon back so she can lift the lid and poke at the fire. I think I can feel my heart beat, hear myself breathe. "We had it all," I say to the air around me, and I have to stop remembering and go outside. But I'm still seeing myself do what I always did next—worm up on that old white stool tucked in the narrow space between the wall and the wood burning stove. I weave my fingers through the spools of its half-back in my mind, and I hear her.

"What's on the docket for you today, anyway, Mouseket?"

"Mouseket!" I snicker again. As I hum and sing beside the stove, I scoot a little piece of bark across its surface with a fork.

"What is that little song of yours?" my grandmother asks, looking up from her breakfast preparations. "Are you singing, 'The Mouseket Makes the Tours'?"

"Yes, I guess I am." I bend to tie my shoelaces, still humming. "Was there a real mouse in the cabin? Was that what I heard you and Gramp talking about?"

I listen as my grandmother tells about my grandfather finding a squirrel in the cab of his truck. This is it. This is the best life gets—here by the fire to warm me, my grandmother stirring the potatoes and onions frying on the stove and saying what was a squirrel doing where a mouse usually goes, my grandfather answering, his voice husky and full of humor, "Why wouldn't it be a squirrel? They're as bad as mice." My grandmother pours herself a cup of coffee and adjusts the damper on the stove.

"What about you? I suppose you'll be going where a squirrel goes today. You're poppin' inside this morning, I can tell that in half a look. Something big in your life?"

"I'm doing something—I've started something down on the creek. Building something—Kent and me."

"Good for you. Must be the biggest thing yet to keep you from your Grand Tours. I never saw you leave that past your first hour up." She slides the coffee pot to the back of the stove and goes to the kitchen table and sits down.

"You must be able to read my thoughts," I say. "That's what I'm going to do today—my Tours." I run through the route. I'll go across the little bridge that is straight in front of our cabin, then along the path through the willows to the planer where my grandfather works.

"A test?" My grandmother is chuckling.

"Yes. I took him a plate of treats while he was listening to the radio—half jelly beans and half Spanish peanuts. He snapped down every jelly bean first before he took a single nut. Isn't he the finest man? Just think about his hair."

"I didn't mess with slouches. By the way, your grandfather was sorry to miss you this morning. He'd barely left for the planer when you wandered out."

"He had?" But I was giggling, disappointed as I was to miss my grandfather. "Slouches! Every slouch—it's sure, every slouch in school likes me. Then I feel riffy because I know they're slouches."

"That's why I didn't mess with them, I guess, although I found you can be wrong about slouches." Laughter comes into my grandmother's voice again. "Riffy?"

"Just what it is."

Make me egg cake, I said to the meadow before me. I miss you, Phaedrus. Like I'd miss this air. But you're closer than you've ever been. You know just where I am, don't you?

If my father is the catalyst in taking me back, I see that my grandmother is the rescuer over and over again, even in revisiting. Anything could make me think of her. I fell asleep that night holding onto the sound of her voice. I knew I had gold. When I woke in the morning, I saw my possibilities, knew I could resume the long exchange with her. I was looking for the position of her mind, its mooring and disposition as much as the words she'd given me. That will be my mooring. Because I was unmoored.

So as the scene outside that kitchen window changed from the apple green of spring to the full palette of summer, I made arrangements to stay longer, and I felt myself led by my grandmother. In the end we found a rhythm that was otherworldly.

She hadn't just been my rescuer. She was Kent's protector as well as his rescuer, right to the last day he was home. On the morning my mother couldn't manage any longer, there were doctors and then boxes and Kent was packed up as he stood staring and trying to formulate a question. I was trembling beside him, violently trembling. Then my grandmother arrived, and my grandfather.

"I couldn't have done it without your grandfather," she is telling me. I hear her voice as clearly as I've ever heard it. "I barely could do it then." I was finishing junior high school. It was 1946, and we had moved again, further into the desert. I was clumsy. And I was lost without Kent—Kent who was now irretrievably lost. He fell off bikes. He walked in front of cars. He got disoriented between classes. He entered people's houses—friends, strangers, they were all the same. Hiya doin', he'd say. A slow blur lay over his speech now. People who were wary I disdained. "Your brother's going crazy," one of our friends said to me, and I brought back my fist and it shot through the air and he dropped like I'd hit him with the old fish whacker.

Everything changed. My parents were rehearsing their separate guilt. I was afraid and standing alone watching Kent drift off, but no one seemed to see, and I was suddenly managing things I'd never done before—shopping, helping Kent get ready for school, keeping him in the right class, doing his homework for him, and all with a terror that he wouldn't be back and I wouldn't have even this.

I loved Kent. I didn't know there was more to lose on earth than him. I couldn't envision a step without him. It was in those years that I began spending hours in the evening talking to him, casting about for an anchor.

Remember how we fished, I'd say to him.

Tell me.

I call those our chestnut-colored days. We'd get a ride up to the mill with Grandpa. You loved to ride back there on the bed of the truck, especially if there was lumber on it. But I liked to sit up front and listen to Grandpa barely whistle or barely sing.

Kent would smile. *Quiet.*

Yep, he's a quiet man, an elegant man.

Elegant?

He has charming ways. You're a lot like him, Kent. You look like him. And you're going to be tall like him.

Tall.

We'd get up there and line out our fishing gear the night before.

Get ready.

Yes, Kent! That's my brother! We'd get ready side by side. I've got plenty of tippet, you'd say. And I've got some floaty stuff. Gink. And I've got some Royal Coachmans. I tied us about a dozen, and a few Sandy Mites.

Sandy?

The connections are going, I'm watching them break down one by one and something flutters in the back of my throat, clear through to the back of my neck, but I keep going.

We'd always string our poles up the night before. We never called them rods. They were hardly rods. Hand-me-downs from Daddy. Those damned automatic reels.

Kent would laugh. *Zip.*

That's right, zip *your fish right out of the water. I don't know why*

Daddy liked them. You did have one he gave you, and every time he looked at it, he'd say 'seventeen jewels' or 'thirteen jewels.' You'd have thought it was a damned watch.

Kent would laugh again. He loved me to swear, and I frankly loved it too. I swore a lot more than he did.

Then it was morning, Kent. And we'd come out of our rooms. You slept out there on the porch when they put that little room in. And my bedroom window still looked right out there so I could push back the curtain and open it and talk to you. Get up. It's time, I'd say.

Up.

And then we'd fly for the pond. Be back with a fish, Gram, we'd call.

Back with fish.

About ten minutes and we'd be back with two fish. We'd start with your Royal Coachman and the morning was so still and you could smell the willows. Hup, they're rising! you'd call the minute you saw a stir on the water. They're just sipping, though.

Sipping.

Remember how the fish would come up from under the fly and just sip it in? Sometimes they'd slash at it and come right up out of the water. You'd go crazy when they did that. But you were good to get them when they just came sipping. I think you could see into the water.

I loved it. Oh my Rennie.

I loved it, too, Kent. Smell the grass and the pines and the wild-flowers? Remember? Like new grass in the spring. Like white dust in the fall. We'll get back there. We don't want to hang around here. The trees are weird. Oranges on them, and lemons. Daddy says it's the San Joaquin Valley, but we're right on the coast and so far from the mill.

I went to Kent's doctor's appointments with Mother. My father never went to them. I asked all the questions I could think of. I kept a list of what to ask next time. I watched out for him at school. I talked to him endlessly. "What's happening, Kent?" I said. "Kent, how does it feel? Where should we look?"

"I'm gone away," he said. "I'm fog." There was no play or lightness in him, and it made such sentences terrifying.

"Can you come back?" My voice trembled.

"Back?"

"Kent, come back." I was crying again and I turned my head so he wouldn't see. When I looked up at him, tears were streaming down his face.

"I'm...I'm reach...I can't find..."

I put my arms around him and held him like I'd done when we were children. We went forward together in whatever way we could. When he couldn't make me understand him, he drew pictures for me. And when I couldn't reach him with words anymore, I drew for him. And so it was images, not words, that were our final bridge.

It was not a time without solace, and we steered around fear for a long while. We had always found great amusement in each other, and we were almost never not together now. If I can just have Kent around, I told myself, I'll manage until we find the answer.

Just about the same time I began to paint, I began to read about the brain. I started with the encyclopedia and then went to the school library and read all the sections on the brain in the biology books. Then I took a bus to San Diego and found my way to the university. I found *Gray's Anatomy* and started its curious section on the brain. I could have drawn the brain when I was through with *Gray's Anatomy*, could have illustrated it for the next edition, but I knew no more than when I'd set out. Then I'd get out my oil paints in the evenings and paint birds.

Little by little, Mother began to break apart. She was like a raft that got caught in rough waters. Parts of her flew off, she upset. She could be patched, I was sure, and taken to gentler currents and reloaded. But she'd never take the full river again.

And one day when my brother couldn't get his shirt on right, she began to scream. "Stop it, *stop* it, you've got to *stop* it!" And she put her hands in her hair and arched her head back and stood there screaming, and I knew Kent would go and that sound would remain.

Fear came to me then. I got Kent's shoes on him and a jacket and got him outside. He was trembling and holding on to the front of his shirt. "Let's play like we're going for a sleigh ride," I said to him. And we went into the garage and got the wheelbarrow and he climbed up in it, big as he was, and I begged him to let go of his shirt and hang on, and I pushed him out of the garage. "Let's imagine snow," I said, and I could hear the runners screeching as I pushed him up into the scant snow of March. I pushed him across patches of snow and across bare spots in the lawns and over driveways. I pushed him around and around what I recast in my mind as Dirke Street, hard as life there had been. I couldn't even think of the mill or the cabin.

I was in my late thirties before I asked my grandmother about the day Kent left home. "It was the worst day I'd had since Lilly died," she told me. She didn't dramatize, which gave every word weight.

She filled things in for me so that I understood we had gathered on the sidewalk in front of our house at the end of summer, and we had sent Kent away.

He had a new haircut, a bad haircut. He already looked institutionalized. He had a new shirt. It looked like a shirt he should have worn ten years earlier. It was faded blue with yellow umbrellas through it. Mother had started buying his clothes at thrift shops. He clung to the front of that shirt as though to keep from a precipice.

I took him into the house and combed his hair. I dragged him back to the bathroom and combed it again, sitting him down to oil it and smooth it.

"Do I look...Rennie...?" he asked, and I'm standing beside him, the tips of my fingers in my mouth.

I walked through the forest every day, finding quietude. It's loam floor cushioned my steps, the movement of the trees loosened me. I was in its trance, taking careful note of the ways of a pine tree, a flower, a squirrel. One morning a mountain lion jumped in front of me, his long body unfolding, his legs extending behind as he disappeared.

When I'd return to the cabin, I'd make my ritual fire, take my place in front of the kitchen window, and study the changing meadow. By the end of June, the yellow daisies started to fade and the tiny white flowers were almost gone. It began to smell like summer. An attentiveness came to me. I remembered how my grandmother could shed the details of a tragedy, and she'd had many. She'd begin in a turmoil of housework and she'd end restored to the present—cooking dinner for us, Grandpa coming up that path.

And I suddenly knew I had found how to summon her. It was something literally beyond my comprehension, and I had a moment like no other in my life. She had come back to me. They were all gone, David and Carlos and Daddy, terribly gone, and she was gone, had been gone longer than any of them. And of all of them, I missed her the most. The most totally, the most frequently. I was filled with the weight of my losses.

I didn't ask how her music had come to me. All I knew was I had her words. I would have been someone else if I hadn't found the way to her. After that, I didn't make the journey alone. It changed everything, changed it absolutely as I listened to the account my grandmother gave me of the worst day she and my grandfather had lived through since their own baby died. God in heaven, the strength those two had. Comfort wasn't the right word to use. I felt awe for them, and in a way for myself, as I listened to her.

> He hardly said anything, and I could hear the song you two sang together as you combed his hair. "There'll be bluebirds over the white cliffs of Dover. Just you wait and see."
>
> You came out of the bathroom singing, your voices fading to nothing but whispers. Your mother was just white and so nervous all she could say was hurry up. Your father walked up and down in front of the house like a madman. His face looked like somebody had taken him by the back of the neck and started tightening.
>
> Kent didn't say three words during that long drive. He kneeled at the back window and watched for you until you were miles behind. Your mother couldn't watch him leave, and she'd gone inside. "I want to go back," he said. He said it over and over. "I want to go back, I want to go

home, can I go home? I want to go back." We were clear to Twin Falls before he stopped watching for you, and he didn't say anything after that. He wouldn't eat a thing.

And then we took him into that cold, bare hall and they came for him and dragged him away from us. He was clinging to us for all he was worth and kicking and screaming and barely whispering, "I want to go home. Will you take me home?" Your grandfather and I were asking each other, "Should we do this? Is there another way?" And suddenly attendants had hold of him, and they dragged him down that cold bare hall. I couldn't even let myself imagine what he was going to. We watched them drag him away, calling "I don't want to go, I don't want to go."

And we left him like that. Your grandfather held me in his arms in that dismal hall and we both shook with sobs. I could feel your grandfather just trembling, and we could still hear your brother, long after we couldn't see him.

I accepted the comfort of the forest like a pilgrim after that—the cold mornings; the long, slow afternoons; the lingering end of day. I felt my former life fall away, not gradually but altogether and all at once, like dropping a coat from my shoulders.

And I was where I wanted to be. I don't know that I ever wanted to be anywhere else in my life. Even the residue of what had been when we were together had more in it than my life in the city.

I'd make a fire in the mornings like my grandmother had done and heat water for tea. As soon as it was dry enough outside, I'd put on my grandfather's old fleece-lined work jacket and walk through the Douglas fir and quaking aspen. I noticed the trees; before the first week was over, I studied them like a botanist. The small quakies, just slim stems still, looked like something Degas could do with chalk—all limber and swaying. The pines were another thing entirely. They had mass and mood—Spanish more than French. I could have discussed each one individually, and each offered me a distinct companionship. And under them were the opulent wildflowers—the yellow dogtooths bobbing on their long thin stems were gone now. The elegant white columbine were in full bloom, and the rambunctious sticky geraniums—

geranium viscosissimum—were everywhere. The sunflowers were up, their faces 3 inches across. The mountain hollyhocks were blooming and along the streams the golden monkey flower and the modest pale fleabane. I hadn't seen Indian paintbrush yet, but the larkspur were beginning to flower. They seemed to cascade upward. Occasionally I encountered a delicate primrose.

The animals were still down, and I saw a moose every morning. He could have been made of chocolate. The deer would come right up to my door. There was a little squirrel that waited for bread, chattering his head off if I was late getting it out. He liked what my grandfather called cakiebread, and I got so I made him a new loaf every few days, just as my grandfather had done.

One morning I saw a great horned owl, grand and remote in his silvers and browns and whites. I was close enough to see his ear tufts. He scared the hell out of me, actually, appearing almost in my face as I came through some branches. I looked up and there was that improbable, inscrutable expression. I was startled, and I had to say to myself *he's unflappable* to regain my composure. When I looked right at him, he gazed back, as direct as a headlight.

"What do you knooow?" I said. Something traveled across his face so faintly I imagined imagining it. "Whooo could say?" He didn't answer. He could have been dead for all his expression changed. The one other time I saw him, I was looking for him, and I could tell he'd let himself be seen. He was supercilious, and something about it made me feel fragile. Anything supercilious makes me feel fragile, has always made me feel fragile.

The tawny mountain cat I had glimpsed above me at the end of the week was the only animal that really frightened me. I hadn't seen eyes like that since my father's mother died. When I got over the first wave of fear, I observed the head, the paws, the tail to see if I could relate my own cat to this austere stretch of a creature.

Then he rose suddenly, stood on the bough, and stepped out toward me. His ears went to the pounce alert. He could have hurt me if he'd just slipped. I shrank away, making myself smaller.

I drove into Pond's Lodge when I had to make arrangements, extensions. I always missed Maraya when I was running things or coming to terms with things as they were. I'd lost touch with her and it wasn't easy getting her phone number, but I did get it. The prefix was 801. So she was back in Utah. "I wish I was coming over, Miss Rennie," she said. "I wish I was bringing you yams and turkey and dressing and mashed potatoes and gravy."

"It has been a bunch of years, hasn't it? But you still do turkey the regular way, don't you? Give you four hours and bring my plate, that's how I remember it."

I heard her trademark laugh. She'd lived in Florida for a while after she left Nicaragua, and then she'd followed an aunt to Salt Lake City. She did housekeeping for a friend of mine and once in a while I'd be over there when she came. She was amusing to talk to and it wasn't long before I saw the kind of skills she had. She was a very capable woman, and responsible. I began asking her to do a few things for me. She was a good organizer; I wasn't. "This is the way it is, Miss Rennie," she'd say to me, "and this is the part of it we can work with, awright?" She never put an l in there. "Just what we can do and no more."

Sometime after that first dozen years, she left Salt Lake. She'd said goodbye but she was vague about where she was going. "Nicaragua?" I'd asked. "If the creek don't rise," she'd said, or something like that.

On those trips to the lodge, I would call my neighbor about my dog, my lawn, the mail, the fruit trees. Then if the weather was just right, I'd drive on down to Harriman State Park, the old Railroad Ranch, and fish. It sits along a meadow that traces the river. The breeze stirs the tops of the grasses beside the North Fork and the Tetons off in the distance get hazy and purple as spring moves into summer.

One day you're going to be out here and it will be brisk, and you'll look up to see those peaks turned white. And the air will be clear as glass and the fields flat and gold. Every color will be here then, from apple green to gold and all the shades of gold that go dark, as dark as russet. Only the grass at the edge of the river will keep this apple green.

I attempted to go back to Salt Lake City once. When I felt I couldn't extend my stay any longer—it would have been before the middle of July—I drove down out of Targhee National Forest and into Ashton. I got the old lump in my throat when I saw the town at the beginning of the valley floor. I was almost in tears by the time I'd pulled into Dave's station and filled my gas tank. When I paid the clerk, she looked at me and said, "Ah hon," her cigarette never leaving her lips.

"Yeah," I said. And then, as though I owed her an explanation, I added, "The town's so ugly."

"Ain't it," she said. "But don't let it get ya. They're fixin' the lights."

"I've been with animals," I said, and by then I was wiping tears from my face.

"I know, hon," she said.

"You wouldn't know a Thelma Myzeld, would you?" And as soon as I asked, I realized I couldn't even remember her last name—her true name.

"Thelma who?" She'd had about ten puffs of her cigarette by then, and she'd never raised her hand to it. Ash would fall from it periodically and manage to miss her.

"Thelma Maylor—I'm not sure. I can't remember exactly. I guess the cigarette made me think of her. She loved to smoke." I made a sound that was meant to be a chuckle, but it could have been mistaken for a small rupture. I thanked her and left, telling myself to say as little as possible out loud.

I talked to myself through the little string of towns along the highway, trying to hang on to what I'd had up there in the forest. I imagined it was my grandmother's voice I was hearing, although I recognized my voice.

"And then you arrive. The forest is still as sleep. The mountain is just waking from winter. The golden dogtooths lay down a path for you. Something you didn't know you were carrying slides away. You breathe as though it were a new thing. Everything around you slows down and speeds up all at once. You walk into that cabin and you're home. I missed you. How I thought of you with your load of snow, fell asleep imagining your wooden floors, your wooden walls, your grayed beams and rafters and decking.

"Daddy's gone," I said and began to cry again.

I stopped to visit my mother on the way down. I'd talked to her on the phone, but I hadn't seen her since the fire. I began to cry again when she walked out of the trailer, her temporary residence, and stood beside the charred old family house, waiting for me to park.

But she was more cheerful than she'd been in decades. A burden had been lifted. If I thought about it, it was hard to imagine anything harder than my father himself.

She led me into the kitchen, which was the least damaged room. The smell of smoke was sharp, and after a few minutes I was coughing. My mother didn't seem affected by it. There were samples of wallpaper, paint chips, carpet, wall coverings spread everywhere, all in pastels that made me remember coloring eggs with her.

"I ought to get rid of this big ugly dining room set," she said. "I'm surprised it didn't burn." That was the only reference to the fire, surprised this was left, surprised that was gone.

"I'll take it. I'll buy it. It's got that battered look."

"Maybe I'd better keep it then," she said.

I was supposed to be in Salt Lake City. I had an art show to hang, but I turned my old yellow Scout around and headed back up Highway 20, back toward the cabin. The thought of managing in the city ruffled me, and I knew when I did return, I'd unplug the cell phones, answering machines, faxes, and probably the telephones themselves. I didn't miss television. I might keep a radio around. I'd get out from under the web of codes and menus and shortcuts. The coldness and clutter of it wasn't worth ten minutes of convenience, and I was unspeakably glad not to return to its tyranny.

I thought about my grandparents and how simple and satisfying their lives were—the same friends, the uninterrupted pleasures, the familiar places for eighty years. Continuity—almost a lost thing.

The cabin looked peaceful and secluded tucked in the jack pine and Douglas fir. As I drove up, I remembered how we'd lived there. Dinners at five o'clock, right after the guys had finished work and cleaned up. They'd come back to the cabins and get their towels and bars of Ivory soap and clean clothes and retrace their steps to the mill, where the shower was. One at a time. Maybe some of them showered after dinner because it was a long process for all of them to get into that bit of hot water the boilers heated. The shower smelled like soap and wet wood—it was nothing but a little wooden stall with some kind of a spray deal rigged up and a bench to sit on. We thought it was poetry.

Everyone helped with the dishes after we'd eaten. Grandpa always took the dishwater and threw it up on the hillside. Us kids dried the dishes. Then we'd sit in the living room and chatter—about the load of lumber that slid a little on the steep incline of the Ashton hill, about the early morning rain that ran down the inside of the root cellar, about Uncle Tom's dog running off with a Utah poodle, about Claine burning his lip on the cook stove when he took the lid off and bent over it to blow on the fire. Eventually the stories got more elaborate, some of them familiar—the time the horse kicked Nola and everyone was out picking huckleberries, the time D. H. pulled Mother up the face of Sawtell with the barrel of his .22.

The cabin was cold and I built a fire, chuckling at Claine burning his lip. He thought a lot of his face. I hadn't packed much for my short stay, and I got right to putting things away. I spent the evening straightening and cleaning, knowing I was settling in for a while.

When I went to the lodge later that week, I arranged for my canvases and paints to be sent up. As soon as they arrived, I began painting outside every morning—big, almost abstract scenes of the river and the forest and the sun glimmering off water. I tinted each canvas before I went out with the deepest red I had and then the earthiest yellow until the surface had a glowing effect, and when I got underway, I was surprised how much of that color I could leave showing and how much it held those endeavors in its hue. Even where I painted over that wash, a luminescence remained. I began to leave more and more red showing until little by little I almost quit using cool colors, except a straightforward cerulean. I went to bigger and bigger brushes and finally the side of my palette knife and then a three-inch putty knife, dragging one color across another.

I got closer and closer to what interested me until I was painting two or three inches of the bank, its red grasses, its dirt swirls, its colored rocks. It was like an archaeological discovery to get that close to nature, to peel back what you thought was there, what you believed grass looked like. I wasn't interested in the big, handsome landscape of a sky, a sweep of mountains, a slash of pines, and a field of wildflowers. I was after the heart of the thing.

It's complicated to paint outside. You've got to haul a paintbox. I'd brought mine back from France, and it was versatile but heavy, with its drawer for paints and its built-in easel that could hold a good-sized canvas. And you had to bring along a palette, turpentine, a medium, brushes, a palette knife or two, paper towels or rags, along with as many tubes of paint as you could stand to carry. It's another kind of gear, like fishing, and I loved all of it, the materials, the equipment, the process—laying out colors on the palette out there in the sun, swatting flies off, trying to keep them out of the little rounds of ultramarine blue, earth green, cadmium yellow, cadmium orange, yellow ochre, alizarin crimson, naphthol red, Indian red, burnt sienna. The colors were like the names of lovers to me.

I was all set up to paint the swirling water at the edge of the North Fork one morning. I was entranced by the red and brown and green rocks seeming to waver and disintegrate in the current. Instead, I turned into the woods. I didn't see it at first and then there it was—a single white columbine rising up out of the tangle of the forest floor. It was exquisite, detailed and refined amid the chaos—the dark greens, the red-and-brown bark, the broken branches, the tall tufts of grass—a moment of clarity in an abstraction of dark. I'd found the essence, and I began painting as quickly as I could. There was the old urgency—you know it will change—the light will change. But it's something else for me. It is not unlike the urgency of making love, not at all unlike it and as impossible to define. As I worked, I let everything dissolve by degrees from that one white moment.

When I stepped back, I was thunderstruck. The simplicity of the white petals, the delicacy of the pale green stem, the echo of the white in a bud partway down against the dark reds and cocoa and velvet greens was triumphal. It was an altarpiece. Everyone wanted that painting, but I wouldn't sell it. I felt its ministrations, and I slept under its watch.

The paintings I made through the next weeks stacked up around me and gave me a sense of protection, as though the sheer numbers of them could keep me from the hand of trouble.

Sometime after those first few months, I drove into Pond's Lodge and called Maraya again. I felt like talking, and she was a good talker. I wouldn't get pity from her, that was a relief, although there was always some baloney. When she answered, I smiled at that theatrical hell-oo of hers, high on the last syllable. I was back in the makeshift phone booth, tears in my eyes.

"I've lost my father, Maraya," I said. "In a fire." And there were those words. "He lost his ears."

Her answer was a long time coming and then she said that *dā-em* of hers. "Oh *dā-em.*" That made me laugh, it always did. "Maraya, you're just what I need. I can say anything, can't I? You won't be offended. You won't be alarmed. Not at the news but my *saying* the news. Say damn for me again. 'Oh *dā-em.*' Don't lose that crazy accent of yours."

"Us fureigners," she said. "We get no respeck. You're fureign enough in your ways to count for something, Miss Rennie. But *dā-em*—this about your father."

"By the way, wherever have you been for the bunch of years you were gone?" I asked her.

"I been here and there," she said. It was nothing new for her to be evasive.

"When you're home I'll bring you yams and turkey and dressing and mashed potatoes and gravy."

"Don't make it sound too good." I leaned against the counter. I was happy to be talking to her, and slightly disconcerted. "You're still doing turkey the regular way, aren't you?" I said.

I heard her trademark laugh. "You remember how we do it in Nicaragua. It's an advanced culture, Miss Rennie."

I laughed. "What's advanced about not wearing shoes?"

"We cope with the environment. That's advanced." There was the Spanish lilt in her *advanced*.

I was still laughing. "Bit of therapy, that's what you are, Maraya."

"Listen, kid, come out of them woods soon—that's where you are, isn't it?"

"Soon, Maraya. And you're in Salt Lake City. I'll come find you."

I stopped at the mill pond on the drive back to the cabin. Sitting out there looking at that gray-blue mirror of the sky, I went over the details of my father's death I'd kept at a distance. "Good hell!" I'd said to the fireman who'd told me about my father's ears. "Why would I want to know any of it?" And then I could see by his face that he couldn't stand having seen it himself. "You put yourself in danger for him, it must be…"I mumbled.

I'd entreated my mother never to tell me details. "I can't…" I'd tried to say, and she had interrupted me—angry, it seemed. "Don't worry," she'd said. *Was* she angry? Anger scared me at that time more than it ever had. But whatever I said, details slipped out, and I'd finally been the one to get hotly angry and say, "I don't *want to think* of…"

It was full summer before my mother and I really talked about the fire, another phone conversation with me leaning against the wall outside the bar at Pond's Lodge. It was as though each of us sensed the other could say something that would ruin the frail scaffolding we'd built around ourselves.

Kent could say what we couldn't. A few months after the funeral, I had gone to Rexburg to the group home he was in now, and he'd noticed I was losing weight. "Sick?" he'd said the minute he saw me. "My daddy passed away, didn't he?" He must have heard that term at his school. "Yes," I told him, "he did." And then he said that sentence he always said. "Is there some way we can go and get him back?" That was his longest sentence since he was twelve, and his biggest thought. He was more than he'd ever been.

I stood there that day talking to my mother on the phone and carrying on a conversation with Kent in my mind. I imagined him precisely, and I studied him for signs of how he was doing. I bought him coffee and tried to simultaneously follow what my mother was saying and what I was telling Kent, *There might be some way we can go and get him back. We could take the mule Daddy always talked about. We could go to the Mojave Desert, and wait for the right constellation, camp out under clear skies. We've got to see Jupiter.*

I know, he answered, and he watched the night, his hand clutching the front of his shirt. I noticed his one eye had begun to droop and he held his mouth differently now. *You're adorable, do you know that? You're starting to look like Walter Matthau.*

Walter? he said with a wild giggle.

Did you see the movie—what was it, Grouchy Old Men?

Grumpy *Old Men!*

You don't miss much, do you? You look like that old guy, kid.

We waited until we saw Jupiter. *I think I see it,* Kent says. *Is that it?*

I think so.

And we loaded the mule and started out in the darkness, a small knapsack each, no maps, no plan, just the two of us—Daddy's children. *We'll go by heart,* we said to each other.

My mother was repeating a sentence over and over. "Rennie! Are you there? Are you all right?" I came back. There was the edge of anger in her voice.

"Don't drift *off* like that. Kent started..." She stopped there.

Again I asked my mother about the fire. "That last night, your father knocked on the wall," she told me. "And that's when he fired that sawed-off .410."

"We never dared shoot that thing," I said. I had a lot of trouble coming to terms with his firing that gun.

"He fired it that night." Her voice had that matter-of-fact quality again.

"What time was it?" The time had become the key to something I couldn't name.

"It was three-thirty in the morning," she said. So he had an hour and a half to live.

"I remember looking at the clock. He asked me to sit on the edge of his bed, and he talked and talked."

"What did he talk about?" I could hardly breathe again; I was almost praying. And then, as though I couldn't control it even long enough to hear her tell me what they talked about, I asked her about that key in his door, tentatively, as though I didn't remember it. But I did remember it, and I was angry with myself that I'd brought it to her mind. I was sick at myself.

But she didn't answer. It was one of those false moments that makes you feel the air is too thin. She acted as though she didn't hear me. She was telling me, "I went into his room and we talked for a long time. Your father said, 'Do you know when I first knew I was in love with you?'" and the leap away from what we were about to approach thinned the still air. I concentrated on breathing as she told me the story of the night Daddy fell asleep in the car. She became dreamy and sentimental. I hadn't heard her talk like that since the forties.

"He laid his head down in my lap and fell asleep. I remember looking down at him and thinking what a cute guy he was. He had the most beautiful eyes, and dark, almost black hair. And the most beautiful mouth. I leaned over and kissed him and he woke and looked up at me.

"'That's when I knew I was in love with you,' he said to me."

I was confused, I was embarrassed, actually. I couldn't imagine why the key was in the door. She waited for me to say something.

"He always called me 'Sug.' From sugar, I guess. Then he quit calling me that, and he didn't call me Sug again until just before he died."

"What else did Daddy say? Did he say anything about us kids?" My words revealed so much to me I made a little sound. I sounded like Kent.

"Yes," she told me. "He talked about Christmas Eves and the songs and the camping trips. He got remembering when we were camping with Ginger and Val and Roger at Krupp Siding and the guys and you kids had gone fishing and Val said, 'You listen, you'll hear a splash in a minute,' and sure enough, there was a splash.

"'And you watch, pretty soon you'll see Roger come dripping up over the hill.'"

I remembered those trips. It did happen every time, and Kent and I came giggling behind Roger. I laughed, picking up the story.

"And you listen. He's going to start bawling just about when he gets to the bottom of the hill." And there he came, dripping from hair to socks and bawling his eyes out. And there was Kent, not yet twelve, and me, the two of us trailing after Roger and laughing our hearts out.

And then I started to cry again. I was getting crying down. Anyone's loss does it. I sat sniffling and remembering my father telling that story and our laughing about it year after year. "It happened every time we went camping," he'd chuckle. "You watch." I didn't think I could stand to hear my father telling it again when he was telling it.

My mother became aware of my struggle. It floated to me through the air. She was just realizing a daughter had lost a father. She had to put that beside a wife losing a husband she maybe wanted to lose. I saw her running back and forth under that window calling his name. And she was telling me, "Your father said how much he loved you and how proud he was of you." She paused and then went on. "Your father was very romantic and sentimental when we went together. He was tender and gentle." She offered this.

A flutter ran through me. How were we connected? These were their last words. How many people was he? Am I? How much time do I have left? And my mother? And why don't I wonder yet about her? Will that take a death? Pay attention.

And I let myself fade from the equation and imagined them young together.

My father was no stranger to deception, and perhaps my mother wasn't either. But they must have begun in tenderness, she was trying to tell me that, and I saw the day. They were outside. It was an early spring Idaho afternoon, on the banks of the Snake River, above the little town of Ashton. You could smell the grass and the wildflowers, the pungent alpine daisies, the flower with a thousand names. The meadows were gleaming with them.

This is the geography. She lives in Rexburg, he lives in St. Anthony, and then there is Ashton, where they've come for the afternoon, and then the forest and the sawmill. Up the line. You go up the line to St. Anthony and Ashton and the sawmill, and then West Yellowstone. And then Canada. And then Alaska. And then Russia. This earth.

I was conceived on the line to the sawmill, that's all that matters to me. I'm sure of it. Because that's where paradise will be for me. That's where my grandparents were and where I found my grandmother again, and where I took David.

It's evening and I go to my bedroom and get in bed, the bed I'd slept in with David. I prop myself up high so I can see out the little window. The first trip with him was about this time of year.

I can remember it down to the sometimes bantering, sometimes languid conversations we had, and I reach for a pencil and paper and write it out as I remember it, so I'll have at least this record.

On our way north, we drove through Ucon and noticed we were low on gas. "We'd better *fill 'er up*," David said. We were well into Idaho, somewhere past Blackfoot. When David would trot out a phrase like that, imitation Western, he'd give it an ironic emphasis. "We wouldn't want to be mar*ooned*." He began to read the signs along the roadway—"Bess and Henley Potatoes, Bisle Jenkins Saddle Supplies. Where *do* they come up with those names?"

"Don't you have any Bisles and Henleys in Philadelphia?" I said as we pulled up to a self-serve gas pump. "Was everyone in your neck of the woods named Franklin or Price or Wanamaker?"

"Or David Braniff," he answered. "Listen, England, you love local fla*vour* as much as I do, and if there's a snob in the car, there's two." We were beyond rapture at being in my Idaho, and everything amused him.

A woman came to the doorway of the grocery store that was part of the station and threw a suspicious look over us like a net. She wore Levis, straight-legged and rolled at the cuffs, and a puffy, short-sleeved blouse.

"My mother had a blouse like that," I said. The woman stood looking at us. Her hair was dyed brown, clipped back from her face. Here and there she'd made a little twist and secured it with a bobby pin. She was pasty-looking, her lips the same color as her eyelids. In the ten minutes we were getting gas and glancing around, her only comment to us was, "How much?"

A few more miles, McCrea's Bridge, another mile and then we were pulling off onto the road into what was left of the saw-mill camp. We couldn't get very close to the cabin so we loaded our gear and walked across the meadow. The last of the alpine daisies, dried now, crunched underfoot and their tangy smell rose up. And then we were at that familiar door, and I reached for the key under the grayed porch steps, and I was saying, "It's old now, it's in disrepair. All the others moved their cabins so it's the only thing out here."

"I've been waiting for this," David said. "Our time. Time has no rest energy."

"No rest energy. I love your mind. That's what I have in mind for you." I began to unbutton my shirt. When I looked up, David was unbuttoning his, and I felt the rush he always brought.

"You're so unfalse," he said to me. He leaned toward me and traced the line of my face with the tips of his fingers.

And the afternoon escaped us.

Sun fell in slanted bars across the bed. It made an angle where it dropped over the edge and down the coverlets and another where it fell across the floor. My back was warm from it.

“Tell me about your grandparents,” David said. “The edge of the sunlight runs right across your shoulder, and if you turn over, it will—yes, it runs right across there.”

“You don’t make it easy to talk,” I said to him.

“Always talk to me, Rennie. It’s the deep side, isn’t it?”

“How much you are. My grandfather would have liked you. He was born Royce Glenn Douglas in a little town in Idaho that no longer exists.” We were lying on the high bed in the room that had been mine, the room I’m in now, our words spoken so near each other, they were muffled. “A little town not far from where we are. Our stories and our histories, David. Weave us together.”

“A full portion of intimacy,” he said. “Tell me more.”

“My grandmother was always amusing, and vastly colorful. She enjoyed herself, took pleasure in her own sense of color and humor, but she wasn’t self-absorbed or affected in the least. She was the same warm, fun, witty woman with highbreds or low. If she had a preference, it would not have been for the high side.”

“A granddaughter who came along and saw it all. I see it all, Rennie—how beautiful you are, and how connected. Do you take after them, Rennie?” He put his arms around me and lay alongside me.

“I’d like to take after them,” I said. I loved how David felt against me—the after-love between us like being in a nest. Nothing separated us, not space nor air nor thought. “We’re like sleepy little animals, you and me. Subdued and content.” I raised up and leaned on my elbow so I could look at him. “I do take after them, both of them. I have my grandfather's round Scottish nose and my grandmother's almond eyes. I have his shyness, and his wry ways a little, I suppose. And I have her curiosity and sense of adventure. Maybe I'm not so bad a talker myself." I looked at him carefully.

We dressed in languor despite the cool night air that had settled into the cabin. The fire we'd half built had gone out hours earlier. I watched David slip a flannel jacket over his shirt.

"It's all different after, isn't it. It's the real beginning." And I was not hungry for anything outside our room. "You take me otherwhere," I said to him.

Remembering David, remembering full intimacy, where one's beginnings, one's dreams and yearnings, and one's abilities are present in the powerful current, filled me with gratitude for having had it and bewildering sorrow for having lost it. I wondered how it had been possible to live without joy after such moments. I could see him, I could feel him, the impressive size of him, his scent of soap and fresh air, the warmth that radiated from wherever his hand fell, his eyes assuring, embracing. And they could be so sad. I felt myself respond to him all these years after his death. My pages made it almost too real, and I went outside and walked to the mill pond where I'd stood with him in the evenings. I came back in when it began to get cold and fixed myself fried potatoes and onions for dinner. That's how we used to eat, and I was returning to it. There wasn't much else.

My grandparents were in love like that. My grandmother had said to me once, "Your grandfather has a beautiful body, and I mean all over." How wonderful to be told such a thing. It made me rejoice in my inheritance. It was a pleasure—like sun, like food—a very physical pleasure to think my mother came out of that kind of love. Then years later, when my grandparents were unable to fully care for themselves, I was helping my grandfather change nightshirts, and my grandmother said, "See what I mean by beautiful all over." Those two sentences were probably spoken ten years apart. She astounded me. They both did.

I went into the kitchen and sat looking out at the flourishing meadow in the dimming light. I felt comforted; I had had abundance. And I sat perfectly still and at peace and summoned my grandmother's voice, and there she was.

> The trip up for us used to really be something in the early days, but uncomplicated in its way.

I remembered it all, and I listened. I knew I was at a crossroads, knew I was being given something I would rather have than anything else in the world, and I listened to her in a different way than I had as a kid. I didn't want to miss a word.

> We mainly wrestled with what seemed like easy things—the laws of nature and such. We would go up with wagons and teams, herding the milk cows as we

went. It would take anywhere from a week to ten days because the roads were so bad. They were so corrugated and miserable the men had to stop and corduroy them—that's when you cut poles and lay them across so you can get through. I remember one especially bad season. We corduroyed that strip in there between Cooks and Last Chance when you leave the flat—we used to go through the flat, not around it—we corduroyed that clear to Pond's. We'd get the horses down in the mud and the wagons nearly out of sight.

On the trip up there the summer after Lilly died, we went as far as St. Anthony the night before and stayed with Royce's sister, Maggie. Royce's mother and his brother Clyde and his wife went with us the next morning. We started from St. Anthony at eight o'clock that morning and we didn't get to the sawmill until eight o'clock that night. It was only forty miles of travel, but we had one flat tire after another, just one flat tire after another. When we got to Ashton, which wasn't even halfway, we'd had so many flat tires that Royce decided he would go in and have a hot patch put on, but we didn't have a dime left. That was right after he had been in Orofino working all winter, and when he came home he had been beaten out of so much money, we didn't have a dollar between us. Anyway, there was a guy named Spike at the service station—he got kidded about that—and he put a hot patch on this tire so we could make it the rest of the way to the mill. Roy asked Spike how much it was. The fellow said it was ten cents, but Royce didn't have a thing. He wanted to write a check, and the guy said, "Oh, never mind. The next time you come, you can pay me."

Another thing in those early days—groceries were shipped up on the train. An order would be mailed down to the store in Rexburg and the groceries would be shipped up. And pigs and horses and cows were kept at the camp. Royce still says, "I don't believe those kids of ours milked, Mother. I don't believe they ever milked." I tell him I know they didn't. Sam hated to milk because the damned cow would run right through you.

One night Royce and I got home late from delivering lumber—sometimes I'd ride with him—and this night we could hear the pigs just a'squealin' when we came into camp. Royce thought they hadn't been fed so he took slop right down. On the way to the pens he could hear the squealing was coming from the side of a hill. So up the hill he headed to see what was going on. When he got to it, he found a bear eatin' on the pig while it was still alive. He picked up a stick, drove the bear off, picked up the pig, and took it back to the pen. Then he went and got Clyde, and they took guns and watched for hours but never saw the bear. However, the next morning, the pig was gone.

Royce never was afraid of nothing.

I got up from that old kitchen table and walked out the screen door and stood looking over the meadow. The path my grandfather had strolled to the mill and back was almost filled in now with grasses and wildflowers. The merest line was visible in it, as though a cat had just trod carefully through it. We'd scampered up and down that path—we'd had those days—and something relaxed in me. I stood out there smiling and listening to her.

Old Charlie Pond had built Pond's Lodge, and he had the biggest dances within a hundred miles, maybe two. The place wasn't anything when Ted Kent owned it. Then Charlie Pond bought it. He was a corker, Charlie Pond. He wouldn't take a regular shovel to shovel sand, he'd take a scoop shovel. He was one of the outstanding personalities up there then. It was a colorful area. Doc Mack built Mack's Inn. He started in the tourist trade at Krupp Siding. He built a few cabins there, then as the time grew on, he moved down where Mack's is now.

Another personality was Doc Riggs. He was the doctor who delivered you and Kent. And the Harrimans were up there at the Railroad Ranch. Averell Harriman went on to be a Washington figure. And the Krupps come up. They were a very wealthy family from Chicago. The old man, J. P. Krupp, was a big criminal lawyer. When they'd come in, they'd come to what we still call Krupp Siding in two or three private cars. That's where our groceries were shipped, to Krupp Siding.

And McCloughs came up. Then there was a couple others who came up to join the poker gang—a couple of deaf-mute boys always came. Anyway, they'd all gather in the back of Doc Mack's place—all the men—to play poker. Ling See would come up from St. Anthony for the game—he'd bring a car up about every weekend and lose it. There were cars and houses and ranches on the table in those games. Doc Riggs won the Deer Creek Ranch in a poker game. Zlake ran it for him and when Doc Riggs died, he willed it to Zlake. Wes, that was his first name, had built everything and his wife, Ruth, had run the dining room. It was one of the outstanding dude ranches of its day.

The Krupps were just terrible during hunting season. They'd kill thousands of chickens—we always called them chickens, but they were sage hens, to be specific. Then they'd dig a hole and bury 'em. I don't think they ever ate a bird.

We used to deliver a lot of lumber to Willard and the boys. Willard was the oldest son, I believe. He made his money in speakeasies in Chicago, that was the word we had. I think he was the one built the big white house they tore down when they put in the reservoir below Pond's. Anyway, the Krupps had a big party at the house this one night, and Senator William E. Borah was there. Old man Krupp went down into their cellar to check the whiskey keg, and it was about half empty, so he told his boys to add some water to it. Well, Willard went right down and added a couple of gallons. Later in the day, Seth thought he'd better take care of it so he went down and added a few gallons. Just before the party, Claude remembered and he rushed down and added some more water.

During the party, Senator Borah—and he was one of the best senators Idaho ever had—was asked to make a few comments. He didn't say much. "Friends," he said, "whenever I want a good drink of Snake River water, I'll always come to Krupps."

It took me a while to come back to myself and the present moment. I walked out into the night. "Your very considerable inheritance, these people, this bold and colorful time," I said to the moon.

Early the next morning I went over to my car and opened the trunk and got out my easel and a canvas, a 20x20, and my paint-box and turp and liquin, and set up partway out in the meadow, where I could look back at the cabin against the ridge of pines behind it, defined against that pure fresh sky.

The first color I applied was that heartrending blue, and something in the clarity of it made me think of the unusual sky on the day of my father's funeral.

I remember the sky on that day because just before we went into the chapel, my mother stood talking with my brother. They were framed against that March landscape, bright and sharp, no dust or pollen dulling it. Then we walked into the chapel together, and I went up on the stand. There was a song and a prayer—I don't remember them. Then I was facing the gathering, and I heard myself say, "We would go down to that river with my father." And it all rushes back, and I'm trying to give a funeral speech—a daughter paying tribute and saying goodbye to her father. And nothing is further from my mind. I'm saying, "Our days together. We get our gear laid out. Father says 'Let's leave first thing, right after breakfast, early breakfast. Be there for the first hatch.'

"'Yeah,' we say. 'First hatch.'

"'We don't want anyone in this family fishing the Gentleman's Hatch,' my father says.

"'No,' Kent laughs."

I look down at Kent. He's sitting on the second bench. I never see him in a suit and tie, and he is sitting so straight and smiling at me—that private smile between us that embraces the history we share. I speak to him.

"'The Englands don't fish the Gentleman's Hatch.' And we dart about, grab our poles, reels already in place, check our hooks, number six, and quick find the shovel and get some worms, get the right ones, he hates those short worms. 'Don't break them, ugh, Kent, put that one back in the ground.'"

Kent smiles again.

"'Daddy won't use it. No, better get more, he likes more than ten. And flies? Daddy will have the flies. I better take a few. Sandy Mites.'"

"And we set out, excited, afraid. Kent holds the pickup door open for me. I try to let him slide in first, by Daddy. 'No, go ahead,' he says.

"And we go up the hill in the old Ford and down it and across McCrea's Bridge. The grass alongside the road is just beginning to turn red. And the Oregon grape leaves are already scarlet. We don't have much time left. The trees make slices across the road and I hear them in my mind, *blip blap blap blapblapblap blap blap blap*."

People are nodding and crying and looking worried. And the only thing I can do is tell this story. My voice must be hushed, must be low; I can see people strain to hear, and I'm looking at Kent.

"'Shall we walk in or drive up Stamp Meadows?' my father says. We don't answer. We know it's not a question.

"'Stamp Meadows,' he says, he always says that. 'I think we'll drop down there past the creek. Can you walk a ways?'

"'Yeah, sure,' we say, right together.

“’Twins!’ He laughs. ‘How’d I get me a set of twins?’” and he slaps me on the leg and I grin. I can feel my silly, quick flash of a grin, and I slap Kent on the leg and he smiles as fast as it’s possible to smile.” He looks cute when he does that and I wonder if that’s how I look. Even with Kent there in the audience to look at, I feel singular and meditative. I continue.

“There’s the smell of the river. Chills run through me. My grandmother said she could smell the fish when she got near water. Mist is still rising off the Coffee Pot when we get to it. We hike down the steep road, way too steep to drive, watching for moose and sniffing huckleberries. I stumble around trying to keep from sliding in the dust and loose pebbles. I want to get there and get my line in, watch it float out, watch the fish rise, take fish home and sit in my corner by the stove as my grandmother prepares them. I see us telling about the river, all sitting around the kitchen table, looking out at the meadow, evening falling.

“Kent caught the first one,” I say. “‘Spinner fall!’ he cries out, and all at once the water is covered with spinners, their spent wings laid out on the water and the trout beginning to rise.

“‘They’re slashing!’ Kent cries. Or ‘They’re sipping! Hurry, Rennie. We’ve got to find our best match.’ And we take out our boxes of flies and pore over them. Kent gives me the best fly if I don’t have it.

“We stay out there for hours, the sun warming our backs and shoulders, the fish flirting with our flies. And Kent does get the first big fellow, and it's furious action for what seems like an hour. 'Keep your tip up!' Daddy calls. 'Get him on the reel!'"

I look out over the audience. There are people I haven't seen in thirty years. Tim and his playful mother who was our renegade church youth group leader. "I'm LuDene," she'd said, "and if you ever plan to play hookey, let me know so I can skip too." I can see people taking seriously a difficult father's death by fire. I have to get a handle on the emotions they call forth.

I've stopped talking and I'm only barely aware that I'm just standing there, listening to my father and I out on the river. *"Damn, that's a big fish, Kent," I hear my father say. He comes over and takes the fish out of Kent's hands. Kent is trembling, he's so thrilled. "God damn, that's over two pounds. What'd you catch this on?"*

"A Sandy Mite. Rennie tied it for me." Kent's voice trembles.

"Lemme see that fly," my father says. And he takes the tip of Kent's pole and gets hold of the line. "What'd I tell you about letting this line just dangle? Keep it in the cork on your rod. Jesus Christ, you'll snag one of us."

And he's taking that fly off Kent's line and saying, "Where'd you throw this in?" And Kent points.

"Can't you speak?" my father says. He's just about got the fly on his line.

"About there, in front of that rock."

"How far in front?" my father says. "What'd I tell you about being precise?"

"About five feet. Just exactly five feet. The first big riffle," Kent says. His voice has a different tremble now.

I can feel myself hate my father, hate the dark skin on the hand that ran through the lathe, hate the way it looks slick, hate the way his hair hangs down. I get out my little box and look through my flies. A splash falls on them and I swipe at my eyes. The minute my father steps out and casts, I slip Kent another Sandy Mite. His shoulders shudder.

"He's a nice fish, Kent," I say. "You played him just right. Gram will love him."

And we watch Daddy cast and cast into Kent's spot. I can feel Kent's bewilderment.

After a while, my father comes over and says, "Here, let me show you how to tie a really good knot." And he takes us up on the shore and sits down between us and does a blood knot, slow and exact. "Let me see you do it now," and we both do it just right.

"You're good fishermen," he says, and there's pride in his voice. "Real good little fishermen." And his hand is making that deft wrap, showing us one more time.

"You'll know every knot. You can always take care of yourselves if you can tie these knots and catch your own dinner. I don't ever want you hungry."

I know he's apologizing. He looks shy and sad, and I feel something for him, I don't know what. I don't understand it's love. I wish I could go over to him.

And I begin to talk again.

"Now let's get a big one for you, Rennie," he says. "Let's get right in front of that rock. Big old clever boys stay back there. They don't have to work hard and that snag will bring them food. Cast just in front of it, Rennie, that's right, that's right, that's good, mend your line, that's right, roll it right over him. Hup, there he is, he's on! You've got 'im. Two good fishermen! Keep your line tight!"

And I see my hands shake. *He's big, he's bigger than Kent's fish. If I lose him...My father says "Son of a bitch! Don't rush it, you'll lose him," and my hands shake so bad I'm afraid my father will see and I grip down and the shaking stops and I reel him in gravely.*

"God damn it. That was handsome work, Rennie."

And I have to steady my voice when I begin speaking again. "We sit on the bank and clean our fish. 'Should we have some lunch?' I ask. I'm so hungry I feel dizzy.

"'Let's fish for a while longer,' my father says.

"It's about four o'clock when we stop for lunch. The sun drops below the tops of the trees and it's suddenly cold. We get our sandwiches out, smashed tuna and melted Hershey bars. We devour them, legs stretched in the grass.

"'Here, I don't think I can eat this one,' my father says, and he splits his second sandwich and hands us each half.

"'Peanut butter and jam,' Kent says. He's got almost the whole thing in his mouth, and he laughs. And my father sings one of his favorites, standing there in his waders with his fishing pole, reel in the grass, swaying along to the music.

> It's a Barnum and Bailey world
> Just as crazy as it can be
> But it wouldn't be make believe
> If you believed in me.

"We stay up on the bank, crawling to a spot in the sun. We sit in a pool of light and lay our fish out. We've got fourteen. We line them up in order of size. Mine, and then Kent's, and most of the rest are Daddy's.

"My father comes over, kneels down, puts a hand on each of our heads and ruffles our hair. 'Fishin' with ya,' he says. 'On the Coffee Pot. I used to come here with my Daddy. Put grass over the fish to keep them cool.' And he leans and pulls out a handful of grass and covers our fish.

"Daddy goes off and fishes the deeper holes, and we lie up on that bank, our noses at the edge of the water, and watch what is happening. Hours and hours and hours. Out there changing our flies and mending our casts and wondering when Dad will take us home to dinner and watching the surface of the water, the Pale Morning Duns, the spinners gone now and the duns almost gone, and then the Caddis all over the water and the fish working seriously. And Kent saying 'We're ready for the Caddis, Rennie.'"

And what I hang on to is the calmness, that was the biggest part of those days on the water with my father and my brother, and the present condition of both of them reaches me and I have to handle my voice again. I begin to cry, but I'm still talking.

"We always ate so late we didn't care about eating. We gave Daddy all our best holes if we happened to have them. He carried our fish in if he didn't get any. We pack up dead tired, beyond being able to get back to the truck."

I pause. I'm unaware for a moment, and then I realize I've stopped talking and I resume.

"And as we leave, the water would be so smooth and so richly colored, the greens and browns and golds in a kind of rocking motion and occasionally a slash of red. That would be a trout's mouth.

"'Watch for any piece of fish,' Daddy would say. 'You won't see all of him. You'll see his tail, or his head, and you'll know he's there.'"

And I speak to my father.

"That's what I'm doing, Daddy, looking for any piece of you. You crazy bastard, I can't believe I miss you."

I can't keep the tears back, and I realize from the faces looking up at me how deeply personal my comments have been, realize I've just said all this at his funeral.

Where will I be when I have finished remembering? Who will I be when I only know forgetting?

The currents David was moored in were changing, were of a different order. What had been demanding in the waters he navigated had become relentless. He had less time, he was almost never not within reach of news sources, of staff, of calls; he could rarely be unavailable. The weight of it made him remote from time to time—an attitude I'd never seen in him before.

I knew it had to do with the hazards of world currents; I knew enough about fissures and pressures to be alarmed myself. We both worked on government projects that were classified. Like a lot of artists, I had developed other skills that were marketable. In addition to doing on-scene sketches for various agencies, I could teach and I could write, and that led me to guide others in articulating their own classified projects. So while I usually used my skills in the art world, I too was drawn into different currents. I suppose I became an important asset to David; he would have said indispensable.

Even now I'm saying more than I should. I don't speak of those projects, and we never did to each other. We wouldn't necessarily have known if we were working on the same assignments—

there was that much built-in security. But he was more and more in…something, not quite trouble. In pursuit. The price was near and so was the payment.

So there was yet another way our lives were secret. The layers and layers of code. I found myself instinctively removing more and more of the evidence of David in every record of my life. As I did so, Rennie and David, their fragility, became more understandable. Or maybe forgivable is the word I'm looking for.

What were we to be protected from now? We hadn't stepped up and chosen each other, chosen each other outright, that is. And I see that in my way I'm trying to make up for that now.

One of the things I am struck by is how little difference there is, really, between fact and fiction, between East and West, between a man and a woman, for that matter.

David and Rennie have been more the present reality than the life I have lived for many years. The numbers float through my head, and I feel a jolt as I realize the years I spent with David no longer outweigh the years he's been gone.

Only my days with my grandmother were straightforward. There wasn't a time when our relationship seemed convoluted or camouflaged. David must have had that too. I had asked him about his grandmother once when we were at the cabin. "Tell me about her," I'd said to him just before we left. "What was it to be ten east of the Snake River? On the Hudson with her?" We were sitting out on the little front porch looking over the meadow.

"We had an old family cottage," David said. "It was hers, had been in her family forever. She was a big and elegant woman. I loved the combination. She was solid and robust. She loved to throw balls to us and take us out on the creek—we called it a creek, but it would have been a river in the west. 'Let's tack out,' she'd say, and we'd get the boat readied, attach the rudder, and she'd steer us out of the creek. If the wind was just right, she'd unfurl the mainsail, drop the centerboard, and pull up the jib. Then she'd just hold that rudder as delicately as a violin bow and the wind would take us out across the silver bay. She's very frail now. I always made her muffins."

"You're lovely telling about her. And you still make her muffins? You're her delight, aren't you? What about your grandfather?"

"He had been dead five years by the time I was fifteen."

"You're interesting, David. Even your math is interesting. Go on and on."

"When we came back in from the creek, she'd disappear for an hour and when we saw her again, her long pants and fisherman's shirt were gone. She'd be in a dress, smelling spicy, her hair redone in the bun she wore. I only saw her let her hair down from that bun twice in my life.

"We'd have tea in beautiful cups, and then she'd read to us—*Treasure Island* or *Huckleberry Finn*. She had beautiful ways and lovely manners and gentle comments. 'How fair you look, David,' she'd say to me when I came in for tea."

"She sounds wonderful, solid. You do look fair. Was your grandfather like her?"

"Yes—a sweet and gentle man, but off running a bank or two. When he was away, my grandmother and I made pickles together. It was often just the two of us. I stained the shingles on the house. I picked cucumbers at the outlying farms."

"You made pickles with her?"

"Yes, we made dills and bread-and-butters. And mustard pickles. We've done it every year for forty-some years. Since before I can remember, I'm sure. Then I make her the muffins and a pear pie and she sings to me. She sings 'When your hair has turned to silver.'"

"Sing it to me, David," I said to him, and he sang, holding me in his arms there on the porch and we rocked back and forth, wanting to stay, wanting that oldest of things—wanting to turn back the clock.

"A pear pie. You're not—replaceable, imaginable. I couldn't..."

"I still go to her on Sundays if I'm in the United States. That sounds a little more heavily...traveled than I..."

"You don't like being important, do you?"

"No. I like my endeavors, though. I like my pursuits, my hopes for..." He didn't finish the sentence; I knew he couldn't. He must have seen that in my face, and he smiled in answer. That smile gave me whatever it took to walk out the door with him.

When we had our things in the car the last hour of that first trip up, I said, "Come to the mill pond with me one more time, David." I talked to him as we strolled down that familiar path.

"I can take you up through the mill any way you want, David," I said to him, still as enchanted as a girl by the spot where it had stood. "I know it so well, I think I could still come out of it with a sliver. How can it have been gone twenty years?

"Come back with me, David. We'll go right to where it was, and you watch my hands and I'll reach up—I always remember the handles I jumped for as a girl, up over my head—you'll watch my hands and see if a sliver doesn't come right at the moment I cross in memory over the place on those handles that was always rough.

"Ready," I continued, and I could hear the weight of the past in my voice. "These are the docks in the clearing between the cabins and the mill pond. Actually, it isn't much of a clearing, is it—there are a lot of trees in there. I call them docks because my grandmother did. Some years they'll be all white, then another year they'll come in both white and yellow. You never know what you're going to get till they come up. I can hear her say, 'What's the difference between a daisy and a sunflower?'

"Step over to the sloggy spot and watch for frogs. You don't see frogs like you used to. It smells different—dank, mossy. Slip along over these planks—wet and rich-smelling and slick as owl shit, to use the phrase we used to love. The planks are thrown down to help you get over, but I think they make it worse. I don't know where the water comes from. It's always wet here, not from a creek or a spring, just a nice smelling soggy spot where the water subs up from the pond. Drenchy," I smiled at David, at how beautifully he listened.

"There's the pond now, just across the little bridge. See the big A-frame rising at its edge—can you imagine it?—the meadow behind running off to the north up into the high country. All that is there now is the meadow and a big square of cement, but I can call it back, down to the last bit of grass.

"A cable from the frame hooks to the logging truck, red—a sun-baked red, and the truck engine tightens it—don't ask me how—and tips its bed and dumps that load of logs helter-skelter, and the pond monkey has him a job untangling those logs.

"He'll skip about on the logs and sort among them and bring the ones that are needed for the day's cutting. He pokes them along over to the chute with a peavey or a pike pole. When he gets them ready to chain up, he'll use a cant hook, and then he'll drop an enormous heavy chain around them and they'll be snaked up that steel chute by a donkey—a winch affair, one of the last of its kind. Sometimes a log will slip loose from the three or four or five that are being chained together and hauled and then look out! Logs come a'flyin' down every which way and the pond monkey could become acquainted with a widowmaker if he doesn't pay attention."

"Widowmaker," David said, and I stopped and stood out there at the edge of the pond and looked at him.

"Come out over the pond onto the gangplank," I said. "Come out over the water. The planks lead us to the chute. See the walkway to one side of it—the east side? A little precarious here and there. Walk on water for me, David. What do we need with reality?" And I tried not to put my head in my hands and weep for it all, for leaving it and leaving him.

"Did you smell the fish? And the tadpoles? And the water and willows? You can always smell willows here, and wildflowers, and if you get above the old wooden shower Grandpa built beside the boilers, you can smell the slaked wet wood that makes the shower in there so slippery.

"Let's go up in her now," I said to him. No one could be to me what he was. Nothing could be, not even the mill.

"Stay with me. Take the sway in the chute. Make it spring under your feet, swagger up it like a working kid, like a pond monkey. Feel the railing—it's as smooth as a willow from the men's hands running up and down it at least four times a day for thirty years. How many of them can I remember—Lester and Bill and Darrell and Tom and Cal and Dan and Clyde and Boon and Blaine and Royce, of course, and Seth and Ronnie, Claine, Kenyon, Billie, D.H. I can't remember the fellow's name who used to stay in and caretake in the winter—Gaskell Fiske, that's it. And a few women, and a few girls. All those hands smoothing this rail. Very few women's hands.

"Maneuver past the logs lying in her right at the top of the chute, step around them lying there side by side like sleeping soldiers. Smell the pitch and new sawdust. The light comes only from the east now, where the mill faces and is open. It's open at the other end too, but it's dark the long distance of her.

"Look at the carriage over to your right."

And I saw myself jumping along the logs and crying, "Eeeeeeeeeeyyyyyaaahh!"

"Come over here on the carriage, David—a little railway cart is about all it is—and I'll take this cant hook and bite its clamps into the log waiting there for a ride. Roll it onto her flat side. We call that doggin' it. The sawyer usually dogs her down—he runs the carriage. But today I'll step over to the controls, tip my hat down a little, *de rigeur*." And I act it out in my mind, with my hands, looking at what used to be.

"The oldest brother," I told David, who was watching me so carefully, "we called him Boon—he was the sawyer. He'd look at a log and see two-by-fours or two-by-sixes or log siding—that was our specialty—and he'd set his controls for what he wanted, hat dipped down. You do it like this—take that control that moves the carriage in hand, the shining wooden rod that comes up from the gears and machinery—beautiful with the redness of the years and the polish of the human hand and grayed nicely at the top where Boon's hand has rested for three decades. You don't move it so much as fondle it—it's a light motion, playful, back and forth, easing that carriage and that log toward those two whirling saws.

"Listen now. The big one will make one sound, a deep steady whirr, and you won't think you're hearing two sounds, just one, but there are two. And watch—here comes the log back through—we've reversed directions and she'll give a high hum this time.

"That's the carriage. I used to sit on the end of it when I was a girl and hang my feet over and ride back and forth all day long, the smell of the tree escaping with each cut like breath—pitch and sawdust and sap and sun released from bark, and the saws singing and a kind of sweetness and safety—up here, up in the heart of the monarch of the meadow."

We were standing out there in the meadow beside the mill pond, my arms up around David's neck. I held the back of his head and spoke against the side of his face. "If you look up in the eaves, you'll see the little barn swallows. They build their nests up here. The whole mill will just shake and they'll sit peacefully in their nests up in the eaves. 'The men are always real tender to those birds. Nobody better knock one of those nests down. I think every one of those guys loved those birds—they're so pretty, colored real deep bright blue and black and some light blue and green that blends together elegantly—and a long forked tail.' Those are my grandmother's words.

"Before we leave it as it was, David—what I come from, David—come out to the west end and look over the camp straight ahead of us. My grandparents' cabin is the first one in the line of them. The five brothers have their five cabins facing the meadow. In front of them in that stand of trees on the other side of the meadow, you see the commissary and the office and the garages. They're just old rustic wood buildings. Those garages used to be full of horses and carriages. Then they were full of Lincolns and

Cadillacs—that's all the brothers drove at the last of our milling days. And one Chrysler.

"Beyond the first line of cabins, halfway up the hill, are the woodsheds. Notice the little additions on them? All of us grandkids built little rooms on the ends of the woodsheds when I was fifteen, and we wallpapered them with newspaper. They leaked like sieves so we'd keep freshening the paper, and we acquired some dabs of information that way. Just a start.

"Up on the hill are the cabins for the hired help, and the waterhouse and the cookhouse and off way to the left, damn near down in a bog, is the bunkhouse. Way beyond—you can't see them—are the sawdust piles we used to play in. And you see some outhouses and some rooftops of cellars dug into the ground sprinkled through the camp."

I looked out over the one cabin left and the dead trees before me, and my voice shook as I said, "Take a look, David. You're looking at America."

He said to me, quietly, "Are we part of what's soon to be unrecognizable as well?" When we got back to the cabin, he continued, "I saw it all, Rennie. Rennie, I love you time beside God."

"Did I get a sliver?" I said, examining my hands. "Did I bring back that much?"

"May nothing come between you and your lives, between guarding the dream you keep alive in you, in me, Rennie England." And he put his arms around me. "There's something left to do, isn't there, Rennie? We've missed something, haven't we? In this holy place. Have we had it all?" And we were late getting away.

I found a yellowed piece of paper in the old roll top desk at the commissary a few mornings later. It was, how can I say it, *evidence* of those wonderful days. It was as though it were proof of me.

Monthly Statement

Douglas Lumber Company, Inc.

REXBURG, IDAHO and MACK'S INN, IDAHO

Rexburg, and Mack's Inn, Idaho, Nov 24, 1937

TO Harry Hare

Butte Montana

TERMS: 30 DAYS Net.

8% Interest on Past Due Accounts will be charged on the 15th of each Month

DEBITS	CREDITS	BALANCE
Balance due		$256.74
Nov Slabs		26.00
		$282.74

Mr. Silver wish you would please have this taken care of at once. Please mail to Rexburg Ida.

Right under it was the little sketch I'd drawn of the mill. I trace out my route, my Grand Tours. I walk my old paths in my mind, carrying the drawing outside and sitting on the little front porch steps that face the meadow.

Nothing essential has changed up here. The docks, the alpine daisies, are up now and their stalks and leaves are beginning to take on that pungent smell. If you walk through them in a few more weeks, they will crackle when you step on them. The kill-deer continue to make their call. Everything is always moving in the meadow and at its edge, the new quaking aspen stirring their leaves like a handful of tiny kites. The June grass is getting tall, and it sways in the breeze. Some of the lodgepole pines have died. It's quiet. It was never quiet here when I was young and it was a mill camp. And the old paths leave only that faint line now. You wouldn't see them if you weren't looking for them.

I watched a butterfly execute a luxurious, languid exploration. Sun and this meadow make me feel the richness of my own investigations, my coming to terms. And I go inside and light a fire, my main endeavor these days.

Tell me more, I said to my grandmother as I warmed myself. I could pick up her voice as soon as I grew calm and listened, and I knew we would resume our exchange.

> It's no wonder you loved the mill like you did. If anything was in your blood, that was. It didn't take Royce and me an hour to fall in love with our life there. The first time we were alone, as I look back, was when we had a little cabin at the mill. To this day I love every detail of it.
>
> Royce started working in the sawmill when he was real young. His grandfather had bought a sawmill before

Royce was even born, and the boys in the family had always worked it. By the time he was twelve years old, Royce was driving a horse and wagon—he hauled lumber from the sawmill down to the siding, Krupp Siding. That's where they loaded the lumber onto railroad cars. After that Royce worked in every part of the mill.

The early mills didn't have a pond like the one you grew up at. Instead of dumping logs in the pond and then snaking 'em up into the mill, we just stacked 'em on the ground and rolled 'em up onto the carriage that took them into the big saws. The carriage was up off the ground a ways—not way up in a second story like it was at our last mill. And I don't think it had a green chain. In our later mills, trimmed lumber come down the green chain, although it wasn't a chain, really—it was a wooden chute that the boards slipped down. They come down sideways on a conveyor-type deal—they slid down horizontal—and it's true, they made that green chain just as slick as a willow. You kids loved to play on it in the evenings after quitting time. You would skate down it and roll down it and dance down it.

The only men hired at the early mills were the choppers. They went into the timber and chopped out the trees and come out with logs. I guess the trees become logs the moment they're felled and limbed off. The choppers would bring the logs down to the mill and the boys would saw a few days, then they'd load a few days, then they'd start again. At that time, they had enough boys in the family to do the rest after the chopping.

The equipment in those early mills was real primitive. They fired the boilers with slabs. Later they had sawdust piped into the boilers. Royce done some chopping. He hauled logs. He hauled lumber. He used to haul lumber down to Krupp Siding and load it on boxcars by hand. The railroad would spot a car. Then when it come up, the boys would fill it with lumber.

The cabins at that time weren't very good, they were just shacks really, because they moved the mill often—moved it to be near the timber they were cutting. We had just a little sleeping cabin our first summer. There was no more than room for us and our clothes. Royce had a little dog and that crazy dog had to sleep on his pants. He'd roll them in a roll at the side of the bed and the dog would sleep on them. But we were alone, and we were in love, and there was no more saying goodbye when we heard the Yellowstone Flyer and knew it was already too late.

The first mill I lived at was on Hotel Creek. Then we went to Bootjack Pass. I was crazy about that little mill at Bootjack. We had a creek that flowed right through the camp and past our cabin, not off from us like it was at Hotel Creek. Then we moved to Yale Creek, and that's where we were when you were a girl.

In most of the cabins, we'd have a little porch where we'd keep the wood and the buckets of water. A dipper always hung above the buckets and everybody would drink out of it. It was the same at church—everybody drank out of the same sacrament cup. Makes you catch the flu just to think about it.

Off the porch was the kitchen. It was the main room of the house. Everybody would collect there on the benches—they'd pull them up close to the fire. We had every kind of good time up there together. We sat around in the evening and we'd light the kerosene lantern. Everybody ate and ate. We'd slice tomatoes and fry up a mess of fish and sit around and eat and talk until there wasn't anything left but a table full of skins and bones.

I couldn't help thinking how different my father's parents were. I don't remember anyone sitting around a table talking until there wasn't anything left. It was rancorous and tense. My grandmother England used to grab one of those heavy blocks of pig iron she kept nearby and wham it against the radiator to call my grandfather and my uncles to dinner. It echoed through every radiator in the house, but particularly the one downstairs where he was. And she went on and on, slamming away until my grandfather appeared at the dinner table. I could burst into sobs today at the idea of being dropped off there for a strange few days.

And then I quiet myself, listen. I can't afford an interruption.

Royce was a wonderful storyteller. He was kind of a quiet, shy guy, but could he tell stories! He'd tell about the time he and a bunch of his friends got expelled on April Fool's Day. They locked the teachers in a faculty room, that's what done it. Vern, one of Royce's cronies, brought a rope and they tied the rope to the doorknob and they had themselves some prisoners. When the teachers got ready to come out, they couldn't get out. The principal got a chair and got up to the transom and looked out and one of the boys hit his fingers with the end of the rope. They were real strict at the school—it was the old Ricks Academy, which was the church school so there was hell to pay.

Royce said he started smoking cigars in the big flu epidemic of—let's see—was it 1917 or 1918? He said nobody in his family got the flu. You gave your grandfather trouble over that. You always asked Royce if that was because everyone in the family smoked.

But back to our cabin. Off the kitchen of our place was a little bit of a bedroom—nothing to it but a bed and a slop jar—that's what we called the chamber pot. Nobody up there would have known what you were talking about if you'd said "chamber." We didn't stand on ceremony, I'll tell you that. We had all we needed in those funny little cabins though, as I look back, except when we were sick.

It was darn hard being sick with no running water nor no bathroom.

When we had you and Kent with us, we were down the hill from the cookhouse and our crazy cook, Edith. But that was our last mill. When we first knew Edith was at the first mill on Hotel Creek. She run the cookhouse and at the time it was right next to us. I helped her for our board. She was a real tasty cook. And funny with the guys. She never threw anything away. She had a real good way of using everything. And when she'd finally get tired of it, she'd throw it on the table and say, "Eat it, damn ya, you'll get it every meal till you do."

She had dyed black hair, brown eyes, and she was just as jolly as could be. She had a bedroom off the cookhouse, and she was scared to death of thunder and lightning. If it stormed at night, any one of us could look for her to come, saying, "I've got to have a bed. I'm not staying over there alone in this." She was just a lot of fun. Your mother wasn't much better when it thundered. She always had you twins standin' in a closet with her through the merest little storms.

When we were on Bootjack, our cabins were a little bigger than they were on Hotel Creek, and we had some real parties there. We always had family up and our old gang from Rexburg. Some of the boys had been to California for the winter and they'd made friends. One was an Italian and he was one of the big guys in the Bank of America. He came up to see the boys, and he barbecued a whole lamb—made the sauce and all. Us women made the cakes and pie. We put long board tables up, and did we have a shindig! He come back and we did that every summer for years and years. He was the nicest guy, just a peach of a guy.

We bathed in little round galvanized washtubs. You always called the one you had by its number—Number Six Common. That was stamped on the bottom of it, if I'm not mistaken.

At the mill at Bootjack, Royce was the plumber and he instigated an improvement. They built on a little room off the side of the boilers and piped water from the steam boilers into this little bathhouse. We couldn't bathe until there was plenty of steam up. We always tried to get out there and bathe before the firemen let the steam down. It didn't have much of a roof on it. We had to get together because we couldn't use that much water. So us women would get together and then the boys would throw buckets of cold water on us from that bit of a roof.

One time they piled ashes up too close to the bathhouse and it started a fire in the night and we nearly lost our sawmill. One of the guys went out without any shoes at all and another with his shoes on the wrong feet and they fought the fire.

We didn't have linoleum in our cabins until later. We had to scrub a wooden floor on our hands and knees. We just had bare walls, unfinished inside, and I'd line up all our things on the two-by-four bridging. Every Saturday I'd take it all down and dust off those two-by-fours and wash off everything.

Even a word like *linoleum* changes the balance in me—the glides, the rolling sounds! I remember my grandmother's linoleum, that one patch of it—wheat-colored squares with a terra cotta line around them and a tiny apple green square in each corner. I swept it, I mopped it, I dedicated myself off and on to keeping it spotless.

If we ever done any canning, we did it at the cabins or when we first went down. I took corn off and laid it out on an old door with a mosquito net on it. Before you put it on there to dry, you had to cut it off the cob and put it in the oven for just a few minutes to set the milk. It seems like we used to put a little salt and sugar with it in the oven.

Then other times I put it in sacks behind the kitchen stove to dry. When I went to gather it in one year, the chipmunks had chewed a little hole and carried it away just as slick as a button. There was hardly anything left of it.

We used to dry apples. We'd peel them and quarter them and then thread string through them and put them outside on the line and dry them. They dry best if you have them in a good, hot sun. My grandmother used to dry sacks full of apples and greengage plums and peaches besides all she canned. My dad's favorite pie was dried peach pie.

As I get to remembering, I think that was the year we got our first pieces of furniture. We got the library table and the phonograph for Christmas. You could get one for about $45. And it was the first you could make payments on things, but we never done that. Years later, Royce came driving up the dusty road into the mill in a dark green Cadillac, and he'd paid cash for it. You and Kent were there, nearly out of your minds with amazement. I think you just figured we were poor. Heaven knows we were for a long time. Not so bad as some, even in the Depression.

We had a worker from the area of all the dust storms and he used to say, "We was starved, we was stymied, we was stepped on." We never knew anything about that kind of poverty. But in the Depression, people didn't have money to buy lumber. It was a poor price during that time. Some guy in Ashton said he was goin' to run the Douglas's out of business right at the outset of the Depression. "You'll play hell doin' that," one of our customers there told him. "You give the Douglas's a sack of beans and a side of pork and they'll be right there."

Royce always scrounged around and found a job when no one else had one. He never didn't have a job, and he never didn't have a little money with him. He never spent everything he had, except for that damn tire.

We had some grand times as well as a lot of work up there. There were several events we never missed. One big one was the Dog Derby at Ashton. Ashton is the little town just about right between the mill and Rexburg—it's the last town before you get up into the timber.

People came from all over that area to see the Dog Derby. Royce never missed one till I married him. I asked him why he quit goin' the other day—we got talkin' about the races some way, and he said, "I missed a lot of things after I married you, Mother."

"Yes, and there's a lot of things you didn't miss," I told him. Anyway, the Derby was real big. They run a special train up from the towns below in the middle of the night to get spectators there for the next morning. Boy, was there a lot of booze consumed and a lot of dancin'.

That's where our Scotsman Larry Hutchinson's drinking buddies were from—two little brothers, not either one of 'em five feet tall. One run the liquor store there in Ashton and the other the post office. Terry and Togo was their names. They were drunk from noon to midnight every damn day. Thinking of Larry puts me in mind of when you kids were little. We were playing cards in the afternoon—some of the wives met every day at one o'clock, no matter what, and played pinochle. It seemed like we were always at my cabin, I don't know why. Well, this one afternoon you pestered and pestered and pestered us. Larry was our old handyman, and he was up on the hill digging a cellar for us. We thought we'd get rid of you—you'd sit in the corner by the stove and roar with laughter all to yourself at the swearing that went on in that game. It was bad, I'm ashamed to admit how bad. When we got so we wanted to forget you—you were practically inside the stove you'd sit so close to it, asking us questions about this phrase or that—we sent you out to see Larry. Pretty soon here you come back and we said what are you doing back and you said, "Larry told me, 'By God you, Rennie, ya better get outta here, too.'" You got an earful from everywhere.

LaRue, Clyde's wife, used to be the worst. Our cabins were side by side and we could all hear her shrieking at her kids, "Get out of here before I beat your brains with a turd on a stick, you damn dirty roaches." She talked like that to them, talked just terrible, but she could be a lot of fun, and she made you laugh. We played pinochle every afternoon for twenty years and a lot of words slipped out of us, I know that. You used to fall over laughing when I'd say some of my specialties. I'd be trying to get the damned kitchen cabinet to stay shut, for example, and I'd invariably say "I'm so mad at this damned thing, I could kick my butt up on my shoulders." I think that was your favorite.

That and "I'm so t-u-r-d tired I could f-a-r-t faint." I'm ashamed of that one. I'd hear you mumbling around "I'm too t-u-r-d tired" to your mother and I gave it up.

My boy Sam was a real corker when he was a kid, not that you weren't. Sam was taking care of this white rat he had one summer. He was working to get its cage right one afternoon and I come along and said, "Your rat looks awful big to me." I'd let him do pretty much as he pleased, but when I saw his pet was going to have babies, I told him I thought we'd have to get rid of it. Well, his face went as white as that rat and those eyes of his even paled out and right then, up and down the path to the cabins, he went asking, "Do you want a white rat? Ours is going to modify."

That reminds me of your mother when she was little, for some reason. We used to play a record called "Loving Sam," and Deborah loved it—she'd play it and play it and play it. After Sam was born, my father came over and he said to Deborah, "Well, Deborah, what are we going to name him?"

Deborah said, "We'll name him 'Loving Sam.'" She was only three years old then. She'd come and say to me, "Play 'Loving Sam' for me," and she'd have the right record every time. She must have had a little secret mark on it somewhere—she knew exactly which one it was and we'd play it for her and damned if we didn't name our last boy after that crazy song.

You were just like her later on, only you made me sing instead of play records. You used to love to sing with me, although you couldn't carry a tune in a bucket. At the last you'd always have me sing, "I'll Take You Home Again, Kathleen." Now I see it made you think of the life you didn't have—the home you didn't have to go to. I was sorry for that, just plain sorry. To have what you want and have it part-time. Royce and I had to deal with a lot of difficulty, but we didn't have to deal with that.

After that first summer alone together, we didn't go to the sawmill for a few years. Royce went up on the dry farm and worked. His father had dry farms, too—up in Teton Basin and one over in Antelope. They were miles apart—twenty or thirty or fifty miles apart, a long way. A dry farm is where you plant your grain in the fall, most of them do it that way. Then they just depend on what moisture comes naturally. There's no irrigation. That's all it is. It's usually in a hilly place where there's no way you could irrigate. A lot of money was made up in the hills behind Rexburg that way.

We got a davenport when we come down that first summer. By then, we had a house of our own and we thought we really had it fixed up nice. We had an old coal stove in it and a little rocking chair. And we got a decent bed.

I walked outside and strolled through the wildflowers, savoring what I'd been given. Instigate a little improvement. That one made me burst out laughing. And the linoleum.

I wondered how my mother, my grandmother's child, could be so different from her—different in outlook, in style, in manner. But naming her baby brother Loving Sam—*this* wasn't so different.

Was it my father who eventually took her into such brooding waters? And I remember something my grandmother told me. It wasn't said critically. It was said mercifully, at a time when my mother had left my father, fallen pretty thoroughly apart, actually more than thoroughly apart. And then, to our horror, she had gone back to him.

"Your mother," my grandmother remarked, "goes where she's the least unhappy." And Kent and I burst out laughing, because, I guess, she got it too right.

"You'd better instigate your little improvement," I said to myself the next morning. I got the sketch my farmer friend had made and studied it. When I had it in mind, I laid out the rolls of pipe that were still in the back of my truck. They alarmed me when I saw them all lined up in the meadow. I put the bits and pieces that would link them in a bucket. Then I went to that wonderful top drawer at the end of the kitchen counter—Grandpa's drawer. Everything was still there—his hunting knife in its leather sheath, old postcards of the Park, screwdrivers, shoelaces, rubber bands, a chunk of pine gum, and tucked in the back, a tin of Copenhagen. That brought a smile. I took the knife and screwdriver and put them in the bucket. Finding a wrench was a little harder. There was a pair of vise grips beside them in the wooden toolbox in the shed and I took them. At the last I added a small hammer and grabbed some matches and a few sheets of newspaper from the little banded barrel beside the stove. Every paper that ever came into camp was put in that barrel and saved for starting fires. I knew that pipe was going to be hard to handle and might have to be warmed up.

When I had everything organized outside, I cut the bands from the nearest roll of pipe and began laying it out. The black line it made cutting through the meadow distressed me. I nearly rolled it back up. Nothing could have been more intrusive than a length of black plastic running through the wildflowers. There were places where they'd been knocked down. "The destroying left hand of progress," I muttered, the one line I remembered from Sarah Orne Jewett. I might have abandoned my project if it hadn't felt so good to lose myself in an endeavor.

I proceeded more carefully, fitting the pipe down into the grasses and wildflowers, lifting them up over it until it was almost covered. Only bits of black showed through when I was finished laying that first hundred feet. I went back for the second roll and carried it to where I'd join the two. I laid it out with care, allowing for the coupling. That word always comes up.

Getting those two pieces together was going to be an education. I tried to think it through before I began to fit them into each other. Then I took one of the couplings and tried to push it into the pipe. It was tapered and ringed at both ends so that it could be slid into place and form a compression seal. *Slid* is the wrong word. I couldn't get any leverage holding the end of pipe. One hand wasn't strong enough to keep it steady, and the other hand wasn't strong enough to work the coupling into place. I put the pipe between my knees and gripped it while I maneuvered with that damned little coupling. Finally I put it down, twisted a few sheets of the newspaper into a kind of torch, and lit it. I held the flame under the pipe, moving it back and forth as I'd seen my father do with a blowtorch. I could feel the pipe heating up, and I crushed out the burning paper and turned that coupling into place neatly. "Yes!" I said to my audience of wildflowers, and I lay down in them for a few minutes. I felt something like happiness. I twisted more paper, warmed the end of the second roll, and fitted it over the coupling. I was engaged now. I had two hundred feet toward water. I'd forgotten how much I liked physical work and how good I was at it.

I should have rolled that second section out all the way before I started making joints, and I should have put the clamps over the end while I had an end. Now I had to go back to the beginning of it and slide two of them along the hundred-foot length to get to the joint. It was easier than taking the pipe apart. When I had the clamps tightened, I went back for another roll and walked with it and the bucket to the end of my line and repeated the process. I had a system worked out now, and before long, I had six rolls laid. They nearly reached the mill pond. If I'd had a pump, I could have quit right there, but I didn't want the complications of a gas motor.

The next roll took me alongside the pond and out into the willows. A creek smells different where there are willows, which is almost everywhere there is a creek. It's a heavier, danker smell, yet fresh, minty. I spent a lot of time in the willows as a girl. I used to take my little homemade fishing pole into them with a worm or two and catch fish. I hate to think how small they were.

By the time I had those seven rolls out, I was tired and hungry. And excited. It wasn't so much that I wanted the ease of having water at hand as that I wanted to see if I could make my idea work. I tried to imagine water streaming through the black tubing to the door of the cabin. The first thing I'd do would be to heat a few bucketfuls in the big dishpan on the stove and fill the Number Six Common and get in there and refresh myself. I'd had some very chilly baths in the creek.

I suddenly missed music. I wanted to bathe to Mozart's "Eine Kleine Nachtmusik." I'd have to pick up a battery-powered radio when I went to West Yellowstone and see what I could tune in.

When I got back to the cabin, I took a piece of ham out of the ice chest and diced it. I found the grater in its usual place and grated some cheese and made myself a proper omelet for lunch. Then I sat down and looked out the kitchen window to see how much I'd disturbed the meadow. Not as much as I would have thought. I pictured taking the waterline apart when I left, but I had no real sense of leaving.

The destroying left hand of progress—was that what it was? Was there a way to provide and not dominate? Could the gentleness excuse the incursion? I hadn't been a dominion-over-the-earth thinker for a long time. I found far more comfort in the Indian idea of stewardship. I imagined a sentence from Chief Joseph: "Let me not take more than I need," and I added, maybe not even quite that much.

Water, my grandmother used to say—that's what people shot each other over. That night I dreamed about the Mediterranean.

The week David and I lived together in Provence, we went by different routes. He met me at the airport in Marseille. I'd flown first class, something I never did, and I was as rested as though I'd slept in my little room off the porch of the cabin. My mind was as still as the surface of the sea.

We were unhurried. We had not known days without the shadow of imminent departure for a long while. David was tanned and rested as well. He wore the short-sleeved woven shirt I'd gotten him in Italy. Blue like his eyes, a mix of the harbor and the sky.

He held me as I stepped off the plane. We stood there in people's way, embracing, breathing in the first of many days. "Bouillabaisse," he said.

"Yes," I answered, and he led me through the perfunctory customs to a dark gray Renault. He drove along back roads, away from the already heavy traffic of Marseille to L'Epuisette. It was wedged between the harbor and a building that looked like it housed fishermen below and fishing equipment above. The water lapped beneath us as we crossed a walkway to the restaurant.

And there we were, another table between us, photographs of fishermen on the wall, their wooden frames knotted together with fishing line. We had wine this time. Appetizers came at once—codfish mousse on a bed of lettuce. A basket of bread, farine de blé. Salads with tart Dijon vinaigrette.

"Live with me in France, Rennie," he said. "While we can."

"Yes, I will live with you here."

The bouillabaisse arrived like a painting, or more like a processional of paintings. A waiter brought a silver tureen of broth and ladled it into our bowls. A second waiter brought a plate of fish that had been participants in the preparation. Ingredients isn't the right word. They were arranged on silver with garnishes of parsley and rosemary—red crab, white fish, encircled in green. Out the window, fishing boats rocked in the harbor. It was one of the first really warm days of May.

"Take these little rounds of bread," David said to me, and I pictured us opening the gates to Mas des Sablières, and closing them and locking them and carrying our bags up those stairs, entering our rooms, opening the blue shutters.

"Float them in the broth,"

"Broth. I can barely say such a word."

"Say bouillabaisse."

"Bouillabaisse, David. Bouillabaisse me."

He half smiled. It was the smile I'd first seen at Reading Terminal. His hair was silver-white now.

"First put a little garlic paste on these small breads. Or herbs." He put a daub of each on the pain grillé and dropped it into his sea of honey-red bouillabaisse.

"Two little rafts," I said.

And we ate sumptuously but more and more quickly. No dessert, just a chocolate with a petite framboise in it.

"Come see the lobsters," David said on the way out. And he led me across the restaurant and down a flight of stairs.

"The sea is coming in," a waiter who let us pass told us. We made a turn and stepped up to a low, deep cement wall, and there was the sea and the smell of the sea as it washed into the holding area. "High tide," David said. "They'll come down here and pick out fresh lobsters."

And we made a brief walk through the ancient narrow alleyways with sleeping perches for fishermen cut into their stone. We walked to the harbor, past Fonfon and the colorful boats jostling and sparkling in the sun. And then we were speeding along the autoroute, away from Marseille, into the green hills, past the turnoff to Aix and along the edge of Cavaillon, through Robion, where we would come for bread.

"Oppède le Vieux," I said, looking out the window. "See the ruins up on the hill."

"Layers of lives there. Back to Rome, if I'm not mistaken, and on to revolutions. Robespierre, who extended the use of terror, named it." I looked shocked, I'm sure, and he added, "A bit north of here and over two hundred years ago. We're here now—where civilization leads."

And we were walking through that gate into the courtyard. I can smell the flowers. Clematis and peonies and honeysuckle and scarlet roses. And the rosemary growing wild through all the countryside. And lavender about to bloom. And vineyards all around.

Our bedroom was on the third floor, but we had the whole *mas*—the entire four- hundred-year-old farmhouse compound. We could have chosen from twenty beds.

And that was our life for a week. I cooked him dinner—golden potatoes and haricots verts and butter lettuce salad with fresh avocado and white asparagus one night, green the next. We studied their merits. I made vinaigrette while he snapped the ends from the beans. We talked about the markets in Apt and L'Isle-sur-la-Sorgue. We drank a little wine. We both said we never thought of meat with all this produce. We ate strawberries for dessert seven nights in a row.

Our bedroom had glass doors that opened out onto a balcony, and we left them open and lay looking at the soft, almost evanescent light. It didn't get dark until after ten. When we woke, sunlight was streaming in the window.

"Tell me about that crazy bird Charlie your grandparents had," David said the first morning.

"Old Charlie got out of the cabin and flew into the forest," I said.

"How'd you get him back in?"

"I'll give you my grandmother's account. I think I can do it word for word." I fluffed myself up in bed and began. "'He just give out.'"

"This is going to be good." David pulled himself up beside me.

"'He stayed out all day. Finally Royce come home from work,

and I told him Charlie was down by the bridge. So he took Charlie's cage and went down there and set it down and said "Where are ya, Charlie? Get in your cage." Charlie just slumped in. We'd been shagging for him all day and couldn't get near him.'"

"Perfect!" David said.

"'That bird did the darndest things. He was just full of antics. He'd march up and down the table just a bobbin' his head like this, just bobbin' back and forth, back and forth, entertaining everybody. And clear crazy for water.'"

"Clear crazy for water," David repeated, laughing.

"'Clear crazy. He'd march up and down in front of the sink making the darndest racket until you came and turned the tap on and put your finger out and he'd jump on it and let you hold him right under that water. He'd shake and puff himself up and preen and flap around, having a regular shower. He all but used soap.'"

"How often did he shower?" David asked. "I love your crazy stories, Rennie."

"He showered every day. He was American, after all. Back to my grandmother. 'We took that crazy bird everywhere. He'd ride in the car on the steering wheel or on Royce's shoulder. We'd tell him to get in his cage and he'd get in. When I'd write letters, he'd perch on my wrist and nibble the paper.'

"It's true," I said. "Every letter came scalloped. 'He'd eat my stationery, he'd sit on my coffee cup and drink my coffee, he'd eat off my plate.'"

"How long did he last?" David asked. "I sense an ending."

"'He got sick and he drooped for quite a while.' That's how my grandmother said it."

And I picked up her voice again. "'Sick and drooped. We didn't expect him to live very long. Then one morning I slept in a little and when I got up, he was gone. I said to Royce, "Did he die?" and Royce said "Yes." I said "What did you do with him?" and Royce said "I wrapped him in a bit of paper and put him in a box and buried him under the pines. I thought it would be better if he was out of the way.'"

By then the sun had enveloped us.

"This story—their lives together. . . ." And I couldn't go on.

David heard all those stories. "The tales we tell—is that the deeper thing, the real embrace?" I asked him.

"Rennie. I want to live with you. Get a parakeet."

"I understand that you can't do that."

"Do you know why?"

"I do," I said, looking at him. His eyes welled with tears. "You're very much like my grandfather. Very much."

"Every man has two countries," David said to me when we walked out into the soft evening. "His own and France."

"Thomas Jefferson," I answered.

"You never miss." He drew me closer to him. "You have three, if you count Idaho."

What would it have been to have had his son? I came home without David and went to Carlos. I'd never imagined Carlos so much our child as I did then.

Carlos Luis Salazar—he loved the whole thing. I had taught him to say that name as clearly as a hearing child, and he said it with considerably more style than most young boys could deliver. Carlos Luis Salazar, he would sing out in his high, birdlike voice, and every head would look up. I'd tapped the rhythm of his name on his wrist. I'd turned his face lightly toward mine so he could see the sounds being formed. And I'd been successful. Now I wondered what David would have brought to him.

His dark eyes flashed in those early days, and his dark hair flew about. He was always barefooted; boys and girls crowded around him in the little yard on Patterson Avenue. It's a fragment of a street, really, his low stucco house tucked at the edge of an overpass.

I wouldn't see him when I'd first drive up, but I learned to look across the street. There he'd be, leaping up like a little fish, his head appearing in the stalks of the sunflowers growing out of the dirt and gravel. The sunflowers were ten feet tall, their brilliant faces the size of a golden platter, a sun. He'd make his jump, jackknife, and drop through the heavy foliage. I thought he would kill himself every time but then he'd soar upward again. My own childhood would take me as I watched Carlos catch his breath.

Cavorting, celebrating—that's what being ten was to Carlos Louis Salazar. Seeing him shining and vibrant in his escapades, I wondered what language could give him. And what would he do with the cards he'd been dealt? What did he have to make it in a shifting, tempestuous world? And what could I bring to the equation?

I comforted myself with questions, then as now. I learned about him. He was born in 1953, the middle of the century, a century I think about more all the time. As a baby, Carlos's mother Lilly told me, he was tiny and he didn't say much. In fact, he didn't say anything, although he made sounds. Still, until he was five, Lilly thought her last child by Aurelio could hear. Five was very late to get started with language.

Remembrance of times past changes with the vantage point. I can see now that for a few years yet, only occasionally did someone protest an injustice, a layer of nonsense, a cruelty, and it was frequently done by a nut, or seen as done by a nut, or both. In another century, who would have had the gold, who the sage and the rabbit brush? And how much of my investment was for Kent, farther away by far than this boy who couldn't talk, the boy I let myself love as a son?

Carlos used to say of life—all of it, its ups and downs—"What happened, that's all." I wonder if that's what he thought the night

I abandoned him to the Yellowstone bear, the famous old Snaggle-tooth. The demands of motherhood would have been far-reaching. And I imagine telling my latest bear story to David and Carlos—the two together. But I was alone with David when I told it to him.

"Here's a bear story for you, David," I said to him that week we were in Provence. We were outside Oppède, Oppède le Vieux. We'd driven to Auberge le Fiacre and spent the afternoon sitting at a little table in the garden. The smells of lavender and rosemary were in the air. Our talk was lazy. We ate between words.

"My neighbors, not too close luckily, loved chocolate, and they kept a lot on hand. Bob and Dorothy. They had a storage refrigerator, a spare kept out on their screened porch. They heard a terrific noise out there just after they'd gone to bed. They were dozing off, and they didn't get up at first. Finally, Dorothy said, 'I'll check it out.' 'No, no, I'd better do it,' Bob said. They were in their sixties, fit and lusty."

"Don't tell me," David said. We'd finished our salade d'aspèrges and were working on the gigot d'agneau aux herbes Provençal.

"Yes, exactly. Bob came flying back into the bedroom. Split pine. He'd done it all himself. 'Come quick,' he said to Dorothy."

"'Give me a minute here,' she said.

"'Don't take a minute. Just come, come quietly.' He scared her, but she followed."

"He took her right into..."

"Right into. Try this bread, David. How can we do without this? Yes. There was a window in the kitchen that looked out onto that deck. Like my room at the cabin out in the add-on."

"I suppose it's going to be a grizzly."

The plateau de fromages had arrived by then. "Have some of this bright yellow bliss. What did she say it was? Monchauneuf?" I asked, making something up. "No supposing. It was an outright grizzly. A big grizzly—over six hundred pounds and looking to gain. There he sat, leaning against the wall, scooping chocolates out of a five-pound box. Cummings—the best Salt Lake City had to offer. Not Birnn Chocolates of Vermont or Fortnum's Favourites, but good."

"Fortnum's Favorites," David said, laughing.

"Fortnum and Mason of Piccadilly, since 1797. They'd had time to master chocolates. But this bear was very content with Cummings." I could just see that bear leaning back, eating Cummings Studio chocolates. Just then a plate of cherries dipped in chocolate arrived. We both laughed.

"You scare me, Rennie. Going up there alone," and the word alone made me start to cry, just like that.

"I don't know why I'm crying," I said. "I've never been much of a crier."

But it wasn't true, none of it. It was because we were living together. Seven days at Mas des Sablières.

When is the moment you step back and see it all starts to add up to a lifetime?

A curve can change overnight in this part of the country, and it's never funny when it's one you've loved for nearly six decades—in fact it will be six decades in a few weeks. When I came back up that old familiar road to the cabin from a trip to West Yellowstone, something yellow—large and unnaturally yellow—stood out at that curve that had always calmed me. It was some kind of sign nailed to a tree, but it was obscured by branches until I was right on it. It alarmed me—I always moved into a protective stance up there at the first suggestion of invasion. But that! It looked thirteen feet tall on a little mountain lane. I was furious. And then I could see—couldn't avoid seeing it. Dead End.

Whose dead end, do you think? I worried myself with my muttering like a fool, like my father, actually, but I kept right on. Some bastard is going to find out whose dead end this is, I said, driving too fast.

When I pulled into the cabin, I could see silver glinting ahead of me, and I felt fury rise in me again. There hadn't been anything out here but Douglas fir for half a century. Maybe there never had been anything but Douglas fir. I knew these trees, had walked through them so many times I was familiar with the way their pine cones fell. Whoever is up there, I nattered, that's the fiend who put up the sign.

I parked, took my gear into the cabin, and stormed up the hill to see what was going on. Some guy from down the line had run a tractor all the way from my place into where he'd pulled his trailer, and he'd torn tracks six inches deep into it. Grass and wildflowers and saplings were strewn right and left.

Maybe Jewett was right; progress does seem to bring destruction. Environmentalists are her heirs. In all these years, no one had brought tractors or any kind of heavy equipment in here. Dead end. It *is* a dead end. Newcomers come ignorant. And they don't learn one feddering thing.

My grandparents were like bridegrooms to their part of the forest. They made everything on the smallest possible scale, by hand if it could be done, and with native materials, dead trees if they were available. So did my father. So did I. You didn't see any aluminum around except for an outbuilding roof at the mill. We wouldn't have had it glaring at us where the cabins were. Now this circling of Airstreams where they can't even be taken without felling a dozen trees every half mile and widening every foot of the old road. Damn it. Krupp's kids must have divided up his ranch.

I talked to the fellow up there the next day, trying to think how my grandfather would have handled it, although it didn't do me much good. "Temporary," he said. "Failed dreams," I hollered out the window.

That's the modern West. Call it temporary. I was still storming around in my mind when I got back to the cabin. I was beyond comfort. It was bone cold, and it rained all the rest of the day and all night, and the meadow turned to a web of white the next morning. "Maybe you're in the stages of grief," I mumbled. It was the end of June, three months since the fire.

I thought of all of us in this kitchen, grandmother making hot chocolate for us. Building a fire in that stove. Heating the water. Mixing a little Carnation Evaporated with Hershey's chocolate and a touch of sugar. Filling the rest of the old blue-and-white mugs with water—mugs that stayed warm in our hands. The ceremony of it, all of us together, no two cups alike.

And I remembered the last cup of hot chocolate I'd had in this cabin with my grandparents. It had been the end of the season and the end of any to come. The mill had burned a month earlier.

At the beginning of the week the mill burned to the ground, my grandmother and I had talked about what could happen to sawmills. We started talking about the derrick horse. I was fascinated by the derrick horse stories. "They wouldn't let you ride the derrick horse?" I said. "Friggy fedderings." My grandmother laughed that easy, comfortable laugh of hers.

"I think I felt damned feddering when I couldn't ride the derrick horse on the farm," she said. "I'd stand at the window when I was a little girl and do dishes everlasting."

"Drenchy," I said.

"Yes, drenchy was it. And I watched my brothers take turns riding the derrick horse. Then one day I went out and I said, 'Get off. I'm helping this time.' And I always rode the derrick horse after that."

"Ho! I could do that with Ronnie and be the pond monkey."

"Insurrectionist," my grandmother called me. "Little insurrectionist, and I can't say I'm innocent in it." We talked about the pond monkey throwing his chain around the logs and giving the signal for them to be snaked up into the mill. I asked her about the carriage—way up there, riding along, back and forth, taking the logs into the big saws. Why was it up so high, high as the derrick, higher?

"Yes, higher, much higher," she said.

"Maybe high because of the sawdust piles? So the sawdust can drop down somewhere?"

We'd chatter like that about everything. "Maybe you have something there," she said. "And the boilers had to be up out of the way. And they had to be real careful with the sawdust piles. A spark in the sawdust could just take the whole thing."

"Hoppers! Don't say that!" I felt liquid inside, and that's what I told her, and my grandmother reached over and ruffled my hair.

"Why would it be so fast?" I was speaking low and carefully, really like an insurrectionist, feeling danger in the words, the thoughts.

"The fine sawdust that seeps down is always full of pitch. All the posts out around the mill below the green chain and on inside are always coated with sawdust. It just coats everything because the mill vibrates and shakes it down and it's real pitch-soaked. The guys never smoke out there."

I went out to the wood box and brought back a piece of kindling with red veins of pitch through it. I lifted the lid of the stove and put the piece of wood down in the fire. It flamed up.

"That's right, Rennie. Pitch burns about like kerosene. In fact, turpentine and kerosene are closely related to pitch but don't ask me for details."

"Glides and swivels," I said. "I'll have to get my white bird's wings around me tonight or I'll never sleep."

"Is that how you put yourself to sleep? What does your white bird feel like?" she asked.

"Like the moss on stones. Smooth and good. When he's not there in the mornings, things feel riffy. Especially on Dirke Street. But this mill won't burn," I said. "Because I'm going to marry someone here and run it. I've decided. I don't like the city. It isn't even riffy. I have a word for it, but I don't say it."

"You do like your sawmill, don't you, sweetie," my grandmother said. And she fluffed a white hand through my hair and I could smell cinnamon rolls.

"I love it here," I said. "It's where I stack my memories up before winter comes." I looked out the kitchen window. "Pidg," I added. "From the movies."

And she laughed and repeated it—"Stacking up some memories...Pidg," and she began to sing to me. "It's one of those songs that's so easy to hear. You can listen just once and you can play it by ear. Dadadada da da some other year...Dadadada da you may shed a tear.

"I can't remember," my grandmother said that day, humming and laughing. "Dadadada lifetime belongs to one of those one of those one of those wonderful songs."

I remember. I remember everything we said that week. It was all about to be over. But that morning I broke into a grin, my head bobbing along to the rhythm of the song. I joined in on the last lines, off-key but intent. I had this now, and what I'd started out there in the willows, and my face caught the light in my grandmother's face.

Such fragile, such buffeted creatures. When I go from her to thinking about my father, I understand the word chiaroscuro.

The last time I was with him comes back to me almost daily now. I couldn't have imagined that. He was like he'd been when Kent and I sat in the grotto of his arms. Climbing up there in the chair with him. Returning to the river to fish. He was as gentle as the young man who'd sung to us, and I had to wonder if I'd been the one to change and retreat more than he. I had forgotten absolutely what caring he sent out of himself when you were in his embrace. I lay my head on his chest, his ruined lungs struggling beneath my face, and a great gulf closed. He put his hand on my head. It was as familiar to me as air, although it had probably been thirty years since he'd done that.

"I was a bastard to live with," he says.

"Yeah. Bastard pretty well covers it." We both make a slight sound, not quite pain, not quite relief.

"I'm sorry I didn't know more." Again there is the simplest of sounds between us. I notice how alike they are.

"Thank you."

"Let's go," my mother is saying. But I stay a long time in the little hospital room, the music I'd brought to him playing. Frank Sinatra. "I wonder why I spend these lonely nights da da da." We listen and my father begins to sing, "The memory of love's refrain." And again I drift. Maybe the worn planks of memory is my own phrase.

The first time he reached out to us once we were grown was about fourteen years after Kent and I were born, a year after Kent had gone to his school. Then on Kent's first visit home, my parents had quarreled. I think my father had been drinking, and my mother packed her things, left Kent and me with him, and went to her mother and father. That's where I wanted to be, with Gram and Gramp, but we'd been left home with Daddy. We were in the Mojave Desert, far from the mill, and to us it was as bleak as our hearts. My grandparents were in Los Angeles for the winter. As I look back, I'm more surprised at my mother than my father.

In the night, my father came into my room and got me. I was even less comfortable with him than usual, not because he was frightening that night, but because he wasn't. It was somewhere between dream and nightmare, but I couldn't tell where. When he got close to me, I smelled the bourbon. He never drank, and the unfamiliar smell of it made me tremble.

"Your mother has gone," he said. I felt a track of fear up my spine.

"Come get in bed with me," he said. A clatter began in my stomach and spread up through my head. I felt the flutter that came to the back of my throat take its route down my neck.

"I'd better stay here," I said. My voice shook.

"Come talk to me for a while." That was the most irrational thing he'd ever said, and I felt myself shake.

"Come in for a little while." He was pleading. His voice was edged in sorrow, I realize, looking back. "Let's go get Kent."

My mind flew up. "Not Kent." I got up. "Let's not bother him." I became aware of myself standing there in my pyjamas, and I reached for my robe. "We better let Kent sleep. He gets so tired."

But my father was walking down the hall to Kent's room. I got ahead of him and sat down beside my brother and shook his shoulder. He jumped. "It's Rennie, Kent," I said. "It's okay. Daddy's here, too." My father was standing in the doorway.

"Trouble for us?" I could hear the alarm in his voice. We're really afraid of him, I realized, and I could see my father make the same discovery.

"Come get in bed with me and talk to me for a while," he said, and his voice took into account our fear. It was an apology. He sounded like the father of my infancy. Sweet man, lost man. Even so, I felt Kent jerk back. I kept my hand on his shoulder. Then he sprang out of bed and stood between my father and me, and my heart welled up. This was the old Kent, quick to act.

"We can talk here," I said, and it was a question.

"Come be with me," my father said. "I don't want to be alone."

Is there a choice for a child? Could a child discern between pity, bewilderment, hope, fear? So I guess I too had usually done what he told me to do.

My father got in bed and said, “Come over here, Kent. One of you on either side of me. Like old times.” My heart that had leaped in joy to see Kent so quick again went down in a cold drop. I stood there picturing it still dropping through the cement in the basement. “By Rennie,” Kent said. What was happening was an illusion, a dark film, a nebulous, unknowable world, silent and cold and untrackable. We’d never talked to this man. Our father had never expressed the slightest uncertainty, let alone shown a need for us.

Kent got in bed beside my father. I moved to that side of the bed and began to crawl in beside him. I was shaking violently now. I could hear my teeth chattering.

“Come over here,” my father said. I waited for him to storm, to scream his command and end it with the Jesus Christ! I hated most. He was quiet, and I went around to the other side of the bed and got in beside him.

He lay perfectly still and silent for a long time. I was blank and rigid. I wished I could reach for Kent’s hand. And then my father said, “I don’t know how to make your mother happy.” I could feel Kent’s mind stutter, as mine did. The idea of my father making my mother happy, any of us happy, hadn’t occurred to me. “Can you tell me what to do? If you see some things I can do if she comes back, will you come and tell me?”

Kent started to cry. “Is my mother coming back?” he asked. “I want Mother. See her again?”

“You will see her,” I said to him. “You will, Kent. It’s okay.”

"Yes," I said to my father. "We'll tell you if we have any ideas." I thought that I could do these things, that they could be done.

"Yeah," Kent said. "Yeah, we will."

"You can talk to her, Daddy. Ask her what she wants."

"I'll try to do that. I'm not very good at it. I get so...I'm too high-strung." So sorrow rose in him, and it stilled him, set him adrift on unfamiliar waters. He was losing, and he felt the slippage. I remembered what it had been like to be a little girl with him and my mother. Once he'd written her name on the ceiling of the house on Dirke Street with wallpaper cleaner. That old pink wall cleaner we all used in the forties. I can smell it. And I see Deborah + Blaine with a heart under it.

"Do you think she'll come back?" my father was saying.

"I think she will. She told us she would only be gone a week. We didn't think she was leaving..."

"Sometimes I think I should just get a mule and some water in a canteen and a little cheese and jerky and tie it to the mule and get on him and ride out into the desert. Maybe take Kent."

Kent started to cry again. "I don't want to go, I don't want to go." We were in Inyokern, in the Mojave Desert, where my father was working. I see him drift off from us, his mule small, his pack small, not enough to last a few days. He disappears into the horizon, something out of Steinbeck. I stand there crying, looking at where he'd been, like I did when he'd left us in Idaho.

"We'll help you, Daddy," I say. I can't see Kent going off with him at all. "We'll go back to our beds and think about it."

We did go back to our beds. Kent said, "Jeez." He touched my hair. He was so relieved. I remember that touch. "Okay?" he said.

I lay awake until morning, trying to find a place among all the violent scenes with my father for this bewildered, reaching man. I missed the certainties of my grandparents.

Morning came and I fixed breakfast for Kent and my father, and we talked about Cheerios and how shredded wheat was better if you ate it fast, and maybe meat for dinner.

Childhood. So little between you and the inconceivable world.

I got in bed with my father one other time, about two years later. We were hunting in Wyoming. We left California and drove twelve hours to Afton and found a room in a nearby lodge and slept the last hours of the night before we rose to walk into the mountain. I wasn't paying attention when my father reserved the room. I followed him to it. We went in. There was a double bed, a door beyond. Adjoining rooms, and I walked to the door with my little pack still in hand. It was locked. My father said, "What are you looking for?"

"I thought it was another room," I said.

"Oh, I should have gotten another room. Do you want...I can get a room with another bed. Another room. It's just a few hours till we hunt."

I hesitated. I never wanted to cause any trouble. That's the gift of turmoil. I especially didn't want a Jesus Christ! What did I bring *you* for.

"No, it's okay," I said. Money was always a factor, in what he did, in what I accepted.

We lay down together, each of us right at the edge of our side of the bed. I was as still and wary as a cornered mouse, and I think my father was, too. We lay like that until a ray of light fell across the wall, and my father stepped out of bed and put a leg into his pants, another leg. "Let's be the first ones up there," he said.

He was an original man, left out of noticing how other people did things, how things ought to be done, were expected to be done. We walked the hills together that morning, we got a little fire going, we were at home in the mountains we loved. He made sure I was wearing the one orange vest we had with us. I was tired, I could hardly keep my eyes open, and I walked beside my father with a kind of pride. He'd been nice to me, and I'd just been elected senior class vice president of my high school in California.

My life seemed strange to me, strange beyond my imagining. How could it be mine? Could I have designed it?

And I need my grandmother's words in a way I hadn't before. The thought that she was *alive* when my father got in bed with me makes me sad. I never mentioned it when I had her, not at the time and not in the forty more years I had with her. Nothing told me how overwhelmed I'd been like that did, how isolated a child can feel, and what a child will do when a parent says 'do this.'

I walk in full humility to that kitchen table and wait for her words.

> We're more than our creations, and we don't even realize it. I think I learned that from you. You're more than

your creations, Rennie, wonderful as they are.

You were about as good a creation as I ever had a hand in. Oh brother, seeing you and that twin of yours. You were just tiny, four pounds four ounces apiece. Rabbits is all there was to it. You were covered with the finest film of hair. But the hair on your heads—your heads weren't as big as a baseball—was already full and curly and two or three inches long. And when I touched your face, you ducked that tiny head into my hand just like my old cat Curly. You had me with that. I'd never seen a baby do that. And with the other hand, I touched Kent's face, and damned if he didn't do the same thing. You were the most loving little babies, and right at first the only way to tell you apart was to pull down your diapers.

You were kept in the hospital in little incubators for weeks. I tried to get them to leave you together, but they wouldn't do it. Your Dad used to come and stand between your heated boxes and sing. You'd stop anything you were doing when he sang to you, and you'd turn your heads to him.

It was hard to watch you begin to turn away from him, but you did. That's not to say you didn't have very good reason. He was so rough and touchy in those days. He'd just gotten over osteomyelitis, and he'd have flare-ups and literally cry out in pain. I could get a call any time of the day or night from your mother. Usually she'd be sobbing, and she could just barely say 'Can you come and help me?' I'd go out and tell Royce, and he'd wrap up what he was doing and we'd come right now. We even closed the mill a few times to come. We did that the day you fell off the slide and fractured your skull. You were a lot like your father. You were a death-defying little thing, far more than Kent was.

By the time you were ten, the summer of that big auction, you'd fairly fly out of your bedroom, still buttoning your Levis. You never in your life, not even the day you were supposed to get married, stayed in a bedroom, or the bathroom for that matter, long enough to finish up. I'd see you stretching up to your bedroom window to see the sky if I happened to be in that little hall we had—hall is a bit elevated for what it was, really. I knew you were looking to see what to get ready for. You had to stand on tiptoe to see out. You weren't more than four-and-a-half-feet tall, and you didn't weigh eighty pounds, even with Levis on, and your yellow socks—I can just see them—rolled down once. You could hardly face a morning without those. I washed them forty-leven times for you.

You'd come out of your room circling your fingers around your rabbit's foot that hung from your belt loop. You were already a complete mystic. I think you scared your mother, but you amused me. You'd be running your other hand, fingers spread like a comb, through your dark hair. I liked to feel it curl too.

You'd tuck in there on your stool beside the stove. It was so tight no one else could get in there without burning themselves. And you'd say, "I've seen the color of this sky before." "Where?" I'd ask. "Along the edge of swimming pools in the city," you'd tell me, or "In the National Geographic—the Mediterranean." Never the same answer. "It makes me homesick when I see it and I'm not here," you'd always add. Your father gave you those paints. That little wooden paintbox—that was his when he was a boy. That just thrilled you, and it surprised you.

You come out from that stove starving every morning. "The road has dusted down the trees," you'd say, or "The baby moon was lying in the mother's arms." The damndest stuff. Or "The sun was a nighttime sliver last night." "Was it the moon?" I'd ask.

"Is the moon the night sun?" you'd answer. "Not exactly," I told you. You had me jumpin' for answers. "The moon's another thing." I liked thinking about it being another thing. You were wonderful to talk with, and I wasn't the only one who thought so. You could amuse your father to death. He asked you what you learned when you come home from your first day of school, and you said, "Move along, get along, get in line." I knew more about your teacher from those few words than I would have if I'd been there with you myself. He called you "Move Along" for a few years after that. It pretty well described you anyway.

You were kind of a sad little muffin. When you'd bless the food, you'd pray for Kent to come up to the mill if he wasn't there with you, and you'd pray you didn't have to go down. You hardly mentioned the food. It took me a long time to see you were mumbling, "Thank thee for no Dirke Street." I didn't know what in the world to do or say at a time like that.

You and Kent were up to something in the willows from sunup to sundown that last summer. You were both always looking out to the line of willows that ran from the mill pond along the creek. You used to tell me it was a nice nature border between the cabins and the cookhouse and the well and the bunkhouse and, on the other side of them, the mill with its planer and pond and washhouse and blacksmith's shed.

I happened onto what you and Kent were up to out there by the creek that summer. I was picking wildflowers for the church bouquet out by Brown Sign and I stepped around a curve in the stream and back up into the willows to get a few Indian paintbrush, and there it was. It was—what would you say—it felt like it had *life* in it. You had the whole thing there, you'd made a whole mill camp. You had your natural border and your sawmill and the cabins and the cookhouse, even the hill it and the other cabins sat on. And a little line of willows. It was big, it was a big enterprise. And I stood there studying it and wondering what it meant to you. One sawmill camp wasn't enough, was it? You were so afraid of losing your heaven.

That was the summer you started drawing pictures of the mill. You'd get every detail there was in there, and then you'd take them to Dirke Street and put them all around your little basement room, all around its cement walls. Sometimes you'd make me heat the iron on the stove and you'd get out a piece of waxed paper and put it over your coloring and iron it, melt it was more like it. It got the most wonderful effect. It looked like it had come through the Renaissance. Or through your dreams.

One day you come in and said to me, "Maybe I shouldn't be doing what I'm doing out there in the woods. It's marvelous"—that's the word you used—"marvelous, especially when I'm away from it."

I wasn't worried because I knew by then. Twigs and sticks and moss and rocks. It was astonishing and beautiful. My heart stopped when I stumbled on it. I could see how delicate your balance was.

When my grandmother began to decline, I stayed with her almost constantly. My grandfather had died years before, and I had been out of the country, unable even to attend his funeral. I sat with my grandmother for hours, and when I got tired, I climbed up on the bed beside her. I'd done that all my life. When she dozed off in one of those early days, I went downtown to the drugstore and I bought a little glass jar of scented oil from Paris—Recherchez or something like that—and brought it back to her. I bathed her and anointed her skin with that oil. The phrase was important to me.

I knew entirely what I was about to lose and what I'd had, and there was a kind of balance in that. "I think of only you now," I said. "I don't want to keep you in the unevenness of age—some of you worn out, some of you still vital, some of you already dying." She'd stopped speaking—all those glorious words interrupted. Her arm seemed to have become detached from the rest of her, and it would rise up and flail down on the bed rail. I could scarcely keep myself from crying out when that happened. It made something come loose inside me as well. The nurses wrapped the rail in foam, tried to restrain her, but whatever we did, the moment would return like a nightmare, and that right arm would get free and slam into the bed rail.

I talked to her by the hour, telling her the stories she'd told. Roses don't last worth a shit, I said to her, nurses coming and going. When Royce got a look at you, that finished Darrell, and all of us got our start. I haven't thought how weary you must have gotten out there in the meadow, corduroying the road, Phaedrus. Those hats you wore, great big, beautiful hats. I have a picture of you in one and a fur stole and it's signed Sincerely, and your name under it in your elegant hand, not exactly a flourish but very close.

"Go back to Rand's, Phaedrus," I said to her. "Find Royce." She watched me, her eyes still birdlike. And then last words. "I love you, believe you me," she said. I brought a tape in and played a waltz. "Go back to Royce," I said to her. "We're okay." And in my heart I said Take her up. I was confident in God where she was concerned.

I sat beside her in the last quiet hours and listened to one of our conversations, listened as though my life depended on it. We were back at the mill, of course, living the simplest of days.

"You like that cousin of yours, don't you?" my grandmother is saying. "Well, so do I. He's a peach of a fellow. He's got the eyes of a cardinal, and he's not even thirteen, is he?"

"No. He's a month younger than me. I'll be thirteen next month, Kent and me. What do you mean, 'the eyes of a cardinal'?"

"Sweetness is a good word for it. Good eyes, Rennie. There's a lot of caring in those eyes. Do you know what he calls you? He calls you and Kent 'my twins.' He was up here last week, right out in front of my cabin, flippin' and sailin' through the air like he'd lost his mind. I watched him till I couldn't stand it another minute, and I went out on the porch and asked what the air show was.

"'Practicing cartwheels for my twins,' he said. Cutest damned kid. Not the least bit braggy and not the least bit bashful. Just getting ready for his twins. You're blushing, Rennie."

"I am? Do you know what I'm thinking—can you tell?" I ask her.

"Yes, most of the time. It's no credit to me. What you're thinking is fluttering all around you. It would take a dolt to miss it."

"What's a dolt?"

"The opposite of a-dept," my grandmother says, laughing at herself.

"You know every word, don't you?"

"Oh, by all means," and she laughs heartily.

I see her. She was so robust, so young, younger than I am now. She goes back to the stove, she was always at that stove, and she puts dishwater on to heat. "What are you thinking?" she asks.

"How come Kent and Claine sound like twins, not Rennie and Kent?"

"That mother of yours was just like you are with your cousin Claine. She was never apart from Claine's mother. It was Deborah and Nola, Nola and Deborah. And they picked those names, Claine and Kent, for their first boys."

"How did they get pregnant at the same time?"

"I'm sure I can't answer that," my grandmother says, "but they did and they were in the hospital delivering together. You and Kent came very near sharing an incubator with Claine."

I knew where the name Rennie came from. In fact I knew the whole story by heart. When I'd asked about my name, she'd told me my mother had a surprise—not one baby but two—and she'd had to use one of the names she and Nola had picked out for a girl. She'd picked Rennie, and, as it turned out, Nola never needed the matching name—all she ever needed was boys' names. "Maybe Kent and I should be thinking of names," I say.

"I wouldn't rush into naming babies," my grandmother tells me. "I wouldn't really. So you're taking your Grand Tours today?"

"Yes, and you'll hear me when I get to Aunt Lucinda's place, won't you?"

"Yes, I'll hear you and I'll see you when you get that close, and I'll be able to tell you you're too late for lunch and you missed your peach pie and you've got pitch on your britches."

"Glides and swivels, I'd better hurry up. I'll have to really hurry to do everything, won't I? I should get up earlier. This morning I was lying in bed thinking about all the things I'm going to do this trip. But the main thing I thought was, when I'm happy in the morning I can stay in bed for a long time and feel my white bird's wings. I have to get up fast at home or he goes away."

"You didn't happen to go back to sleep this morning, did you? You and that bird—you find your way, don't you."

"Riffy without him."

"I believe I felt riffy when your grandfather went off to World War I. What would your word be for when he came back the next morning because the war was over?"

"Was it? Is that how he came back? That would be glissful. Glisss." I say it to myself now.

"You're entirely right." She's taking bread out of the oven. She bends a little stiffly—she's stiff in the back like I am. "It was glisss," she says, looking up at me. I'm on my little stool beside the stove. "It was glisss. It was one extra s."

"Whenever I think about growing up, I know I'll come back here and I'll stay when I don't have to go to school, and someday I'll never leave. Maybe I'll run the commissary like you. That makes me feel like glisss, not all riffy and frailly."

"Maybe you'll marry someone in the city and have a station wagon full of kids and be a den mother," she says, looking right at me, opening the door to other possibilities. "Lots of things could happen. Sawmills don't last forever."

I had an idea I didn't have enough pipe to reach the intake for my waterline, so I waited for a rainy day and drove down to St. Anthony. I left in time to get to Housley's before Wes was out on a job.

"You got water out there?" he asked, looking up. "Told the wife about it."

"I *do* have water, I've got ever-lovin' loads of water," I said. I'm sure I had that childhood grin on my face I was always teased about. "The quickest grin in the West," my grandfather used to say.

"Good for ya," he said. "Makes a difference—water."

"I got a barrel at the Co-op and they finagled a faucet at the base. Then I built a kind of saddle to get it up off the ground so I can nip out there and fill my buckets and I'm not crawling in the pine needles. Old times. Even found the water dipper."

"You're ready for an advance, aren't ya?"

"Taking it into the cabin."

"I thought you'd be back for that." He communicated a lot of approval.

"I've got a covered porch—I could easily drill through that wall.

It isn't insulated. There's no complications—wiring or anything."

"Perfect for ya. If you can get that barrel up higher than the washstand, you're in business. You can't go too high or you'll lose your siphon."

"I could make a little stand. There's still plenty of lumber out there." Workmen always liked me. You think you're going to be a bother to them, but they're glad to see you do for yourself.

"You got a saw?" he asked.

"I have a good saw." I envisioned everything as he talked—my grandfather's handsaw with the green grip.

"Cross brace all four sides of your stand." He took out his notebook and drew a rectangle with an X through it. Then he erased one part of the X. "One diagonal will be enough. Make a two-by-four frame and put that diagonal two-by in there to brace it. You'll have to hold it in place and mark the angle. Toenail that in, then lay two-by-fours over the whole thing—cover it with two-by-fours. You don't want to mess with trying to hand-saw plywood."

"I can round up two-by-fours. And the barrel won't be too heavy to lift in place empty."

"Here, let's get you a few things." He grabbed a basket this time. "Use a threaded piece at the end of the line near the cabin, and we'll send you a length of hose. You can use the hose to fill the barrel." He was moving down the aisle collecting parts, assembling them loosely as we went along. "You'll need a pipe wrench," he said.

"I've got my grandfather's pipe wrench. He did a lot of plumbing."

"Those Douglas brothers could do anything," he said. "Everybody liked working with them."

I could feel his words revive something in me. "They were wonderful," I said.

He took a minute and then went on. "You're going to drill a hole in the side of the house. Here's your drill and bit. Run this pipe through that hole. Stuff steel wool around the opening—mice hate it." Exactly what my grandmother did. "It's really very simple," he was saying. "And you're going to use this assembly on the outside of the house." He drew it out for me.

"It isn't too complicated, is it?" I said.

"Not at all. A right angle is all that is involved. Where you come in, is there a little place for a washstand?"

"Yes, there is! Right on that back porch. I'll carry the little stand over to it."

"Fine." He had that half-smile. He was lining up a job, completely at home. I noticed he had long fingers for a man of his build. Not rough looking. He made me think of David—not in a take-his-place way, just the good, nice feeling of looking at a man's well-formed hands.

"So this piece is going right through the house," he reviewed. "This metal piece. Now let's take this right-angle piece and you see this is threaded at the end. It might be too long. What do you think?"

"Three feet will take it to a perfect spot."

"Okay. Three feet. Let me cut it at that," and he reached for a clamp affair and twisted it back and forth over the end of that heavy galvanized pipe until he'd cut through it. "Now, I can step in the back and put a thread on this."

"You can? Could I see that?" It seemed good to me to be around someone—I was aware of that.

"You're set for this," he said with that half-grin. "Hell yes, come and see how it's done." I followed him into the back room—more parts, pipes laid along arms that held them. I liked this work. I'd been around a lot of it in the blacksmith shop at the mill. "So we're going to thread this," and he clamped the pipe in place and brought an instrument down—I don't remember it—and threaded the end of the pipe. "Now it's easy. Here's a right angle. You'll put it on—use a little of this plumber's grease, and now we'll come up four feet—that should clear your stand and put another right angle here and extend it—what—eight inches? Will that just about drop into your washbasin?"

"Wow. I've got the old basin. The old buckets. The dipper."

He walked me through the last steps deftly. I knew I was making him late for his first jobs.

The next morning I woke with real purpose. I'd gathered my tools and laid everything out. You'd have thought I was getting ready for surgery. I got on my knees outside that covered porch before breakfast and began drilling. I'd forgotten the satisfaction of a hand drill—the circular motion, the feel of the bit grabbing into the wood, the shavings curling away. I slipped the pipe through, put my attachment on the outside and clamped it in place, greased the threaded end inside, formed the right angle and tightened it. I was to the second right angle in less than five minutes, attaching the faucet and sliding the little washstand in place. I put the old washbasin on it and raced outside to turn open the valve from the barrel. I came back to that washstand and stood there majestically, as though I'd discovered America. I turned on the tap. I don't think I expected anything to happen, but water spilled like diamonds into my grandmother's wash-basin. I put my hands in it and lifted it to my face. I found soap and washed my hands, my arms. I took my shirt off—I'd given up bras weeks ago—and washed myself.

Then I went to the kitchen table with the old green-and-white striped towel and cried—cried for the past and for the future and the life I was living, inventing. "Come to me, Phaedrus," I said, and she did.

She talked to me about water and the West.

"You're safe now, Rennie," she said. "You've got water."

And I realized I'd feared the fires, the defenselessness.

Of course I came back to the cabin where I could take comfort and maybe direction from the elegance of spring moving into full summer. July slid by in bedazzling sunny days and cool nights, the colors in the meadow deepening from whites and yellows to its full palette of reds and oranges and blue-violets. At the end of the month, I found a twin flower, deep pink and delicate. I took it back to the kitchen and put it in a glass of water until I could dry it in a handful of silica from the shore of the reservoir.

I walked through the last half of August. I was out every day, usually following the waterline, checking for leaks, tucking new growth up around it. It would be well covered by next spring. I'd continue walking along the creek and up into the high meadow.

Then we had an early frost, and the larkspur and lupine went down. The meadow seemed to turn gold almost overnight. The low Oregon grape bushes turned to scarlet, their leaves a dark accent in among the wheat-colored grasses. The huckleberries were late. The whole bush was amber and translucent except for the purple berries, few and small. I savored a handful each trip out. Above them the quaking aspen let go of their apple green and turned to yellow. Higher up they'd already darkened at their edges. Entire hillsides were a burst of dark gold and yellow gold. They seemed to give off light well into the evening. Just before dusk the sky toned down, the local colors keyed up, and that hush that comes with end of day fell over everything. The yellow grasses and the reds and golds and violets and blues were a symphony. It was enough to break your heart.

I took big canvases out into the meadow and painted its ochre and sienna and every shade of yellow and buff and red. Then late in the afternoon I went up on the hill to paint the aspen. I came back with canvases nothing but broad strokes of yellow with a few thin white lines of trunks and branches through them. I stood right among the aspen to paint, and when I'd step back from those paintings, there was that sense of being awash in the shimmering gold. I'm outside even remembrance when I'm painting. It feels like flight must feel to a bird. And those paintings stacked deep around the walls of the cabin were like gold themselves to me. They measured something valuable.

When I stopped in at the lodge at the end of the week, I noticed a message for me on the bulletin board, if you could call it that. It was from Thelma Myzeld, out of the blue. I called her from the old familiar payphone, and her whisky voice said, "This must be Rennie."

"Myzeld?" I said. "Thelma Myzeld?"

"Yes. Myzeld. I'll never live it down."

"Damn, I thought I'd lost you. Are you back in Bozeman?"

"More or less. What would be wrong with your driving through

Yellowstone Park and then the other park, Grand Teton—that puts you in Wyoming—and meeting me in Jackson Hole. From there we'll make our way to Kemmerer for an early Thanksgiving, very early. You won't be out of the forest for long. A day. Two, maybe."

I burst out laughing. "I expected that on behalf of Kemmerer," she said. "Now that's out of the way. We could have a smoke. My father has a little deal there."

"Any deal in Kemmerer is a little deal, Myzeld, begging your pardon. Utahns hate to cross into that end of Wyoming, but at least I'd be coming at it from the north."

"North for thirty minutes at the most." Thelma Myzeld's voice was droll, very.

"This is a serious invitation, isn't it, Myzeld."

"You could call it that. I wouldn't take it *too* seriously. There'd be antelope to watch. Maybe a coyote, deer, bear, elk, moose. Eagles—maybe a very late fledgling. Trees, rivers, lakes, meadows, paint pots, geysers. How much do you need?"

"You make it interesting. Of course you've got a lot to work with. I can't remember if the trees just stop and the sagebrush begins or how it goes."

"Not so much sagebrush, Rennie. You'll see boxwood and poplar, hemlock, birch. And my father has quite a few flowering trees."

"In Kemmerer?"

"In Kemmerer, Lincoln County, Western United States—part of the world, Rennie. Such a snob."

I was chortling. "And you have a father?"

"You could call him that. Just the one. Pretty abrupt end of pines, it's true. We'll be smoking by then and we won't notice. And then my father will have his yellow Cadillac and he'll pick us up. We'll be a local sensation driving into Kemmerer."

"A local sensation in Kemmerer. Kind of a dream of mine."

"Good. Don't underrate the fish fossil capital of the world."

More laughter. "I'm crazy about fish fossils, Myzeld. I actually am."

"Sure. It's all right there—the fish fossils. That's where it started. Don't be fooled by the bird-and-dinosaur stuff. We'll be out of that in a few years and back to fish. If you want a fossil, bring your chisel."

"You can go chisel yourself a fish fossil?"

"You can. If you find something as good as a stingray, you have to hand it over."

"Stingray! How far back are we talking?"

"Before Noah, on a broad scale."

Chuckling again. "We wouldn't want to just meet in Bozeman?"

"My father has a little closing out to do in Kemmerer. Besides, we've pretty well done Bozeman."

"So I'll be going north, then east, then south?"

"Whit won't put up with any of this indirection."

"Whit?"

"My father."

"Did you ever call him Daddy?"

"Never. Not ever. Of course not. I'll meet you at the Silver Dollar Bar or whatever it is—with the big silver dollars in the counter, you know, at noon in two days. That will be Saturday by my calculations, Rennie."

She knew I wouldn't be there. The next day I cleaned out the Scout. I was prompted to do that much, and I tried to give myself a haircut standing out in the forest where I wouldn't make a mess, but I ended up doing just that when I came in and got a look at myself in the little mirror on the back porch. "Take care of yourself for a minute, you aging goat," I said, giving the rough image in the mirror a thumbs up.

I would be sorry not to meet Thelma's father. We'd had a talk about him once and I remembered our Whitman routine. She'd told me her father was named Whit and I'd said surely not after the Good Gray Poet.

"Yes, purely," she answered. And I could hear her say, "'Twenty-eight years of womanly life, and all so lonesome.'"

We'd carried on. I came up with a line: "'O if I am to have so much, let me have more.'"

And I stand there remembering Whitman. "Plenty of persons near, and yet the right person not near." It took me to David, to a night in Edinburgh, arm in arm on Princes Street, the evening sun lighting up the castle on the hill at the end of that green sweep of gardens.

"'Scented herbage of my breast,'" I said to make myself laugh. He did have range.

"My father's favorite line to quote isn't from Whitman, though," Thelma had told me. "It's from Shakespeare. Can you guess it?"

"Oh, just guess from the greatest *oeuvre* in the English language, probably any language." She liked *oeuvre.*

"'Whoreson cur,' or whatever it was," she'd said. Of course.

"'Whoreson indistinguishable cur,'" I added, snuffling with laughter.

"'Whoreson jackanapes.'"

It all made me miss her, and I was aware how alone I'd stayed.

The conversation had ended seriously. She'd asked me what I thought about more than anything. "I think of those I've loved," I told her. "And I think of atonement."

I remember her saying, "That was an interesting answer. Do they go together?"

"In my constellation, yes," I told her. "What are your thoughts on atonement?"

"The more the better," she said, and somehow I couldn't help laughing again.

Later that week I called her. She didn't even ask me about not showing up. "You don't sound like you're from Kemmerer or somewhere around here," I said. "You do sound very, very Western."

"I *am* very, very Western," she told me. "My mother had me in Montana at a tender age."

"So just trips out to see your father?"

"Just trips out."

"I wonder how that would have been." I was quiet for a few minutes and then I said, "Something happened to my father," not intending to.

"I thought something had happened. And you went to the cabin to fill your lungs."

I talked about the cabin, not my father. "I store the scent of mountain hollyhock and the feel of pale green moss on the north side of the trees and the pungent pitch you lean into and the sun setting while you're still on the river and the moon rising like a dream of a moon, and daybreak with a deer at the door." I went on and on.

"It doesn't sound bad, Rennie."

"To drive up that road to the cabin. My grandmother could draw anyone into her peace and her joy. When I'm not here, I put myself to sleep every night walking up the path, through the meadow, and into my cabin, the screen door with its curve of pine bough for a door pull. I slide my hand into that curved slicked wood, my fingers fitting right into its bend, and I start to drift to sleep smelling wood fires and hearing laughter and feeling joy—that's the only word for it. I never heard a voice raised in anger between those walls. And the conviviality of family and friends. The stories told, the meals served. My cousins would get homesick, but I never did. I never had a second thought about staying up. I've never thought of that before."

"This is a *rendering*, Rennie, a *holding forth*. I've been through five cigarettes, and I'm willing to go another five."

"The cabin. I just go to mush. And Kent is the same way."

"What is its future?"

"Don't even ask. It's on Forest Service land we'd leased so…I didn't even know that until the sawmill burned down."

"I hate to hear that—that's hard to forget."

"I'm very careful now. I never even thought of…" and I stop myself, and I'm glad I can leave it at that. I had the feeling Thelma knew the rest.

"How long are you going to stay?"

"I haven't seemed to hit the planning stage. I do plan to drive back to the place and pile into bed, however."

"I'll drink to that," Thelma said, and I knew she was raising a glass.

A few days later, there was a message for me at Pond's. *Call* was all it said. I walked over to the payphone and dialed her number. "Ray knows where his cashmere jacket is," Thelma told me. No preliminaries. "*Knows*."

"I wonder how it would look on a white bird." The minute I said it, I realized why Thelma had asked me to call. She knew how far away I was. Her answer brought me back to the moment.

"I should have taught you to really smoke. Maybe nicotine

would have done the trick. It's a good thing you're here where there are plenty of birds, if killdeer and wrens count—gray, I know." Thelma's voice had her usual wry edge, but I didn't miss the fellow feeling.

"What was your last name? I must have known it, but I can't remember it."

"I *beg* your pardon."

"I know it's pushy."

"My last name was..." and there was the significant pause. "Ronnefeleur," she said, already laughing by the time she let go of the *r*. It was the quintessential mimic of the quintessential Parisian.

"Pleeeze don't make me larf," I said. And then I was back to that darkly thoughtful mood. "Did you understand your father?" I asked.

"No. Of course not. Because he was *my* father. You might have understood him."

"Is there a Mrs. Ronnefeleur?" I was laughing again, spluttering before I got to the *r*.

"Not exactly," she said. "What's on your mind?"

"If there was a key in the lock," I said.

"Key in the lock?"

"There was a key in the lock. At the last. I thought there couldn't have been. I mean—everyone went right in. Firemen. Detectives. Agents. *We* did. It was still smouldering."

"So your father died in a fire, Rennie?"

"He died in a fire in his bedroom."

Thelma Myzeld was quiet, then she said, "You'd better drive up here."

"I think I will," I said.

"So this accounts for the black widow dream you told me about?"

My heart caught. "I hadn't even thought ...I asked the neighbor what happened after my mother ran over there. 'Your mother was running up and down under that window. Black smoke just rolling out,' she said."

"Black smoke stays on your mind, I know that," Thelma said.

"I had an assistant in Nicaragua. Maraya. You would have loved her. She ran my household, totally ran it, even the garden. I was away so much. She called me Miss Rennie. She'd give me more than a little folk wisdom right now, or superstition, depending on her mood. 'Oh, Miss Rennie,' she'd say, 'Come quick, come quick. My sister-in-law is coming back to haunt me, the bitch.'"

Thelma chuckled. "Back to haunt her?"

"'She slams doors in my face,' she told me. 'They just slam when I'm all by myself and I know it's her. She hated me when she was alive and she hates me even more dead.'"

"Hell, she's worse than I am." And I could tell Thelma was worried. I've never known her to be worried. "What brings her to mind?" she asked.

"I don't know. She didn't ever talk about black smoke, although her mind was full of smoke and mirrors. My mind is as skittish as hers once in a while. Maybe it's the midnight hours I'm keeping. Am I disturbing you?"

"Don't be silly. I'll be disturbed if you don't get on the road. Why don't you run over. Bozeman's not that far. Your old yellow thing is up there, isn't it?"

"Yeah, it's here—good old Scout."

"We need the laughs—a Utah license plate is always good in Bozeman."

I left the next morning. On the way I tried to remember the words to a hymn, and I hummed it to myself. "Who can I turn to when all is..." and I couldn't remember anything else.

Go undefending toward the truth, I say to myself. Some Zen follower had said something like that. It made sense to me now.

And I noticed that as things had begun to get better, they were in some ways worse.

"You cannot serve two masters," David said to me, so softly I thought I'd misunderstood, and I wished I had. "Beleaguered," he told me. He was beleaguered. It was just a few weeks before he went to Jerusalem. He was melancholy, almost distant. He had come to what most people manage to avoid. He was standing over the split in himself. We didn't quarrel. It wasn't a quarrel.

He left me with the Roethke poem, "Wish for a Young Wife."

My lizard, my lively writher,
May your limbs never wither,
May the eyes in your face
Survive the green ice

Of envy's mean gaze;
May you live out your life
Without hate, without grief,
And your hair ever blaze,
In the sun, in the sun,
When I am undone,
When I am no one.

On the drive back to the cabin, I remembered Kent coming to our father's funeral. I see him in the beautiful blue suit he wore. I didn't know he even had a suit. His tie was maroon and blue. It looked like one my grandfather had, and it felt as though a talisman had been extended.

Kent got out of the car at the funeral home with a great deal of tentativeness. It was like bringing a deer out of that sedan, and my mother walked over to him. I had dreaded this moment above all others on my return to Pocatello. I was afraid I might be the one to tell Kent our father had died, and I wasn't sure I could do it. I knew I had to maintain enough equanimity to get up there on that stand and talk about a difficult man, a complex man whom I missed, unexpectedly missed. I'd thought there might be just ten or twenty of us at the funeral, and I'd been saying to myself that would be all right. I knew what I would do—I'd go into the women's room or out behind the chapel so that I wouldn't see anyone until after.

Then Kent was getting out of that car, and my mother walked over to him without hesitation. I was proud of her, and I could barely hear her say something like, "Honey, I have some bad news for you." I started to cry, and he looked up and saw me.

"Daddy has gone," she said. "He was real sick, and he's gone to heaven."

"Won't he be here?" he asked.

"No, he won't."

"Won't he be coming back?"

"No," my mother said. I was standing there crying helplessly, astonished at myself that I couldn't have more equanimity, that I couldn't stay steady for Kent.

"No, he won't," my mother said. "He'll wait for us up there."

"Will we see him again?" he asked.

"Yes, we will."

"Do you think he drives his truck?"

I realized how few certainties remained for me as I heard this soft conversation, how direct Kent's questions were and how amorphous my own thoughts. And then Kent walked off by himself, just walked off and stood twenty feet from us with his head down. He was as still as an animal in the forest. He stayed there for a long time. We held the service up for him. Then he came back and we all went into the church, and I walked up to the stand.

Not everything is headed toward resolution, you figure that out after a while. There is disintegration, there is entropy. I could see it after Kent left home, but I couldn't understand it, or stand it. My father's behavior may have changed more than anyone's in the subsequent years. It's another thing I didn't notice at the time. And when I came upon the pages I'd written that defined the extent of the change, I couldn't do more than just flip through them, looking for passages about my grandparents.

I'm surprised I wrote down what happened that Thanksgiving. I can't imagine I thought I'd ever want to remember it. But I did write it all down here at the cabin and that's where the pages stayed. I wrote about my reluctance to go home for Thanksgiving—I would have been thirty-nine and it was the last time I went home for a holiday. I wrote about my change of heart when I heard my grandparents would be there, the corrosion between my parents, a little girl mentioned over and over.

When my grandmother entered the picture, I read very carefully. We were in the kitchen together, having one of our conversations. I could always remember dialogue precisely.

“What hurt lasted the longest for you, Gram?” I asked, pushing pieces of celery into a design as I formed my question.

She didn’t say anything for a long few minutes. When she talked again, she too began making a whimsical arrangement with the celery stalks. They looked as though they were going to spin into a spitfire before we were through with them.

“Your mother came all dressed up with your father one evening when they’d been going together quite a while. We were up at the mill. I knew something was wrong when I saw them. Your mother burst out crying, and your father looked subdued down to nothing. He was quite a little dandy in those days.”

“He was? Old Sweatshirt and Slippers? Old Spider Belly?” I never said things like that around my grandmother and I winced.

“Rennie!”

“Awful of me.” And I remembered the big portrait of him in the oval frame in its place of honor in his parents’ home. He gazed out, intent and sweet-faced, untested. I always tried to see if he looked like Kent had as a boy, but I couldn’t find any connection at all.

My grandmother massaged her arthritic fingers. “Anyway, that was my worst hour. Your mother cried and cried and told us they were going that night to get married. I knew right then what was in store for her.”

“What was Mother like as a child?”

“Well, to tell you the truth, she was a lot the same. Nobody could be more fun and she had some starch, but she was inward, quiet. I don’t know what made her that way.”

"Was she like that before she met Daddy?"

"Yes, only not so bad. Your mother's always been afraid of him. Although I don't know why, the little bit of a shit. I'm worse than you. Don't take after me."

I was laughing. "I think you're Mediterranean. I think there's a mistake about Denmark and Wales. You've got all the cards right out there on the table."

"Speaking of, how's your canasta?"

"Right after dinner," I said.

She restored me. I think that Thanksgiving is when I began writing down on scraps of paper little things she'd say, things like, "Your mother has to go where she's the least unhappy." I had drawers full of them by the time she died, but it wasn't like I was going to forget the gold she spoke.

"Let's go put our feet up for a while and visit with your mother and father," she said.

The smell of turkey and Thanksgiving preparations seemed never to have reached the living room, with its worn-out white shag rug and its worn-out pink couch, where Mother was lying, eyes closed.

"Well, Blaine, are you going to eat more than your father-in-law this year?" My grandmother did most of the talking for us. My father nodded at me. "Good to see you," he said. He didn't hug me in those days, and I can't have made it easy. He must have been outside when I came in, but I hadn't gone looking for him. On the contrary.

"I've pulled way ahead of the Bishop, haven't I, Royce?" he answered my grandmother.

"I might not eat as much anymore, but I eat better," my grandfather chuckled quietly.

"You can eat better, but you'd better not eat my cranberries," my father responded, pleased with himself. He'd gotten fat. It must have been happening for years, and I hadn't noticed. He'd been so skinny he could hardly keep a pair of pants up, but suddenly he was fat.

I got up from the chair. I was cold, I was always cold when I came home, and I walked back to the kitchen. "Light for a minute," my grandmother called to me. "Come back in here and light for a while."

I went back into the living room and sank into the big, sloppy chair across from my father. He always sat in his undershirt in the overstuffed rocking chair. Beside it was enough medical equipment—salves and pills and tubes and oxygen tanks—to revive five patients. I looked at it all, and I felt as though I were the sick one—I'd need all this before long, I'd never be out of this thrown-together clinic. And there wasn't enough of something in the room. I didn't know what it was, but there wasn't enough of something I needed.

"How've you been feeling, Dad?" I asked.

"Not too bad, not too bad," he answered. "I'm going blind is all."

I'd forgotten what it was like.

"Heard a weather report? I'd like to get back to the cabin." I looked to my grandfather. He was dressed and groomed like a gentleman. "Might leave in time to spend the night there."

"Snow. You can't get there," my father said.

As I left the room, I leaned over my grandfather and said, "You look handsome. Is that a new suit?"

"I feel handsome," he replied, squeezing my hand with his big, well-shaped one. He took care of those beautiful hands. They were sheathed in leather in any kind of weather or work. "Yes, it is new."

A chill ran through me. I see what my father and I did to each other. He wasn't even a present figure for me. And maybe I was the first to leave, but God knows I couldn't have survived staying. Even being there a few hours was difficult then.

"Let's peel the potatoes," my grandmother said as she came into the kitchen. I turned around to see her lowering herself into the chair at the table, something she could just barely do. Her legs were so bowed she looked like she would sink into the space between them. And her knuckles were swollen. She winced when they bumped against the table edge.

"Where's your cane, Gram?" I asked, coming around the table to stand behind her and rub her shoulders. "Why don't you use it?"

"Oh, the damn little kids. They get it and play with it and then I can't find it. Speaking of kids, your Aunt Lucinda is never going to get over her daughter moving away."

"Wasn't that a while ago?"

"Yes, it was, but it's no different. She called me all het up about it the other day and said, 'You just don't know how I feel about it.'

"'I do too, Lucinda,' I told her. 'I lost one completely. What I mean is, Lilly didn't just go on a trip.'"

I smiled at that. My grandmother wasn't wearing herself out trying to be perfect. Or worse, look perfect. Then I came to the account of the mill burning.

"I can just see you coming up the path after work, Gramp," I said, looking over at him. "The whistle blowing and we're out the door, scooting down that path to you."

"I scooted down it the day the mill burned," my grandmother said.

The day the mill burned. It blazed through me like ice. It seemed in reflection that it must have been cold that day, that it must have been ice, not heat, that had thrown us back from saving it.

"You did sail for it that day all right," I said quietly, remembering that terrifying afternoon my grandmother had emptied the water buckets on the floor of the porch so she could rush with them to the mill pond and the fire. It was so vivid for me I thought I smelled smoke and my legs felt weightless.

"I came just a tootin' and fell flat on my face, and got up and started in again. I formed the brigade. We used our slop jars and everything."

"Cars stopped along the road, and people ran over to help us. Everybody did. You did," my grandfather said. "We saved the planer. One woman got right down in the mill pond to fill buckets. Did the washhouse go, Mother? I can't remember."

"No. Just the shed. It and the mill absolutely exploded. They just exploded." She showed what it was like with her bursting fingers.

"Did it roar? Was it a huge fire?" my father asked. He looked at me as he asked it.

"Did it roar?" my grandfather repeated, surprised at the question. "Whhhuuh! A fire creates its own wind. It just whipped through her." His hand came down in a flame.

"What caused it, did you ever know?" my father asked.

"Probably some kids smoking down in the sawdust piles," my grandfather said.

"Whoever that was ought to have the living hell kicked out of him. God Almighty."

"What does it matter?" my grandmother asked. "It's done, whether someone was smoking a smoke in the sawdust piles or the boiler threw a spark. What would the good of knowing be? It wouldn't bring back one board of the old place, or one hour of the good times there."

My grandmother must have seen something in my face, and she reached to ruffle my hair. "Remember it happy, Rennie, that's what you can do—for me as well as you."

"What did you think when you knew it was on fire?" I looked up and asked my grandfather.

"What did I think?" he said. "I thought it was a dirty shame!"

He looked across at me and saw me trying to come to terms with it. "It took a lot away from you, too," he said. His words fell over me like a blessing.

"At least you got out."

"I would have been back up in it after lunch. I'd just come down to grab a bite, and I was going back up to fix a pipe up in the roof."

"Gram and I were afraid you were in it. We ran...we didn't know."

The dinner proceeded. My father talked about the Jell-O salad he'd made, which hadn't set. I tried to kid him about apologizing for it. He explained that he wasn't apologizing, he was explaining. Mother didn't eat. By the time the pudding was served, everyone was silent again.

I felt gray and stilled inside. I tried to put the Christmas to come out of mind. What is it we expect? I wondered what David's day, surrounded by his family, was like, and I was mad at myself for having had the thought and having said the words I'd said to him when I left.

I skipped another handful of pages. And then I paid close attention.

That night I played solitaire at the dining room table. "I've had my red pains and my black pains," I said to my grandmother, quoting her.

"You have to have if you're going to live in this world. And you know something else? Don't puzzle over them too much, Rennie. I haven't ever known anybody I gave two licks for that wasn't half a mystery to himself and a full one to everyone else. To hell with it, live your life. You're doing just fine with yours, as near as I can tell."

"You're not like anybody else. Nobody says what you do. You hear so much."

"You're easy to talk to, little Wren. You were named for the bird, you know. We couldn't name you Wren and Ken so we changed it to Rennie, but then Kenny seemed going too far, even at the beginning of the forties. We laughed and laughed when we all sat around thinking up two names, not one."

"You help me go back and stop feeling wrong about the wrong things." I looked out the window. "I always thought I'd caused the mill to burn."

My grandmother looked up at me. "Oh, Rennie. I didn't know you were packing that around."

"I...Claine and I...Kent and I had made..."

"Oh, go on. I knew right where you were—down there in that little camp of yours making your miniature sawmill and playing house. What else? What generation on earth hasn't done it?"

"I didn't know anyone ever saw our little world down there. It seemed like we shouldn't have done it, like the real thing should have been enough. We loved it so much."

"You loved it more than any of us, Rennie, I do believe you did. I worried myself what you'd do without it."

"I thought..."

"You thought your adolescent smolderings had set the world

on fire, honey. But that's the wonder of life, not the destroyer. And do you know something else? Kent felt like he caused the fire. So did Julie. So did Tess's daughter. You know what she done? She asked her mother if she could go to town and the answer was no. Little Annette said, 'Oh, I wish the mill would burn down,' and she looked up and there it went. Do you think she caused it?"

"Yes! It was her. I had nothing to do with it."

"That's right. That's better. Laugh while you can. Your grandpa thinks he caused it because he couldn't get the pump to working right. One more day and we'd have had the fire truck filled. But it wasn't one more day, and that's that. To hell with it, that's what I say to such thinking. What's the good of it?"

"I'm glad when we have a chance to talk. I'd felt like I'd done something terrible with my private little world. Maybe I'd let it stand for other private worlds. As though the apparent world weren't enough. As though I weren't grateful."

"Very little is enough, Rennie—I'm pretty sure that is one of the things you've figured out. And when something is enough, it's God-given."

My father had left the room for a while and when he came back in, he stormed around at something my mother had forgotten to do. Then he started on me. "I suppose you're going to duck out of here now that your mother needs you," he said.

That's what I did. It's what I always did when he lost his temper. There was more to that day than I can bear to remember. But

I do remember feeling that if I wandered through my life with him from that moment until the next world, the shale and crackers would still be breaking inside and the white feathers falling and there would be nothing to cling to but David, farther away than he'd ever been, and my grandmother reaching for me, believing that I'd know how to grapple with my gray sadness. And she was sure I'd finally win.

Even with my grandmother there, the day was sad.

I don't know what going forward would have even been if I hadn't had my grandmother.

What she was comforted me beyond what being helped is. And I heard her again.

"Phaedrus, I don't want my life," you said to me in one of those summers in San Francisco. You weren't even in high school yet, and you didn't know what to do with yourself with the mill gone, and we didn't get to see you much. "You've got it," I said to you on the subject of your life. "Take care of it."

I've never told you this but it meant a kingdom to have you with me the day the mill burned. You loved it like I did, and you were a lot like me and you understood me. You have an understanding heart, Rennie, and it's blessed a lot of people.

Do you remember how you helped me? You'd been sick. I'd taken you to Rexburg to the doctor, and he said it was some kind of virus and there wasn't much he could do. I was working in the commissary, getting my order ready and adding up the charges in the books, when I heard a lot of screaming and yelling outside. I thought somebody had been hurt. Some of the guys were in there and we all ran out and when we got outside, we looked toward the sawmill and it was just in flames, absolutely enveloped.

I went running to the cabin first to get buckets and to see that you didn't get up because the doctor had given you strict orders to stay right in bed. When I got there, you had your Levis on and you were mumbling and sometimes your voice would rise up out of you all of a sudden, and tears were streaming down your cheeks. I tried to say something, but I could hardly speak myself, and you threw your arms around me and then we both headed toward the sawmill as hard as we could go. We'd grabbed all the buckets we could carry, even the slop jar. I fell once and when I looked up, there you were, leaning to help me up and looking too sick to make it yourself. I'd have hated to be alone that day, Rennie, I would really.

Royce had been up on the roof of the mill about five minutes before the fire broke out, and the first thing we done was find him. If he'd been up there when it started, he'd never have had time to get down. We always figured it began with one of the boys smoking a cigarette and starting the sawdust burning.

It was a new thought to me that I had helped her too.

David and I stayed at a place called the Jolly Dodger in Cairo at the beginning of another end, in the early spring of 1982. It's the end of that day I remember, too. "You mentioned a poem," he had said when he took me to the airport in Cairo. "Your poem. Read it to me." The traffic was moving at about the pace you would walk. Life on the sidewalk teemed and bumped against us as we crawled past—men with their languor and their laughter and their assurance, women demure and veiled, children darting in and out so quick and shining they seemed made of film. There was a call to prayer and all was still among those who faced the east, found the minaret in the familiar skyline—Qalu'un or Barquq. You could hear the voice single and clear—more incantation than chant. It seemed to rise up over the rooftops.

"'Houses bunched together untidily,'" David said. "Naguib Mahfouz would make you love it if you didn't already." I studied the side street we'd taken. "Isn't it wonderful," he said. "Did you get high enough to look down at the scramble of roofs?"

"I did—I walked up into the sweetest assortment of angles and extensions and vapors and scents when I had time in the evenings."

"Read me the poem," David said.

"It's not the right poem for right now." I handed it to him as we sat stalled in traffic, mumbling that it could use more cinnamon and saffron while he read it.

When he looked up, he said, "You have always astonished me," and behind his words were the sounds of horns honking, donkeys braying, shopkeepers crying out their wares—limes, they call them lemons, their nasal *Ashara! Ashara—Bae beriza!* Ten for a dollar. And David's voice. "She will try to help him out of the briars with her urgent eyes, telling him of the autumn that has come to the open country, telling him, when the time comes how he was like a last slant of sun dropping across the roll of the earth as he left her quickly, just ahead of the cross hairs of instinct and claim."

A vendor stepped up to the car, waving socks. "Two dollars a pound, two dollars a pound." I turned toward David so I could see his smile.

"You make me sound very good," I said to him. "You and the symphony of Cairo."

"Tell me about the riot when you were here before," he said. "I couldn't get to you," and his voice was wrought with the anguish of not having been there at the right time.

"We were guests of the government—you know the Minister of Education was with us—a lovely, lovely man. Omar something; we called him Omar although perhaps we shouldn't have."

"Yes, I'd..."

"I wondered if you'd arranged it. He met us at the airport and said he knew we were coming and would like to show our group around Cairo. We had just those few days, and the first thing he did was take me to the museum. Everyone else went to freshen up and rest. It was a quiet morning, and he took me directly there."

"Did you see the treasures of Tutankhamun and the papyrus of Mesopotamia?"

"And the gold and the jeweled utensils, the very fine copy of the Rosetta Stone, the collection of obelisks. I had two of the best hours I've ever had in a museum. And when we came out, Omar said that Sadat was speaking that night and he had tickets for our group. You probably know all this. We'd just come outside and the Nile was within view, heavy and refreshing. 'It's our Independence Day,' he told me. The palm trees surprised me. And the air—not as dry as I'd expected, at least not that day."

"Not today, either," David said.

"Perfect today." I paused and then continued. "Omar dropped me off at the Nile Hilton, and I stood looking out over the river and the sprawling city." I traced an arabesque design on David's arm as I spoke. I could not have imagined that the sprawl before me would eventually extend through the sands of the desert to the feet of the pyramids. It had been an hour's journey for us by camel, I should say tourist camel. The Egyptians didn't go by camel.

"Did Omar take you to the stadium?" David asked. I knew he knew Omar. I was pretty sure he knew Sadat.

"Yes, he picked us up in a trim little bus in the early afternoon—there were about twenty in our expedition—and drove us to the big soccer stadium on the outskirts of town. Was it the tenth anniversary of Sadat's presidency? I remember it as the tenth, but I could be years and years off."

"The tenth anniversary would have been at the end of Sadat's presidency. It already seems farther away than six months ago. It was in October, in 1981. Your trip would have been a few years earlier. But go on, tell me about it."

"I love what you know about this part of the world," I said to him, and then I continued. "The streets were packed. Omar gave each of us a pink ticket, and we got out and queued up with what looked like most of Cairo. Then he went on through the line of guards and into the stadium while we waited in line."

"I see you standing there, looking cool amid the press. Did you like it? Being in the thick of it?" David looked intent as he spoke.

"I loved it," I said. "It was like being at sea—a sea of Egyptians. They were courteous to us, but it didn't last. The crowds swayed and pushed and pressed in an abandoned way—tired of waiting but not impatient. Dressed in everything—pajamas, western pants. We waited a very long time—nothing like waiting with Westerners."

"Amid the animated sounds of Arabic," David mused, "as unfamiliar as its alphabet. And the snap of garlic filling the air."

"Yes—and fatigue," I said. "Everyone was cheerful, enjoying the evening air, and suddenly it changed. Omar had gone back through the line of guards that were keeping back the crowd, and he motioned for our group to come forward. I shook my head no—I tried to signal to him that we'd rather wait. I hate being singled out. 'Will the American guests come forward,' one of the guards called. 'Hold up your tickets.' And my group did just that, held up their tickets and pushed forward."

"It seems to start with something like the tickets, but there is more behind it."

"I felt dread, David. I feel dread hearing you say that. I hate that preferential treatment. And what more? There we were, pressing past people eating fōul sandwiches—their beloved fava beans—and koshari, humming and shouting to each other. And then the guards began taking us through the security line—I don't know if they were police or not."

"Probably not," David said. "At least not hashishin." He was in despair, and I wondered whether to go on, but he insisted.

"When the first of us stepped through, a great cry went up from the people. Just spontaneous and at once. It surged up from everyone, as if on cue. They were outraged, and the whole crowd swelled forward in a wave that overwhelmed the guards. They went down like a line. Or more, they were absorbed—one minute they were a line, they were swinging their clubs, then you couldn't identify them."

"Rennie! And where was I? I'm always out of sight, out of reach. You could have been killed in an instant. That kind of death isn't even reported, isn't...you can't sort out what's state-sponsored..."

"It seemed so spontaneous. You wouldn't have been proud of me, David. I felt the heat, the oppression of that many people in the heat. Babies were crying. I was trembling, violently trembling. The batons were swinging, and I felt a crack against my hip."

"Dear God!" David said. I'd never heard him say that.

"I dropped to my knees and scrambled through legs. Like an animal, David. I could feel my clothes tearing. I had no thought of the others..."

"That's why you didn't end up in the hospital—or the morgue. You did just right. Your instincts are for survival."

"But David..."

"I know." And he looked about him. "Here we are leaving, and we should be in the coffeehouse sipping espresso, waiting for the sun to set, watching the coffeepots steam in their big braziers, watching the ashes piled up over them." He slowed the car and pulled to the side of the road. "Can we get along, Rennie?" he said, "from island to island? Can we learn to float in between? Can we? Can we?"

I'd never seen despair take him, and I felt jeopardy again. With a jolt I remembered the first poem he'd quoted to me at Reading Terminal. I knew more of it now.

> I offer you that kernel of myself that I have
> saved, somehow—the central heart that deals
> not in words, traffics not with dreams and is
> untouched by time, by joy, by adversities.
> I offer you the memory of a yellow rose seen at
> sunset, years before you were born.

> I offer you explanations of yourself, theories
> about yourself, authentic and surprising news
> of yourself.
> I can give you my loneliness, my darkness, the
> hunger of my heart; I am trying to bribe you
> with uncertainty, with danger, with defeat.

He looked at his watch and saw that we were going to be late. "It's hard to hang on to water from the moon, isn't it?" he said. That sentence of his comforted me long after I didn't have him.

"And yet we do go somewhere." I barely spoke. "We do sail out to open sea."

And by then I was reaching for him, and looking at my watch, and trying not to simply put my life in his hands and weep. I was silent until we entered the air terminal parking area. "You've been better at it than I, that is all," I said to him as he parked the car. "And you think I'm the one who knows how to manage."

"Well, you don't tie up all the loose ends in a lifetime, do you?" he said. "I guess we've learned that. 'Can understanding come stumbling across the fiery years?' Mafouz again. My Arabic isn't good enough anymore…"

He reached for a pencil and turned my poem over and wrote on the back of it. I could see the words as they came out of him. I watched him write, and pause, and cross out, and write again. I couldn't imagine the speed of his mind or the depth of his heart. He handed me the piece of paper, and I watched him walk into the terminal. I sat there reading his words, holding the jacket he'd left. It's the first lines and the last of it I remember.

Where she was there is
Such a pool of reckless ecstasy
Where her mind has moved
everything is set in motion,
yet subtly, like Jerusalem and the scent
of cinnamon and saffron through
its Souks.

There remains the fierce betrothal
of instinct to extravagance and audacity
of soul to air and sanctified bone
of judgment and mercies to lovingkindness
where she was.

I sat there reading those words, overwhelmed at the need to love him and the fervent need to never say goodbye again. And yes, overwhelmed at his sense of me. And I thought of all the layers in his answer in Reading Terminal fifteen years before when I asked him what he did. "What I do," he'd said. "If it could be enough."

The next time I saw him was in the Ben Gurion Airport in Tel Aviv. Our fifteen years had been full of…I guess I would have to say assignations. I couldn't have known that the last time I'd see him would be in the Ben Gurion Airport in Tel Aviv.

THREE

"What happened?" I said to the meadow when I thought about David dying. "What is it that happened?" It was many years before I found my way back to Carlos's response to trouble or loss, chirped out in that high voice of his: "What happened, that's all." *That's all* was a separate sentence for me, and it closed my womanly years. After that, I made my bed from room to room. I still do.

I didn't stay anywhere for long after David was gone. But I did begin to trace out my grandmother's wisdom, over and over. "A lot of life is an accident, Rennie," she said to me once. "Things will come along and you'll figure and you'll figure, but it don't figure."

To shake myself from remembering the days I couldn't figure, I reached for my grandmother's plaid Pendleton jacket that was still hanging from its nail on the porch and went out into the meadow to find some sun. I walked past the crooked pine Kent and I had always called the camel tree and up to the woodshed. It was brisk enough that stacking wood felt good. Rearranged it is about all I did—I was there for the smell of the pitch and the pine. Then I wandered out toward the mill pond, assessing the day. The weather was going to make its big shift soon and I'd be making my final pilgrimage to Sawtell. The meadow was in the last of its gold, burned gold.

"Take me back to ordinary days," I said to Phaedrus, "ordinary losses." I thought of my grandmother in that meadow. "Teach me what I need to know." And I let her give me words, knew she was going to. I didn't go to her when David was alive; I could have gone to her, but I didn't. Now, when everything was at stake, I did.

> A lot of life is an accident, Rennie. Think about it. You don't live as long as I've lived without noticing it. And when you really see it is when your kids try every which way, but it doesn't work. Your life with David was nothing like my life with Royce, and yet you began in the same place, wanting the same things. Did Royce and I deserve what we got? No more than anyone else. The plain truth is I'd have done what you did to have Royce. I can see the times changing is what I can see. Complicating.
>
> Our lives were more straightforward, and so were our accidents. Once when Royce and I got home from our first little trip together—we'd gone into the Park and stayed a couple of nights—just as we pulled into camp, his brother Clyde come to meet us. He was in his early teens at that time. He come running for us just as hard as he could run. When he got to us, he said, "Hurry up and come on. We've got to have the car. A horse has stepped on Nola."

The men had unhooked the horses off the wagons when they came in from the timber, and the kids had been playing hide and seek. Nola was laying up against a log. She was laying flat behind it, hiding, and the horses had run through the yard and one of them come over this log where she was and stepped right in her face. It left a hoof mark on her forehead, just laid the scalp right back. She's got a horseshoe across her forehead to this day.

Nola's father was the oldest and Clyde was the youngest of the Douglas brothers, and it was sad to see Clyde come up to Boon and tell him what had happened to his pride and joy. Boon went to pieces for everything. She was his daughter. He just tore his hair out, he couldn't do anything. They were waiting for the car to take her to the doctor when we came in. So that ended our trip. We knew we were home.

We were always having accidents at the mills. Another one we had that summer was when we went up on Sawtell picking huckleberries one Sunday afternoon. We were just loading up to come home when Darrell shot a shotgun.

What were these connections? I listened in astonishment. There seemed to be a plan here. This couldn't be random.

The team heard that shot and they were just pounding up and down. Royce stood up and tried to hold them and he was white as a sheet. We come flying off that moment, I'll tell you. The horses run out of control clear to Stamp Meadows Road, right nearly to the bottom.

In those days we didn't stay at the sawmill very late. However, that year I stayed up until the weather turned bad. I was expecting your mother. My mother and father came up and visited me, but I can't remember if I went home with them or not. Anyway, I went home earlier than Royce. All the women went down when the weather turned bad, and there were just men in the camp. The women had to go home to put the children in school.

My grandmother's words took me to solid ground, anchored in the reality of things. She didn't enshrine anything. She met it head on. And I picked up her voice again. I could get her back exactly, and I knew it said something very fine about me.

"I want every detail, Phaedrus," I said to her. "I'm in no hurry."

No, by gosh, that year the other wives took me down and left me with the kids, and they all went back. They took me down and left me to keep Clyde and Alice and get Royce's sister's two children in school, since I was expecting my first baby, and I had to get all my baby clothes sewn and ready. I came down and I put four kids in school. I had a cow to take care of. I didn't have to milk it, but I had to take care of the milk. It wouldn't have got milked if

I'd had it to do. That was a real hard time for me. It was all kind of new to me, and I worked like the dickens.

Along in September when I was about six months pregnant, Clyde and the others went out to feed the cow one morning. They got in a hurry and they picked up a lot of real pale leaf and put it out for the cow to eat. I was down helping Mother when the telephone rang. We had a phone by then. It was one of the kids, and they said to come quick, the cow was dying. It bloated. So, anyway, the cow died.

I stood beside the mill pond looking out over the meadow.

Pale leaf.

It bloated.

So anyway the cow died.

My grandmother's whole nature was right there—the exquisitely observed detail, the fact, matter-of-fact, and the result—a little narrative—its own haiku. That sense of irony—she amused herself no end. I could hear exactly how she'd phrase this, and she'd know Kent and I were going to collapse with laughter. It helped you deal with the loss of a cow.

"In the fall," will be next, I say to myself. And I heard her.

In the late fall, we went up to the dry farm again. We had an expression at the time and it was really true. We used to say we worked from "could see to couldn't see." Then we dropped all in a heap.

When I dropped all in a heap at the end of those autumn days, I dropped like a cylinder. I was so big I looked like a cartoon of a pregnant woman. Speaking of accidents, there was another one. My labor began, clear up there on that farm, and we left in the middle of the night, Royce driving hell bent for leather to get me down to the doctor and me seeing that we weren't going to make it.

How did I feel about having my first child? I felt nervous. I was with my mother when she lost her third baby, for one thing. I'd seen that baby born blue, just dark blue. And the last month at the mill I'd had a lot of trouble I didn't tell Royce about, and I won't bother you with it either.

People say you forget the pain. It's propaganda. You don't forget. I can still feel my hands get cold and my knees draw up when I remember my first delivery. I thought I was giving birth to a submarine is what I thought. And if I'd ever thought about it after that, I might have quit right then and there. But hindsight is left out of me.

I wasn't a boob though. Deborah was born in the old Model T. I was turned so I was leaning up against Royce with my feet pressed nearly clear through the door, and I could feel the baby's head. "Royce," I said, "stop the car and come around and get your baby." He could hardly quit trembling—he barely managed to get the truck shut off and get around and open my door.

I must have passed out and when I came to, Royce was shaking me and telling me to wake up. I remember him saying over and over from a long way off that we had the most beautiful little girl, we had the most beautiful little girl. He was just shaking me to beat the band. She *was* beautiful, she was the cutest baby I'd ever been near.

I thought of the distance from this baby girl to my mother, whose life wasn't what she wanted—and wasn't what she deserved either, if deserving plays in there. Have a wider mind, Rennie, I told myself. Take note.

Anyway, when Royce saw that baby, all at once he quit shaking and he said, "I'm so proud of you," and he laid her across my stomach. There was a membrane over her face, and he leaned down and drew that membrane away with his mouth and cleaned out all her passages until she could breathe easily. I don't think I ever loved him like I did watching him do that, steady and careful and somehow knowing just what to do.

I was sitting in a pool of blood and Royce got back in the truck and drove harder than ever for town. Suddenly a big buck leaped right out in front of us. He leaped right into the ring of light from our headlights. We felt a jolt and heard a terrible thud, but Royce held that wheel and went for town. I'd never heard of a deer being that far down before. I couldn't look back to see if the deer bound off. I couldn't even ask Royce about it.

On his way back to the farm next day, Royce stopped along the side of the road where Deborah was born and heaped up a little monument of rocks. He's a man who knows what sentiment is, I knew that, but thinking of him placing his rocks of remembrance choked me right up.

Does that kind of sentiment get in the molecules of something like rocks and stay there, I wondered? I went looking for that stack of rocks once. I thought they'd call out to me. It wasn't silence I heard, but it wasn't differentiation either. Every rock called out.

I went back from my thoughts to the everyday wonder of my grandmother's voice. I saw that I could control the shift.

When Deborah was little she was plump and fat, and her feet were so limber. You could take her foot and lay it right back against her leg. I remember I thought something was wrong with her, and I bawled when I discovered it because I was sure she was deformed.

We slept right with our children in those days. They slept right with us. In fact, they slept right in the middle. We never thought of putting a baby in a bed by itself—we had to keep them in bed with us to keep them warm.

We would cover them clear up, their little heads would be clear under the covers. I think that's terrible now. It almost scares me. Deborah used to sleep on my arm all night long. It's nice to cuddle babies for a while, but you get so you would like to turn over and really sleep.

We didn't feed babies like we do now, either. All they got was milk—breast-fed or bottle-fed. They didn't get anything but milk. The poor things were hungry and we had to feed them every few hours all night and all day. And if they had a diaper rash, we put some flour in the oven and burned it and put that on their little bums. I don't know where we got the idea. We just done what somebody else done.

And the sugar tits, that's coming up. I chuckled out loud.

You and Kent used to love to hear me tell about the sugar tits we gave our babies. Kent done okay with it, but you could hardly say it. Both of you had me telling you all the time how we quieted our babies. You couldn't hear a baby cry without asking for the story. You made me mention sugar tits in the damndest places, and then I'd have to listen to you two titter. We took a little piece of rag and wet the end of it and twisted a little bit of sugar in it and give it to the babies to suck on. I think it's a pretty good idea—no worse than those pacifiers hanging out of kids' mouths today, except I guess for the sugar. I used to dunk Deborah's in fruit juice, but I guess that wasn't a terribly lot better.

Deborah was practically addicted to her sugar tit, whatever I put on it. I used to pin it to the front of her smock. She'd grope around for it all in a frenzy if she got the least bit upset. Nothing made you laugh like thinking of your mother fumbling around for her sugar tit. I don't know why you couldn't say the word—it wasn't ever hard for me to say and you heard that kind of talk all your life, around me anyway, I'm ashamed to admit.

Remember the roses someone sent for one of our anniversaries? I couldn't tell you which one. You were there when they came, and I looked up at them, and really without even thinking, I said, "You know, roses don't last worth a shit." That's all it would take to set you off. I loved to hear you laugh and you laughed that day for half an hour and I said, "Well, it's true, they don't, they don't last."

I was off. I was laughing heartily out there in the meadow and I was filled with how deep our companionship was, how much I still had her. I knew I should write this gold down. And I was taken with her voice again, simply taken.

When Kent was with you, it was double everything—I had a symphony of laughs in you too, and when you got started, it was five movements. That laughing got you in trouble once in a while. You used to laugh so long your father would get annoyed. Actually annoyed was never the word for him. He'd just flame up suddenly and reach over and grab you by the hair and bang your heads together. Then the laughing would stop and you'd be wiping bloody noses and looking stunned and the silence after that was terrible. None of us knew what to do but just slip away when Blaine got like that, slip away with you kids. Our own kids never had a hand laid on them. I can't stand to remember wondering whether to leave things to Deborah or step in there and get you kids out of that situation. I never had that in my house. We lived in peace and quiet with my mother and father. And Royce never touched a child in anger.

We lived with his folks the rest of the winter Deborah was born. There was a little more noise there. His father could act pretty tough, but that's all it was.

Phaedrus, you're somewhere within me, and I think of my own father, think about telling David about him. My father had been out of my thoughts for days, weeks. That might be progress.

And I'm back at the cabin with David, our last trip there together. And he asks about my father. "You don't talk about him, Rennie."

"I'll tell you something early, something happy. All the good times were early—the first five years of so. My father was nothing whatsoever like my grandfather. He wasn't imposing or handsome or gentlemanly. My idea of a fine man was my grandfather."

I study David beside me. "My grandfather— not my father—led me to you. How terribly lonely for him," and I'm shaken by the thought. I'm curled in his arms. "Are we spoonering? Tucked into each other like this?"

"I can't tell if I'm spoonering or spoonered," he says, bringing his knees closer into me.

I laugh at him. "Well, my father *could* make me laugh. In 1938, he laughed with us. We'd put our buff-colored coats and leggings on and then our caps, which had little ears, honest to God, and he'd say to my mother, 'Look at my two little deer. Shall we paint their bottoms white?' which made us prance and squeal. And he'd take us outside and make a big circle in the snow, not lifting his feet so the snow packed. And then he'd cut it in half, crying out to us, 'Come little deer, stay by,' and then he'd cut it again.

"We'd shuffle and slide along behind him, giggling our heads off, and he told us about Fox and Geese. 'You are the *geese*,' he'd say. And he'd *swing* around facing us, 'and *I* am the *fox*,' and we'd screech and flee on the path cut through the snow—the slices of pie—laughing and sliding into each other, falling down and leaping up to race through the white world."

Sometimes the neighbor kids would come over—Carol Ann and Jim Leish, but they stayed at the edge and watched. Jim Leish was never more than at the edge of things. And for once we were a completion—literally a family circle. It took away the fear of people like Jim Leish and how close he came to killing the little Dolf boy.

I turn my head so I can look at David. "Did you play it, David, in the snow in Philadelphia, a world away? Did you grow up playing Fox and Geese? Did you think you'd be loved like this? It lifts me beyond my…my regrets."

"Pasternak had it figured," and he quoted *Dr. Zhivago*. "'I don't think I could love you so much if you had no regrets.'"

We spent the entire day in our little room. The sun was beginning to set before we noticed the time. When we finally came out into the kitchen, we were being silly again. For one thing, we were half starved. While he built a fire, I fussed in the kitchen and chattered. "Further back on the other side of the family was my great-grandfather, David Douglas. My first David."

"Tell me about him, about his lovely name. All about it."

"I know I wanted it and not my father's name. I used to introduce myself as Rennie Douglas up here when I was a girl. I guess I started out a snob, it's true. Everyone knew the Douglas's and our sawmill. I was a rotten little trader."

"I hope you were," he laughed. "But I think charmer more than trader."

"Douglas, a family whose origin is lost in obscurity, but which in the beginning of the fifteenth century was thought to spring from the same stock as the Murrays." I was peeling potatoes and I put the peeler and potatoes down and made the deaf sign for *spring up*. "The Murrays, Sir William de Douglas figures from…"

"Figures?" David said. I noticed his eyes. "Your language gets us…"

"Come over here and figure me," I said to him.

He put his arms around me from behind, and I leaned my head back so my mouth was against his ear. "Yes, David. You're listening to my Douglas's and Murrays and figuring me…"

"What was the worst of it with your father?" David asked me the last hour of the last day in that cabin.

"I can't tell you here," I said to him. "When I'm home and you've gone away, I'll write it down and you will read it and it will be…can it be neutralized?"

I did write to David about my father hanging Jim Leish. I was careful. I never addressed anything to him. His name doesn't appear anywhere. He called me after he'd read it. I don't remember what we said. I don't think we used words. I could hear that he was crying for the heavy sins of the past.

I kept a copy of what I wrote to David, I'm not sure why, but I have it here with the things I saved:

My father was overwhelmed—not all at once, a little at a time. I think he registered life as a series of accidents. And it wore him out. Fox and Geese in the snow was a brief interlude.

"Your father could be ugly like nobody's business, he could really, that's for sure." That's how my grandmother would say it. "Like nobody's business." She had that right. She didn't step back from the way things were. And you don't need to, either.

He said, "*Jesus Christ, didn't anybody look after the fire extinguishing equipment?* How could they lose the whole mill?" He always knew what someone should have looked after. "Didn't anybody check those hoses? That's the first thing I'd have done. I'd have done it every day if I could have saved a business like they had going. I told them to open a lumber store down below. They'd have been wealthy people if they'd done it. They could have supplied lumber for all of southeast Idaho. Did supply Montana up into West Yellowstone. They couldn't get the pump to work? Of all the *stupid, idiotic...*" A lot of the sentences that started with Jesus Christ ended with stupid idiotic. Telling you, I don't feel the old shudder. I see how desperately he was engaged with us—and how ill-prepared.

Accidents. Maybe if Jim Leish hadn't...if Daddy hadn't... or if Carol Ann hadn't come over and slumped into the big kitchen Daddy didn't finish, slumped in the way she did, trying to be someone at fourteen she hadn't been at thirteen. We lived from maybe to maybe on Dirke Street. Maybe they knew quite a bit about what happened, and they took us away.

I was somewhere I shouldn't be that night—in my own house. I felt like I was inside everybody. Carol Ann felt like oatmeal. Jim Leish felt like breadsticks. My father, when he came, felt like liver. I felt like smoke, and I wished I were. I wished I could swirl up away from Dirke Street and find my grandparents and the cabin.

Carol Ann caught my eye. She saw something there that gave her courage or made her crazy, two things she hadn't been until then. "Jim Leish, awful Creish," she called out. It sounded so stupid I wanted to cry, but I burst out laughing.

Jim Leish was in the house—just him and me and Carol Ann. He was leaving and she taunted him, and then it goes into a dream sequence—Jim Leish walking out the door and away, becoming a mass, a turning, a martial player, knees bent, sinking, spiraling back toward the door.

Carol Ann managed to slam it against him. He turned to leave again and Carol Ann, pale but not finished with Jim Leish, opened it and cried out, "Too baaaaddd."

His foot was in the door. Screams, in a neighborhood where nobody screamed. Kicks, a flurry of feet. We were jamming our feet against Jim Leish's big foot. Carol Ann came down on Jim Leish like a spike. His foot ripped back automatically, a piston. The door slammed shut. Trembling. Laughing now, a desperate thing to do. Slide that bolt.

She started to cry out something else. My voice went over hers, sad and loud, "Nooo." Maybe the Nooo brought him back, wailed against the lid of the sky.

The night had changed once and it changed again with that one syllable. I heard his hard word as though it exploded from inside my chest. The door was flung open. We worked to get it closed, Jim Leish's strange leg mostly inside, looking dissociated from him, from anyone. We struggled for leverage. No one said anything. It was intense. It was adult. There was no play—this was not Fox and Geese. Breathing, lips white-edged, no time to wipe away the white edge, lungs gusting with effort, the door cutting against the big leg, remembering what he'd done, how the little Dolf boy had looked at the end of Jim Leish's arm. And then no more Jim Leish for a year.

As the door began to give against Jim Leish's weight, Carol Ann sank to her knees and threw her head back, her mouth so wide open you could see the back of her throat, and then she came down into the flesh of Jim Leish's leg. She clamped down like some sea creature, as though she knew only this one function.

The door was closed and locked in the next moment, and the blind drawn over the window in it. I couldn't have said which one of us pulled it down. We looked at each other with odd faces. I had never liked Carol Ann.

My throat felt like it tore and my face twisted as a fist shot through the glass and a hand groped under the blind for the lock. The hand looked like some freak of nature, like that leg, grotesquely dissociated from its body, its function, and I wanted Kent. Then a hammer was there and Carol Ann was saying, "Get an ice pick," and I had a terrible picture of that hand by itself, feeling its way toward an ice pick.

Then Jim Leish had the hammer and there didn't seem to be any more logic, or sequence even, to what followed. A piece of the lock smashed into my hand. Jim Leish was inside, his face full of white wildness.

Then Kent was there. He said two words to Jim Leish, two big words, although he was much smaller. Those two words seemed like the only two words in the world, maybe the only two words Kent knew then, and I felt them make it out of him and into the night. "Get out," weaving the air back together, and Jim Leish leaving.

When my father came home that night and looked at the lock, I saw the maniac behind his strong nose and full mouth. He looked like Jim Leish had looked. I didn't—how could I tell him how Carol Ann had taunted Jim Leish, how dark everything had become, what Jim Leish had done with Carol Ann the last time he was over and how strange it had been for me, standing there bewildered, cut off. I had no words for what Jim Leish had said to me, had tried to do to me in the shed weeks earlier. No whimper, no scream, no sentence.

It was late, but my father kept Kent and me up.

"What the hell have you done to the window? What happened to this lock?""Not Kent," I said. I was trembling.

"Did you do this?" His voice was so loud the words bounced back and forth in my head and I couldn't understand.

"No," Kent said.

"Kent scared him off." I was shaking too much to continue. My father grabbed me by the shoulders and shook me.

"You tell me what happened or I'll never let go of you."

"Came. And."

"Jim Leish," Kent said.

"Came. And Carol Ann. And...."

"Did he get in here? Was she in here?"

"Tried and...."

"Tried and?" My father's voice was low now and quiet.

"Tried and we fought and kicked and his leg and the door and his fist and broken glass," and big sobs took over and my chin was trembling and Kent was holding onto me.

"By God, tomorrow we'll see what Jim Leish has to say for himself," Blaine England said. My father—someone I didn't know. Then my mother was leading me to bed, those waves of sobbing making my breathing shudder and Kent silent again.

I got in bed, but I didn't sleep. I watched the designs the headlights of passing cars made on the wall, first a hand, then a leg. Finally there weren't any cars and I watched the wall. Something was trying to make its way out of the shadows, but I couldn't tell what it was and I curled away from it, the tips of my fingers in my mouth.

"Come here," my father growled to Jim Leish when he saw him in his own back yard the next morning. I had seen Jim Leish do a lot of things and look a lot of ways in the seven years we'd lived across the street from him. I'd watched his boy pursuits drop away and lengthen into awkward tallness and his loose curly hair stiffen under Brylcreem that couldn't be too much and couldn't be too often. I'd seen his soft cheeks harden. You could tell it from across the street.

The one way I had never seen Jim Leish in those years was frightened, but I saw him beset with terror when he heard my father's voice. "Here Jim, here Jim Leish." My father stood out on the street and called him like a dog, and Jim Leish shook like a dog. There was something more unnatural than insulting in it.

When Jim Leish could make himself move, he ran on old lady legs. His face was the color of cream, but I knew it would be hard. His lips seemed frozen; he didn't form words when he made sounds. My father ran after Jim Leish in what was left of broad daylight, and people came out on their porches to watch the tall boy veer down the street like a rabid animal, my crippled father's course even more grotesque.

I stared. How had I set this in motion? The two disappeared behind Nillson's house, came into view again in his cherry trees, and then disappeared for several minutes. When they reappeared beyond Mr. Spencer's half-standing garage, my father was limping heavily; I could hear him breathe from where I was. Then they disappeared behind Diggot's, and when I saw them again, my little father was pushing big Jim Leish in front of him. He had Jim Leish in an arm lock. He was twisting too hard and Jim Leish would nearly go up in the air, then he'd drag down. Over and over he sailed up, then dragged down. His hair hung in streaks about his face, all the curl oiled out of it. Only his hair looked like my father's, my father's when he was furious. The resemblance ended there. Jim Leish was tall and husky and blond and terrified, and my father was short and thin and insanely sure of himself.

When he and Jim Leish arrived under the tree that I was almost always in, he said, "I'm going to string you up." My father said, "Get a rope!" He wrestled with the rope that was suddenly on hand, and I realized I was going to stand there in a pool of shock and watch Jim Leish be hanged. I felt like my bird wings had come off and were fluttering madly inside my brain.

Then Jim Leish looked at me. He looked pleading and something in his eyes made me remember him climbing into Mr. Brown's shed after I'd gone in.

Jim Leish was staring at nothing as my father tossed him up against the tree. I finally pushed a sentence up past my trembling. My father was making a noose with the rope. "Daddy. Daddy, we're not mad at Jim. Not mad. You can—maybe—you don't need to..."

"Shut up." He worked with the rope. "You're going to show him what it's like to be scared. Ever been afraid, Jim?" My father laughed. He was almost gone. "You're going to be goddamned good and afraid now." There was that jeering laugh.

Coming toward him with the rope in a noose, my father said in almost the same kind of cooing that Jim had made to me in the shed, "Are you scared now, because I'm gonna teach you a lesson you won't even want to look back on."

Jim Leish was mumbling too, but there was no cooing in him. It was the disjointed, illogical rattling of terror. "No, Mr. England, don't, don't—God! God, Mr. England. Don't with the rope. Don't put my neck. God! Somebody! Get my father. Please. Get me my father. My father will kill you for this, Mr. England."

Suddenly something happened that made the tree trunks stop weaving in and out of the stabs in my brain. Something was flying up in the air, but it wasn't Jim Leish following his neck. It was Jim Leish following one leg. My father was sweating and wheezing, his eyes bulging and full of hatred. His hair hung away from his head and down over his eyes. He didn't even look like himself.

When he ran out of rope, one of Jim Leish's legs was sticking up toward the limb I always sat on. The other leg was dangling straight out from his body. His arms dropped down past the blood vessels already standing out in the sides of his head. He put his fingers in the dirt, right next to where his hair was hanging, and pushed so a little of his weight was supported. Then he went limp, and I gasped, expecting to see the rope give a few inches and his head hit and turn to the side. I knew just how it would turn and how his eyes would roll back.

My father called me over. Jim Leish was sobbing, "My father will come over here, Mr. England. God. Get him. Get him!" I was as scared as Jim Leish was. I'd never seen anybody like this.

"Now you do to him whatever you want," my father said, satisfied and leaning against the swaying trunk. "Get a board and bash him. Slap him, kick him in the teeth, throw dirt in his eyes. Use your imagination. Just so you scare the goddamn living hell out of him. Go on!"

I see myself sink away, I feel my knees give. My father grabbed me by the arm. "Go on! If you don't do what you want to him, I'll do what I want and it won't be pretty."

Pretty hung there in the air. Would I ever know pretty. Pretty good kid. Pretty day. Pretty girl.

"You'd better get busy before I have to," my father said. I could smell Jim Leish's smoky sweetness with something acrid layered over it. Fear, I thought. What a dog smells.

"I don't want to," someone small and far off said. "Can't." I fell back, my knees like water. Then Kent was there, and I leaned into him, and he put his arm around me tighter than he ever had.

"Don't want to? I don't care if you want to! Do you think I'm doing this for me? What have I told you about carrying a big stick. Who tells us to carry a big stick?"

I can hear my father, and I can see me. I stood there bewildered. Bewildered is a little tiny word. White, biting my fingertips. Jim Leish turning purple, his whole face pulsing, that color draining down into his hair.

Carol Ann had come over from her house next door. She was pale, and I could see her hands trembling. Then she turned and left. No words.

"I'll show you what to do," my father said as he pulled me away from Kent and took my skinny hand in his crippled one. He brought it down violently across Jim Leish's ear. Striking him felt as though a stick had jutted up into my shoulder and neck, and when it was done, my hand hung limp at the end of some world I couldn't remember belonging to. I heard Kent make a low, angry sound behind me, and its protest was like my bird wings to me.

"Not Kent," I moaned.

My father had his finger right under Jim Leish's eye so that he could push the hanging, almost lifeless mass back and forth. It was the finger that had gotten sliced from joint to nail in a lathe, cleaning off the top half. It had been mended with strips of skin from his hip, and it looked now like someone had sewn pieces of beef jerky over it.

"See this!" my father screamed. "Do you know what I can do with this? You tell me some of the things I could do with it."

Jim's mind was gone and he couldn't answer. He couldn't even care. He wasn't whimpering or murmuring or holding his weight up with his hands. I thought he's dying now. He's never going to get down. He's never going to get me. I realized the alliance of the young against the old, and I felt as lifeless inside as the boy hanging before me.

After that, David, I wrote stories about a girl who looked three years younger than she was, who stayed outside until it was dark, even in rain. If something threatened her, she took out her bone-handled pocketknife, opened the blade, and made tiny slashes with her ninety pounds behind an arm that looked like a wild twig waving.

I give this to you, David. It is enough. I see my resources. And I see maybe for the first time that my father was a very lost man. He needed help and he didn't get help. And none of us around him got him help. That includes me and my mother. And my grandmother. It wasn't a very enlightened time.

Telling you, David, I feel the hand of mercy.

When the weather changed the next morning, I began preparing for my annual hike into the Utmost Source. It would start getting cold up there on Sawtell soon now. I got out my Danners and oiled them. I should have done it the night before, but they already had a good waterproofing. I still hadn't rounded up a backpack, so I found my old green fishing vest and took most of my equipment out of it and lay it in a neat row on the kitchen table—the boxes of colorful mayflies, the tapered leaders and rolls of tippet, the gingko. I left the clippers and knife and clamps and added my standard hiking gear—matches, a few strands of tinder, a compass I didn't trust, extra socks, a length of thin nylon rope, gloves. I put a windbreaker in the wide pocket in the back of the vest and filled my water bottle and put it in its sling. I added some nuts and fruit because you're way back up in there and you'll need all you've got.

I took Stamp Meadows Road, the beautiful old logging trail lined with stands of jack pine that open into meadows and quaking aspen. It's only a few miles to the foot of Sawtell, just below the Indian Head peak and just above the Bootjack mill that looks out over the flats. Then the road winds up through huckleberry patches and thicker timber, around and around on those hairpin turns. When I was about three turns from the top, I started watching for a slight widening in the road, just enough to leave one car. A handful of people know that turnoff and even fewer know where the faint trail begins. It's high enough that some of the pines are burled and twisted from the wind.

I could see over the whole caldera from up there—the North Fork a silver ribbon wending through the valley floor, joining the Buffalo below Pond's Lodge and spilling over the dam into the reservoir. I could just make out the big lodges along the rivers. They look like match boxes. Big Springs is the hardest to sight, sitting off to the east at the headwaters of the North Fork, then Island Park Lodge, the only one some distance from the river. And from there they line up along the highway—Mack's Inn on the Fork, Pond's Lodge on the Buffalo, and five or six miles below where the rivers merge, Last Chance. They're all a little grand, a little ragged.

I hiked for a couple of hours, the earth soft and loamy. Birds were twittering, and high above, almost out of sight, a red-tailed hawk rose and fell on the air currents. It was cool and I settled down. I knew what was ahead, and that made me peaceful. The trail in is like a lot of mountain trails up here—alpine, strewn with the yellows and pinks of wildflowers and the greens and grays of mosses along springs, the jumble of pines—lodgepole and quaking aspen and Douglas fir and then the fanciful limber pine and the rare white pine—not much of it left.

At the last, everything changes. The trail narrows suddenly and leads toward a rock formation, and you have to know just how to make the final steps to enter a high, wide, hushed grotto, the only sound the creek falling from the tops of the rocks, the utmost source of the headwaters of the Missouri. Everyone feels the spirit residing in that ground. A small meadow spreads out, but it is somehow part of the enclosure, and all through it, wherever you move, there is that hallowed feel. It is tangible—it isn't anything you could conjure. It's like a force field, and it ends at the parameters of that grotto and meadow.

"Who was here?" David asked me when I took him up—that would be over ten years ago now. I hadn't told him the history of the place. And when I said Chief Joseph and what was left of his tribe, he said, "They must have stayed here for a time to invest it with this much."

I stood there in the sunlight that had broken through, remembering him saying that. Then I hiked out quickly and drove back down those switchbacks to Mack's Inn and went to the payphone and called my neighbor in Salt Lake City. "Hal!" I said on the second hello. I had trouble making the shift. He sounded like the idea of a former life, not a fact in it, and it took me a minute to get oriented.

"Rennie!" He kept saying my name. "We're all wondering how you are. I'm glad you called." He sounded worried, and I hadn't expected that. I particularly didn't want to impose that on anyone.

"I'm okay, Hal," I said. "I'm in a good place."

"All around?" he asked.

"Yes—pretty much. But I miss Thalo. How did I come to name her that?"

"Old Dog Blue or something like that," he said.

I laughed. "Is she okay?" I asked him. "I miss her. I've been so.... Thank you for taking her. Maybe I'd better...would you send her to me, Hal? She's flown a lot—she doesn't mind it."

"I can't believe you take her to Washington, D.C., when you go on those trips," he said. I heard him laugh.

"Would you—this is presumptuous on top of everything else, but Hal, could you drive her? There's a carrier for her in the garage and if you'd drive her to the airport—to Western Airlines—and put her on a flight to Yellowstone, I could meet her any time."

"Hell yes, I'd do anything for you, Rennie, we all would. We're all worried about you. I thought you'd be up there in those mountains. If you get back here, we'll have a barbeque and I'll make you that red-pepper-yellow-pepper-raisin dish you love. Get back here and let us look after you."

"Soon," I told him. I could see the street in my mind, its crowding of houses, and I wondered when I'd ever go back.

"I can take Thalo down today, Rennie—any time. I'm off work—out of work, actually."

"Oh, Hal, I'm sorry. If you need something to do, go water my aspen and laurel. I'll cross your palm. There is a flight that gets in here at ten o'clock and one at three—somewhere in there. I'll call for the schedule and call you back."

"Don't do a thing but go to the airport in West Yellowstone. I'll leave now and get her on the afternoon flight. I'll load her up right away. Can you be at the airport by three?"

"I can, Hal. I'm close to it. You have no idea how much you're doing for me."

"Shall I come with her?"

I couldn't imagine the loss of my solitude. I was stunned to think of it. I paused for a long time.

"You need to be alone right now, don't you, Rennie?"

"Yes," I answered. I couldn't put another word with it.

"Thalo will be with you by afternoon. I'll take care of everything on this end."

My heart raced. "Put one of my shirts in the carrier for her. Does she still tap the floor with her paws when she's excited? Beg for peanut butter?"

"She most definitely does. Honestly, Rennie, you have not changed one bit," he said, and I was thinking how much I had changed, how much everything had changed.

I drove into the Park and stopped along the Madison. There was a picnic table and I took a yellow pad and pencil from my backpack and went over to the bench and sat there in the early morning sun and sketched an eagle and her fledgling atop an old tree across the river.

I stayed until it was time for Thalo to arrive. When I got to the airport, she was being carried off the plane and I ran out onto the tarmac and got her. "Girl, Thalo, damn Thalo, I missed you so much. I didn't even know how much. It was so quiet. I was so quiet." And I looked up at the attendant. "I missed her," I said.

I talked to Thalo all the way back to the cabin. When we pulled into the circle of pines that surrounded it, I told her, "Something's happening in there, Thalo." I found her bowl and gave her water, food. And I knew what was waiting for me. I had that gathering feeling. When we'd unloaded, I got her lunch and I sat at the kitchen table. I knew I was going to hear my grandmother again, and this time I was full of joy. I was not so needy.

> We really had a time that fall. We had nothing but trouble and storm. It was a hard time for lumbermen and farmers right after the war—prices were way down for what we could sell and way up for what we needed to buy. I cooked for the men, and I'd have anywhere from four to six to eight of them every night. I baked about six or eight loaves of bread and a pan of biscuits about every other day.
>
> Then I discovered I was pregnant again, and Deborah was just nine months old. We lived in a little tar-papered shack. It was entirely covered with tar paper. We had screen doors and screen on the windows, but where the stovepipe went through the ceiling, there was about an inch cut around it. Nobody had triple walls in those days. The flies would come in there so thick. When we would spray and put stuff out to kill them, they would fall on the floor, and Deborah would crawl along behind and pick

them up. Oh, I had the worst time with her, and I was sick from being pregnant, and all those men to cook for.

We had to haul water in from the tank, and where they had to go to get the water to fill the tank was just a little shallow, warm ditch, and the cows would stand in it. They had to drive the cows out of the ditch in order to fill the tank. That was our drinking water. We tried to be careful. We boiled most all of it. We used hardly any water unless we boiled it. I think I boiled everything we gave to Deborah, and I did for myself more or less. But the men out in the field would get so thirsty they'd take a drink out of the ditch, and that water would taste just like cow manure.

We had one breakdown after another that fall. All our farm equipment was old and it just give out. I had my first experience making chokecherry jelly then. The men couldn't work all one day because of a breakdown, so they went out and picked chokecherries and brought them back and I fixed them. Some of the chokecherries started fermenting because I hadn't done them fast enough. I didn't really know how to do it.

Lilly was born on the tenth of May, right in the home. We were here in Rexburg then. Royce had plumbed all winter with Carlson. My mother was there, and Royce's mother Molly. But they were such boobs. All they could do was sit up on the stair steps and bawl. Royce gave me the anesthetic. I think it was just chloroform. I had quite a hard labor, and they had to put me right out at the last and use instruments.

We went up to the sawmill in June of that year, 1915. I had a real tough time. Deborah was only eighteen months old, and Lilly was tiny and had colic all the time. Half the morning I walked the floor with Lilly, and Deborah would hang onto my skirt, bawling. And the afternoon and night were just the same. I used to have to put Lilly in the buggy and jiggle it with one foot and rock Deborah with the other.

We had some real bad accidents through that summer. First we lost our best team of horses, Buck and Spider. The team was skidding out the logs, the felled logs, and getting them out of the way. When the accident happened, they were tied back from where the men were working. Suddenly a wind come up, just as they were felling a tree. The wind whipped that tree around, and it hit across the backs of those horses. It drove one of them's legs right into the ground, its hind legs. The horses just stood there and moaned and the men had to shoot them. The word "accident" got back to camp before any of the guys were there to ask about it.

Yes, we saw a peck of accidents in our sawmilling years. You can't imagine how that word accident went through us. It was like the word cancer is today. We were miles and miles—always over fifty miles—from a doctor up there. When someone said there's been an accident, we went all loose inside. Those were the accidents that run through our lives, and almost none of them could even happen today.

We went back up to the dry farm in the fall. When we came down after we finally got the crop up, Royce started feeling sick. We didn't know what was wrong with him. He was just sick and miserable, and he acted miserable along with it. He wouldn't let us do a damn thing for him. It just went on and on, and he felt so terrible. I wasn't like I am now, I wouldn't stand up to him for anything. Anyway, when I saw how sick he was, I did. I said, "You're going to bed and you are going right now, and I'm calling the doctor." He said, no, he'd be okay. "That's all right," I said, "you go to bed. I'm going to call the doctor."

I think that was the first time I said what I really wanted to. I called the doctor and the doctor came in. He walked up to the foot of the bed and he said, "You've got typhoid, I can smell it." That was the contaminated water we drank. You know typhoid takes a long time to develop.

After that I learned to stand up for myself a little more. Royce's father used to say, "A woman's place is in the bedroom." I didn't see it quite that way—that's where I think women's rights come in a little bit.

I'll tell you one time I stood up for myself. We had an outhouse that was just loaded—it was just full to the brim.

We nagged and we begged the men. Every night we'd tell the men move it, move it, move it. So finally I said to Sarah—that was Boon's wife—let's burn it. And she said okay. We took some coal oil and put it around some papers and lit it afire. It went up in flames and the men came runnin' and when they got right up to where they were staring, I said, "Never mind movin' it."

Phaedrus could play all the strings on the violin. She could especially play the one-liner note. Never mind movin' it fell in with our favorites. Even Phaedrus got tired of us tossing that off, the less appropriate the better.

We went down the line at the end of the fall, and that winter we didn't have enough money to live on. When Royce got over his typhoid, we just didn't have anything to go on, so he tried to find work. He went up and worked in the beets for a while, and oh, it was terribly hard work. His wrists got so swollen that he could hardly lift anything. Then he got cheated out of his money.

Right after that he got a chance to go up and work on the institute for the—oh, the insane asylum—I'll say it right out and then you'll know what I mean. We had forty 'leven things we called it. He went up there to work—I can't remember whether it was before Christmas or after Christmas.

I gave up the apartment we had, and I went home and stayed until after Christmas. Then I went to work in the Rexall drugstore and Mother took care of the kids for me. Royce wasn't going to be through with his work until February, so I got another apartment and got all moved into it. Just before he was to come home, the kids and I went to stay with his mother to be at her place when he got home. She wanted to have us stay for a few days.

While we were there she went over to take care of a little child that was real sick with erysipelas. When she came home the next day, she picked up Lilly and played with her and that very afternoon Lilly took sick with her first convulsion. The doctor said there was nothing we could do for her. Erysipelas is highly infectious. Royce's mother was real careful when she washed and everything, but we just didn't realize. Lilly had a little place on her leg—almost up on her bottom—and that swelled up in great big purple blisters and developed into meningitis.

We called the doctor as soon as she took bad and the ornery thing wouldn't come until morning. He said, "I can't do anything for her until tomorrow." I had him come once when she had a convulsion, and he said it was something she had eaten. And then I called him when I found this spot coming on her leg. I knew what erysipelas looked like, and so did Royce's mother. I told him I thought she had erysipelas. But he didn't come until morning. Then he gave me some salve for it, but it was a very, very severe type of infection. Another doctor said that almost all infants who get it die. You don't see it much anymore.

Royce's mother said she was scared to death when Lilly had the first convulsion. I was nursing her and she would hardly eat. She was in such pain and out of her head with fever, although she didn't really push up a very high fever. If she had done, she would have been better off because she might would have burned the poison out. When I'd try to nurse her, she'd just grab hold with her teeth and bite and just shake her head.

We hurried up and sent word to Royce because the doctor told us there wasn't much hope. I never said anything to his mother. I don't think she really realized that she was the one brought the germ home. I wouldn't have made her feel bad.

Royce had to come down from Orofino, clear up in northern Idaho. We sent someone to Idaho Falls to meet him and bring him straight home. He got in sometime after midnight, and he came over to her crib and took her up in his arms and put his face down against her little white dress and the sobs just shook him. He had delivered her too, and he was crazy about her. While he was holding her, her little dress slipped up and I noticed she had a dark streak right down her spine. I came over to the two of them and lifted that little white dress up, and she had that streak clear to the base of her spine.

Oh Phaedrus, Phaedrus and Royce—young and up in the mountains with no telephone. I don't know if you had cars then, but if you did, you had that rough trip across the flat—you had to corduroy the road, and you didn't have a handful of spare change, and you were losing your second born. I wish I could reach into those pages with modern medicine and modern transportation—a lifeline flight out, antibiotics. And I ponder the juxtapositions—the price of being where the serenity and the solitude are rarely broken.

> Royce didn't put her down until she died along about five o'clock that morning. Just before she died, she took one convulsion after another. I was holding her the first time she had one. She just stiffened right out and her eyes were set, absolutely set. She stared up in the corner of the room, just still as a board. It was terrible. I don't think I could have stood it without Royce there.
>
> You asked me once if I still thought of Lilly. "Every February," I said. I thought of her every day for maybe twenty years. You were so tender-hearted, you could hardly stand to hear me tell about Lilly.
>
> Lilly and Deborah had been real close, and I thought

Deborah was going to die of grief for a while. They had played together all the time. Lilly was only nine-and-a-half months old when she died. She would creep and Deborah would walk when they played. Deborah would dress her up in everything she could find. She even painted all over her head with lipstick once. Lilly would crawl right along behind Deborah with all those clothes Deborah would drape on her. She would creep right behind her. I have one little picture of her, but you can't see what she looks like.

For months after Lilly died, every time Deborah would see anybody with a little baby, she would go up to them and look at the baby and say, "We had a Lilly once." That's all she'd say, "We had a Lilly once." She was just past two years old. She wasn't very old.

When we went to the mill that summer, I was like Deborah—I missed Lilly too. I'd go over to Royce's mother and sit for a minute, and then I'd get up and find myself halfway home to see if the baby was awake before I'd realize there was no baby to feed. All that year George Gershwin's "Rhapsody in Blue" was on the radio, and it always set me to thinking about her.

We buried Lilly the first or second of March, I can't remember the date without looking it up. I do remember it was the most bitter cold day I have ever seen in my life. We had the funeral services at home. She looked so pretty,

> like a little angel. The most beautiful flowers had been sent to us. We had to go out to the cemetery in a sleigh, in a bobsleigh. It was not too far out of town, just out to the west a few miles. But even before we got from the house to the bobsleigh with the flowers, they were frozen rigid. The petals of the carnations and roses were just sheets of ice, they'd just break off in your hand if you touched them. They were absolutely stiff. We had to take that little thing out there in that terrifically cold blizzardy weather and put her away.

My grandmother's tragedies weren't of her own making. Even in the account of the death of her second child, her attention is on the child, the weather, the day, the flowers. It's not on her.

Phaedrus. Nothing diminishes her, not loss nor suffering. She is enough to stand up to time itself. And she is the key for me.

"Take her mantle and step beyond your burdens," I hear, and I know they are my words.

I thought I would lose Kent in the Teton Dam flood, like Phaedrus lost her Lilly, like we later lost Daddy. I thought it would be another accident that wouldn't figure. That flood, with its pounding water and its debris and its destruction and then its mold and rot, was the biggest accident to ever hit our part of Idaho. Expectation. I didn't expect the Teton flood to end the way it did. David had said to me the day before, "Can't you remember how good it is and get along on that?" So it wasn't like there weren't cracks. And then one appeared in the Teton Dam above Rexburg. I was at the cabin for the ritual spring opening. It was 1976; there's no way to forget that. David and I were to meet that evening in Reno, each of us flying different degrees of west. I'd hoped to see Kent in Rexburg on the way down and to drop Thalo off in Salt Lake City before catching a flight the next morning. I turned on the radio as I was leaving the cabin, and there was the news. Engineers were up there on the flat brown expanse of that dam watching sand drop through a hole in it, like you'd turned an hourglass upside down. They were on graders riding back and forth looking for cracks, watching that hole get bigger and bigger.

I knew that territory. I knew that if the dam broke, the little farming town of Sugar City would be the first to go. Rexburg and Idaho Falls would flood. The announcer was suddenly serious. "We'll need homes in Blackfoot and Pocatello—prepare for victims, friends." Down the line took on a new meaning.

That's when my heart stopped. I knew Kent's shelter home had a fishing trip planned for some time in the day. I grabbed my keys and bag and called my dog. That's all I took that day. When I got to Pond's Lodge, I went in and called David. I couldn't get him, and I left a message I shouldn't have left and got back on Highway 20.

"Be okay, Kent," I said as I drove. When you hear real fear in your own voice, you pay very close attention to what you're doing. I thought about my grandmother. What an ability she had to simply do what had to be done. I was doing it too, I noticed.

Pines dropped away behind me. I talked to myself for the next hour, the sound of my voice was the fuel I was going on. "Think of the course of that water," I said, and I saw in my mind the stretch of farmland from Ashton to Rexburg. "It's going to wash Sugar City out. They'll stop traffic at Ashton," and I made a U-turn and headed north again and then west to Dubois. "Come in behind," I said aloud. "Get below everything before you enter Rexburg." I watched the sides of the road where the pines rose up. "A deer could step out of there in a second and meet your bumper and then your windshield before you identified him, let alone swerved." I was giving myself advice, hope.

I found the Rexburg radio station I'd been listening to at the cabin. It was a Saturday morning, and all the farm reports were being interrupted with accounts of the flooding. "Give me specifics," I said, and I realized I was anticipating ahead of the newscaster, and I was running out of time. I looked at the speedometer. I was going eighty on the worst highway in Idaho, the graveled western spur to Kilgore and Dubois. Old 191, old 20 South that I'd abandoned, ran right through the path of the water, and I knew I'd played a good hunch. Eventually the announcer got to it. "Nothing is allowed in from Ashton."

The radio station went back to playing Western music. "Next up is 'Help Me Make It Through the Night,'" the announcer said. "I cannot believe this," I said to myself. And when he came back on, he said, "It looks like Rexburg is going to get its feet a bit wet."

"I'd get your feet wet right now if I could," I said to this witless stranger—my only company through what I understood could put my brother in danger. I thought about what the announcer would be operating on and realized he wasn't getting his data fast enough, and he wasn't someone who could make any kind of a forecast ahead of the facts. Maybe he didn't dare. I looked at the speedometer—eighty-nine miles an hour.

The traffic slowed when I got off the highway and came into town by the cemetery. "Too many people thought of this entrance," I said, still talking aloud. I pulled off the road and walked to my grandparents' headstones. I couldn't say why I did that. When I got to those big gray stones with pine trees etched into them, I looked up to see if the sky had clouded. It was bright blue and the air was very still. It all might have been a painting—the green cemetery with its bouquets of flowers scattered about, the motionless trees, the river, looking as motionless beyond. The trees were bigger and floppier and looser-looking than the trees at the cabin, even though they were so still. I studied it all, knowing it was going to be submerged.

Then a breeze came up, but not enough to make me feel as cold as I suddenly felt. My hair was blowing, and I shivered. I went back to the car to get a jacket. "You hated wind, even as a child," I remembered Phaedrus telling me. "You went inside at the slightest whiff of wind, but you could play forever in the cold." I looked toward the line of cars stalled now, and zipped up my jacket and began jogging toward town.

The Tetons rose straight up from the valley floor like a cutout of a mountain, an alpine mountain, something from Italy or Canada. I'd never noticed how flat it was under those peaks. It wasn't just the shift from that stark vertical ascent. The farmland was as flat as a platter below those three Grand Tetons, with almost no transition through foothills. I glanced to the east, and my throat closed. I felt the gooseflesh come up, and I felt like I'd been iced. My mind slammed up against something. I talked to quiet myself. "It's a wall of water; keep perfectly calm, and find Kent." I began to run.

Thalo was whimpering beside me. "You jumped out!" I said to her, muttering "Good girl, good good Thalo, how to deserve you." She was a young dog then. I broke my stride and reached down to her. She was reluctantly staying with me. "We've got to go this direction, Thalo," I said to her. "Keep by me."

I looked back up toward Driggs at the foot of the Tetons. The dam was right up in there somewhere. The wall of water was in full view now. It was as tall as a man and thirty feet wide, moving over the whole valley in front of me. I guessed it was moving at twenty miles an hour or so, taking everything with it. It looked as though someone had spilled millions upon millions of gallons of muddy dishwater. Its color was as threatening as its mass, opaque and dark, nothing in it blue or calm or reflective. Water, I knew as a painter, should reflect the color of the sky. It's partly the angle. You've never seen water from a horizontal slice—you're seeing the front of the wave.

The first wave wasn't very high, but its depth rose quickly behind it, following as though pulled along by the little gray-brown, turned-back flap. As it moved, it swept houses, cattle, telephone poles before it. It happened so fast, it created the illusion that everything was popping out in front of the water. I felt my body jerk. I stood gaping until a trailer house to the left of the mass was snapped off its moorings. For a moment I had thought it was going to be spared, then the edge of the water caught it. As far away as I was, I could hear the wood shriek as it ripped apart. The trailer whirled like a toy. I could smell the water now, dark and heavy and unfamiliar, and I was trembling. "Kent," I cried out, and I heard the plaintive wail.

"Never, never expected to see anything like this," I said. My voice was heaving now with the effort to run, and to articulate something I couldn't grasp. "Stay right with me, Thalo. This isn't the evening news." I thought of David, and I talked to him. "What do you have to do?" I said to him, and the despair in my voice told me more than the flood waters had how serious the converging forces were.

In order to get out of the cemetery and away from that wall of water, I made my way back to the Scout. I got in and got Thalo up beside me and turned it around so that I was headed straight toward the water. It was one of the boldest things I ever did, and it confirmed for me that I *was* my grandmother's daughter. But it was my father's savvy that stood me in good stead through the next hours. He knew how to estimate, figure, and act and I'd been around him doing it a lot of my years.

The water rose in front of me like the side of a barn. "Dear God!" I said, "it's eight feet high." I noticed very few people were taking the back route. The water had all been off in the distance a moment ago, and I found myself thinking about physics and time. But I had just enough to get to the highway and get somewhere high or south before the water cut across the road.

Kent would be by the college, and that's high ground. If he hadn't left for his fishing trip. But once I turned out of the path of the water, I was back in traffic, frantic traffic, and I was stalled again. I was almost alongside a farmer in an old rig. He rolled down his window and hollered through his puckered mouth,

"Waited till I seen the waters to git." I was just turning off Main Street to head up the road that led past the hospital and behind Ricks College. I was very near Brown's Café—good ice cream, and I see my father taking his twins in there, a hand in each of his. There we are, the three of us—another time, another place. He is looking out for us. I'm at the movies, one vignette after another.

I could hear the water behind me now. My last choices had been bad, and I had run out of luck. Then one tire pulled strangely to the left as I was calculating how to get up to the campus, and I felt the whole outfit pull down. I wished at that moment that my father was there with me. I tried to think the way he'd think, and it helped me see that actually just the opposite had happened to my truck. It had been tossed up in a spout of water. I knew I had to get out of the truck and hold onto something, maybe work my way over to the Porter Printing Company on the corner and get upstairs. I rolled up the window and stepped out as the full force of the water overtook the truck. "Clumsy Scout," I mumbled as it swirled like a bug in the cluttered water. I was thrown ahead of it—virtually tossed out of the pounding ferocity for a few seconds. It was long enough for me to get my feet on something solid and grab for a tree.

I was alert and working, and I had gained another four feet by the time the water had moved up the street. I looked down at a giant milkshake churning and twisting below me. Logs, some of them as big as telephone poles, slapped at my tree, nearly shaking me out. My legs snapped back and forth like the limbs above me. I scrambled higher. A streetlight ahead of me dropped. From every direction came the cracking and ripping of destruction. Only the air, I guessed it was the air, kept that unearthly stillness, and it made what was going on separate, as though the sky and the earth no longer bore a relation.

I heard water rushing into the printing building behind me, and at the same moment there was a deafening crash. The tree I was in trembled as water shot out the second-story window of the building, spraying me. I wondered if we had an earthquake on our hands as well as a flood.

Below me an old man churned by. I could see he was drunk from the blurred face that rolled up twice. I scampered as far down the tree as I could and clutched at his worn coat, and then I saw that it was the farmer I'd stalled behind before my truck was caught up in the water.

"Woom!" he roared. "What the H E double L." I had a hard time hanging on to him. The water pulled at him like an enormous Maytag, and he spun away from me. He was entirely unconcerned at the rinsing he was getting.

He suddenly reversed direction and came back toward me. I managed to get hold of him again, and I turned him around and kept a firm grip on his belt. I started up the tree again but couldn't gain an inch with him squiggling off my right hand. "Fella," I said to him, "my name is Rennie. Rennie England. Glad to have some company. We're in a flood. Let's help each other. Can you give me a nudge up this tree? Get your knees around it and..."

"Nudgle yourself up the tree," the man said. "Yer young. I can't be fishin' out the young women."

"Just get your knees around the tree and give me a shove with your hands," I said. "Then I'll give you a hand."

The man was half singing when a wave snatched him out of my grip. I looked down at the gray, thoroughly soaked coat I was holding. I must have let go of his belt and grabbed for his coat. It had slid off him like a banana peel. I looked around frantically. Then I heard the rest of the tune and looked to where it came from. The old fellow was ten feet away, bobbing unabashed in the water.

I dropped his limp coat and jumped for him, but it took me what seemed like half an hour to maneuver through the foaming water and the gathering debris. I watched as the old man's head went under. Just then a cow floated by. I thought it was alive until I saw its eyes fixed in a stare.

My father had told me about floods, told me about getting to high ground, about being wary of narrow canyon gorges and heavy rain, about thinking of all the routes out—not just one. And about taking care of the animals. He'd talked to me a lot more about floods than about fires. Looking back, I see him training his twins. He'd always wanted us to go to college. He was telling Kent and me before we were walking to get all the education we could. He stood and applauded when I walked across the stage to receive my first degree. We'd taken his ball cap and his slippers off him just as we were going out the door in time to be slightly late for my graduation.

"He'll humiliate us," my mother had said. I hadn't wanted to think the word. "He's got new shoes he won't wear. He won't wear his new shirt you got him. 'It's too good to wear,' he told me." I see him rise alone when I begin my walk across that lengthening stage, see him stand and clap. A single stander. The only one clapping. So he was proud. I felt a great emotion, but I didn't know what it was. I do now. No other father.

Is the price of experience that its endowments carry a sense of expectation—not from others but from within?

"Keep your mind on high ground." My voice was reassuring. I felt able and canny now. When I finally did reach the old farmer, he seemed glad enough to have a friend back. "The water is already polluted. We've got to get up out of it," I said, and I remembered the talk of snakes on the radio. The force of the water was tremendous out away from the buildings, although it wasn't more than six feet deep. I half swam, half dragged the old man over to an entrance and pulled him a few steps into what seemed like a shelter. I heard a sudden slamming and stepped out a little to see a house plant itself squarely in the middle of the street we'd just been struggling in.

Distrustful of the shelter I had found, I jerked the drunk and headed wildly for the house that had landed in the street. "Don't be floating in this, Kent," I said, and I noticed the fear in my voice had subsided.

I spent the next couple of hours sitting astride the top of a yellow farmhouse in the middle of a business street in the town I was born in, my drunk friend chatting beside me. I wasn't sure how long it was before Thalo paddled up to the house. Those were my only tears, and I blinked hard and scampered down the shingled slant of the roof and reached from its edge into the water to pull Thalo up. "Dear God, I forgot you, Thalo," I said, and I had a hard time not crying.

The old man was holding forth on matters of great import and small—from keeping warm to not noticing. "Never get cold," he told me.

"Sure wish I had a warm coat," I said. "Any idea what keeps you warm?"

"Wish to high heaven and deep hell I had some of what keeps me warm. Light o' my life."

"Where's your place?" I asked him.

He fixed his glazed eyes on me, cricked his mouth to the right, licked his lips as quickly as a cat, and said, "All over this valley, don't you reckon?"

"Going to start again?"

"Gonna give it H E double L," and he snuffled deeply.

"Ever been in anything like this?"

"Saw action in the War. Saw a lot of chaos and blood. Different color than this. Same feeling. Saw my best friend's head roll down the hill. Couldn't decide whether to cover his torso or go for his head. Decisions of wartime." He turned and studied me.

"Hey, you eat shrimp at Chiz's, don't you? I've had a chat with you there! The waterline girl. And look at us watered now!"

"How's this water staying together with this much land to spread out over? Did the dam burst?"

"Did the dam burst? Remember sweet yesterday? Did the trout swim? Did the goat eat grass? Did the dam burst! Try it from Hog Holler."

I laughed. "Do you mind if I call you Alfred P.? Are you Welsh? Listen, Alfred, I've got to go find my brother. Stay right here."

"Call me anything at all, but don't make it Alfred."

"Stay right here. I'll be back with my brother and some lunch, if I can find some. Where's Hog Hollow?"

"All over this valley, Daughter, that's where the Holler is. All over the plain. It's gone, 'n its residents is gone, 'n its rodents is gone. Its topsoil is gone. I wouldn't be surprised if its bedrock is gone. And what took 'em? Not this puny little splasher we're sittin' in. No, me. This is a by-Jesus sweet bathtub. A worthy wash took Hog Holler. First thing it did take. Took 'er slicker 'n a brook trout."

"Stay. Wait for me. I'll be back. Wait here. It's safe. I'll get you coffee."

"For coffee I'll wait, no offense to you. But you can't swim with coffee. You've got to let 'er subside."

"I guess that's right," I said.

"Your brother look just like you?"

"Yes, he does. Everyone says we still…"

"I think I know him. Quiet. Comes in to get coffee where I'm sippin,' comes in regular."

"We're twins. He's tall. He's damn good looking."

"Never thought of a fella looking like a girl."

"He doesn't look like a girl."

"Woah, woah, what I mean is resemblance. You resemble. "

"He needs me right now. Can you take me to him? I haven't been to his new place. Is he okay? Does he seem…is he…"

"Yeah, he's okay. He's slow. Everyone's nice to him. He's pretty quiet most the time. I'll help ya find 'im. Ya saved me out of the mud soup."

"Tell me how it happened. You were right up under it, weren't you? That's the Hollow?"

"Was the Hollow. Yes, Jesus, yes. I was sleepin' in a spud cellar on the farmland above it when I hear a couple of cannons roar. Then explosions follow. My Gawd, I'm back in the Bulge, and I jumps straight to attention. I reached for my rifle and found a filthy reminder of my night's spree. Needn't go into that." His mouth made its little crick to the right.

"So I poked myself up and wandered out into the most hellish sight I ever seen. Here comes a three-hundred-foot wall of water, comin' at me on hell's hinges. Picked up the Wilford place and it fair flew apart. Pring! Like that," he said, making his fingers fly out. "And every time it snacked down a little more brick, here comes another explosion. I'm standin' there dribblin' down my own legs and mumbling God bless me for once, I'm on high ground, 'n God forgive me for I'm a changed man."

All the time the old man talked, he picked at a thread in his work pants. It was an interesting gesture to me—playful, not nervous—as though he had just dived into the weave of his pants with two fingers, in the way he might have done for a grasshopper in tall grass. And every few minutes he would lick his lips in that cat-like motion.

"Givin' thanks for my own fortune, I was almost too late to see Mr. and Mrs. Caw's truck moving up one of the canyon roads, tryin' for all it was worth to gain a little more ground, just another ten feet. Where is it now? Out in the sand dunes, no doubt. And who was that in it? And who sitting beside him?" He shook himself a little and rubbed his knees and continued.

"'This ain't polite,' I pronounced, strugglin' to revive my vigorously spare sense of humor. This called for more than change, ya see. This called for something a man must be careful not to trifle with—this involved repentance. The terror of perspective had come to me. I was a six-foot man, or used to be, and I was starin' at water more than half a mile high.

"You know the word eerie, Daughter? Haven't used a word like that since my weddin' night. This was eerie. Ever heard of brown caps? Ever heard a telephone pole scream? Not snap like we're hearin' here in this little bathtub. ZEEEEEEEEEE. Like that—high, fast.

"I saw a family in a rubber raft just ahead of the wave. Saw them look back, see this nightmare, and flail like flippin' virgins. Hopped straight up the canyon wall like seven flailing virgins indeed."

"Your account is pretty damn good," I said, laughing.

"I saw old man Reynolds right after that—ran to his barn longin' for human company. His house is down in the Holler. Or was. He was there at his barn with his wife. It's up on the bluff, up high.

"'My wife wanted to save some things,' he told me, just a shakin' and shakin' his head, tryin' to hide his shakin' all over. 'We got our lives, and that's all we got,' he told her.

"That's how it looked from above the Holler, Girl. Allemand South and a wave's a'crashin'. Allemand North and the water's creepin'. Allemand West and a cow's a'bloatin.'"

David, I said to myself, I won't be with you tonight. Hear me. Wait for me. And I'll tell you. And I said to the old man, "You've got to tell my brother about it when we find him."

"Much obliged to do that." He tipped an imaginary hat.

I could see myself giving Maraya an account of this quick fellow. "No respek," she'd say. "He's as good as a fureigner, and he'll get no respek."

"How's that?" I asked the old man, who was still talking.

"I says nature has no respect," he said. I stared at him.

"None whatsoever," I said. "Shouldn't surprise us."

"Where ya from?" he asked, turning toward me and studying me with those small, intent, if slightly blurred, brown eyes. "Ya don't sound like from here, and yet ya do."

"I am from here, but I don't get here much now. My cabin used to be part of the Douglas Sawmill, and now it sits alone, not far from the old mill pond."

"Ya don't say! I knew 'em all—Royce, Clyde, Boon, Darrell. Which one was yours?"

"Royce!" I said it as though he had just arrived. "Royce! He's my grandfather."

"He was your grandfather?" He emphasized the grandfather just the way I had. "I see where he died a few years back. Manly man. Everybody up here liked that man. And his wife too—she could dance."

"She loved to dance. She got up and waltzed me around her living room once and said, 'See why I was considered the best dancer in Idaho,' and I did see why."

"I wouldn't split anybody from that view. Had some meals out in that Douglas meadow."

"The big spreads? The Harrimans, the Krupps? Once in a while a Guggenheim?"

"And the Ponds and Doc Mack. Man!"

"Do you remember a set of twins, a boy and a girl?"

"That would be your brother. Rippin' and tearin'. Pair 'a scamps? Fallin' off stilts?"

I had to mop up the tears. "I've got to find my brother," I said. "You're not making this up? You remember those days?"

"Best of it—right up there—huckleberry pies. Hospitality. Laughter. Here's what you gonna do. You gonna find your brother in one hour, when this water recedes. And you'll be back in that little cabin a ' yours. Fireplace. Old kitchen stove. I got all my lumber from up there. Went after it myself."

He made that quick little crick of the mouth. "You keep yer mind on yer brother, kid. And I'll keep telling ya what happened up there, and the time'll pass. I went with Reynolds, up around the end of the dam. My Gawd, they had cats and dozers out on that mound of controversy ten minutes before she tore. Hole twenty-five feet in diameter at her north base had the engineers puzzled—bunch 'a schoolboys. She didn't leak from it, but sand kept spinnin' into it from above, like one of them sand timers."

"You saw it right before it went?"

"Saw it. Suddenly a huge piece of her north side fell in—she came boiling out of that hole and ripped all the way up then. Came out like the Pacific Ocean out a rodeo shoot. Every time a piece of the dam fell in, she exploded. Reynolds saw it comin' from over the top 'a his two-story barn.

"June fifth, Kiddo. Nineteen hundred and seventy-six, year of our Lord. Today's a black day for Idaho. And blacker for the U.S. of A. Today's the day water was goin' to come off her spillway. Sweet Jeezus, it makes me tight as a goat on the bottle. And a birthday comin'."

I couldn't help laughing.

"Yes, Rexburg got it today," he continued, "but not like the Holler. Rexburg, who hasn't let her hair down since Prohibition."

"How long they been having trouble up there?"

"If they'd known trouble when they saw it. With this goes the pieces to the puzzle, ya know. This here is the result of a lot of fightin' and resistin' and belly-achin' and gettin' ignored. I said it would never hold water. Gawd, I wish't I'd never said it. The environmentalists said it would never hold fish. The experts said it would never fill, not in less than three years, anyway. This is two of 'em, and Gawd only knows where we'd be if it had been full. Full of fish and experts ourselves."

I swung both legs over to the same side of the house and pulled my knees up under me, turning so I could see my friend better. "How did you manage to get down into Rexburg from Hog Hollow?" I started to ask him, but I wasn't in time.

"They say not a drop ever went over that spillway. Everyone said the dam was just sucking it up. It had two deep cracks two years ago and they poured a little cement into them and said, she's new—every dam has a few leaks. Hellamighty, I thought so myself. Used to fish up in Box Canyon. Dam up there in Island Park spoutin' from everywhere."

The old fellow leveled his eyes at me. He didn't say anything at first. Then he reached over and patted my leg. "Best not to take bad luck too hard," he said. "Douglas Sawmill," and he licked his lips. "If you can figure out how not to."

The two of us and Thalo sat it out until dusk, when the water began to recede, then we half-walked, half-waded to Ricks College. That's where information would be. "Are calls getting out?" I asked the volunteer positioned at the door of the Student Center.

"Some are, most aren't. People are having the best luck with the payphone over by the David O. McKay Library—right over there, just north."

I said goodbye to my friend in front of the Center and walked over to the payphone and got in the line. I thought how I could get a message to David without making a direct call but that's what I did when I was in that phone booth. I sat there counting the rings and hung up after four.

"Think of folk wisdom," I murmured and I thought of the crazy advice Maraya would give me when things fell apart. *Be cahm and take the ginger tea*, something like that. Her blend of superstition and street smarts and her sardonic take on life were like a reset button.

I stayed in the phone booth. I could see how annoyed people were with me. Almost outraged. Instead of trying to find her number—finding her mother in Nicaragua and asking for it again—I sat there imagining our conversation:

I need the native ways, I say to her. *Anchor me.*

Miss Rennie? You okay, kid? You sound rough.

I'm in a flood. I'm in Rexburg. In Idaho. I can't...and I knew my voice would be warbling around.

My God, Miss Rennie. I knew that's what she'd say. I kept inventing the conversation. It was better than having it—it occupied my mind in just the right way.

You do sound rough, kid. What's happening?

I've got to find my brother.

Oh Miss Rennie, that's bad. I hate to hear that.

The water just broke through...he was supposed to be up there fishing...

Dear God, Miss Rennie! That the dā-em they talking about on the radio? Teetin or something?

Dā-em, yeah—it would be Teetin Dā-em to you. You crazy fureinger. It's about time for your famous We get no respek. I was laughing now and hearing her say *Do this, Miss Rennie. Get some hot water some way. Grate your ginger in it, and boil it for twenty or thirty minutes if you can. If you can't, just let it steep, you know what I mean. Drink the water, all of it, just the water. That will cahm you, Miss Rennie, and keep you from getting down—you know, with anything, a cold. There is the damp.*

Ginger? I say aloud.

You know, kid, I'm always telling you keep fresh ginger nearby.

I'm making myself laugh. *I'm in a flood*, I imagine telling her. I actually say it aloud, and I tell her she's nuts—just what I need. *Everything is contaminated. I'd have to get this stuff from the Red Cross.*

They should have it, Miss Rennie.

They should, I think to myself. My grandmother would say they should really.

And I listen for Maraya. *They should. And if not ginger, garlic. Then this is what you're going to do. Stay cahm.*

Cahm, I say out loud, like her, like cat.

Whether it's ginger or something else, this is the way you'll take it and this is the way you'll feel. Some people feel very well, some people do not feel very well. It's not there and now it is, you know what I mean.

I'm really laughing now. I've got straight access to her.

I know, Miss Rennie. But now the thing is this, my advice to you I would say is go and look at the shelter.

The shelter, I say, long ē in the.

Where there's a problem, everyone lookin' for the shelter. Whether it's here or Nicaragua, anywhere—everyone will be wandering from shelter to shelter. If at the first one you do not find him, go to the second, and on and on. You will find him. That's what I'd do if it hit my place, and that's what I'd do if it hit yours. Lookin' for you and the pets, them, from shelter to shelter.

The pets, them. Looking. My brother, him. *You've learned more than learning, Maraya,* I say.

Oh, Lord. I imagine the Lord going way low.

Pigs are floating by. They're already swollen. You can't tell them from cows.

Oh my. Oh dear. All these snakes can drown or die for all I care. But the pigs. And the horses?

I've got a feller for you to meet. Like to sit around and listen to you two talk.

Oh Lord, the voice dropping. *You can keep your man. I don't want another one. Now get your ginger tea, and then you'll go right to your brother. He's close.*

See me finding him, I say to Maraya, the universe.

The town had begun to smell like the slop we used to keep for the pigs at the mill. "Take this to the slop, Rennie," my grandmother would say. She knew everything that could go in it and everything that couldn't and it always came out smelling the same, whatever combinations went into that barrel.

I tried to call David again, the third time that day I'd done something I never did. He didn't answer, and I didn't leave a message. It will always be like this, I realized. And eventually that will be worse than the loneliness between times together. He'll never even know those times are happening, however urgent. And it will be the same for him. We've been lucky—that's just what it has been. And I knew how many fissures I'd been unwilling to see. Now they stood before me. You can't see David flawed, can you? And the two of you? But it was there for me to see.

I thought of his boys. I'd met them once. He'd brought them to a museum where I was exhibiting. They were handsome but not certain of themselves. They looked to him even in where to be seated. From his talk I knew they adored him—the able, energetic, fun-loving, always good-natured father from whom they would never get enough and never be free.

It was an ever harder life for him, I saw for the first time. And mine was getting harder too. It was not designed nor planned any longer. We were both whirled in something like what had hit Rexburg this afternoon.

That was the first time I saw the configuration that could overwhelm us.

My father was still alive when the Teton Dam flooded. He wasn't well enough to come look for his son, and my mother wouldn't be coming—she didn't leave my father alone by then. I was still sitting in that phone booth and someone rapped on the door and signaled for me to get out. I picked up the phone, fed it a dime, and called my parents. It was much harder to get a call through in the area, but finally my father answered and I said, "I'm looking for Kent, I'll find him, I'll call you. He'll be all right."

"Take care of yourself, Rennie," my father said to me.

I'd made myself sound in control on the phone, but I was frantic. The day Kent had fallen into the mill pond, he hadn't even struggled to come to the surface. He'd stepped off the gangplank that led up into the mill and sunk like a stone. I had leaped off that gangplank the same moment and brought him up by the back of his collar before he could inhale. "I drowned, Rennie," he said. I didn't even know he knew the word.

"You're no fish, kid, " I said to him, standing there shivering beside the mill pond, holding him, muffling him.

"No fish!" He laughed. He was shivering too, and laughing, almost hysterical. We dripped down the path together, joking, but I was shaking inside. He didn't know what was danger out there anymore, and he didn't fight for life.

I hurried back to the Ricks campus, which was an outpost by now. I couldn't think what to do except to walk the town and check back in. My winsome drunk was coming out of the main entrance to the Student Center as I walked up. He was considerably steadier. "You," he said. "You saved my life, may the Lord forgive you. You with the R."

"Rennie." And we shook hands. You shook hands in this part of the West, no matter what was happening.

"Your brother's in there hoppin' all over the place. I told him you'd be comin'. I was settin' out to look for you myself. He's got a chair and he keeps picking it up and carrying it closer to the door he's watchin' for you to come to. He loves you something. Facing that door. He's about right out in the middle of the room now. Wouldn't come to eat, so I brought him a tray. Where's yer dog?"

"Kent is in there? Wait for me here." I looked around for Thalo, and I flew into that room and Kent saw me and he flew for me. "Kent!" I finally cried.

He had his face buried against my hair. "How ya doin'?" he said, without stepping away from me or looking up. So he'd been afraid; I could feel him trembling. We both trembled.

"I watched for you, Rennie," he said.

"I searched for you, Kent. Are you hungry?" I stepped back to look at him. "Did you get wet? Did someone find dry clothes for you?"

By then the drunk had come back in. "Please my heart and lift my soul," he was saying. "Those two are from a loving family."

"No," Kent said. We all laughed. "Damn dirty dogs."

I took note. He remembered the worst of it in the worst of times. Mother had always said that. I'm nothing but a damn dirty dog.

"Listen, Dirty Dog, we were pretty bad."

"Pretty bad," he repeated.

"Sneakin' into the commissary when we weren't supposed to."

"Sneakin' in," he said and chuckled.

"Tryin' to walk on water at the mill pond."

"Tryin'. Drowning. Oh, Rennie!"

"Throwin' dirt on Old Lady Hansen's clean clothes."

"Dirt bombs."

"Foolin' around rolling our city friends into the mill pond."

"Walkin' logs."

"That's right, Kent. And who was the fastest? Who won every round of our lives?"

"That's me!"

"That's my Kent. Let's get to Thalo and feed her and walk her and then lay a plan."

"Lay a plan," he said.

"Lay a fabulous plan." And we held hands and walked down the streets of Rexburg. We must have looked like something out of Oz.

"Better get out of town," Kent said. His sentences were wonderfully animated and expressive.

"Are you worried about your friends?"

"Worried sick."

"Course you are," I said, laughing at the way he'd said it. He had had a funny way with language, an irony, and it was returning. It was a glorious gain. "'Worried sick.' Who says that?"

"My mother. 'I'm worried sick about you.'"

"I was worried sick. What a day to go fishing." I couldn't bring myself, then or ever, to ask him if he'd seen the wall of water that came down that river. Maybe it had slid out of focus, and he never needed to feel again the fear it would have engendered. That's what I think happened. I think he was very close to the dam because we had planned to meet near his old fishing hole. He must have had to scramble, or someone scrambled for him.

At the end of that day, David walked into the Student Center just as we were leaving. I thought I'd lost my mind when I saw him.

"It isn't..."

"It is," he said. "It's me. I'm finally where I should be, and even so, it's late.

I came as quickly as I heard. I knew you'd be here. I knew you'd come down from your cabin. For once I did come."

We moved the two or three steps that separated us, and we put our arms around each other in a still way and stood there in the mud and the sun, engulfed in the inevitability that had led us to so little time together and so much time apart. I had the same feeling I'd had the first night with him. I didn't want life to go on from that moment. I didn't want to draw back from David and the utter home he was to me and walk away in a few hours to something I didn't care about and wasn't good at.

I introduced my brother to David. They shook hands, and I imagined a life in which David came home with me, took me home. I couldn't have guessed how overwhelmed I'd feel seeing the two of them together.

We had dinner together. I listened to them talk to each other. I prayed for it never to end.

"I love you, Rennie," Kent said to me when we took him to his shelter and said goodbye. He said it against the side of my face, and he put his arms around me and said it again.

"Rexburg," David said, looking out the window at the flooded streets as we maneuvered out of town. "We're fugitives in our own way."

"How did you get here?" I asked him. "What do we do? Where do we start?"

"With us, Rennie. There is a lifetime of work to do here, but we're going to start by making a home for ourselves for enough hours that I can..."

"I don't know anything beyond tomorrow. Let me have you." I could hear how slowly I said the words. They were wrung from me, and I put my head in my hands. It was more the prayer of a supplicant than anything. I could hear him saying my name as I drove to the Jolly Roger Hotel. He registered us as Mr. and Mrs.

D. R. Braniff. I watched him write that on the hotel form and I felt our promises and compromises more than I ever had.

Then we were in that room. "You're beyond time and place, Rennie," he said. "Inside and out. You would have put yourself in any danger for your brother."

"I would."

We drew a hot bath and sat in it, my back to his chest, administering to each other, serious and loving. There was something final about that evening, although it wasn't the last time we'd be together. We could always close out the weight of the world when we had time with each other. We became like forest creatures—abandoned, fearless, foolishly playful, and then intent, and then playful again. We delighted in each other, rediscovering the thousand paths we had wandered, now moving luxuriously over an almost forgotten one, now soaring into the dazzling familiar path we inevitably came back to. Hours passed. The light in the room dimmed. And then it was dark.

The way things end. When David left that last morning, we were in Jerusalem, the beautiful spring of 1982. Portentous is one of my least favorite words. I hate to think about that now. I'm surprised I didn't see what was coming, but I didn't.

He said goodbye to me in the rooms we had rented on French Hill and took a cab to the airport. I drove back to Ein Karem with its green-and-white tiled tables and its luxurious flowers enclosing the patio. We'd discovered it by accident, and after that we hadn't eaten anywhere else, and I thought I'd have one more lunch there. It was May and the air felt like it was made of the blossoms of flowers. We could smell them even in the car. Fifteen years and 13,000 miles lay between us and the first table we'd shared at Kelly's in Philadelphia, with its oyster plates lining the walls and its gold coat hooks that looked like music staffs.

Ein Karem was just outside Jerusalem, west, the direction of home. I loved it because wooded hills rose from its narrow streets, and you could look out into the countryside and rest your eyes from the white of Jerusalem. An artist lived nearby and we always took the walkway that led around his house to the studio to see if he was in. He never was, but we kept going along the path that led through flowering bushes and potter's wheels and tables full of bits of old tiles and clay jugs, perhaps because it was at once familiar and foreign. As was Jerusalem.

We sat in the night air and listened to the birds and the call to prayer. The last of the sun glinted off what looked like a church up ahead. The cars nosed by, bells rang, horns honked, but they sounded lighter and less insistent than they did in their restless dialogue on the streets of Jerusalem. Languages mingled with the smells of evening—German and French and Arabic and Hebrew and English with jasmine and geranium and roses and honeysuckle.

We'd stayed in Jaffa the first few days, always eating in a lovely old boat that had been outfitted with wooden tables and tablecloths the color of the Mediterranean we floated on. Shrimp, Israeli salad, babaganoush—the old lighthouse behind us, the sea stretched out ahead. It looked like a silver plate. Then the boat would rock, and you felt the shifting history of an ancient port.

We went from there to Jerusalem and found that beautiful, light apartment on French Hill, its floors marble, its views of the whole of old Jerusalem. It was a ten-minute walk from the Mount of Olives. We walked everywhere that next few days—along the ancient wall, into the old city through Damascus Gate, through the souks to the Temple Mount with its golden-crowned Dome of the Rock, the minarets rising into that clear blue air. Out Jaffa Gate, past the Tower of David. It was Jerusalem, the walled city, seat of hope, mother of faiths, island of contention, everything, and it kept that foreign and familiar feeling.

We'd discovered the little restaurant in Ein Karem when we went out to Hadassah Hospital to see the Chagall stained glass windows. It was a tiny church, standing freely beside the high walls of the hospital, and it was nothing but glass, glass the colors of heaven.

The restaurant was buried in greenery. I could go to my easel and paint it today. Those green-and-white tiled tables drenched in the last of the sun. Flowers brushing the tables, outlining the patio. We almost had to push back the roses.

"Ein Karem," David had said, raising his glass.

"Ein Karem," I answered. "'Caravansary of the Spring of the Vineyard.' All the tables we've eaten at—they're as indispensable to me as children."

We never looked away from each other. Only the most intimate of lovers, I later knew, do that. I had thought my eyes never grew accustomed to him, but what they'd never learned by heart was his absence.

Wild geraniums and lobelia and hollyhocks ran along the stone wall and climbed beside the steps that led up to rooms. "Should we forsake French Hill and stay at the top of those stairs?" he said. The sun was still so bright on them there was hardly a distinction between the vertical and horizontal surfaces. I wondered how that could be. The white stone steps rose up through the flowers in that pattern of light that seemed to lead into sky. Flowering branches hung out over them, laying soft outlines of themselves in the rose white. The air was scented not just with flowers but with cinnamon and saffron and lemon and butter and garlic.

"Your friend will come today?" the waiter said to me when I walked in alone. We always had the same man, young and handsome and enigmatic and gentle. He wore a nametag that said Jamal, but we never addressed him by name, nor he us.

"No, not today," I said. His eyes sent the most subtle condolence, and behind that, his notice of the mysteries of the world. There were hellos and goodbyes and wars and ruins and retrenchment and enslavement in his look.

I ordered a bitter lemon with ice. It's all we'd had to drink all week.

"Pesto as usual?" Jamal asked. "And watermelon?"

I nodded. "And water from the moon."

"From the moon?"

I smiled. "Water."

In the first hours after David left me to return to his work or his home, I didn't want words, as though they might interrupt the level of connection that had been given between the weight of life, this heaviness of earth, and the lightness of soul, the evanescence of arrival. We were anything but lost from here to eternity. We'd found the opposite of the Whiffenpoof Song even though we'd had to meet in obscurity, in secrecy, yes, in complicity. Unaccountably, it was the one right thing I ever knew, as fitted and fitting as strawberry to stem.

I was in that suspended state, sitting out in the sun in Ein Karem, when a guard appeared. "Empty the place," he called out. The faces at the tables around me bore in upon me. "Come with me," someone was saying. There was no margin here. By the time the guard's words had floated down over the pesto, soldiers were everywhere. A dark resolution took even the air.

I felt myself falter. I knew my life and my future were in these strangers' hands. I remember thinking how much red there was in the military greens that surrounded me, how muted the green was. Already I was merely an observer.

Jamal was coming toward me in the gathering chaos. "This way," he said. He led me quickly up those stairs, now growing pale pink in the diminishing light. I watched the pattern of faded terra cotta and gold alternate on the surfaces as we hurried up.

He opened a door into a small room with a double bed and windows looking onto the street. "Stay," he said. "I'll find out what it is. I'll come to tell you." I didn't even thank him.

I knew immediately. I could tell you the instant he fell. "'Good-bye my rowan tree,'" I murmured. "'My rowan tree, my own flesh and blood.'"

Jamal wasn't gone long. "There was an attack at the airport—in Tel Aviv," he said. "Several...your people...I think your...." He led me along the corridor, out into the setting sun, down through the first roses of May, toward a car that would take me back to the city that had fostered the faiths of the world, that had darkened the hopes of the world. Jerusalem, O Jerusalem. Even Christ wept here in this city that was destroyed twenty-five times. "If thou hadst known, even thou, at least in this thy day, the things which belong unto thy peace! But now they are hid from thine eyes."

"Christ," I called out, and the word rose like an ancient wail and I didn't recognize myself.

"What happened to you? Rennie?" Kent said when I went home to him, and he cried the tears I didn't have.

I dreamed I was La Dame de la Licorne. I had the beautiful, the dangerous animal. I touched his horn. "So set apart," I said. I knew the legend. I held the mirror so he could see himself. I saw him see. I was the virgin who could do it. And he was the animal who had the antidote to poison.

Grace was between us.

I went to the cabin after David died. It was in the middle of May and the little yellow dogtooths were in bloom. They grew all through the meadow and right down the road. I got up in the morning, made a fire in the kitchen stove, and then went back to bed. I didn't want to get out of that bed, and then I would think of David in that bed with me, and I'd feel the life in me slow to nothing.

I walked all day long. I walked to McCrea's Bridge, I walked to the west end of the reservoir, I walked up Yale Creek, through great patches of snow. I walked along Hotel Creek, I walked to the mill pond and back again and again and again.

At night I got on my knees and I prayed. "David," I prayed, "send me what you can, whatever you can. Send me news of everlasting life. With things as they should be."

After a few weeks at the cabin, I drove through Montana to Glacier. It was starkly cold there, and I reversed direction and drove to San Francisco. I made my way north again, this time to Alaska. I drove until it was September and the country was in its sweetest month—every day sunny but cool. It all looked indestructible.

I began writing about David then. It stilled me to sit in a café in Missoula or Monterey and listen to the jukebox and put down words and find a thought within them, like dropping sand from a bucket and kneeling to shape it.

I threw most of those pages away. The ones I kept, I put in my grandfather's old green knapsack. I had dated them, and I'd sometimes drawn the logo of the café I was sitting in or the lodge where I was staying at the bottom of the page. Those pages ended up back at this cabin, and I went to the little closet between the two bedrooms, got a chair, and reached up to that top shelf, back behind the photograph albums, and dragged out the old knapsack.

I took it to the kitchen table and laid the pages out. I saw I'd kept the unsparing ones. They were hard to read again, but I did read them, starting with May 24, Kalispell, Montana.

May 24
Kalispell

History has bequeathed us too much. And posterity—did we turn our backs on her, David? Except in our gift of art? Was it enough?

June 5
Moab

I hiked last week in the narrow gorges of Canyonlands, one so like another I could only follow the trail if I watched for the piles of rocks heaped up by the Pueblo tribes before the carved red delta knew car or bus, the air jet or spacecraft. They were friendly, those stacks of rocks placed at points where I might have gone a dangerous way. They were better than a map if I thought I was lost. One day years ago I was there in a flash flood, and I was earnest then for all the world in making my way from one to another.

Everyone on the trail protected those cairns. If you brushed against one and a rock tumbled, you bent and tucked it back with the care of a surgeon, but most of them would stay in those amazingly high, whimsical formations for what appeared to be centuries, pilgrims on the trail, moving reverently past them.

I think sometimes, David, of what we didn't do, didn't have, and I end imagining myself not always a traveler but stopping on some familiar trail to rest there in a not-altogether-haphazard formation—large stones and small wedged into each other, the color of a quail's egg. Marking the trail.

June 22
Summer solstice—is it
San Francisco

We saw it as sin, absolutely, whatever that is. We talked about it. I know we both prayed about it in our ways. But it was not "Help me overcome this." It was "Forgive me, help me protect the others. But this one thing—I don't give this up." Better to have all the rest of my years in repentance, eternity—whatever it takes—than to say no to this fullness of life.

When I read this, I penciled in a Samuel Butler comment that had provided me some refuge from my thoughts. And I added an observation.

"I do not greatly care whether I have been right or wrong on my part, but I care a great deal about knowing which of the two I have been."

Scientists say about a bad theory, "It is not even wrong."

I liked that as much now as I did then.

The cabin

July 24, 1977

I asked my grandmother once what she thought memory was. "I think it's a little glimpse of eternity," she said.

I stopped there. I was astonished all over again by her words. I went out to the mill pond and sat at its edge and drew the mill, and put it in with the sheets of yellowing paper. Then I continued.

Will this looking back unloose tomorrow?

July 24

I don't understand the times, but I understand the times have something to do with how my life left its expectations.

July 25

I found the quote I'd given you, David. You'd changed the names.

"David, will we take up again—beside what river?—this uncertain dialogue, and will we ask each other if ever, in a city, lost by a plain, we were David and Rennie?"

I changed city to meadow and plain to pond. And the names. My last rearrangement, I told myself.

Would Borges have allowed it for the sake of lovers?

September, Alaska

I have always with me the feeling of having been a traveler who came from another time, another place. Everything in this world seems to me astonishing, unintelligible, sometimes beautiful and somehow ageless. I wonder if I ever belonged, was ever meant to wander into this time, this place.

October

Lord I believe; help thou mine unbelief.

I've never forgotten the visceral loss of David. But there was another quality in those pages I could see now—how self-absorbing grief is. That is its prolonging mechanism—as though you had to stay until you were chastened to the last cell. Or if not chastened, instructed.

What was it Menalhces, however you spell it, said? Maybe it was Mencius. Time takes all that we have away from us?

I called Thelma Myzeld and said "What's the *whole deal*, Myzeld, the *complete* look?"

"At life?" she said. "These small considerations of yours. This is the whole deal, Rennie. There are two ways to tell a story. You can tell that the loser lost or the winner won. Grantland Rice, sportscaster."

I went back to that cabin bedroom with its one narrow bed and my big high bed across from it. I lay my pages on the narrow bed and sat at the foot of the high bed, where I could see out the window. "Go back to ordinary days," I say, and this time I will words from my grandmother.

This time and this place is the best you'll have, Rennie.

Don't be too quick to judge time, or the times.

"*Phaedrus*," I said. Chills covered my body. "She's speaking to you, Rennie, hear her," and I could hear my own voice.

You take me back to the time I first saw you—and how I got you. I loved you from the moment I laid eyes on you, believe you me. And I loved Kent the same way. You two looked like little rabbits when you were born. You barely lived, you came so early, but you did live and you were my delight.

Thinking about you and your losses—I don't know about Phaedrus, wherever you got that from—but I do know Penelope. She was good at weaving and unweaving. I've got just like her, thinking about what got you underway. And that led me to getting a husband.

I think it's unimaginable to my kids that Royce wasn't always my husband, but he wasn't. I never was too eager to fly into a marriage. Some days I didn't care if I married or not, and I waited a lot longer than most girls my age waited.

My life before Royce was full of friends, just a whole lot of friends. You've heard all these stories. You and Kent were fascinated with the pictures I had of those days. We used to pose in some of the most dramatic poses. Cameras were the sensation then. There was one picture of

Zim, and she was sitting up against a tree, leaning against it, her dress—I believe it was organdy—flowing out in front of her, and she was holding a wide-brimmed hat with ribbons on it. She looked melancholy for all the world, there under that huge tree, a little bridge just in front of her, her auburn hair falling down over her shoulders. You and Kent made me get that picture out every time you came. You got off with all those photographs so you had them to look at.

Zim was the sweetest friend. She was always the sweetest darn girl. She wore her hair loose over her forehead, and sometimes she wore it pulled back and tied kind of low and loose, and other times she flipped it under some way and other times she'd pile it all up on her head. But it was free and natural. I used to fix her hair. If I wasn't at her house, she was at mine until the day she got married.

Anyway, Zim and me and a bunch of our friends used to go to dances every darn night. Or swim. I could swim like a fish. And I could dance too. Somebody at the time was rantin' around—maybe it was a few years later but I don't think so—that dancing was the first and easiest step to hell. But I didn't worry. I figured I'd taken it and I'd liked it. I didn't care, really. As I look back, I'm glad too. After my crazy years, when I was having babies in the twenties, the "Flaming Youth" come along, flapping up a storm to "If You Knew Susie (Like I Know Susie)." But I wasn't one of those housewives who was jealous and whinin' about my lost youth. Everybody that wasn't wanted to be young again for a while in those years, but I didn't. I was content. I had my day and I made the most of it, and then I got on with my life.

But when I was having it, I sure had a time! A bunch of us girls would get together—Irma and Ella and Sara and Lorrie and Zim—and we'd all go to the dances. Sometimes I'd go in a turtleneck sweater and skirt. Sometimes I'd wear a hat. Hats were my hobby—big beautiful hats. The milliner used to say I could wear any hat in the place. I had one, you used to call it a leghorn hat. It had a wide rim and underneath the brim was pink chiffon, sheared. On the top of it, it had a black velvet ribbon that was held together with a bouquet of pink rosebuds. It was just the prettiest hat. Then I had another one that was purple with grosgrain ribbon in flat loops against the brim. Then I had a red velvet that had a rolled rim with a band of red feathers around the crown of it—it was very simple.

We didn't usually wear our hats to the dances. I only did once in a while. We wore them on the street—we nearly always wore them on the street and to go to church. We used to wear suits a lot too. And we always had a spring coat.

But I loved hats above everything else there was to put

on. I had a little black cloche hat with a little pompom stuck on the side. Another thing you always wore you don't see now and I hated them was those damned corsets. The stays dug clear into your ribs. Held my belly in and that's all. I didn't have anything else to hold in. I was skinnier than a rail, but it didn't matter anyway. The brassieres were wide and had no shape at all—they just pushed you down. When the busts made it into prominence was when they first come out with the sweater girls. I can't remember just when it was—it was before World War II, though. I never did put any weight on until after I had a baby. My father used to say, "You eat so much it makes you poor to carry it around."

Royce got into my life this way. I had met his brother Darrell at a dance and danced with him a lot. Darrell was a good dancer and I liked him all right. I went out with him quite a little bit. He and Royce looked a lot alike, and they both wore their hats pulled down over their eyes. Anyway, one afternoon I bumped into Darrell down by the post office. I said, "Hello, Darrell." He didn't say anything. He just looked up and grinned, and when I saw his face, I saw it wasn't Darrell, it was Royce.

That finished Darrell.

I'd heard this story more than any of the others—dozens and dozens of times. There was a time when I quit paying attention when she told it. But now I did, remembering how animated her face was and her voice, how clearly in love with Royce she still was.

I thought Royce was a darn good looking guy—when I say good looking, I mean good looking, and I liked that he was shy. He wasn't anything like Darrell, who couldn't mind himself, especially his hands, for two minutes. Anyway, Royce was so shy and so darn good looking, I guess he was kind of a challenge to me. He wasn't long kissing me—he wasn't that shy.

After that when I'd run into him on the street, he didn't say anything for quite a bit. He told the boys about me calling him Darrell, but he never said anything about it to me. I know he talked about it because when I'd pass him with his friends, the other boys would snicker and say, "Hi, Darrell." Finally I got so I thought, "Well, I'll fix him. I'll make him speak to me." So I'd say hello to him and he'd just duck his head, and it was quite a head. He'd go around the block to keep from meeting me, and I'd go around the block and meet him the other way. I can see those streets exactly—lilacs and hollyhocks and Royce walking past the big stone houses—gray stone—it must have been granite.

Anyway, he carried on that way for a while, then one night at a dance he came and got me. All us girls were at the dance together.

Royce didn't like to dance much in those days, but he'd come over all cleaned up. He wore the cleanest white shirts. And I remember his white handkerchief. He always wore a hat. He used to wear corduroys when he didn't wear a suit. He'd wear work shirts and corduroys. The corduroys weren't as fine a wale as they are now, but they were real soft. He used to wear corduroys to work and everything. He never wore Levis, never wore them in his life. Isn't it funny what you remember?

In the middle of the dance, some of us girls walked down to Woodman Hall. We just wanted to get out for a minute so we walked down by the post office, which was a common meeting ground for all of us. Then after a few minutes we were going back to the dance. That's when Royce come up to me and took ahold of my arm and walked off with me. He didn't say so much as "by your leave" or "if you please" or "go to hell" or a damn thing. He just walked off with me.

We had a little place called Rand's, a little confectionary store, with a marble-topped counter and stools up to it and little, kind of gay tables. My friends and I used to go down there all the time and a bunch of boys would always be sitting around the store, joshing and flirting with whoever come in. Royce told me after we were married, "I saw you walk into Rand's, and I thought you were the prettiest girl in Rexburg."

Us girls didn't care if we went with boys, to tell you the truth. The craziest things entertained us. One thing we did—we'd walk around the blocks where we lived, a whole gang of us, and sing as loud as you please. Sometimes we'd dress up like boys and go out and walk around. We'd get our brothers' pants, or our dads', and put them on. We never had any of our own, but nobody paid any attention to us. Nobody thought it was dangerous. Plainly, it wasn't.

I kept in touch with most all those girls, and now I get letters from their children saying they've died. Sara is dead now. She was a real good friend to me. She moved to San Francisco and Royce and I went to visit her and her husband nearly every year. He was a smart guy but I can't remember what he done—I think he worked for the military some way.

Lorrie married Darrell and told dirty jokes to the men on the street corner for the rest of her life. Her boy Boyd—really he was the only child I think she knew she had—was killed out in Stamp Meadows. His best friend brought him down during hunting season—just shot him as though he was wearing antlers or something, and Boyd just standing out in the middle of the meadow.

One of my friends—he was a boy but he was just a friend—used to take pictures of us from sunup to sundown. Pictures of us sitting up on the porch, making out like we were smoking a pipe, pictures of us with our heads flung back, our hats held out in a gesture of some kind or other. There was just stacks of me doing every crazy thing you could imagine—one of me being pushed around in a wheelbarrow with a bunch of kittens, and Zim was pushing me. One was of a friend of mine that I took. He was a caution. He used to come take me dancing—he'd come to the door and cry out for me. I'll make what he said rhyme with the name you gave me, which won't sound as bad as it was. "Silly ahss Phaedrus," he'd call, "let's go steppin!" I don't know what in the world my mother thought. Boy, he was a dancer—he just cleared the floor. Everybody stood back to watch him.

Most of us girls worked for the telephone company, and Sweet Sabbath, if we didn't have fun. We'd laugh half the day till we couldn't take the calls coming in. Anything would make us laugh. Zim used to strut around there sweepin' to one side like our boss and poppin' her eyes and clackin' her tongue like he done. She was so proper we couldn't hold together seeing her 'a sweepin' and 'a snappin' like him.

We used to do what we thought was an awful daring thing. We had Royce buy us a package of cigarettes—Quebebs or Cubebs, I can't remember—it was a herb cigarette for asthmatics. Lord, we done crazy things, now I think about it. None of us smoked, of course, because we were Mormon. My Dad was a bishop and I'll tell you I'd better not have smoked. And even if we hadn't been Mormon, women didn't hardly dare smoke in those days. The flappers were just coming in and they begun to smoke some.

We'd go down by the river before work—six or six-thirty in the morning—and cook breakfast and after we ate our pancakes and fried potatoes and eggs—it's a wonder we weren't as big as moose—we'd light up our Quebebs and laugh until we could hardly get packed up and to the telephone company on time. I'd forgotten how odd those herbal cigarettes smelled. At that time we wore those middy tops taken from navy suits. They had white navy collars and a tie. We'd toss our hats up in the willows and kick our shoes off and lay along what little beach there was and eat breakfast and smoke.

Oh the ecstasies Kent and I had felt at the idea of our grandmother smoking! It had led us to try smoking grated carrots, cinnamon sticks, stalks of weeds of all kinds. "Just a Quebeb," we'd say, and howl with laughter. Somehow it hadn't led us to Chesterfields.

All us girls used to sing a lot by the river too. Lorrie loved to sing. Another thing we done—we used to go down and watch the train come in. It was the Yellowstone

Special—we called it the Flyer because you had to flag it. It seems to me it came through once in the afternoon. And I remember exactly when the late one shuttled in—between four and five in the morning.

There used to be horses and buggies and wagons and cars on the street, all together, and then an airplane would come overhead and we'd all run out on the street to see it. And they used to sometimes—in the wintertime when they had bobsleighs—whirl them and you'd just turn round and round right on Main Street. The horses were so frightened of the cars when they came in and we had a lot of runaways. It was a kind of free, crazy time. Maybe part of it was my age.

The first summer I went with Royce, he didn't go up to the mill. He went on into Montana to drive stagecoach at Yellowstone Park. Boon, that was Royce's oldest brother, and Royce were supposed to catch the train to get up there—I'll never forget that—so they come over to our place early and got me and we walked around and around and said goodbye forty-leven times. And finally Boon called out, "For hell's sake, hurry up or bring 'er with you!" You used to say your grandfather was a Titan. I asked what the hell a Titan was, although I had my ideas. "It's the race of the gods," you said. Remember that? "You both are," you said. "You're his match."

One night I remember his mother telling me they wanted him to go to Logan to the college there. It's a hundred miles away at least—in Utah. "Well, I'm not going," he said, and they said, "Why aren't you going?" He came right back. "Just as soon as I go, Darrell will take my girl."

Then came World War I, the Great War we called it, and we really had a hectic time. Whenever they set up the draft, a bunch of boys would be sent all at once, and everybody in town would go down to the depot to see them off. All us girls would go down and we'd kiss them all goodbye, every one of them. I wrote letters to boys I never saw and I wrote letters to boys I did know. Every day we'd get the newspapers or go over to the post office and read the casualty lists. They were posted there and then they came out in the papers too.

I remember as plain as day the first time my heart went clear out of me during the war. I was standing there at the post office readin' the lists when Zim came up to me and said she'd just heard some news I should have heard first. We all had people in that war, of course. I had uncles and friends and cousins over there till I couldn't count them. They were the ones I thought of right off.

"Royce's enlisted," she said, and I'd never even thought of him. He wasn't old enough until then. I walked right over to the draft board because I knew I could find out all

I wanted to know. My father ran it, and I went up to him and said, "When does Royce leave?"

"In the morning," he said. He was a kind man, and it gave him some pain to tell me, I could see that. He took off his little wire-rimmed glasses to tell me. There was some dried up old woman that worked in there with him. She was the kind of woman you know died a virgin, although she had a couple of little sticks for children. She swept up to study how I was takin' it, but I had my back to her before she found out.

So then it was my turn to go home and think about if I wanted him to do it. I felt way more than bad to think he might be going, but I wanted him to go. That was how we felt about the war. We didn't think of withholding.

I walked home up along Center Street to our street, and all the way I was seeing his blue eyes and his big handsome hands. And I was being surprised all over again by his dry wit. He was a man full of surprises from the first look I looked at him, and that was a good one.

On that walk home, I realized I couldn't even imagine what it would be like to have him gone, let alone way off being shelled—and me listening to the Yellowstone Special fly by in the middle of the night with him not there to give me everything I wanted. I guess that says it pretty plain. Anyway, it was then I knew how much I could never get enough of him. You've found out how that feels. What comes next is you find when you lose that person, something very real, very rich, remains.

Phaedrus, you've never spoken more eloquently of your times, and I knew I must look to my own time.

I drove into Pond's Lodge and called Thelma Myzeld. "Friend," I said.

"Friend," she said.

"Friend, I'm thinking about the *whole deal*."

That's all. And I went into the restaurant and sat by a window looking south, where you could see the trees and a glimpse of the river. "I'll have soup," I said when the waitress got around to coming over. "Is it homemade?"

"Nah, not anymore," she said.

"Good, I'll have it."

FOUR

This *is* what is happening. I'm Penelope too. I'll be in my cabin unraveling. And raveling. And one day I'll come to the end of it. Even Penelope didn't go on forever. I wake in the night and the room is orange and I can see orange billows of flame and gray billows of smoke. I turn on the light.

This isn't necessarily about my father. I've been waking to orange and gray for ten, fifteen years. I've always thought it was something crossing in the brain—well, assuredly that. I get up and walk out into the forest. I don't last long out there. I sit in the old kitchen chair with yellow showing through the chipped white. The shushing of the pines isn't as comfortable a sound at night.

"That crazy pig gave me a testimony," I hear my father say. He had always tossed around religious talk in a sardonic way. He made people mad mocking their religious terms, but he was funny with this. He carried on and on. "Look, the Lord has sent me a pig. I finally have my own conviction."

I'd been helping him build a pigpen. Hand me this, hand me that for two days. I went into the house to get a Coke, and I heard him call, "Come quick, Rennie."

Our talk had started where it always started—with him catching the biggest fish of his life on the Salmon River. We weren't five words into that until we got to the Coffee Pot.

"How it's tucked down in there," my father said.

"Trees running up from the side—but not dark and cold like Box Canyon," I said.

"Smell of huckleberries. You kids loved to scamper for your berries."

"You loved to eat them. I once calculated a huckleberry pie. I came up with eight hundred thousand berries to make you a pie." He liked that. He looked at me with admiration. He didn't expect anyone was going to do anything for him. I'd never expected admiration.

"My papa took us to the Coffee Pot when we were little," he said, "but he loved to fish in the Park."

"Those strings of fish he's holding, one in each hand, on the cover of that magazine—was it better than we had it in the forties?" I ask.

"Hand me that saw." And I was walking back into the house to get the Coke, and I heard him holler. I thought he'd hurt himself, and when I got out on the porch, he was laughing and slapping his leg. "Come quick. I'm a believer." He was funny with it—it wasn't his usual Mormon disdain. "Look at this. Wilbur's come home."

And I'll be damned if the biggest pig I'd ever seen hadn't walked into his pigpen.

"Help me lift this gate, Rennie," he said, and we lifted it in place—that's how far along we were. "He just walked right in," my father said. "I went into the garage and when I came out, he was standing right there."

"Where *did* he come from?" I asked, chuckling. I was sure my father knew that pig, knew he belonged up the road.

"Don't ask," he said.

"You've set this up, haven't you?" I laughed.

"No, I'm telling you. God sent him. The pig walked in here."

I half believed him, half didn't.

You can't say where the delay is in a nightmare, but there is a delay. When the phone rang early in the morning in the weeks after the fire, my hands began to tremble and I had to work with my voice. I'm not much better now, although no phone rings up here. Any sound early in the morning will do it. The call itself when it came felt like an overseas call years ago when you could hear the other voice slogging toward you through the transatlantic cable. Momma? Is this Momma?

Everything was out of time. The beginning of a beautiful day. I stood on the lawn when I got to my parents' house under that blue sky and managed to avoid the side of the house my father was taken out as long as possible—with the black hole at the window and the guns all lined up, and the knives, and the little bottle of arsenic turned black. All that, lying on the lawn being photographed. He'd always said he had arsenic, but we hadn't—of course we hadn't believed him. And the gun shells, the bullet loader. What were policemen to think? And a key in the lock?

Nothing was supposed to happen. My father hadn't hanged Jim Leish in the ordinary sense. He hadn't killed my mother. He hadn't shot me. He'd talked. He'd stormed and roared. There had been professional advice. No, after that long, the behavior would stay the same. No need to fear he'd take the knife and slice, pick up the gun and shoot. The plot doesn't usually thicken; it thins out.

But he did pick up the gun and shoot that last night. That's how he called Mother. "That's how he got my attention all that week," she told me. I'm incredulous. I see the house still smoking. A Browning pistol and four rifles with stocks he'd hand-carved had been under his bed. A few pocketknives. A hunting knife. Photos and newspaper clippings from the family paper and pictures and books and rocks and the jewelry he'd made, and his trumpet. All charred.

"Why did he have guns in there, Mrs. England?" I remember that question.

"Did bullets go off? Momma?" I asked that day. I can't find the right words. "Mother?" How could I have asked her if he'd started the fire? However it happened, the pattern went to its end. Fate had been tempted. Fate had been invited.

"Yes, bullets were going every which way," she tells me. "That's where he kept them."

I try to imagine my mother in that room. She would have been throwing water on the fire when it might have been fairly easy to drag my father out of there. Then the lights went out.

"Did the smoke alarm go off?" I ask.

"Not until I opened the door."

So the door *was* closed.

"When I opened the door, it started to shriek and your father said, just as calm as can be, 'Deborah, I think you'd better get some water in the bucket in the bathroom and throw it on these flames.' No, first he said, 'Deborah, grab that little rug and smother these flames.'"

I review it in my mind. She said to him, "I can't get it. You're laying on it.'"

"What did he…" I start to say, and she goes on.

"Then he said, 'You'd better get some water in the bathroom and throw on them.'" And that's when she must have gotten the water in the yellow bucket and thrown it. And she went back for another bucket of water, and this time it's different.

"I could hardly see him in the room," she is saying. "And that's when I noticed little flames starting to lick up under the bed-clothes."

"The sheets?"

"Yes, they were starting to burn."

Finally I ask her, "Where was he?"

"He was on the floor."

"By his window?"

"No. He was more between it and the door."

"Was he…?"

"He was laying on his stomach."

"His head?"

"Right there by the flames." She's as matter-of-fact as a news report, and I can't tell if she has to be or if she just is. What can't be said here shouldn't be said.

"They took pictures," she told me much later, "and I…"

"Oh no," I cried. "Don't go down there. No, you don't want to see those pictures. You don't want to do that, Mother."

This is what I thought. I thought this isn't my family. We aren't those people on television who stand sobbing before the cameras, nothing left of us but rasps, the bone of emotion. This isn't how we lived—what's on this lawn, this blackened house. We got up each morning, loved each other, more or less, kept clean like other people. We drank from glasses, forks on the left. We washed the Buick once a week, cared for a garden, preferred geraniums to marigolds. We drank root beer floats together at the drive-in, slid the window neatly up one-quarter for the tray.

But this. Is there a history for what's lying on this lawn, always present for me now? And the black house behind it? We got into trouble in the schoolyard, knocked each other's teeth out. But we came home, had dinner together, played kick the can in the vacant lot. Changed to limeade.

This. Does what's here now stand between me and what can come after? Where *will* I be when I have finished remembering?

A lot of time goes by between talks with my mother about that morning. "Do you think it was fast?" I ask. "Smoke inhalation—if your lungs are compromised? When do you think he was gone? Mother?"

She answers indirectly. "I ran to the neighbors when I saw all that smoke and flames. He'd said you'd better call 911, just as calm. And I started to dial it and the lights went out and the phone went dead, and I said, 'Blaine, I've got to go to the neighbors and get help.' And he said 'Yes, you'd better do that.' I was in the living room, and I just—I dropped that bucket. I could feel it getting hot. And I heard him say 'Deborah.'"

Did his spirit guard her out? Let me think so. Because he was gone before she ever got to that door.

I leave the cabin and drive to Rexburg. When I find Kent, we walk and walk and walk. He asks again, "Can we go and get him back?"

All the fires I've built at the cabin. All the danger up here where no one could get to you. No phones, no neighbors, no fire trucks. You build a fire and the whole cabin changes on a rainy, overcast day. The warmth of a real fire sinks through the wood, the bones. Even the preparations cheer you. You might have to duck out into the rain to the woodshed, and you scramble back, connected to the animals around you, the rabbits making it for their warren, the marmots sliding down into their tunnels, the squirrels nicking up into the trees, the birds fluttering, finding a nest.

And the pleasure of expertise. Twist the paper just so, like Grandpa did. Not too tight. Place it well back for a good draw. Don't skimp on kindling, and don't try to get away with big chunks, not with that old Monarch. And don't hurry the next piece. Let it really start burning. Listen to the *cacacacapapa* of the wood.

And finally I try to know what it was for my father. Did he have a comprehending moment? Did he say to himself *I'm Joan of Arc here. This is what will happen.* And I see the black smoke pouring out. I've heard my father cough all his life, wrenching coughs, wracking wheezes.

I drive to the lodge, Thalo sitting up in the seat beside me. It's cool enough for her to stay in the car while I call my mother.

"How big was the fire," I ask again when I hear her voice. I try to breathe regularly and I have to breathe stealthily to breathe at all.

"Not very big," she says.

When I see her, I'll say "Show me," and she'll make a circle of her arms, and much later I will say "How high?" and she'll indicate three feet. So the flames were higher than I thought, or than I thought she said. But the story shifts a little. And I think of trying to reconstruct the order in which I did things after that call, and I know how much goes, how much order, how much detail.

"So you couldn't get to him?"

"No, it was so crowded in that room. He'd dragged his gun loader up from the basement and he had that chair in there and his bed was just covered with paper—books and magazines. He'd dragged his high school yearbooks up. He could hardly get into bed. He sat all that week with the window open and looked out at the pasture and down at those pictures of him and Blake stealing horses. Us going up to Bear Gulch to ski. You kids in the little bed we made for you in the trunk of the old Plymouth. Those are all gone now."

"Was he frightened? Mother?" The sky outside is opalescent. It's a perfect night to go fishing. Days on the Coffee Pot Rapids, eating our smashed sandwiches, licking up our melted Hersheys. From there to here.

"No, he wasn't the least bit frightened. Or angry. He didn't boss me around. He was just as calm. Actually, he was as nice as he's ever been. 'Deborah,' he said, 'I think you'd better get some water.'"

So she ran out into the dark March morning, barefooted, in a nightgown, through snow. Angels weren't home so she ran to the next house, stood pounding on the door. "Come quick, my house is on fire." Did she always use *my*? "And my husband is in there."

And she'd started out into the living room, still carrying the yellow bucket. I can't figure it out. And he called Deborah.

"Not frightened," she says, "not loud, just like he'd say my name, like he said it when we first lived together. He wasn't calling me back. I knew I couldn't drag him through those flames, and I ran through the living room and out those doors."

I walk myself back outside his room in my mind—out to where he would have been looking from his window. "We are those people." I hear myself say it.

We are those people. We did ask that the television crews turn their cameras off. The whole gaggle of them nodded with understanding, went up the street five hundred yards, and got out their telephotos. Maybe everyone asks them to leave, then sees themselves on the evening news.

I try to stay where I am. I am finding the small ways my father did magic for me. I've always known how to laugh. I'm as good at that as he was. I can fish. I can make things. It isn't nothing.

"I can't help myself—I'm just happy," he said to me once. I'm more interested now than I was then that he saw even a slice of himself that way.

Maybe the best thing I could say about him is that he didn't let her burn there with him.

And my mother? She survived. For the first time I see it with admiration. What she's just come through could have been the moment she stopped moving forward but she didn't choose that—or let it choose her.

On the drive back to camp, I ruffle through Thalo's fur, talking to her. My mind drifts to Carlos, and I wonder if I did everything I could have for him.

His energy went all at once, and then his kidneys. He was eighteen.

"Carlos has Alport syndrome," I said to his doctor. My student had little by little become my son.

"We've never even seen a case of that," the doctor told me, the note of dismissal in every word.

But Carlos did have it—one of those curious combinations: born deaf, early renal failure. His life after that was full of more than one major surgery a year for the fifteen years he had left. A haunting wistfulness began to work around the edges of his style.

"I care, dead or alive," he murmured, his face against mine, and then he was wheeled through the last set of surgical doors.

David held me in his arms, rocking me, when I told him Carlos had died. "'Knowest thou he will give thee living water,'" he said to me.

"David, I love you time out of mind," I said to him. "How could I have imagined you? Meet me at Rand's. Can you? Let's find the little table my grandparents went to—sit there and look at each other and get up after a while and dance in the afternoon." I say these things to him. I'm still talking to him, praying to him.

There was a totality about him—his vigor, his body, his mind, and his rich and sorrowing spirit. The things he said. It takes a good deal of history to produce a little literature. Henry James and King James.

He gave me a lot of the words I live by. "Fear not, little flock; for it is your Father's good pleasure to give you the Kingdom."

I answered him, staying with Luke. "Her sins, which are many, are forgiven; for she loved much."

And yes, he quoted the Song of Solomon: "Kiss me the kisses of thy mouth; for thy love is better than wine."

I walk out into the forest and say to the trees, "The voice of my beloved. Behold, he cometh leaping upon the mountains, skipping upon the hills."

"David, Beloved of the Lord. Thou hast ravished my heart."

I watch myself trying to find a balancing point. And suddenly I know my grandmother is still with me. My heart is pounding. "*Rennie.*" I hear her.

Just that. God in heaven, I don't know how to understand what I've been given. I know I'm somewhere between my own ability to find the precise lens and her capacity to bring it.

She's going to give me words about David, about losing David. Can she reach back through the years and hand me the key?

Rennie, I used to go by train all the time. I like the train. I can remember those trains where you faced each other in the seats. I rode across two states once with a woman who sat looking at me for twelve hours. She did nothing the whole time but look at me and eat chocolate. She had one of those Swiss chocolate bars made in triangles and she just set watching me and nibbling on this chocolate. I tried to talk but it wasn't worth doing. Her idea of conversation was, "Can you imagine the French not wrapping their breads?"

Well, you get on the train and who knows what kind of adventure you'll have. I guess that's how I can envision you now—stepping on a train and you have the idea where you're headed, but you haven't seen the countryside and you haven't been there before.

Her unforgettable way—the train, the countryside, the adventure. And I'm the one having an unfathomable journey with her—an adventure that crosses worlds. The word chosen comes to my mind. And friendship—there is as much friendship here as kinship.

I've had plenty of time since to think what your life was, and mine. I fell in love and was courted and took long rides in the buggy with the horse who knew the way home. I married, I had my children, I did my work. It was a simple life, in its way.

You used to ask me about my life—what would I change? you'd ask. What was the hardest thing? Did I ever want something I couldn't have and couldn't let go of? I never did, I told you. We didn't have time, if we'd had the inclination, to wish for another life than the one we were trying to keep up with. I should have added that was the overview—the whole life. Parts, yes, I'd change. I'd have raised Lilly. I'd change things for you if I could. I'd like you to have what I had. That long view was a blessing. And the time that allowed that view is one of the things that separates my life and my era from yours.

Look what I had—time, and that man that never didn't make me lose my breath a little, and the children playing "Loving Sam" on the wind-up phonograph, and the jars and jars of raspberries and peaches and apricots and cherries I set on the table and watched them relish, and the gratitude from all of you that keeps coming up over me like a warm wave. I had it all. It wasn't even that I tried hard. I made up my mind to certain things—that I wasn't going to sulk or brood, for one thing—and then my hectic life, if not my decision, never let me.

I saw life plentiful. I can't even imagine a quote like that one you wrote about—'some time in a distant place we'll take up this uncertain dialogue and we'll ask ourselves if ever by a meadow, lost beside a pond, we were Royce and Phaedrus.' I can't even imagine our thinking that.

I can't imagine it either. And I let go of being suspended between what I partly had and what I might have had. The uncertain dialogue had been largely from within.

And another thing I did. I tried never to make the mistake you wrote about in one of your letters. Something like it never failed that during the dry years the people forgot about the rich years, and during the wet years they lost all memory of the dry years. *East of Eden*. You sent me that and wrote about it. You have to be a long way off to see that, as you know, Rennie.

Time is a funny thing, Rennie—your babies are small and they grow and then they go off to school. I remember when Terp went off to school his first day and my last baby was out of the nest and I wouldn't have a little one about me. I couldn't wait for your mother to start school, but I felt so lost when Terp went—I shuffled around missin' the little scamp. And Lilly just clear gone. But I was too busy to brood. I had the washing and the ironing. I didn't get so sentimental I wasn't cross when Terp come home without his coat.

What it is about life is this—things change. They do. They change. Life can't stand still. And they don't always change real slow and natural. It's bang and it's this way and it's slam and it's that. You know who taught me a lot about that, Rennie?

I'll say it better here. Remember when you come near to burning the cabin down? You almost smoked yourself into the next world right then and there with putting that stick of pitch in the fire—just a whole big log of it. You were banging around in here trying to shut the fire out when I looked up from the commissary and saw the blackest, the thickest smoke pouring out of every window, let alone the chimney. I wondered what you were using for air if you were in here.

In *here,* she said.

When I got up that lane—and I was bad off enough in the legs even then I couldn't run, I just could hurtle my body along in a fast walk—your eyes were wild with grief and guilt and fear that you'd done something couldn't be set right. I was mad as one of those snotty hens I told you about till I saw that face of yours. Then I would rather have seen the cabin burn down than your suffering.

All children must have a moment when they see they cannot control or reverse what they've unwittingly set in motion. Mine was that day when I saw I was going to burn the cabin down.

Flames leaped over my hands when I tried to reach in there and get that pitch-soaked piece of wood out. I should have recognized it—red-streaked and heavy and almost petrified. But I'd been hurrying, I'd been distracted. And now I was going to burn my hands off or run outside and look back to see the thing I loved best in the world burn. And my grandmother would come up that path and see her home going—her books and her addresses and her clothes and Grandpa's chain watch and that old red- and-white set of hens and chickens in the kitchen and those photographs in the long black book in the closet.

All this was before me and the flames were spilling over the top of the stove and somehow I knew it wasn't enough to put the lid back over it, even though I tried. It wouldn't fit anyway, I'd laid the wood in there so badly. That was a second mistake. My heart slammed in my chest, my throat, my temples, and I could hear myself breathing fast. It was terror, mature terror. And then there she was.

> What I done was this—I took the lid off the stove and flames shot nearly clear to the ceiling and I put grandpa's gloves on that he kept by the stove and reached in there into the flames—you cried right out, I remember that. I had ahold of that piece of pitch in a second and I carried it smokin' and flamin' out to the road and tossed it down, you practically right between my legs with worrying about me. Well, we stood there and you said how did you *do* that and

I said I stuck my hand in there and I pulled that piece of pitch out. Otherwise it was going to burn down the cabin.

What come to me at the end of it all was this. I have set my woman's feet back to my girlhood paths, Rennie. That's because of you. I've gotten to start again with my youth and my age side by side.

Remember me saying I never did want to be young, or anything else, forever? You've gone straight ahead, Rennie. That's what makes me think you will take up again.

And I reflect on what I've heard, as though I could replay it. You get on the train and who knows? Look what I had. I saw life plentiful. Time is a funny thing. It is together we make the spreading tree.

Because of you, she said. Because of you.

"We're going to bake," I hear her say. I'm standing at the window, biting on the tips of my index fingers. It's the first summer after the mill burned, and we're in San Francisco.

"The way I like to bake is to lay everything out. You get things up on the counter as I call them out, how does that sound? First, get your pie tin. Use the little old one—that funny little brown thing with the holes in the bottom bakes better than glass, better than stainless steel. It just puts out a beautiful pie."

"Pie tin out," I say. The countertop is laminated wood, and she runs her hand along it.

"Get your Crisco. Some people use margarine. The dough is easier to handle, but you lose the flakiness. That's what makes pie crust good. I prefer lard myself, when I can get it."

"Crisco out. Gram, you make everything—I guess you are the sawmill. Wherever you are."

"What about you? Don't you think I'm having the time of my life with my little minnow here?"

"Are you? Are you?"

"Certainly I am or I'd send you home. Now get your flour out."

"Flour out."

"Salt."

"Salt out."

"Vinegar."

"Vinegar? In a pie? I don't know where it is."

"It makes the crust. I keep it over in that cupboard by the stove. No, down. It's right—right in there."

"Vinegar out."

"That's it. Now you're ready to mix. Let's make apple, shall we? I've got some real nice, firm Winesap apples. They make the best pie."

"Why do you call them Winesap?"

"Don't ask me, I don't have a notion, but it's the best pie-making apple there is. And Granny apples are good. Jonathans are okay; in fact, they're excellent, but you can't use a Delicious. If you have to use a Delicious, use Golden Delicious."

"How many shall I lay up?"

"Oh, four, five. They're kind of small. Here, I'll grab a mixing bowl while you get the apples."

"Five up."

"Sugar," my grandmother says, and I slide it out of the row of white canisters with red apples painted on them.

"And cinnamon and nutmeg and butter." She helps me round up the last items.

"Now let me show you about pies. You put in some flour."

"How much?"

"Oh let's see, a cup and a half, about that."

I measure a cup and a half of flour into the bowl.

"Now take some Crisco. I use a lot. I like to get my dough real rich. Put in about a cup—let's see what that looks like."

I take my grandmother's big silver spoon—I remember it down to the feel of the thick handle—and fill the measuring cup with Crisco.

"Use this little spatula to get it out." She hands me a little rubber spatula.

"Spatula's a word I can't stand," I say.

"It's a funny word, you're right. Now you can get in the dough and pounce it up with your fingers or with this pastry deal—where is it?"

"I want to use my fingers."

"The trick is, don't handle it too much, although actually you're all right until you add your moisture. Oh, we need some ice water. I'll set down some ice cubes."

I get my fingers into the bowl and begin to squeeze the Crisco through the flour. It feels luscious, like toes in mud. "It's oozy but not slicky or slimy. It's as soft as your skin."

"I'd like to be that soft. That's it. Just mix it up until you've got a whole bunch of little chips in there the size of hazelnuts."

I laugh. "I like pouncing it up," I say.

I'd forgotten the lightness in our voices, the pleasure.

"Now notice how that feels. That's about right. You want it to be the right consistency."

I feel it and wonder if I can remember how it should be.

"Now make a place for your moisture." She hands me a set of measuring spoons, yellow.

"Put a little water in the center, and then sprinkle some around. That's it. Now add a little vinegar, about a tablespoon. Sprinkle a little of it around." She watches me. "A little more, that's it. Now let me show you. You don't want to handle it much from here. The less the better. I hate a tough pie."

I watch as she makes a few movements. They're efficient. They have authority. I pay attention again. The pie dough is in a ball in the bottom of the bowl.

"Now rolling it out is just good clean fun. I love to roll out pie dough when it's good dough. I wouldn't even bother with that stuff the French make. You could throw it clear across the room and it would come out in a little circle just like you started with."

She flours the countertop and her rolling pin and I'm watching her, loving her so much, wondering how she can ever be gone, and she takes a handful of dough. "Flounce it down good in the flour," she says. I repeat flounce it down good.

"You talk so good."

"You talk as good as I do, I know that much about talk." She's rolling by now. "Don't worry about the edges. They'll come out thin. Work on the middle. Roll from the middle like this."

I take the rolling pin and it's like a sacramental thing. I know I will do this all my life and think of her.

"Don't attack it, Rennie. Just give it a gentle roll. You never want to stage an attack on dough, especially pie dough."

I laugh. “I do stage an attack. I like a staged attack.”

“I know you do. You’re getting it just right now. It takes some practice to make a good pie. It takes a real knack, too, if you want my opinion.”

We peel and grate apples and finish up our pie.

“Now we’ll do a little cherry pie. I thought we’d have enough dough. I’ve got some cherries down there in the bottom of the fridge in a little pint jar. That should do it. Just a small pie. Your grandpa loves cherry pie.”

I get the cherries, and I’m listening to everything, the cars going by on Market Street, people chattering on the sidewalks, and I remember the *shshsh* of the pines at the cabin, the chatter of the chipmunks, the sound of the firewood crackling, my grandmother’s movement. Keep this, I say.

“The deal on cherry pie is don’t get it too thick. I hate a claggy pie.”

I burst out laughing and go into the living room where my grandfather is listening to the radio. “Gram hates a claggy pie,” I say.

“Well? So do I.”

“I hate a claggy pie,” I murmur. “Hate a claggy pie.”

In half an hour, the whole house smells like the baking pies. I lurk around the oven, waiting for them to turn golden.

“Don’t you open that oven door one more time, you little whippet,” my grandmother calls from the couch. “You be content to wait. And remember when you get in stormy seas—make a pie. This is where your anchor is—simple chores.”

When we take the pies out, I slip a finger up under a little of the cherry juice that has bubbled over. "Oh Gram, it's good. It tastes like the mill. It's tangy and good."

I draw in my breath. My grandmother comes over and puts her arms around me. She's right there. We're touching. "You're my delight," she murmurs. And the two of us stand there together, slicing and eating pie and calling to Grandpa to get it while it's hot.

I realize I'm in *Our Town*. I'm still making my Grand Tours. I'm getting one more day.

"What did you find out, Daddy?" I ask the trees I'm standing among. I'm getting ready to leave, and I can't make myself stay in that cabin doing the final taking apart.

And there he is before me. He has his long miner's beard and he is laughing—not his leering, lewd laugh that I hated, but the sweetest laugh—and he's sitting up against great rocks, water running behind him. It looks like the Utmost Source. I think I can hike up to him.

I study him. His face is full of something I hadn't seen, full of understanding and joy. We acknowledge each other. He took joy in me, I can see that. I'm his, I see that too. I don't know that it had even occurred to me before, other than as a dilemma, a problem to be solved. "One of my uncles said you died without the light of Christ," I tell my father. I hate talk like that. "Not ours to know," I say, "who has the light and from where." What I'm seeing is the part I'd missed all along—a man grieved by his errors. And a loving man.

And I'd never thought you might have wisdom, one of its bands of color. I say this to him.

I had hardly slept for days and days when Thelma Myzeld came to see me. I was sitting there at the kitchen table looking out the window at that golden meadow, only a few red Oregon grape leaves left. I looked up, startled. "I won't ask if you knocked," I said. "You need a meal."

"How can you know your mother and father?"

"I thought this is where I'd find you." And she lit a cigarette and handed it to me. "You're back to working on understanding. How long have you been here?"

"What if he *was* locked in?" and my hand was trembling. The cigarette was doing this little dance, and we were both watching it. Ordinarily we would have laughed, but nothing at all seemed funny, not even that bobbling cigarette.

"Look at this pathetic little business," I said, and I put out the cigarette. By then I was crying.

"Dear me, Rennie. I've never seen you cry. But feel free. *Dios mios*, what do you mean locked in?"

"Or locked out."

"Or locked out. No one ever had the skill of seeing it both ways since the Iceman, Rennie. In or out?"

"Well, it was a skeleton key. That old house and the old lock still on the bedroom door. So the key could go on either side of the lock. When did locks come along, do you think?"

"They came with the package is my guess, Rennie. I'm sure they came with the fig leaf. Who went in there?"

"My mother."

"So *she* wasn't locked out?"

"No, that's *right*. At least not by then. I've circled in my mind. I haven't walked myself straight through it. I've been going around and around it. She said, 'I opened the door.'"

"That day? What made you think there was a key?"

"Someone said it—insurance agents were asking about it. There were police, detectives. The key kept coming up. Or it seems like it did. The damned media confuses you. Circling. They were all there—small-enough town. Smoke signal." We did start laughing at that, but it wasn't much of a laugh. A little relief—no diversion.

"At least not by then…?"

"By then?"

"'She wasn't locked out. At least not by then…'"

"You mean what did I mean? I don't know what 'at least not by then' means."

"God damn, Rennie…"

"That's what it is. Damn. How's Ray?"

"He found that crazy jacket."

"No. He couldn't…"

"I was in Missoula, and there it was—lining, label, cashmere—the same jacket. And I took it home and put it at the back of his closet. I don't know why but I was delirious with joy when he found it. He came flying out. 'Honey! Honey Pot, I've found my jacket. I don't know how the *hell* I've missed it.' And I was nearly in tears seeing him standing there holding it."

"When you're surreptitious and it goes good…" It made me

smile. "We shouldn't have clipped it. Let's have tea, I mean real tea—a cup of hot tea." And we went to the kitchen and put the teakettle on the stove and pulled our chairs up to it.

"This is what I call a kitchen," Thelma said. "No wonder you want to be here."

"I just built up the fire. Warmest warm."

"I brought you some Earl Grey. I knew you wouldn't have it up here."

"This is deep rescue, isn't it?"

She ignored that. "First, Rennie," she said, her cup at the ready, "what about this key?"

"Key in the lock. Maybe it was switched out."

"Switched out? The key?"

"Like the jacket. We might not even have the right key."

"Are you all right, Rennie?"

"All? Some. But that key deal...We've got something that's not right." I was crying again. I could see that Thelma was beside herself and I got a handle on my emotions—the tears anyway, but I couldn't seem to calm my mind. "Key in the lock." I studied my tea. "I only want to know if it's what I want to know. Do you know what I mean? I wish I had some cream."

"Here," she said, and reached over to her coat pocket and dragged out three of those little restaurant half-and-halfs.

She looked at me. She had a long drink of tea and set her cup down. "It will be what you want to know, Rennie. Two ways to tell a story."

I made an effort at a smile and reached for my cup. "You do get what you're able to construe, don't you? Thank you for the tea and cream."

"That is what you do get. What you're able to construe and not more."

"Read these."

"God, Rennie. Your tea leaves? You've been up here too long."

"I can't remember who was there at all."

"At the funeral? Was there a guest book?"

"Yes! I hadn't…I've missed a lot here. What could it tell us?"

"Who was there. And was there a police record?"

"Why? I guess there was. There was…" A shudder ran through me.

"Maybe a third thing present," Thelma said. She got up from the table and brought the teapot over from the counter and filled our cups. I noticed a slight tremor in her hands.

"Third thing present?"

"D. H. Lawrence made the observation. My father read it to me from a little volume of poetry for children:

> 'Water is H_2O, hydrogen two parts, oxygen one,
> but there is also a third thing, that makes it water
> and nobody knows what that is.'

"That's me, Thelma. Nothing but backward glances. My bid for atonement?"

"That's *very* adult, Rennie. *Very*."

Thelma Myzeld left a message for me to call when she got home. I was in Pond's Lodge the next day and I saw it.

"Whales are bigger than you realize," she said when she answered the phone.

"Yes. Except for the people who swim with them. They realize."

She asked how I felt. "I mean, how do you feel physically?" I hadn't noticed how little I slept, how uncomfortable I was lying down, how rarely food crossed my mind.

I got down on the floor after Thelma left and put my face in Thalo's fur. "Let's get out on the Coffee Pot," I said to her. She sprang up. We didn't go through any preliminaries—no fishing gear, no food—we just set out and spent the rest of the day on the bank of the river. Now and then I'd pick up the faint smell of the last huckleberries. Or think I did. The air had that scented crispness it gets before everything turns white.

We walked clear up to the old Coffee Pot Lodge and watched a few fishermen land small ones. When it began to get dark, we hiked out. There's a lot of deadfall in there and it was slow going. I hadn't noticed how stiff Thalo was getting.

I thought about my father and the household my parents had created as I walked that familiar path. I'm starting to see how much it was driven by what romance was to my parents. The myriad signals between them, sometimes encircling us, often slicing us away from each other, the frequent and apparently inadvertent stumbling into the bedroom or being locked out of it, the quarrels about something—my father getting out of the car at a stoplight, slamming the door, storming off into the rain, my mother crying—sobbing is more like it—and sliding into the driver's seat. The fingers of fear reaching around me. And probably the nick of anger.

And the next weekend we might be getting ready for Christmas. "We'll get the tree together," I hear my father say. Just like always. "And we'll go in the Buick." It's a little pounded now, and we can drink root beers in it.

"Then we'll get out the decorations," he says, and he sings "Oh Tannenbaum, Oh Tannenbaum," and reaches into the back seat and ruffles us. My mother gives him such a look. And we take the tree home and string the lights, and he makes us sourdoughs and sings to us until we fall asleep. Oh night Divine.

I called Maraya the next morning. I can't say why. Maybe now that I'd started talking, I needed to talk.

There was that "Hell-oo."

"Do you see any advances in this civilization?"

"Oh Lord," she said, the Lord going low. "You're another history, I can tell you that, Miss Rennie. Umhmm. That's what I see. But if you mean modern times, it's a *very hard* form of government."

"Unless you handpick the masses."

"Forget the masses, Miss Rennie. What you need is some sweet potatoes and some mashed potatoes and gravy with a few giblets in. You in those mountains? When you get home, come by. I'll have your meal ready. I should have kept in touch, Miss

Rennie. By the way, I'll just say this. You make your bed, you lie in it. That's what I told myself."

"About…? Does that bear on something particular?"

"Not particularly," she said, adding that hnhnhn of hers.

"You're as outrageous as ever," I said. "How could you be anything but bracing?"

"You can't have too many potatoes. What I'll do, I'll fix you some string beans with bacon. I think I'll make you my strawberry dish this time."

"Do I still have to take it home to eat?"

"Now why would we mess with custom?"

What I don't want to lose is what I have left. I go more carefully, seeing where that points.

I never understood why my mother didn't leave my father. It isn't why she might have locked him in that I don't understand. If she did lock him in. But she couldn't have; she's not weighed down with that kind of burden. And she's gentle by nature. He didn't take her nature from her. I'm troubled that in my bewilderment, I'm assigning guilt. Maybe not quite guilt, but too close.

I might have locked my father in myself, or her out, at one time. But what would it have been for her that could obscure the knowledge—and maybe I'm crossing into wisdom here—that the unending chaos between them would carry her past judgment?

And I'm back out there on the Coffee Pot Rapids with that river gathering force and me in the moment when you only have a moment left. And I trace out that obliterating day when Daddy went down just at the head of the rapids. Kent had stayed home, and I was alone with my father. There wasn't another soul on the river. A thin cloud cover and a beautiful caddis hatch distracted us even from each other. We weren't paying attention to anything but the next cast, setting the hook, reeling in, getting him off the hook, next cast. We'd become primitives.

"How ya doin'?" my father called out to me after a while. He didn't look up and neither did I.

"Haulin' in fish," I called back.

"Me too." He was yipping and laughing, fishing downstream. "This is your prime North Fork, your prime Snake River," he called. That was a long speech for him on the river.

When I did look up, I noticed where he was. "Be careful," I called, but he wouldn't be hearing anything where he was. Then he had a hit, a big one, and he pivoted out there, the water roaring, and he was down like that. He hung onto his rod. For a moment that's all I saw—his rod switching around in the water. And I remembered him telling me, "Let your gear go if you have to. Reach down and get your boots off and get out of your waders before they fill."

And I realized he was hanging onto that bamboo rod he'd made and trying to take his boots off with one hand and I was screaming "Let go of it!" and running up and down along the bank and the channel was narrowing—the pines growing what looked like almost together where the big rocks began to let the water drop—ten, fifteen feet at a time, swirling and pounding.

If the rapids take him around that corner, he's dead, I said—I said it over and over. "No! He'll be dead. Daddy, let your rod go. God. Daddy." The day changed from beautiful to threatening, the pines dark, the river menacing.

Then I got a little ahead of him and gestured—I held out my hands. I was right down at the edge of the swirling water—it never once occurred to me to try to go in there and save him. I had nothing at all to save him with—no weight, no authority—nothing. And I hadn't the least plan to die with him.

He saw what I wanted. He was making gulping and fearful sounds. *Buhhh, buhhh*, and he heaved that rod toward my outstretched hands, and I barely managed to pluck it out of the air without going into the maelstrom. I felt the current catch my leg—God almighty, my legs are so thin, and I thought about our tuna fish sandwiches, and I almost lay down in the water to get back to the rock that rose up out of it.

Then I had it and I'd kept that goddamned rod. And I shifted my head around to see if my father was gone down into the white foam and I didn't see him at all and my heart was slamming against my chest—you could have seen it slamming—and I was crying out "Daddy, Daddy, Father, Blaine," and after a long, a protracted time—time in which I wondered how life was going to be without him and how I would find my way off the rapids and home—his head bobbed up in that first pool beyond the foam and he swam out of it. The pool was small and you could see from the darkening shades of blue how deep it was. The difficulty was staying out of the swirling current that took you down over the next enormous rocks. He came up out of that water like a god—his white undershirt and shorts shimmering. He looked like he'd finally been baptized. He pulled his shirt down and laughed and said, “That’s the best ride I’ve had since Bear Gulch. Think I’ll try it again.”

That was life with my father. I could see that he might have lit that candle in his room himself and let it get right to the edge of the edge. He wouldn’t need any key in a lock to keep him in the face of danger. Or her out.

I also saw that he had endangered me, out there on the rapids. My mother had always been in danger, that wasn’t news.

And I turn to keeping what I have left.

I loaded Thalo up the next morning with the idea of going for a drive. I liked being in the car, looking around, and so did my dog. I drove west through Shotgun Valley and when I got to Spencer I drifted onto the highway, not paying much attention. Before long I was seeing signs for Rexburg and I realized I'd been in a steady line south for quite a while. I took the old road that cut over to Rexburg and spent an hour trying to track down Kent, but he was fishing and not in any of the usual spots.

I thought I might as well go see my mother—I was just an hour away. I don't remember being particularly distracted but I missed the turnoff and was too—something—disengaged maybe, to turn around and go back. The towns went by, separated by farmland. It got flatter and drier. Before long I was in Utah. I was listening to the radio and a wacky version of "Swing Low, Sweet Chariot" came on: "If you get to heaven before I do..." It had that jazz feeling to it that made you smile and tap your foot. "...I'll cut a hole and pull you through."

I was crying again by the time I left the freeway. I didn't go to my place on the avenues. There wouldn't be any food and I was hungry, and I'd turned my water heater off—the second thing I wanted was a bath. I drove by the Little America Hotel, circled back, pulled in under the broad canopy and went in and registered. I should have left the car in a more discreet place but Thalo seemed to know to lie low, and she let me sneak her into the suite without making a sound. She sat in the bathroom beside me while I had a luxurious bath. Then I fed her with the promise of more later and went down to the too-opulent dining room and had dinner—cold apple and butternut squash soup, pork chops with rosemary and couscous, a pear and arugula salad. It was a bit much after potatoes and onions every day. I don't think I'd eaten a full meal since I left at the end of March. I was startled that it was almost five months ago.

I went to Maraya's house the next morning. She'd given me her address when we last talked. "You're..." I start to say when she comes to the door.

"Don't even say it, Miss Rennie. I'm old, Miss Rennie. And I've lost half my teeth. And I'm dark, I'm darker than I was. And tin."

"Tin." I laugh. "I forgot how you say that. You don't like the word skinny, do you, Maraya? You never use it."

"A word like skinny is for some rabbit."

"You can say *that*, speaking of. And *this*. What's the deal with *tin*?"

"They're *completely* different, Miss Rennie. And I *heard* them different is the thing. Heard them different than you. I like tin."

"It is more interesting," I said, still chuckling. "And you're going gray, Maraya."

"Look in the mirror, Miss Rennie. Lord, it's slipping away and we don't even see it."

"I just wanted to say hello," I said to her. "I was in the neighborhood. You take care of yourself."

"You be takin' care of yourself, you hear. And come by when you can stay. Or stay a minute now, Miss Rennie. Kid, you look tired."

"There was a key in the lock. I finally said it to myself on the drive home. I wasn't even headed home. I haven't been there yet, actually." We were standing on her porch. I leaned on the rail. The trees that lined the street were golden.

"There was a key in the lock?"

"I don't remember a key ever being kept in that door."

"Oh, Miss Rennie. Don't remember now, Miss Rennie. Your papa's gone, and the dead don't come back and explain. In my opinion, in matters like these matters, there is always *more than* a key in the lock."

She was intent, leaning forward. She wore glasses now and you noticed her elegant face, her high cheekbones. She looked so worried for me, about me. I'd forgotten how interesting she was. I smiled at her. "It's good to see you, Maraya. Have you been all right?"

"I'm aright, Miss Rennie, I'm aright. I got to see to that. Who else is goin' to? But you look…. Would you like to come inside for tea?"

I could feel myself relax, relax in the back of my neck, in my knees. "I like it out here in the golden leaves. Do you mind if I sit in your little chair?" And I return to the subject. "*More than* a key?" I say, glancing up at her. "I should have known it wouldn't be *just* a key with you, Maraya. Is this going to lead to fate? Maraya? Your favorite?"

"Well, something like that, Miss Rennie. Principally, yes, something like that. It's all one continent, and all one world, for that matter."

"Does that bear upon fate?"

"Well yes, Miss Rennie. How did you used to put matters like these? 'If the ducks fly, the noodles will be done.'"

I burst into full laughter. She made that little chuckle of hers—hnnn hnnn. "You said something like that whenever things was..."

"Inexplicable? I probably did. A young and flippant Rennie. When the ducks fly eastward, the noodles are barely done. I clipped the line from somewhere—some hippie, no doubt."

"What don't that cover, Miss Rennie?" she said.

"Oh Lord. I hate to have affected your thinking. Are we having a conversation here, Maraya? Could this be called a conversation? Did you get these skills in English from me? What about a key in the lock?"

"Say no more," Maraya said and lit a cigarette.

"To you?"

"To anyone. What could it possibly matter? Think of it the other way whenever you can, Miss Rennie. Did your mother have him locked *out*?"

"For about fifty years—all of us did."

"Do you know where the key is, Miss Rennie? She so busy keeping him locked out, she don't see what she locking in."

"But she stayed."

"No *but*, Miss Rennie. Principally, Miss Rennie, she stayed because she stayed."

"I see." I was paying full attention and at the same time, trying not to smile.

"No, Miss Rennie. The children them, they don't see. They can't see and *be* children. It's not nermal for children to see. Principally, if you stay until you can't leave, you can't leave."

"Too long," I said. I was all thought now. Maraya might seem to be taking the back road, but it was usually the *route directe*. "Not normal…"

"These are the elements in these matters, Miss Rennie. Too long at the party." Long e on the. "The way the song goes."

"At the ball. Stayed too long at the ball?"

"Exactly yes, Miss Rennie, the party, the ball. Too late is one of the elements. Money is one of the elements in matters like these matters. And someone else is one of the elements which keeps you at the party also. Which of these do you see, if you don't mind my askin'?"

Too long at the ball. Beyond decision. I did see it. I was there too long myself, or I'd have seen what was happening, would have intervened. Nothing left to leave with. The ducks didn't get out for winter. Who knows what happened to the noodles.

"Do you know where the key is, Maraya?"

"Miss Rennie, you tryin' to smoke out what can't be smoked out." And she blew smoke toward me and raised an eyebrow slightly.

"The thing with the key, Miss Rennie, is the onlyest person who knows about the key is the papa." She handed me her cigarette. She had drawn up a chair beside me by then. "This cigarette is just a prop, you know." After a pause in which she studied me, she added, "I hardly smoke anymore."

"I don't think I've smoked twice since I saw you last. Maybe four times. Four times a year, like all bad Mormons. That's not quite right either."

"Umhmm. Equinox, vernal equinox. What would be the other occasions?"

"Smoke means something different to me now," I said. Her face took on that grave, hollowed look as she listened. "And the key is...?" I handed the cigarette back to her. "It's right here, isn't it? Where there's a lock, there is a key."

"It *is* right here, Miss Rennie. The key is *right here*." She thumped her chest with her cigarette hand, and ashes fell down her sweater. "Oh, Lord. There goes another sweater," she said, and we began to laugh.

"Give me a cigarette of my own."

"Absolutely not."

I took the pack, tapped one out and lit it. I drew deeply and did the remove a fleck from your tongue maneuver.

"Lord, Rennie, it's filtered. It is a prop and a bit of a performance for you, isn't it kid?"

"It's the process I like. Something to do while you think." And I looked at her. "If you wait long enough, you won't need the answers, that's what I'm noticing."

"Lord, Lord," she said. "You're no smoker nor no philosopher. Put that out."

"Vision bears, spirit bears. Tea leaves. Fires and floods. I should have known where the key is, and I'm finally finishing a cigarette. But it's my last."

We talked about her sisters in Nicaragua, we talked about our dogs. She had me bring Thalo in, and she gave her a Milk-Bone. Then she said, "Miss Rennie, I was a Mormon for a few months. I had to quit smoking."

"And give up Bingo with the Catholics as well?"

"Yes, and that's not all. They came around and said 'This goin' to cost you ten percent.'

"'*Ten percent*!' I said. 'Yes, for tithing,' the missionaries said. 'Oh no,' I said. 'I been readin'. It says right here,' and I reached over for my Bible and I opened right to it. 'It says I'll pay the widow's mite, ummhumm.'"

I laughed a long time, and it felt good to be laughing with Maraya. "You were ready for them, weren't you, friend? I can just see their faces. You make me think of Thelma Myzeld. If you ever got together with her, we'd have revolutions and counter-revolutions going in the same afternoon."

"This Thelma Misel a friend of yours?"

"Myzeld. True. Truly a friend. And she'd be a friend to you, too. You could count on her if you needed to."

"I'm countin' on me myself, Miss Rennie. That's who I got to count on."

"Maraya, if you ever did need anything and you couldn't find me—can't reach me—if someone named Thelma Myzeld—she calls herself that—if she calls, take the call. You can ask her if you need anything. You can trust her. Just take the call. None of your superstitions."

"God knows, God knows for sure, Miss Rennie, I'm a paranoia woman. Still, even if I wasn't paranoia, us fureigners..."

"You should try it from native moccasins."

"I'm getting pretty damn close to being native, Miss Rennie, pretty damn close."

"Hell, I guess you are. In India—your mama was from India, wasn't she? So you know about the four great cycles of time? Isn't that what..."

"That's right, Miss Rennie. So you remembered my mama. We're in the middle of the fourth cycle. You got plenty of time to eat your turkey. You feelin' sick and wan, Miss Rennie? Look at me. You looks good, tin, but good, but don't take nothin' from nobody on that tin. Tin is good, Miss Rennie."

"Tin. Lord. How could I have taught you English?"

"Well, principally, Miss Rennie..."

"Don't say it. I took you as far as I wanted to go and left some interest in you. No, I don't feel sick and wan. Feelin' good, Miss Maraya. Feelin' ahead is all. I'm not as thin as I look. Remember."

"You make your bed, you lie in it—I'll just say again. That's why I been sleepin' on the couch." Long e in the.

"That's a perfect answer to just about anything," I said.

She made that little sound of hers.

"Just about anything."

I sang what I could remember of "If you get to heaven before me" on the way back to the hotel. I didn't much believe in hell.

I left before the sun was up. I didn't stop until I got to Pond's Lodge. I went in and looked at the so-called message board. Call T was pinned up there.

"Feel like going for a ride?" Thelma Myzeld asked me when she picked up the phone.

"Sure, hell yes," I said. "I've just been for a ride, but not with you. Bozeman?"

"I'm at my old place for a few more days," she said.

I drove the thirty miles to West Yellowstone and thought of flying the rest of the way to Bozeman. I must have been dreary tired to even think of it. It's only ninety miles, and I ended up driving. That afternoon we did take a ride around town. Thelma hardly talked. When we passed the Old Faithful Bar and Grill, she said, "Let's get a bite." I walked Thalo for a minute first and we ate out on the deck, although it was technically closed up. Nobody cared if we were out there with a dog.

First, we went in to order, and Thelma asked the long-haired bartender if we could get something to eat. "Why not?" he said. " Got soup, a few sandwiches." He was a complete holdover from the '60s.

"What's your soup?"

"Chicken gumbo."

"Is it homemade?"

"Absolutely. Last month."

"Umm," Thelma said. "I kind of wanted canned." She lit a cigarette. "That was for you," she said, looking at me, an unsparingly direct consideration. And after the next long drag, when we were back on the deck, she said, "Ray and I are having trouble."

"No," I said. "Oh, I hate to hear it."

"Yes. He drives me crazy. He obsesses."

"Don't tell me."

"Yes, the goddamned cashmere. Now he thinks something's wrong with it. It doesn't fit like it used to. He's hit his *usedtobe* stage. It's come early."

"I can't get the original back now, Thelma," I said.

She took another long drag. "That was my way of finding out. Anyway," long draw, "if he ever wears that goddamned jacket again, it would ruin the marriage."

Late in the evening I drove the ninety miles back to my cabin, through the heavy pines of the Gallatin Gateway, ninety miles of heart-melting beauty. That cabin was like a magnet to me. I'd have driven three hours to get to it, tired as I was. I stopped at Howard Springs on the way back and sat there watching the shadows on that pool of water, the best within a hundred miles. "How could we have done what we did to Chief Joseph?" I said aloud. Trail of Tears. Thirty miles from freedom. Thirty miles from the Canadian border. A thousand miles of walking. "Hear me, my chiefs." My father's favorite line. Everyone's favorite. And to name this after that lout Howard.

I called Thelma the next morning. "What about Chief Joseph?" I asked.

"You stopped at Howard Springs," she said.

"Don't even say the name. Thalo did have a good drink. 'From where the sun now sets.' Pursued a thousand miles. More than. Maybe it's come full circle."

"Pursued? You're thinking of world affairs, aren't you, Rennie."

"When Sadat..."

"I know you can't say—it's clear you're a piece of classified work yourself, Rennie. I've got that much figured out."

"Don't be silly. But after Sadat, that year after... 1982. Where are we from what was begun? And not just us. The race is not to the swift, I see that, not this one. This will change not just what comes after."

"And...what comes before?"

"It already has."

"Dear God, Rennie." I can hear her light a cigarette.

"All those who will make the journey, begin to prepare a place beyond loss. My losses so slight, so comprehensible—even though I'm not quite there."

"Rennie, I'm going to drive over there to that cabin of yours and fix you a cup of tea."

"I'll call back, Myzeld. In an hour."

"I've damn near forgotten where we came up with Myzeld," she said.

I went out on the waterline that afternoon. So much is dependable in the forest. The headlines don't alter the grass or trees or meadow. They keep their own rhythm. And even this little intrusion of mine was unchanged. I always expected to see my line broken up somehow—flung apart by a tripped-up moose or rutting elk. But it never was. It seemed impervious to anything going on around it.

A few days went by and I began arranging my things—the first step in packing.

Then I drove into Pond's and called Thelma. "Black line or whatever it is," Thelma said. No hello. "Have you tried black line?"

"Black line? For what?"

"For snails. A pesticide. You won't have a snail problem. You'll see a trail of tears. Those snails are nothing but tears when they cross the black line."

"Dead line."

"Is that it? How can they market that? I'm going to get in touch with Insect International or someone like that and see if I can do an ad for them. Ray won me back, by the way."

"Did he find out about the jacket?"

"No. That goddamned jacket. Wasn't it bliss." And we snickered like we used to.

But the jacket was on my mind.

"Do you think it matters if he *knows* it's not the right jacket?"

"Let me get your mind off it." She told me about a good old Montana blowout they'd had. "One of the guests—actually, it was the governor's wife—said, 'What a party. You can sure put it together.'

"Ray looked at me for a long time. Then he looked at the governor's wife for a long time. I don't remember her name. She doesn't like me. I think she heard me sing my version of 'Jesus Loves me.' I remember all the wrong names. She was growing uncomfortable with that much silence. Then Ray said, on the subject of the party, 'Now if we can just take it apart,' and he looked at me and we went upstairs. He didn't carry me. He didn't have to.

"Who knows when the guests left?"

The next morning there was another message for me to call. I stood there at the counter at Pond's and dialed Thelma's number. She was singing, if you could call it that. "Remember this one? 'Drop Kick Me Jesus Through the Goalposts of Life'?"

I couldn't help laughing, but I said to her, "The deal with your Jesus songs is that you're no stranger to what he represents. While we're laughing, let me...I'm wondering..."

"Toss it out, Rennie, before my cigarette goes out."

I snickered. "That cigarette of yours. Talk about a prop."

I was quiet for a minute and then I said, "Knowing and not knowing...on this knowing your father and mother. Knowing if there was a key in the lock..."

"Here's what I see. You *know* two things. Your mother was with your father—the last person with him. And he had a candle in there and he died in a fire. Maybe that's three things. What do you know from knowing that?"

I didn't answer.

"It's just about the same as not knowing. If you didn't know the candle was in there. If your mother confessed. Knowing and not knowing, pardon me, Rennie, but they're twins."

"There's something profound in you, Myzeld."

"It's in you, Rennie, or you'd never see it. Let's remember the governor's wife. 'Drop kick me, Jesus.'"

I walked in the meadow most of the next day, Thalo flitting back and forth after ground squirrels. She showed her old verve for a minute. I checked my waterline again. This time I looked it over carefully. I was impressed with how it had held up. I'd need to drain it soon.

The color in the quakies was fading, and some of the leaves were ringed in black. A few kept their brilliant gold.

I talked to Thalo along the familiar route. "So many things to love in this part of the country," I told her. "Think how we live. We drive thirty or forty miles for romaine lettuce, but we're not counting time. We're watching for Henry's Lake and then Staley Springs and the Fiddleback off to the right and then the high peaks of the Centennials rising. We're wondering whether to take the old road, the Bootjack Pass. But it won't matter—it's all in becalming beauty.

"Maybe tomorrow we'll fish the Madison one more time—go on up the highway to Ennis. Get our order for sausage at the butchers and run out to the honey farm. Maybe have breakfast. We'll still be on the river in time for the Gentleman's Hatch." Thalo is listening with her head cocked. "That waitress with a cigarette in her voice—the one that comes to the counter, drops a great box of jelly where you're sitting, narrowly missing the last three fingers of your casting hand, and announces to no one, 'Slicker 'n owl shit.' That guy who tells us what happened at the Blue Moon Saloon while he drinks a Black Dog. We'll hike to the Utmost Source one more time and think of Chief Joseph camping there in that hushed meadow." I ruffle her fur. "It's going to be hard for us to leave."

We were back at the cabin by then and I sat on the front porch steps and thought of the days when we'd all been there together—my grandfather and Kent and sometimes my parents and always my grandmother I watched the light fade on the willows. Be still, I said.

> Lots of things changed in the years before you and Kent were born. The horse and buggy went. And the sweepers on the streets that came along and cleared all the manure up. Scrapers kept the streets and sidewalks cleaned off. One little horse would pull a couple of boards headed into a V to clean the snow off the sidewalks. And snow would be piled high, way high down the center of the road in the winter. You couldn't see the people on the other side.
>
> The cowcatcher on the front of the train engine cleaned the railroad tracks. In the winter they'd put a blade on, and it would just whirl the snow up and away.

All that went. And eventually we lost the good old Yellowstone Special.

We used to have to sweep rugs with a broom or take them out on the line and beat and beat and beat them. We'd have rag carpets on the floor and we'd put hay under them. It was a job. There'd be dust over everything. And when Mother was young, they didn't have mattresses. They'd make a cover and stuff it with hay, then put a feather bed over it. When you got up to make your bed in the morning, all that had to be smoothed out.

By the time my mother was old, there was no more parlor. Boy, you didn't get into the parlor very often—that was special occasions and then you just set around and talked by the big fancy heating stove like we had at our last cabin.

The day passed quickly, as I look back now, that we didn't bother ourselves when we heard an airplane. But when the first ones flew over—you can't imagine our astonishment. We'd all just pour out into the streets. And the first automobiles were nothing but a novelty to us. We didn't ever think we'd have one.

I wonder as I listen to her, what is the cowcatcher in our midst? What are the emblems of our time that will be gone and when they go, seem to take a way of life—a delight in a way of life—

with them? Have we seen so much that astonishments are a thing of the past?

During the war was when we heard a radio—squeak and scratch and squawk was what we heard. Studebaker John was the first one to have a radio in Rexburg, and from my first few minutes with it, I wasn't impressed. Later I was the only one in the mill camp had a radio that got KSL out of Salt Lake City. It was just a little maroon radio, and it could pick up Salt Lake City, day or night. You know the song I remember coming on that little radio? What's the title? I can remember the tune as plain as day, and the last line is "Someone waits for you."

Every dog has its day and that was ours. Our kids grew up in the mountains, and I watched the path coming up from the mill every evening for I guess it was over forty years, and when I'd see Royce, my heart would give a little jump. Oh, sometimes it was too tired to jump much, but usually it could manage a little something.

We were never lonely in that life, children or adults. The kids would play as hard as they could go all day long. Then sometimes at night they'd play Run Sheepies Run, or they'd go out to the mill where the edgings had been wheeled away. The edgings from the lumber would stack up and stack up till one of the guys would come along and load them and take them out of the way. When there was a good-sized pile, the kids would light fire to it and sometimes nearly everyone in camp would come down and sit around and talk and roast wieners and marshmallows. And later, when the moon was high and the air chilly, we'd gather closer to the fire and sing.

The willows leading off of the pond would smell tangy, and the creek—it's a funny thing how you can smell water, almost smell the life in it. I get near a creek and I swear I can smell the fish. I'd stand by that fire and listen to it crackle and listen to the creek. I could identify every part of the mill just by smell—the wildflowers along the path to the cabin, the sawdust and metal around the mill, the slaked-wet wood in the washhouse, the little bridge where you and Kent always fished—all those smells come back to me like old songs. I used to feel all filled up at those times, with Royce beside me and the faces of my kids shining from the flames of the bonfire.

I was lifted by her. Taken somewhere beyond searching.

The next morning I drove down to Coffee Pot Rapids as much to look at the big stands of quakies along Stamp Meadows Road as to fish. I drove slow enough I felt I could watch the leaves change. They were beginning to fall, and the ground beneath the trees was spread in gold.

I threw my waders over my shoulder and grabbed my rod and vest—what was left of it—and set out. It's steep getting down that trail. You're stumbling over rocks and roots of trees and brush. The river was deep blue and the riverbank smelled of mint. I walked along the bank until I came to a cutout.

The current rippled through me. I could feel the life within it around my legs, I always could, and I came suddenly alive, feeling the motion of the water and the rocks beneath me through my flyweights. I walked as softly as I could, not wanting to disturb the riverbed. I hadn't worn boots, and I could feel the stones and sand on the bottom of the riverbed. I knew I'd ruin my waders but I made my way as gingerly as I could.

I strung up my rod and the great peace and the old excitement came together in me. I cast into the sandy bank where the sun fell, letting the fly drift down just above a riffle I'd watched for. I never took my eyes from my fly until a splash went up around it, and my line went tight. Then everything was back to instinct. You know or you don't know fish—I remember my father saying that.

"Get higher," I said to myself. I got out of the river and walked along the bank upstream until the river calmed down. I found stepping-stones back into it and felt the laps of water touch me again. I got my fly on the water quickly and let it float out. But my attention was on the river. I noticed what the clear water did to the stones and pebbles. It was as though the water could eliminate them and then return them in the next ripple. They were there, yet the water seemed to rearrange them.

Things were what they were in the river. There was the current and the objects subject to it, and there were the banks that shifted and adjusted themselves according to the river's whims. I looked at the line eight feet from the water's edge where the water level had been in the early spring, then at all the cuts into the bank where the waterline was now.

Birds hovered at that mysterious demarcation of land and water, the green and gold changing to dappled blue. A few gulls cried out, but I watched downstream now for a sand crane or a blue heron. The songs of the birds were all through the woods, the *Ta wee Ta wee* of one, the *Kaaww* of another, the *Woblwoblwobl* of another. I felt the last of the day take its shape, the river flowing beside and between my legs, the late sun warming my shoulders, and the splendor, upriver, of forest life where a moose might walk out and give you a prehistoric stare.

"Memory," I said. That old vagrant.

The first hit was a good one, and I talked him in. "Hey, Runner, come to me." And there was that feeling of permanence. The fish cut my way and darted back. Then he rose, and I let the line go slack. When he was free, he came directly toward me. I never lost sight of him.

It was almost evening when I got out of the water. I sat on the bank and watched for a long time. "Don't look for fish, look for parts of fish," I could hear my father say. I watched the pattern the water made as it moved. Then a glinting appeared, almost like a sunspot, and disappeared, and the river returned to the pattern I'd memorized. "A big fish," I said. I watched his lie. He was just ahead of the water that broke in front of a large rock. I saw a cut through the surface film, and I knew it would be his tail. I watched.

Where he came up, a great splash spread around him. "It's you and me, Swimmer," I said to him. He came up again, staying on the water for so long I felt my own breath grow short. He hovered there, forming a dream.

"Go down, boy." He went under and came up again. I waded out a ways and cast above him, letting the fly drift to him. He came up again immediately, and he seemed almost to skate across the water, he came up so many times in a row. He took my fly as he went down. His audacity stunned me and I let the line go slack at once. "Go, Runner," I said. "Go home."

I slept on the riverbank for a few hours, and I woke just before sunset. I filed the barb from my hook as I sat on the bank, watching. A dorsal fin barely cut the surface film. Then the fly hatch came down on the water, so many caddis I wondered if my elk hair would have a chance.

"Audacity." It'll take something different tonight, not something the same. I put on an attractor, a Royal Wulff, and watched until I saw a big fish working a hole. He took at least thirty caddis.

"Here's some dessert," I said and cast the Wulff, double-hauling the line the way my father did and feeling it shoot out through the guides of my rod. The fly landed above the fish, and I let it drift down. When it was beyond him, I cast again. Again he refused it. I cast again.

"Selection," I said.

He rolled and gulped the Wulff. The fish was big, and he took line through half of the backing on my reel. I began to walk downstream toward him, reeling him in when he wasn't taking line. I stopped when he turned and saw me. He was off the hook in an instant. I'd been inattentive, but I wanted him off the hook anyway.

I caught a salmon at dark and all the while I was bringing him in, I talked to David. "I stand here in your swiftness, in your cold current, David," I said over the waters. "I know the far side of the moon in you now, and I take this of you—with this current, in this earth, I provide myself with you."

By then the moon had risen, and I stood watching it. The light fell across the tips of the pines, and I felt all my ages present within me. "The third thing," I said. I had looked up the Lawrence poem Thelma had quoted. "It is the third thing," I said. A squirrel stopped his chattering and watched me. I walked along the banks far upstream.

I was light and alive and alone in the words that came back to me.

> ". . . there is also a third thing, that makes it water
> and nobody knows what that is."

I unbuttoned my blouse and laid it on the moonlit grass. I sat on a rock and pulled off my Levis. I stepped out of my yellow socks. I unfastened what remained between me and the shimmering night.

When I arose, I walked into the river and stood waiting. Then I walked upstream, out into the rippling current. "Come, Swimmer," I said, feeling the words part of each other. "Come, Salmon. Come, Swimmer."

I stood quietly, my shoulders and breasts warm in the night air. "I have just these words, Swimmer. I have no imitations. I have no line. I offer you these words, old as the river. Mercy, economy, generosity."

When I looked down, there was a great circle of salmon in the moonlight around me. I went underwater to them. I felt them, soft as a touch against me. A trout came to the edge of the circle and when I came up, he made his leap beside me. The first thing I saw was his rainbow. I watched water run down it, beads flying out from his thrust like jewels and a stream flowing from his tail.

ACKNOWLEDGMENTS

Thank you, David Kranes, who saw the statue in the stone. Heartfelt thanks to Alice Peck and Ruth Mullen, editors who protected the soul of the story—and the writer. A salute to designer Duane Stapp; he understands all the meanings of "finish." And thank you Cill, for making me laugh when I put down the pen. A bow to my cohorts on the trail—the Weasel, Pat, Les and Patty, Jeanne, Kent, Garlene, Ronny, Scott. And last, unending thanks to my grandparents, who let me live in the forest with them.

CPSIA information can be obtained
at www.ICGtesting.com
Printed in the USA
FSOW01n0502021115
12822FS